guardians

praise for

guardians

"*Guardians* is a more than satisfying ending to Heather Frost's Seers trilogy. Packed with suspense, action, emotion, romance, and plenty of heartrending moments, fans of the previous books will be thrilled by this exciting ending to Kate and Patrick's story. Guardians is everything I hoped it would be, brilliantly satisfying this fan. The only fault I can find with it is that the book inevitably ended."

Cindy C Bennett

Author of *Rapunzel Untangled* and *Geek Girl*

"*Guardians* is the perfect ending to this edge-of-your-seat series. I laughed, cried, and gasped for breath many times while I was reading it. Fans of this series will find this is a perfect ending for the characters we have grown to love."

Mindy Holt

Popular blogger, www.minreadsandreviews.blogspot.com & www.ldswomensbookreview.com

book 3 of the seers trilogy

guardians

heather frost

sweetwater books
an imprint of cedar fort, inc.
springville, utah

ISBN 13: 978-1-4621-1035-3

LIBRARY OF CONGRESS CATALOGING-IN-PUBLICATION DATA

Frost, Heather (Heather Marlene), 1989- author.
Guardians / by Heather Frost.
pages cm
Summary: After witnessing her grandfather's murder by a demon, Kate struggles even more to appear normal in her high school life when the powers of evil seem to be too much for her Guardian and Seer friends.
ISBN 978-1-4621-1035-3 (hardback with dust jacket : alk. paper)
[1. Clairvoyance--Fiction. 2. Immortality--Fiction. 3. Demonology--Fiction. 4. Murder--Fiction. 5. Supernatural--Fiction.] I. Title.
PZ7.F92048Gu 2013
[Fic]--dc23
2013005915

Published by Sweetwater Books, an imprint of Cedar Fort, Inc.
2373 W. 700 S., Springville, UT 84663
Distributed by Cedar Fort, Inc., www.cedarfort.com

Cover design by Kelsey Webb
Cover design © 2013 by Lyle Mortimer
Edited and typeset by Melissa J. Caldwell

Printed in the United States of America

10 9 8 7 6 5 4 3 2 1

For Jacob
Thank you for being our Guardian Angel.
"Forever isn't long at all when I'm with you."
Families Are Forever

also by
heather frost

Seers
Demons

prologue

April 28, 1792
Patrick O'Donnell
Wexford County, Ireland

I stood at my mother's side, listening to her soft laughter. The sound was delightful and polite, easy happiness that carried on the light breeze. She was standing with a group of women, discussing a variety of things: vegetables, weather, flowers, children—the things women enjoy talking about. Though I was twelve years old, I was content staying near my mother during social events. Many thought it was a bad habit—a sign of infinite shyness. A few of the women openly pitied my mother, and the men often asked my father if everything was quite all right with me. My parents were patient and kind, though, and, as a result, the neighbors were constantly assured that I was perfectly normal.

I don't know exactly what the other children thought about me and my reticence. Most in the area were younger or older than me, so I didn't care to join them very often in their games. Besides, I wasn't extremely athletic. I preferred staying unobserved, unnoticed. I preferred painting, reading, or daydreaming over playing rough games outdoors.

I was the exact opposite of my younger brother.

Sean was energetic, active, and well loved by everyone for miles around. He was always in the thick of things, for good or for ill. The women adored him, the men often gave my father satisfied looks, and even some of the children older than Sean's ten years looked up to him. Though he was young, his magnetic personality, good looks, and bright mind drew everyone to him. I don't believe anyone said it aloud, but I knew many believed Sean was the superior son.

While I understood all of this—accepted it—I wasn't bothered by their obvious thoughts. Because I knew my family didn't share any of these opinions. My father was the local pastor, and he was well respected. He was equal parts spiritual and brilliant. He'd often told me that my quiet strength was my greatest virtue, and that someday I would find my place and be sure of it. My mother was the kindest woman the earth had ever known, and her heart was infinitely pure. She always whispered to me that I was extremely talented and would grow into a strong man one day. My brother would grin, clap my shoulder, and tease that someday I would be his equal. Their quiet words were enough for me; I needed the respect of no one else.

Perhaps I was unnecessarily hard on my neighbors. They did not disapprove of me, exactly. In fact, many of the women commented on my charming O'Donnell looks, and quite a few of the men believed I was uncommonly wise for my age. Still, I knew that in the privacy of their homes, many heads were shaken on my behalf.

My mother rubbed her hand absently over my back, causing me to glance up at her. It wasn't a long distance to her face anymore—I was already past her shoulder and growing more rapidly every day. She didn't respond to my sudden look, but I continued to watch her beautiful face as she listened to Alana Carroll describe the antics of her youngest child, a girl of two.

I stared at my mother's face until she finally bent her head to give me a fast smile. She slid her hand around my shoulders, pulling me closer to her side before turning her attention back to Mrs. Carroll.

I shifted my gaze to our peaceful surroundings. My father's small white church was beautiful in the early evening light. The rolling hills that surrounded the area were gentle and sloping, inviting the grazing sheep to wander freely. It seemed half the province was gathered in the churchyard. Father sometimes joked that he never realized how many "sheep" he had to care for until they came flocking for a springtime social. There were many faces I was used to—faces from school, frequenters of the church, and the nearby families that often visited our home. Many of the remaining crowd were unfamiliar to me; relations of my neighbors, perhaps. The face of Sarah McKenna was notably absent, but a cold had taken hold of her only yesterday, so I'd known not to expect her.

The picnic portion of the social was over. The sounds of playing children punctuated the clear air, and mingling adults created a low, persistent chatter. I was content here, next to my mother, and could have stayed for the duration of the evening.

My father stepped up behind me, balancing one large hand on my shoulder. "Patrick, you haven't been standing here all this time, have you?"

Before I could answer, Mrs. Carroll was speaking. "Aye, indeed he has, Pastor O'Donnell. And if I'm not too bold to be saying so, I might add that he hasn't spoken a single word. What thought holds his attention, I wonder?" She peered at me with her big green eyes, as if wondering whether I had a single thought in my head at all.

Mother laughed lightly at my side, and her arm tightened around me. "Patrick's thoughts are usually his own. Whenever we are allowed inside, however, I'm always amazed at the depth of them."

Father's palm lifted to rustle against my light brown hair.

"Indeed. Nevertheless, if I might intrude upon those thoughts . . . Patrick, your brother has gone missing, along with the Doyle boy. What's his name . . . ?"

"Colin," I offered, tipping my head up so I could catch a look at his face.

He gave me a small smile. "Yes. Colin. His parents would like to go home, so I assured them you would be happy to find Colin."

I lowered my head with a small sigh. "Yes, Da."

Mother squeezed me thankfully before I slipped out from under her falling arm. I turned and pushed my hands deep into my pockets, though after I'd gone just a few paces I threw a glance back over my shoulder. My father had taken the place beside my mother, their arms casually supporting each other as Mrs. Carroll resumed her tale. They often stood like that, his hand almost imperceptibly rubbing her slender side, drawing her closer. They could remain that way for a long time, not saying anything, whether they were standing at a window, on the back step, in the garden, or on the stairs of the church. Sean told me once that such silence and stillness bothered him. It didn't seem affectionate in his eyes. "They look bored," he'd said once, when I'd commented on their posture.

Personally, I thought it was a comforting stance. It showed me that words were not always necessary, which was something I was relieved to see evidence of. It made me feel less self-conscious when I saw my parents act like I did.

I nearly stumbled on a loose stone hidden in the long, trampled grass, so I returned my attention to where I was going.

I wandered through the loose crowds, nodding to those who met my eye or called out a special greeting. I didn't know where Sean and Colin would be, but I knew they'd be together. I decided to check the cemetery first. I'd found them there more than once before.

I passed through the edge of the lingering party and

rounded the corner of the white church. Though there was not a great span between the church and the crowd, as soon as I passed through the gap in the waist-high stone wall that fenced the small, crowded cemetery, I seemed partially cut off from the noise. It was distant now, as if I was in a place too sacred to desecrate with light laughter and easy banter. I enjoyed the sudden peace, and the thought briefly crossed my mind that I should make this my retreat more often.

The varied gravestones and simple wooden markers were crowded tightly together, but I navigated the cemetery with an ease that came only through repetition. I'd been walking these grounds since my first steps, and I wasn't about to start tripping over the dead now. God rest their souls, of course.

The cemetery ran the length of the church and wrapped around the back. I hadn't reached the end corner before I could hear the small voice of Colin Doyle.

"I don't think this is a good idea," he was saying, voice timid.

My brother answered immediately, confident and faintly panting. "Oh, shut it. I can do this."

I fought the urge to roll my eyes as I stepped fully into the backyard. I saw Colin standing beneath the sprawling branches of the large yew tree, the sparse green leaves just coming in due to the earliness of the season. He was nervously fiddling with the strap on his suspenders, and he was looking to three other boys I didn't recognize. They were young, judging from the roundness of their faces; however, they were not small. The oldest couldn't be older than me, and the youngest was probably nine years—if that. The one in the middle was staring up into the heavy branches of the ancient tree, and I followed his gaze—already knowing who I'd see.

Sean was climbing up the thick trunk, swinging on the evenly spaced branches with an agility that equally amazed and terrified me. He was already more than halfway up the gigantic tree. My neck strained painfully as I followed his rapid progress.

I walked a bit unsteadily the rest of the way forward, stopping when I reached Colin's side. Colin saw me from the corner of his eye, and then—upon realizing my identity—he cupped his hands around his mouth and yelled up to my brother, "Sean! Patrick's here!"

Sean wavered in his climb, but only for a moment before he braced himself against the branch and trunk, gripping the rough bark tightly. Despite the flush in his face, his grin was too wide to miss—even from this distance.

"He can watch me too!" he yelled down, not in the least bit fazed by my presence.

I turned to Colin, glancing at the three large boys who were now staring at me. "What's going on here?" I asked evenly.

Colin was biting his lower lip, obviously agitated. "Sean's going to jump from the tree onto the church roof. I told him he couldn't do it!"

I craned my head back up to my brother, who was climbing ever higher. He'd surpassed the top of the church, the tree shivering under his weight as he came closer to the top. I then turned to look at the church behind us, noting that although the tree was *close* to the roof, it was nowhere near close enough.

"Sean!" I hollered up to him."You're going to break your neck!"

His answer was defensive and immediate. "I will not. I've done this loads of times," he added, speaking primarily to the largest three members of his audience.

Colin and I shared a quick look; I tried to sound more authoritative. "I'll get Da, Sean. I swear I will."

The smallest of the three large boys chuckled loudly. "Let your *Da* save you, then," he yelled up.

The largest grinned hugely. "Knew you were lying from the start . . ."

Even from here I could see Sean bristle. "I can jump it," he declared boldly. He looked to the church—squinted as if aiming—and then he slowly started scooting out onto a quivering limb.

The hands in my pockets were fists. I tossed a rueful look to the young boy at my side. "What happened, Colin?" I asked lowly, a slight variation to my earlier question.

The other three boys glanced at us, though they were still centered mostly on Sean.

Colin's distress was visibly rising with every second. He started wringing his hands as he met my hard stare. "Sean was boasting toward the McCarthy brothers—they're nephews of the O'Briens. He said he could jump onto the church roof. They dared him to prove it."

I glanced to the McCarthy brothers, who were laughing amongst themselves at my brother's imbecilic actions. I would have joined them, if I weren't so worried for Sean.

Sean was creeping toward the end of the branch now, and he was beginning to dip toward the ground far below. I felt the vertigo he never seemed to feel, and I tried one last time to reason with him. "Sean, you can't make it. Come down!"

"I can make it!" he protested. He grunted loudly, shifting his weight gradually as he struggled to a crouching position.

The middle McCarthy brother guffawed loudly, and I rounded on them in an instant, trying to assert my age in my superior tone. "Tell my brother you believe him. Let him climb down."

The oldest gave me a dark sneer. "Bugger off. It was his idea, not ours."

"Yeah," the youngest drawled, head tilted back to enjoy Sean's shivering form as he fought for balance.

The middle one smiled at the sight, and my stomach grew painfully tight. "Let the idiot fall," the boy said, chuckling. "I'll bet he makes a nice scream before he hits."

I stared at them, completely sickened. This was my brother. How could anyone talk about him in this way? Perhaps more important, why had I stayed back this long?

I did the only thing I could think of doing. I looked up into the leafy branches. "Hold on, Sean—I'm coming up. I'll do it with you."

Colin actually gasped, and Sean did a double take as he watched me move for the trunk.

"What?" My brother was clearly taken aback. "Patrick, you can't jump this!"

"That fact hasn't stopped you," I reasoned. I grabbed for the lowest branch, and with a great deal of worming, I managed to pull myself up into the lower reaches of the old yew.

"Patrick, stop!" Sean called down to me, sounding genuinely alarmed. "You can't climb this tree."

I could hear the McCarthy brothers below and behind, laughing at the both of us—primarily me, as I struggled to make progress.

"Why not?" I grunted up to my brother.

Sean all but glared down at me. "You're afraid of heights," he hissed. I think he meant it to be for my ears alone, except the light breeze carried the words easily.

The largest McCarthy turned mocking. "Oho, he's afraid of heights. Is he going to faint and fall, do you think?"

The other brothers laughed, and Sean growled down at me, deeply annoyed. "Patrick—get down, will you? You're making fools of us both!"

I didn't answer—I had to focus on my climb. I wasn't graceful, or fast, but I was steady. For now. I knew my first glimpse of the ground would freeze me, effectively ruining my feeble bluff. I prayed my brother would save me before that happened.

The reaction I was waiting for didn't come soon enough for me; I was halfway up and sweating more from fear than exertion when finally Sean let go of his foolish pride. He started to back down the tree, despite the many jeers from the boys below. I hesitated where I was, watching as he swung down to my side in seconds. He stopped near my elbow, his flushed face upset with me. "What did you do that for?" he rasped narrowly.

I grunted low in my throat. "To keep you from being a big dolt. You'll thank me someday. Now help me get off this thing . . ."

Sean helped me in whispers know where to place my feet and hands, and slowly we made our way down together. He actually grasped my ankle once to guide me to the best foot-hold. Though I slipped once, the journey wasn't as perilous as it could have been.

When we were nearly to the ground, the middle McCarthy began to taunt my brother. "Good thing you had your brother to save you, Sean. He's quite the pretty knight, isn't he?"

I could feel Sean's body shiver with anger. I called his name gently; his eyes whipped to mine. I kept my voice firm. "Ignore them, Sean. What they think doesn't matter."

He ground his teeth a bit violently, but he kept his mouth shut. We continued to descend amid jibes and ribs that became increasingly insulting. Poor Colin was still twisting his fingers together, looking completely at a loss for what to do.

Sean dropped to the ground before me, a second before the largest McCarthy spoke. "Tell us about your brother, Sean. Is he as daft as he looks? Or just plain dumb?"

I was lowering myself from the bottom branch to the long grass, and once my legs were steadied, I looked up to see Sean at my side, glaring openly at the McCarthys.

"Sean . . ." I spoke warningly.

The eldest McCarthy grinned at my brother. "Is he always this pathetic? Or is this a special occasion?"

I don't know if those words snapped him, or if it was a combination of all the others and he'd just been pausing a second to catch his breath; regardless, he was charging the largest McCarthy before I had a chance to grab him. His head was lowered into the brutal shove, and his unexpectedly powerful impact sent them both sprawling to the ground.

"Sean!" I yelled, rooted to the earth for a horrible second.

I watched as the brave Colin Doyle turned and bolted, dashing for the nearest corner of the church. I then saw the other McCarthys moving to converge on my brother, meaty fists raised expectantly.

A side of me I never knew existed burst forth, and I was running for the two McCarthy brothers before I quite realized what I was doing.

The middle McCarthy saw me coming, and he braced himself to hopefully absorb my sudden thrust of weight. I slammed into him, and we both staggered back a step before I was cuffed on my right ear by the younger McCarthy. I let my fist sail, feeling my knuckles bruise against the middle McCarthy's jaw. My fingers popped on impact, and I was grabbed from behind by the marginally shorter McCarthy behind me. The middle McCarthy shook free of me and began to pound his fists in my unguarded face as his younger brother clutched me tightly, pinning my arms to my sides.

Though my face was exploding in a pain I'd never before experienced, I was aware of Sean's struggle nearby. He was still on the ground, the large McCarthy on top of him. Both were letting out grunts of pain, and it wasn't until Sean cried out that I feared my brother was truly losing the fight.

"Sean!" I gulped, blood trickling from my nose into my mouth. I tasted it on my lips, on my tongue, and the horrible taste made me feel sick. I struggled more desperately to get free, but I was held too tightly.

Locked in this world of brutal pain, I didn't realize pounding footsteps were coming toward us until my father's voice assaulted my ears. "Patrick! Sean!"

The fists beating against my pulverized face stopped, thankfully, and I was released. I shook and fell to my knees, my trembling fingers moving up to press delicately against my throbbing skin.

"Patrick!" my mother cried, having seen me fall to the ground. Her skirts whipped briskly around me as she sank into a crouch before me. I felt her cold hands cover mine, tilt my head up, and she let out a wounded cry. "Patrick," she gasped, eyes tortured. I blinked heavily, trying to smile, to reassure her; the effect was more of a flinch, and when I tried to speak the words clogged in my throat.

She pulled out her small white handkerchief and set it against my nose and mouth. It was immediately soaked. She looked over her shoulder and I followed her gaze with my eyes.

Sean was propped up in my father's arms, his legs sprawled out over the grass. He wasn't as bloody as me, but he was already swollen. Father was looking up at Mr. O'Brien, who was apologizing profusely. "They shall be punished, Pastor O'Donnell, you have my word." The balding man glared toward his nephews. "Home! The lot of you!" He waited until they responded before turning back to my father. "Their father's just passed, and their mother—poor soul—she's had her hands full with them."

Father nodded grimly, balancing Sean's head on one straining arm. "Of course. I don't believe any lasting damage has been done."

I felt more than heard my mother whimper, as if she disagreed with my father's assessment.

Colin Doyle cast us pale glances, but his parents were directing the rest of the crowd to fall back, that there was nothing more to be done here. So he followed the retreat until the crowd had all disappeared around the corner of the church.

My mother stroked my hair with her free hand, tears forming in her eyes. "Patrick, whatever happened? You'll tell me this instant!"

I swallowed roughly while Sean began speaking. "Not

much, Mam. Just playing." He cast me a deep look, meant to coerce me into silence.

Unfortunately, my mother could see the look more clearly than I could, and Sean realized this belatedly. Mother's voice quivered with emotion—not all of it fear. "Boys of mine, fighting. I can hardly stand the thought." She looked to my father. "Patrick? Say something!"

He stared at Sean for a moment, then looked to me. "Patrick, who began this?"

I answered honestly. "It takes two to quarrel, Da."

He didn't seem to appreciate his own proverb in the present circumstances. "Who threw the first blow?" he refined his question.

Sean sighed loudly. "That would be me, I suppose."

"You *suppose?*" Mother's voice was quietly shrill. "Did you attack one of those boys, or didn't you?"

"I did. But they were being rude."

"I don't care if they were being insufferable!" she nearly snapped. "I never want to see a drop of blood on either of your faces again. Do you hear me?"

"Aileen, please," Father spoke suddenly. She glanced to him quickly, and I wished I could see her face. I'd never seen her so impassioned before. It was a little disturbing, but inspiring too. I was like her in so many other ways—did this mean that when I needed to be fierce and vocal, I would be able to be so? Feeling the bruises on my face, I decided my chances were good.

My parents finished exchanging their long glance, then my father's voice was surprisingly quiet. "Patrick, Sean—are you well enough to walk with me to the house?"

We both nodded humbly, demonstrating our capability by standing. My mother held my arm until Father gave her a look. She released me with a sigh. "I'll return to the social. But, Patrick, please let the boys go inside and rest. No undue lectures tonight."

Father nodded once, and mother planted a kiss first on my forehead and then Sean's, before wandering back through the cemetery. Once she'd disappeared from view, Father pulled out his own handkerchief and handed it to Sean, who pressed it to his bloody lip. I continued to hold my mother's soiled cloth to my bleeding nose as my brother and I shifted to stand shoulder to shoulder, facing my father.

His face was harder than usual, and I knew Sean was sharing my same thoughts: Was he going to yell? He rarely did, although that only made those rare occasions of raised voice much more powerful and intimidating.

We waited tensely, until finally his tight lips parted. "Tell me everything. Spare nothing—your mother will never hear of this. You have my word."

So we told him, Sean remembering each insult with impressive clarity. I made sure Father understood I'd had no intention of jumping with Sean from the tree—that it had been a ruse to get him to come down.

Sean summed things up with these words and a simple shrug. "I couldn't let them call Patrick those things. I've never felt so angry, Da."

"Anger should never dictate our actions," Da warned severely, though his eyes were no longer burning. He was looking at us with a new light—as if seeing us clearly for the first time. "Not all brothers have this strong loyalty," he continued slowly. "I am relieved to see that, despite your differences, you have this connection. It brings me great comfort."

"What about mother?" Sean asked. "Does it bring her comfort?"

I sniffed loudly against the blood falling from my nose, and Father winced. "Perhaps comfort isn't the best word," he admitted. "But I'm sure she'll someday recognize the importance of your bond. Because, someday, your mother and I will be gone. You'll only have each other then."

Sean coughed, spitting out a bloody tooth into his palm.

Father grimaced. "Come, let's get you two inside. And Sean . . . just toss that anywhere. If your mother sees, you'll be lucky to survive her wrath."

I know my eyes bulged. *Wrath? Mother?* Still, seeing Father's face, I decided there must be something he knew about her that I didn't.

Sean must have felt the same, because as we started to follow Father to the house, he let the small tooth slip through his fingers, leaving it to rest in the long grass.

***

Present Day
Far Darrig
Nevada, United States

I stood looking out one of the floor-to-ceiling windows on the top floor of the Illusion Hotel and Casino. I was alone at the window, as was my way: aloof, always on the edge of vision. But always right where I needed to be. I gazed down at the Strip, watching as the cars below swerved impatiently around each other. Humans were always so impatient. It was actually quite amazing what humans would do to save themselves a few seconds. Risk death, even. Like some Demons.

Across the room, far behind me, Selena Avalos was speaking too loudly. "I just don't see the point," she was saying, her voice approaching a whine. "Why do we just stand here? Kate Bennett needs to die. After her insult to us, she doesn't deserve to live. There are more of us united than any of the Guardians realize; we would meet little resistance, even with their dramatic show of guarding her. Far Darrig alone would be able to penetrate their feeble defenses."

I was relieved once again that Avalos was too intimidated by me to address me personally—that held true for most everyone who served the Demon Lord. I preferred things that way; I wasn't much of a conversationalist.

One of the Dmitriev brothers grunted, appreciating her words. Without turning, I would have to guess it was Viktor—he was the more aggressive of the two.

Takao Kiyota spoke, his voice thin and dangerous. It matched his appearance and personality perfectly. "You Demons are too impulsive. We must stop and think."

Exactly, I agreed internally.

"What good is she to us, anyway?" Mei Li muttered. "She finished her unique task. Surely we have enough gifted Seers. What is one more?"

"Fine!" Avalos said. "Let *me* take care of her, my lord. It would be my pleasure. You would then be free to focus on distributing the virus to our allies."

I cast a long look at an insignificant white SUV as it darted through the traffic. I saw it come upon the slowing black car too quickly and knew an accident was imminent. I closed my eyes before impact, wishing the Demon Lord would finally speak and restore order to his ranks; give *me* an order, something to do so I wouldn't become impatient. Since O'Donnell's narrow escape last night, I'd been aching to snap his neck. Even better, snap *her* neck and make him watch. He needed to suffer. As I suffered.

Music—Chopin—filled the room. The intricate notes grated on my nerves. I opened my eyes, saw the wreckage on the street below. A tangle of metal, a littering of broken glass. That was all that remained of the colliding cars, all because of impatience. I gritted my teeth and swallowed back my rush of anger.

I needed to be patient. I couldn't rush my revenge. I couldn't afford for O'Donnell to escape me again.

Your brother, the thought flashed through my mind. I easily resisted the urge to wince. No. Not my brother. My enemy.

Yuri's voice was low, his words slow. "She did what was

most required of her. She secured Far Darrig. Anything else she could do for us could be done by another."

"Far Darrig?" My master's voice was politely inquiring.

I turned at once, fists tight at my sides.

The white room was occupied by only a handful, the Demon Lord's inner circle. My master had his back to a window, his questioning eyes on me. Takao was standing nearest to him, with Mei Li still close at hand; both were overprotective bodyguards. Avalos was wearing a green evening gown, though it was still morning, and beside her the Dmitrievs looked all the more weathered and ugly.

They were all watching me, waiting for my answer.

I focused on my master, my mouth barely moving. "We need to be cautious. Revenge is only possible with patience."

Avalos rolled her eyes, hands moving to rest against her curving hips. "Patience? That's what you suggest?"

"Now, now." The Demon Lord smiled at me, though his comments were directed to Avalos. "Far Darrig has a valid point. Of course we have the forces necessary to kill Kate. Despite the Guardians' efforts, she could be dead before tomorrow if we wished."

"Well, don't we want her dead?" Avalos griped.

Yuri spoke. "Master, she's insulted you by escaping. Your enemies, your more tentative allies . . . they will hear of this. They will think you incapable of handling the Guardians if you can't manage a single Seer."

The Demon Lord ignored them, eyes on me. "Far Darrig, do you have a specific plan in mind?"

I shrugged. "Nothing specific. But I know how to stalk prey most effectively, if it's a point you're trying to make. This is your opportunity to show the world—Guardians, Demons, and Seers—that you have the upper hand. Let the Guardians think they're winning and then crush them. Let them bring forth their best efforts to stop you, and then destroy them. Let O'Donnell think he's keeping her safe, and then strike. Let Kate Bennett think she's escaped and then end her."

The Demon Lord nodded leisurely, considering the idea. "We can't afford to let them go unpunished," he mused aloud. "Kate must die. But that doesn't mean we can't use this situation to our advantage."

"How?" Avalos asked. She shook her head. "Waiting would be a mistake, I think. Let us attack when they are weakest, before they have time to fully prepare for our—"

"No." The Demon Lord smiled. "I will use Kate Bennett as an example. We will give the Guardians time to scramble, time to panic. Kate Bennett hasn't escaped, and her Guardians at least know as much. I have an idea . . . It will keep them entertained. In the meantime, we'll see what epic plan the Guardians will devise to stop us. This revenge will be sweet, because it will be well earned. Far Darrig?"

I looked up. "Yes, Master?"

"How would you like to oversee O'Donnell's downfall?"

I felt my eyes sharpen. "I want nothing more."

one

One Month Later
Kate Bennett
New Mexico, United States

I was standing in the parking lot of the Illusion Hotel and Casino. I'd been here before, but it hadn't been like this. Last time, the darkness hadn't seemed this black. The lights of Vegas had kept everything lit up, and last time, I hadn't been alone. Patrick's strong arm had been wrapped protectively around my shoulders, and I'd been surrounded by other Guardians and Seers who cared about me.

Not this time.

I was alone. But not without company.

I was staring into the piercing blue eyes of Far Darrig, and just below my line of sight I knew he was pointing a gun at me. He had no expression on his face, and his black aura told me nothing. We simply gazed at each other, neither of us moving, not even breathing. His eyes were familiar to me—almost a perfect copy of Patrick's. But there was a hate inside of them I had no experience with. That hate was all his own.

Suddenly his lips moved. He was speaking to me, his voice low and muted. "He told you to save me, didn't he?"

I swallowed hard—my heart was pounding. "Yes," I whispered, my eyes firmly on his. "He promised everything would be all right."

Far Darrig's expressionless face twitched, the change too quick to interpret; he was back to a blank stare in a split second. "My father is a fool. As you are, if you believe you can change me."

"I believe him." I wasn't sure why I insisted on arguing with this dangerous enemy. What compelled me to ignite that spark of loathing hiding just beneath his carefully crafted mask?

He blinked at last, though only once. I drew in a sharp breath, as if that insignificant action had somehow freed me from this trance. His voice was wooden. "Don't. Faith is for the unrealistic. Only the weak trust in the empty words of others."

I pressed my lips tightly together and tried to make my expression as calming as possible. "I trust him, Sean. Call me weak or unrealistic—but I trust him. I trust in you, your good side."

His eyes closed again, longer this time, and when they opened, I knew something had changed. I knew I'd lost the fight.

A chilling smile climbed his cheeks. "I have no good side."

I heard a gunshot. I waited for the painful bite of the discharged bullet, but it never came. I could see the thin trail of smoke curling up from the end of Far Darrig's gun, but it didn't make sense. If the bullet wasn't in me, where had it gone?

In a second, I had my answer. The revelation had only been waiting this long to build suspense. A body collapsed next to me, and I turned to see my grandpa on the warm asphalt. His aura was gone; he was dead. I screamed, but no sound came out.

All I heard was Far Darrig's low, horrible laugh. "Hold on to your faith if you wish, Kate. But you'll be disappointed in the end. I'll make sure of it."

I fell to my knees, as if predestined to do so. I crawled to my grandpa's side, saw his wide and gaping eyes, and I screamed again. Still no sound, aside from Far Darrig's unhurriedly building chuckle.

Grandpa's lifeless mouth suddenly moved, while his eyes and body remained dead. "Kate. Bring me back. You can bring me back."

I tried to speak—to tell him it was impossible. Yes, I could travel through memories. I could stop that bullet from stealing his life. But if I did, I would die. Special Seers weren't allowed to roam around the years in their own lifetime. I might have enough time to change this one event, but then I would be dead. And I knew he didn't want that exchange. He would never want me to give up my life for his. Although knowing it and then having to tell him that I valued my life more than his . . .

I couldn't tell him. No sound could escape me.

I felt something in my closed fist. Something I'd been clinging to this whole time, though I hadn't realized it until now. I glanced down at my uncurling fingers and saw the knife balanced on my open palm.

I couldn't bring my grandfather back, despite his pleas. But I could avenge him. I could kill Far Darrig.

Kill him or save him . . .

I pushed myself up from the ground and turned toward the waiting Demon. He was staring at me, his eyes wider than before. "Kill me, then," he nearly taunted. "You can't save me. So kill me. Kill me. Kill me, Kate Bennett, before I kill you. Before I kill everyone you love."

My fingers hesitated, then suddenly I was crushing the hilt. I knew without consciously admitting it that I'd made my decision to destroy him.

Far Darrig grinned. I tried to ignore how familiar that grin was. He dropped the gun without thought, spreading his hands and holding them inoffensively near each hip. It was an inviting pose, and his taunting eyes gleamed. "Come on, Kate," he breathed. "We haven't all night . . ."

I zeroed in on his chest, where his heart was beating madly. I thought I could actually hear it pounding. My resolve wavered for only a second, then I was darting forward, holding the knife exactly as Patrick's training dictated.

The second before the blade sank into his heart, I heard Patrick's agonized cry.

I jolted awake, my arms and legs thrashing abruptly against the mattress. I lay gasping on my bed, staring up at the ceiling, trying to steady my breathing.

I'd had versions of that same dream nearly every night for just over a month now. Ever since the funeral I'd been reliving my grandfather's death. The horrible bang of the gunshot, the awful dropping of my stomach as I watched him fall to the asphalt . . .

This past week, the dreams had changed. After hearing my grandpa beg me to save him, to change the past, I looked down and discovered the knife. This was the first time I'd ever decided to actually use it, determined to kill Sean O'Donnell for what he'd done. Last night I'd tossed the knife aside, disgusted by the sight of it. But I hadn't this time. This time, I would have done it. I *had* done it.

I squeezed my eyes closed, dragged one arm to drape over my face. It blocked out the majority of the morning sunlight, but the comforting darkness was not completely calming. The thumping of my heart was painful, and my rasping breaths were taking too long to steady.

These dreams couldn't be healthy. Killing my boyfriend's brother, seeing my grandfather die again and again . . . It had to be the stress. That's what created these dreams that filled me with doubt; that left me so shaken I hardly knew my own emotions anymore. Had I really become the type of person who would kill? The idea was ludicrous. Yet the dream was so fresh I could still feel the thrill of giving in to my murderous urges. I hadn't just chosen to kill Far Darrig. I'd *enjoyed* it.

I was going to be sick.

I placed a hand over my mouth and fought to remember

what else had been different this time. Patrick's cry had been new. And though it had been extremely painful to hear his wounded scream, I was glad it was the resounding memory of the dream. The lingering knowledge that killing Sean would destroy Patrick left me feeling a little more sane. Of course I wouldn't kill Far Darrig. Patrick would never forgive me for killing his brother. It was only a dream. A horrible nightmare, maybe, but in the end it was just fantasy.

The sudden pounding on my door startled me, giving my body its second shock of the morning. "Kate!" Josie called through the door. "Are you up or what? We need to be out of here in fifteen minutes!"

"Of course I'm up," I lied, pushing myself into a sitting position so I could see the clock. Wow, I'd slept in. "I'll be right down!" I shouldn't have bothered with the last words, because I could already hear my sister skipping down the stairs.

It was Friday, thankfully. Getting through school was becoming a daily chore. Senioritis might be some of the problem, but mostly I was just tired of pretending to be normal when I wasn't. True, I had some excuses to be a little weird and distant in public. I was the girl who'd lost both her parents and a grandparent, all in the same year.

Luckily, Thanksgiving break was fast approaching, so I had that to look forward to. Today, then just another week and a half. It would be a great break from school—one that I needed.

If only a vacation from my own life could be so easily arranged. Not all of it was bad, of course, but I'd been living under constant fear and heavy guard for a month. There was no break from it. Instead of the usual one or two Guardians most Seers had, I had four. I enjoyed the help of two additional Seers, just in case someone tried to sneak up on us when I wasn't paying attention. Basically, I was never alone. Not even at home. Neither was my family, not that they were aware of that fact. The twins had no clue about the unusual side of my life. Grandma knew everything now, but even she didn't realize how closely we were being watched. It was just as well—I was freaking out enough for all of us.

I mean, I knew things had to be different now. Escaping the Demon Lord wasn't something we could just walk away from. There would be consequences. And I was completely aware of how much my Guardians were sacrificing to protect me. At the same time, it was hard to be smothered so constantly, when absolutely nothing had happened. From what we could detect, there were no Demons in the area, aside from Clyde. Peter Keegan, a Seer who worked for the Demons, was the closest possible enemy we had, though I didn't perceive him that way. He was dating my best friend's mom and completely committed to their safety. While that opened up the possibility for betrayal, he was, for the moment, protecting people I cared about. Patrick didn't share my optimistic view on Peter Keegan, but at least for now I didn't feel the need to fear the Demon Seer.

I pulled in a deep breath meant to brace me for the day and rolled easily out of bed. I found some lightly wrinkled jeans in the corner that I'd worn yesterday and a little more searching won me a simple black T-shirt. Though it wasn't the most stylish outfit, it would work for a Friday. As I slipped my feet into a pair of thin flats, I gripped the edge of my dresser, my eyes drawn to the framed pictures on the top. The smiling faces of my parents filled me with longing and nostalgia, but it was the picture of Grandpa in his old overalls that made my lips compress painfully. He looked so happy in the snapshot. His arm was slung around Grandma's shoulders, and she was annoyed because she wanted to eat the hamburger on her plate. He was just grinning, his thin hair caught in the breeze. I'd taken this picture myself, the last Fourth of July my parents had spent with us.

I knew my grandpa didn't blame me for his death, yet I couldn't help but feel responsible. Especially when I missed him so much. I knew I wouldn't feel so lost and worried if he was downstairs right now, reading his paper over breakfast, teasing Grandma . . .

I forced myself to look away from the picture. I didn't have time to have a breakdown this morning. I sniffed back my stinging tears, scooped up my makeup bag, and made my way to the bathroom at the end of the hall. I wanted to skip over the whole get-ready-for-the-day routine, but Lee would get concerned if I showed up without doing any makeup. Besides, my hair really needed some attention.

The bathroom door was partially closed, but I didn't bother to knock. Living in a house of girls did that to a person. Unfortunately, I should have remembered more people were living here these days.

Luckily his back was to me as he stood in front of the toilet. Still, when I heard the sound of a short zipper being tugged down, I was pretty sure I'd just walked into my most embarrassing moment.

"Toni!" I gasped in shock.

My Hispanic Guardian glanced over his shoulder. "Whoa, there!" he griped, whole body tensing as he tried to keep his body angled away from me. "Kate, where's your *propriety?*"

My cheeks were flushed, and I wanted nothing more than to close my eyes and slam the door. But I couldn't keep myself from blurting out the obvious. "You're in my *bathroom!*"

"And I'm not taking a bath," he hinted significantly, his expression bordering on pain.

"We had rules!" I snapped, lowering my voice instinctively. (I was getting used to interacting with invisible people, through necessity; I didn't want my sisters to think I'd started talking to myself.) "You're not supposed to come up the stairs," I reminded him heavily, keeping my gaze firmly on his wide eyes. Even though he was turned away, I wasn't about to let my eyes drift lower.

"Yeah, well, your grandma was in the one downstairs, and I'm no pervert. Though I can't say the same for you. Geez, Kate," he whined. "Can you at least close your eyes or something? Or I'm telling Patrick you peeked."

His words triggered my ability to move, and I was quick to pull the door closed. I heard him mutter something in Spanish, and I closed my eyes tightly, wishing I could forget the whole moment.

Jenna's voice was confused beside me, and I barely restrained a jump of surprise. "Is someone in there?" she asked.

Yeah. An invisible immortal guy who's been shadowing you for the past month. "What?" I asked too quickly.

She raised one dubious eyebrow at my startled reception of her. "Josie's downstairs. But you were talking to someone."

"Huh? No, I wasn't."

She folded her arms, regarding me strangely. "Fine. Then why are you standing out here, holding the doorknob?"

For a brief second, I had no answer. And then I shook my head. "Jenna, it's a spider, okay?"

"You always tell spiders they aren't allowed up the stairs?"

I squinted at her. "I thought you were afraid of spiders?"

"I am. But I'm also scared of psychotic sisters."

"Do *you* want to kill it?" I challenged, remembering my dream the second the word *kill* escaped me.

She paled just a little. "I think I'll let you get this one," she said, before skirting past me and bouncing down the stairs. I watched her go, taking note of her aura.

It was brighter today. Good.

A second later, the toilet flushed, and then Toni's voice rang through the door. "The psychotic pervert can come in now, if she so desires." I pushed the door open, watching as Toni washed his hands in the sink. He tossed me a carefree smile. "Good morning. How was your night?"

I got right to the point. "Toni, what are you doing in my bathroom?"

"Pretty sure you caught the gist of—"

"Why didn't you close the door then?" I hissed. "Just because my sisters can't see you doesn't mean you should be in their *bathroom.*"

"Sheesh, let's not bite Toni's head off or anything. I mean, it's not like the guy does any favors for you." He shut off the water and reached for the fluffy blue hand towel. He turned to me while he dried off his hands, leaning against the counter and looking perfectly at ease. "I mean, do you think I *like* trailing two eleven-year-old girls all day? I use your bathroom in return for being a dutiful bodyguard, and the next thing I know I'm getting yelled at."

"I'm not yelling."

"Your eyes are."

I opened my mouth to contradict him when Josie yelled from downstairs, "Nine minutes, Kate. Wait—eight!"

I pushed past Toni into the bathroom and set my makeup bag on the counter. I jerked the zipper open and searched for my mascara.

Toni watched me silently for a moment, and then he spoke easily. "Something's bugging you. Want to share?"

"I don't really want to share anything with you at the moment. Including this room." I found my mascara and twisted the top off. I glanced over at Toni, gesturing with my chin. "Can you turn on the light, please?"

He flipped it on with the flick of a finger, but he continued to hold the towel and stare at me. He settled back against the counter, watching as I began stroking the small brush over my eyelashes.

"You haven't been sleeping well," Toni stated suddenly. "During my last night watch, I heard you from downstairs. You were crying."

I started combing through my other eyelashes, eyes intent on the mirror before me. "I had a bad dream."

"Yeah, I can imagine. Claire and Jason, they've heard you too. I haven't asked the others, but I'm pretty sure these bad dreams of yours are getting worse."

I sent him a quick look, then dipped my hand back into my bag, searching for some eye shadow to help my eyes look less tired. I tried to keep my voice neutral. "Have you told Patrick?"

He meticulously folded and replaced the towel on its rack. "Nope. Wasn't planning on it, either. The guy's already losing enough sleep over you."

"He worries too much."

Toni shrugged. "He's duly concerned, I think. You're a little heavier on the right eye—there, yeah. Anyway, I don't think he's got any plans to help on the night watches, since you keep him busy all day, but . . . if he does, you might give him some warning. Else he might come running up those stairs to save you, and that's obviously against the rules."

"He's exempt from that rule."

"He's allowed in your bedroom? I should tell your grandmother . . ." He squinted into my bag, and before I could stop him he'd snatched something out. "What the freak thing is this?" He blanched, holding it close to his face for a better examination.

"It's for curling your eyelashes."

"It looks like a medieval torture device," he said evenly, cautiously opening and closing it.

"You would know."

"I'm not *that* old, *chica*."

I rolled my eyes. "Toni, don't you have anything better to do?"

"Not really, no."

"Maybe you could *find* something to do? Downstairs?"

He set the eyelash curler on the counter, looking wounded. "Fine," he sniffed. "But just so you know, your hints are so pointed I think you drew blood—you should be more careful."

"Toni," I said warningly.

He surrendered, with raised hands and all. "Yeah, sure, I'm gone. I was never here . . ." He backed out of the room, and I concentrated on getting ready for the day.

I heard Jack's thick Australian accent before I reached the kitchen. He was the only Guardian aside from Patrick allowed to be visible around the twins, and I was grateful my sisters had him. Honestly, I think he was a lot of the reason why their auras were getting happier lately. To them he was Uncle Jack, one of Grandpa's good friends. He looked to be in his mid-thirties, quite a bit younger than Grandpa had been, not that that seemed to raise any suspicions. The twins were just happy to have him around.

". . . Then I said to the bludger, 'Get your own!' " The twins chuckled, more from his eccentric storytelling than the actual story, and then he prompted them to finish their food. "Brekkie is an important meal, you two. Don't laugh at me; I'm serious." More giggles erupted at that.

"Um, thank you, Jack," Grandma interrupted, sounding anything but grateful. "Josie, finish your milk. Jenna, was Kate on her way down?"

Before my sister could answer, I was stepping into the familiar kitchen.

The twins were sitting at the table with Jack, who was sitting in Grandpa's usual spot. Grandma was at the stove, heating some water for her tea. An invisible Toni was standing in the corner, waggling his fingers at me with a goofy grin.

I focused on Grandma, who turned at my entrance. "Kate, how did you sleep?"

"Good," I said, not bothering to elaborate.

Toni snorted, and Jack caught himself before he could completely turn at the sound. He did lift questioning eyes to me, and I rolled mine in answer. Jack smiled a little, then focused back on his oatmeal.

I moved to the table, not bothering to sit down. I reached

around Jenna to grab a bagel, and I asked Josie to pass the knife and strawberry cream cheese.

While I prepared my breakfast, I tried to figure out who was on what duty today. Judging from Toni's presence, and Jack's, it was pretty safe to guess that Claire had just gotten off the night shift. That meant Maddy would most likely be at the elementary school, where—with fake ID and some help from Terence—she'd been able to secure a janitorial position. She and Toni would be on twin duty, then. Jack would be with my Grandma for the day, which meant Jason was the one with the morning off. Patrick, of course, was my personal bodyguard. The occasions were rare when he would let that job fall to anyone else. His presence was the one thing I could count on every day.

I took a few hurried bites of my bagel, and then I motioned for the twins to head for the car. Toni was already moving toward the door, assuring me he'd be in the trunk. He called it the Toni Seat, actually. Jack barely held in a laugh, which he covered by jumping up to help my Grandma with the steaming teapot. "Let me get that billy for you, Charlotte."

She nodded her thanks and then turned back to the table. "You girls have a good day at school, all right?"

"Yeah," Josie grunted. "Should be great. Mr. Keegan's going to show us some boring movie about how great the ocean is."

"I think it's going to be fun," Jenna argued.

"We all make mistakes," Josie reassured her sister.

I waved with my bagel on the way out. "Bye, Grandma. Bye, Jack."

"Have a corker of a day, Kate."

"I love you." Grandma overrode him.

I returned the sentiment with a smile, then turned and walked down the entryway to the waiting front door.

Despite all the negative things in my life, it was great to know I had friends who cared about me. Not just the Guardians and Seers, either. Lee Pearson was one of my greatest comforts these days. She understood me better than almost anyone alive. She'd been with me through losing my parents, so she could basically pick up on my moods with telepathic accuracy. In addition to understanding my needs, she was also one of the only people who knew about my abilities and the danger I was in. She'd been there in Vegas, helping me get away from the Demon Lord. I knew she'd be there whenever I needed her next. That was just Lee. She was loyal and understanding. She was also a little eccentric. This week was the last week of Rainbow Days, her seven-week celebration of the basic colors. Orange, blue, red, pink . . . she'd done them all. This week was green. Though she'd done a lime green shade for the first half of the week, she'd now moved on to a darker color. She kind of resembled a leprechaun, actually. Her almost shoulder-length hair was still dyed a lighter shade, but it worked with the darker outfit.

As I pulled up to her house and watched her approach the car, I could see she'd stuck with the darker theme today. She wore green leggings and a cute green dress she'd probably got at some yard sale. Her green shoes were dressy, closed toe with a thick buckle over the top. Her makeup was green, her dangling earrings were green—shamrocks, by the look of them—and she had on dark green lipstick. Who knew they even made something like that?

I'd been picking her up for school ever since I'd gotten my Hyundai Elantra, but I wondered if my car would have been able to recognize her as the same person through all of her extreme fashion changes. Several weeks ago she'd been gothic, after all, and a hippie before that. There really was no knowing with Lee. I wondered what she'd look like come Monday.

Lee slipped into the car and Josie spoke immediately, unable to hold the words back. "Um, St. Patrick's Day is in March, Lee."

"Yeah, well, you try wearing green stuff for a week. Sooner or later you run into something Irish-y." She gave me a quick smile. "And how are you, Kate?"

"Great. I love the lipstick; it's better than what you used Monday."

"Yeah, I had to special order this one. Bit more expensive than I like, and it didn't get here until after school yesterday. But I got the shoes and dress at this really awesome garage sale. I mean, this lady had *everything*. I'm just about ready for next week too, I think."

"Which is?" Jenna asked, a little nervously.

Lee only grinned. "Nope, not telling. I want it to be a surprise."

Josie laughed once. "Don't worry, Lee—everything you do is a surprise, whether you give us warning or not."

The drive to the elementary school was pretty much an opportunity for Lee to quarrel lightly with my sisters. I didn't contribute much to the conversation, but they didn't seem to need my input.

Once at school we followed the usual routine. The twins slid out with half-hearted good-byes, and once they'd walked far enough away, I popped the trunk. Toni pushed it open the rest of the way and hopped out, invisible to everyone but me. Lee got out of the car to shut the trunk, casting an apologetic look to the concerned-looking lady behind us, and then on her way back to the car she muttered a quiet good-bye to Toni.

"I love her," Toni told me, grinning at Lee as she ducked back into the car, oblivious to his presence. "She knows how to show gratitude."

"Have a good day, Toni," I told him.

"Hey, you—"

His words were lost when Lee slammed the door closed.

She looked over at me belatedly. "Oops. Did I cut him off?"

"Nope," I lied, shifting and pulling away from the curb, leaving Toni frowning on the sidewalk. Once back on the road, I shot a look to Lee. "You know, you handle all of this really well."

She was holding my iPod, searching for a new song. "Yeah,

I'm great and wonderful. So, did you have the dream again last night?"

She always knew what was on my mind, and she wasn't afraid of getting to the point. I sighed, my fingers tightening around the steering wheel. "Yeah."

"The same?" Her concern was obvious, though she was trying to hide it.

"Mostly. Only this time, I didn't drop the knife."

Her hunt for a song was abandoned in an instant. She looked over at me, her voice soft. "What did you do with it?"

I snorted, eyes on the road. "I did what he told me to do. I attacked him. I woke up before it actually hit him, but . . . I made the decision to kill him. I wanted to kill him."

She didn't look as disturbed as I thought a normal person should; even her voice was too calm. "Kate, you should tell Patrick."

"What? Why? He doesn't need to know I'm having nightmares about killing his brother."

"You're not sleeping well. You're getting edgy. It's becoming obvious. I think you and Patrick need to work this out. I mean, you haven't really talked about it since coming back from Vegas, and the topic needs to be addressed. Sean is messing up the both of you."

"You talk about all this so easily . . ."

"Yeah, well, when you have a weird psychic Seer for a best friend who's dating an ancient, immortal Guardian, you get used to strange things."

Her light words tugged a smile from me. "I guess you've got a point."

"I've got a few good points. Really, I think you should talk about this." There was a slight pause, where neither of us said anything. Then, "Will you at least consider it? Just because you can see emotions doesn't mean you always know what's best for people."

"I can't see Patrick's." As if that justified anything.

"I know. But if you'd look a little closer, you'd see how worried he is. And all that worry can't be just about you. Suddenly learning about his brother had to be a shock. He needs to talk to someone, but I don't think he wants to burden you with that. I mean, after everything Sean did to you . . ."

My stomach tightened at the memories. "Yeah. You're right. I'll try and talk to him."

"Good. That done . . . Any plans for this weekend?"

I sighed. "I'll have to discuss that with my probation officer."

Lee laughed, and the happy sound lifted my face with a slow smile.

two

We were nearing the end of the semester. In American Literature we were focusing on Edgar Allen Poe. We had an essay due next week that I was trying really hard not to think about, because I already felt like I had enough horror in my life without reading Poe's gory stories. The great thing about American Lit was the same great thing about all my classes—Patrick O'Donnell. My Guardian, the man I was in love with.

It was amazing how my fears and frustrations could melt away the second we were in the same room together. He was early as usual, the only one in the classroom. He was sitting at the same desk he'd been sitting in for what seemed like forever, silently waiting for me. He was thumbing through the slim book of Poe's most popular works, but he glanced up when he heard me enter the room.

He was wearing a light-blue button-up shirt, sleeves rolled at the elbows. His faded jeans made him appear tall, even when he was seated. A black leather bracelet circled his wrist, a gift he'd received from Toni years ago. He was quite pale because immortals couldn't get tans or sunburns. He had a light dusting of freckles on his face and light-brown hair that brushed over his forehead and curled delicately around his ears. He had a prominent jaw and a heart-melting smile. But it was his eyes that always seemed to capture me. They were startlingly blue, piercing and clear. The way they focused on me—as if there was nothing else in the world that mattered more. It made me wonder what I'd done to deserve this level of devotion.

He laid the book down on his desk, Poe's words no longer worth noticing as he stood to greet me. "Kate," he said, half-grinning. The smile was somewhat cautious, and I knew he was trying to measure my expression. Judge to see if today was a good day, or one of my harder ones.

I didn't make him wonder long. My smile came of its own accord, unable to resist him. I stepped right into his waiting arms, which encircled me easily—backpack and all. I wrapped my arms around his neck, pulling closer against his muscled chest.

He chuckled in my hair, which I'd left down in slightly unruly waves. "I gather your day is going okay, then?"

"Now it is."

He laughed again, pleased that I was in such an improved mood. He pulled back so he could place his hands on the sides of my face. He looked into my eyes for a short moment, his fingertips stroking my sensitive skin, then he leaned in and our lips met softly.

While we kissed my own arms slid down from around his neck. One hand wandered to cradle his slowly moving jaw while the other brushed at the hair around his right ear. His skin was so warm and smooth, his hair wonderfully soft and the perfect length: long enough to run fingers through, while not so long that it covered his face. His lips slid gently around mine, making this otherwise mundane moment completely poignant. Patrick's mouth shifted away from my lips. My eyes were closed, and I didn't bother to open them yet, content to enjoy the feel of this moment. My fingers continued to play with the ends of his hair, his hands still warm on my skin. His forehead tipped to rest against mine. "The bell's going to ring soon."

We were both breathing heavier than could be considered normal, but that didn't stop me from pressing my lips back against his. I pulled away almost as quickly and his fingertips tightened against my face, fighting tenderly to keep me close. I smiled and spoke carefully. "You're embarrassed to be seen with me, then?"

"Hmm, I was thinking of your feelings, actually."

"You don't think I like PDA?"

"What?" He laughed lightly, leaning his head back so he could see my face. "PDA?"

"Public displays of affection," I explained patiently, my eyes fighting to remain serious. Actually, he was really quite good at modern terms, for being over two centuries old.

He shook his head at me. "Texting has become a language unto itself. I suppose I'll have to practice it some more."

I grinned. "I'm happy to give you a lesson any time."

"Yes, but do you think we'd get much done?"

"Oh, I think we could accomplish a lot," I said, leaning in for another kiss.

When the warning bell rang we slid into our seats, though he wouldn't stop flashing me flirtatious smiles. So much for calming my heart rate before the room filled with students.

I decided to distract him. "So, Lee was wondering about my plans for the weekend."

He nodded once, watching me closely as I dug in my backpack for my copy of Poe's works. "What did you tell her?"

"That I'd need to consult with my guards first."

"Ouch. Is that all I am to you?"

I smiled and jokingly nodded, pressing the top of my mechanical pencil to force out some lead. "You're the grumpiest of them all. Toni's the most annoying, though."

"Oh yes? And just what is it he's done now?"

"You know Toni. He enjoys making a nuisance of himself."

"Quite true. Anything specific?"

I thought I'd be able to relay the story without blushing, but that was a lost battle after the first couple words. "He was in the bathroom this morning. I walked in on him. I kind of thought he'd be texting you all about it."

Patrick frowned and rolled his eyes. "Toni . . . I don't know what to do with him."

"Let's face it—you've spent like twenty-five years trying to civilize him. I don't think it's going to work."

He winced a little. "Are you ruined for life?"

"Maybe. It really wasn't that bad."

"You're blushing," he stated.

The flush deepened. "I guess living with only sisters has made me more innocent than some."

"I love you exactly the way you are, Kate. And as for Toni—"

"I think I properly dealt with him. I hope."

"Didn't we have the stair rule?" he asked suddenly.

"I'm glad someone remembers that, other than me. He claimed ignorance."

"He would."

The first of our classmates began meandering in, so our conversation died. He went back to sending me very distracting looks, and I tried to glance over the reading assignment we were going to be quizzed on today.

When Aaron stepped into the room, he called out a quick hello to both of us before settling into his desk across the pre arranged circle from us. My old boyfriend was happy today. His aura was bursting with yellow. I hadn't bothered to ask him about his increased happiness, even though his aura had been getting steadily brighter over the past week. Now, however, didn't seem like the appropriate time to question him. It could wait. Instead, I watched him surreptitiously over the next couple minutes, waiting for feelings of regret or even a hint of nostalgia to come.

He'd been my first boyfriend, one of my best friends for so long. I'd had so many good times with him; sometimes I wondered how my heart had let go of him so quickly. Sometimes I wondered why I hadn't doubted my decision to break up with him. Aaron was just so perfect; so natural. Our life together would have been predictable and pleasant.

Patrick, on the other hand, was a big unknown. Our relationship would never be normal. While loving him was as easy as breathing, nothing was easy about our complicated future. Demons aside, we had plenty of other problematic roadblocks to fairy-tale happiness. One of them being the fact that Patrick would live forever, and when I died I would go directly to heaven. We would be separated forever at that point.

Of course, my more logical side argued that I was still getting to know Patrick. We'd known each other less than six months. Should I really be worrying about these sort of long distance things? Then again, was my possible death really that far away? If I continued opposing the Demon Lord, I could be dead by Christmas, easy.

In the end, it was always my heart that tried to still these inner dilemmas. It didn't matter what conclusions I reached on a logical level, because I knew Patrick loved me, and he'd always be there for me—no matter what.

I was still stealing glances at Aaron, but no twinges of regret came. They didn't come because there was nothing to regret. There was only love. Love for a chapter of my life now gone and a remaining love that would fill me for the rest of my life.

***

Patrick held my hand while we walked to the cafeteria for lunch. Moving through the busy halls, he reminded me of the question I'd posed before first hour—our plans for the weekend.

I shrugged a little. "Honestly, I don't really care. But . . ."

"Yes?" he pressed.

"I was sort of hoping we could do something without the whole twenty-four-hour guard."

Immediately, his face grew concerned. "I don't know if that's such a good idea."

"Patrick, I think I'm going a little crazy under all this protection. I mean, I'd be with you, right? I just want to go somewhere without an invisible bodyguard, that's all. It's not like I'm proposing we go to Vegas or anything."

He didn't seem to appreciate my attempt to make light of the situation. "Kate, I know we've been a little overbearing, but it's for your own safety. No Seer has ever escaped the Demon Lord."

I sighed and tugged on the strap of my bag, which was slipping down my shoulder. "I wish he'd just try something already," I muttered.

Patrick blinked quickly. "What?"

"I hate this waiting. It's making me go insane."

"You want the Demons to come after you?" He nearly choked, struggling with the thought.

I nodded once, unrepentant. "At least then we'd know if all this protection is even worth the effort. I mean, knowing we haven't deflected any of his attempts doesn't exactly make me feel safer. All it proves is that the Demon Lord is taking his precious time to come get his revenge."

"Kate. I didn't realize you had so little faith in me."

He construed things so personally sometimes. Regardless, I felt bad for letting my frustration out. "No, of course I trust you. That's not what I meant at all."

He forced a somewhat pale smile and squeezed my hand. "I know."

I sighed deeply. "Forget it. Forget I said anything."

"No. If you need a break . . ." He shrugged. "I should be grateful you invited me along."

I smiled thinly up at him, searching his face carefully. "Are you sure?"

He nodded. "What is it you'd like to do?"

"I didn't think that far ahead. But as long as I'm with you, and there's no Toni involved . . . I'll be happy with whatever."

He smiled fully. "Very well. I'll pick you up tonight at six, if that works."

"You're taking me on a date?"

"You sound surprised. Isn't that what a boyfriend is supposed to do?"

My lingering smile was still wide by the time we'd gotten our food and taken seats at our usual table. Patrick reached over to help Jason open his water bottle, simultaneously offering a warm hello to Landen. All of the kids at this table were happy—no denying that. But Landen's aura seemed brighter than most. More content than most. He hardly ever spoke, and on the rare occasions he did, words were scarce. Emotions were always strong with him, and they flared brightly in his aura. When Patrick asked him once what he loved most, the answer had been simple: "Mom."

Today, Landen merely nodded at Patrick's greeting.

Trent started asking me if I was having spaghetti, which pulled my attention from watching Landen eat his spinach salad.

"Nope, just a sandwich," I told him.

Trent's smile was still wide. "Spaghetti?"

"What are you having?" I asked, deciding a different approach might better further the conversation.

"Spaghetti," he informed me happily.

"He is not!" David called out accusingly. "He's having pizza!"

"No, spaghetti," Trent insisted calmly.

"No, it's pizza!" David whined.

I gave him a firm look. "David, it's okay."

"Patrick . . ."

Patrick looked up from helping Jason. "David, Kate's right. Don't worry about Trent."

"Fine. I'll never worry about him ever again. *Ever.*"

I fought the urge to roll my eyes, and luckily I had the distraction of turning to see Olivia taking her seat next to me. She mumbled a quiet greeting, and then she started eating her large chocolate chip cookie.

I began unwrapping my sandwich but paused and looked up when I heard Lee's happy voice. "Much more of this, and I'm going to go insane, that's what."

Rodney, who was walking beside her, chuckled. "I don't know that anyone could tell the difference, actually."

She was holding her lunch tray, but she managed to thrust an elbow into his side. He groaned and favored his side with a bent arm, his tray tipping precariously. "*Ow,* Lee. That's what I get, after helping you with the music? Nice, really nice."

She grinned at him with her green lips, and her green hair seemed to shimmer under the lights when she sat across from me. "You secretly like me," she told him.

He took his seat on her side and snorted once. "Yeah. It's so top secretly secret that even *I'm* unsure." He then leaned in and placed a quick kiss on her surprised lips. He pulled back almost immediately, pulling a face. "Ew, that stuff stinks."

Her lips twitched. "You match me now."

He snatched up his napkin and hurried to wipe the green residue off his mouth. While he did that, Lee turned to look at me. "Well, *I*, for one, am glad it's Friday. Does anyone have any great plans?"

Mark glanced up from his food to nod. "Yeah, I am. My mom's taking me to buy a new game tomorrow."

"That's not fair," David complained. "You get a new game every week."

"Sometimes two," Mark confided, scratching absently at a sore near his ear. "I only tell you about my favorite ones."

I swallowed a bite of my sandwich and cleared my throat before speaking. "So, Lee, what are *you* doing this weekend? You seem a little more obsessed than usual."

"So says you to the one in total green," Rodney muttered.

Lee elbowed him again before answering me. "Nothing major. Mom and I are probably going to be cleaning the house all day. She gets like this around the holidays, not that I understand why. As far as I know, we're not doing anything special for Thanksgiving."

"You're always welcome to join us," I told her quickly, a little surprised she wasn't already planning on it. The Pearsons had been celebrating Thanksgiving with the Bennetts for years now.

She shrugged a little. "My mom doesn't want to impose. Things are different this year . . ." She shook her head. "Anyway, that's my great weekend. Peter may come by to help out, so I'll save the bathroom for last. More specifically, the toilet. It's all his, as far as I'm concerned."

"Are things not going well with him?" Patrick asked. He was always interested in anything the Demon Seer was doing, and Lee knew what the offhand question really meant: Was Peter acting strangely or being contacted by the Demons who had blackmailed him before?

Lee's voice was steady, though her aura was a bit more uneasy than before. "No, things are peachy—I just hate cleaning the toilet." She nodded to my Guardian. "What about you? What are you up to this weekend?"

"I'm not sure about much past tonight. Kate and I are going out."

"Oh yeah?" Lee's smile was knowing. "That's really nice of you, Patrick."

"Is that so unusual? Them going out?" Rodney laughed.

"Trust me—you don't know these two like I do. Kate's a party pooper and Patrick's a penny-pincher."

"And you're my best friend *why*?" I asked, wryly scathing.

She grinned. "Because you love my quirkiness."

"All-out weirdness, maybe."

She reached across the table to pat my hand. "Just telling it like it is, hon." She looked to Patrick. "I'm glad. You two will have fun doing something . . . fun." Rodney shook his head at her, but Patrick and I both heard the word Lee had wanted to say: *normal.*

***

As soon as we got home, the twins went to the kitchen to find a snack. I could hear Grandma's comfortingly rough voice greet them, and I hesitated on the bottom step, playing with the idea of joining them. But it was during moments like this the guilt resurfaced, and so I clutched at my bag and moved up the stairs instead. Once in my room, I tossed my bag to the floor and then stared out my window.

The worst part about these past few weeks was the waiting. The nothing. Ever since I'd been introduced to the world of the Guardians, it had been a constant battle against Demons. Dodging attacks, hunting enemies, trying to stay alive. For over a month now, I had nothing to do. We were purely on the defensive now. Terence—Patrick and Toni's Guardian supervisor—assured us that he had people taking care of everything else—tracking the Guardian virus, keeping tabs on Far Darrig and Selena Avalos (our two top worries), and basically solving all our problems with the Demon Lord. It's not that I didn't trust Terence, but . . . it was hard to entrust your fate to someone else, while you did absolutely nothing.

I wanted to talk to my grandpa. Since I didn't have him . . .

For a brief second, I wondered why it had taken me so long to think of this option; after all, it made sense. I wanted to know what was going on in the Demon world, and I had one strong connection to the dangerous underground: Clyde, Grandpa's old friend.

Clyde was a moderately reformed Demon. He owned a pawnshop on the edge of town, a dingy little store. He excelled at hearing rumors from other Demons, which helped him know who to avoid. He didn't exactly want people to know he'd been friendly with a Guardian Seer, but he'd imparted his information to my grandfather anyway. I hadn't seen him since the funeral, but if anyone knew what the Demon Lord was up to, it would be Clyde.

A part of me knew that if Clyde had something concrete, he would have called me, even if he wasn't a really communicative person. He might not know me personally, but he'd owed my grandfather a lot. Still, the sudden urge to do something—anything—was too strong to ignore. Maybe the trip wouldn't be for anything, but it would help my sanity.

I knew without going downstairs that an invisible Toni was in the kitchen, and Jack was also around, somewhere. To keep the twins from freaking out, he went around invisible a lot. Presumably, they were both downstairs.

I glanced at the clock, still turning the idea around in my head. A visit to Clyde would be fast and safe. My Guardians knew about him, though they didn't exactly consider him an ally. Though Patrick hadn't said the words aloud, I knew he didn't approve of Clyde. He wouldn't want me to go; he didn't think the sketchy rumors Clyde heard were worth the risk of associating with him.

I could be there and back easily before Patrick came to pick me up tonight, and then I'd know if our preparations were actually worth the energy. Though I knew going without a bodyguard might be immature and stupid, the idea of just getting in my car and going somewhere without supervision was appealing.

Stupid, stupid, my mind assured me.

But what was the alternative? The need to see Clyde was surprisingly strong. To have the illusion of doing something productive was an irresistible pull. I couldn't take Toni—I'd seen enough of him for one day. Besides, he'd try to talk me out of it. I didn't want Claire to find out about Clyde—she'd be at the warehouse, anyway, with Maddy and Patrick, who would then find out. Jack would probably be game for such a sudden excursion, but I couldn't invite him without inviting Toni; the annoying Guardian would tattle on me before we were out the door, if he wasn't included. That left only one bodyguard option: Jason, the Seer, and he had enough on his plate with classes and homework.

It would be so easy to go alone. If Patrick heard about this—whether Jason came with me or not—he'd be angry I hadn't discussed it with him first. Was the visit to Clyde worth my boyfriend's potential anger?

I answered that mental question with action. I snatched up my purse, patting my pockets to be sure I still had my keys and phone, then I slipped out of my room.

I was just stepping up to the front door when I heard Toni's voice behind me. "What'cha doin'?"

I spun around, noting in the turn he was alone in the entryway, and that I was most likely the only person able to see and hear him. I kept my voice low. "Toni. I'm just heading over to Lee's."

"Why?" he asked, his brown face straight.

I sighed. "Look, I'm going to be honest with you. Lee wants to talk about Rodney."

Toni pulled a quick face, clearly showing what he thought of that. "The band geek?"

"Yeah."

"Why?"

"She wanted to hear my take on his aura this afternoon."

One eyebrow rose. "That can't be done over the phone?"

"You know Lee. She'd rather we do this in person."

"And you were going to ditch your Guardians for this? On my watch? Patty would kill me and you know it." His countenance suddenly lifted. "I'll come with you!"

"You're on twin duty."

He shrugged. "Jack will fill in."

"Toni, do you really want to be there when Lee's trying to talk boys?"

"Heck yes I do. Maybe she'll talk about me?"

"Don't hold your breath. You'll be there visible or not at all."

He looked stricken. "Kate, what in the name of all that is good and holy is the point of being able to go invisible if you can't spy on old girlfriends?"

"Lee was never your girlfriend."

"Uh, check your definitions, smarty. She's a girl, since last I looked, and we were most assuredly friends."

I rolled my eyes. "I'll be at Lee's. Call if you need anything. I'll be back in an hour or so."

"You better go straight there and come straight back here, missy."

I pulled the door open. "You got it. Let my Grandma know where I've gone, okay?"

"Yeah, sure. 'Cuz I love being a message board."

I gave him a wry smile, then stepped onto the porch and pulled the door closed behind me. I was backing out of my driveway in the same minute. I didn't let myself dwell on what Patrick would say if he knew where I was going.

Clyde's Pawn was located in a rather unsavory part of town, and the building itself was pretty rundown looking. As I drove up, I was more than a little surprised to see another car parked out front. I'd never seen actual customers, so hopefully this meant Clyde would be in a good mood. I parked in front of the building, next to a black SUV. I made sure all my doors were locked, and then I walked up to the glass door. A man pushed it open from the inside, and I saw from his aura that he was really excited about something. I presumed it was the purchase he'd just made, which was wrapped up in a cardboard box in his arms. The woman behind him seemed a bit less impressed, but she was the one who warned him not to back over me.

"Sorry." He grinned, and I brushed off the near miss dismissively with one hand. The woman stepped through the door and slipped past me. The man kept his back pressed against the door, keeping it open for me. I nodded my thanks and entered the musty, dimly lit room.

The carpet was probably from the seventies, worn-looking and orange. The shelves were tightly packed, and stuff was everywhere. A narrow path weaved to the counter, which could barely be seen from here. The TVs lining one wall flashed with movement but made no sound. Clyde pretty much had a bit of everything: books, clocks, DVDs, stereos, computers, game consoles, bikes, musical instruments, little useless figurines; he even had a traffic light propped up in one corner.

The door thumped closed behind me, making the brass bell bang against the glass to signal my entrance. I stepped around the shelves, trying not to touch more than was absolutely necessary on my way to the back of the shop. The smell of tobacco was heavy in the air, permeating everything.

Clyde must have already slipped into the back room after helping his customers, because I couldn't see anyone behind the glass counter. There were guns for sale on the back wall, and in the glass case counter there were scattered valuables and some jewelry. I spared it all a quick glance, then looked toward the beaded curtain set against the back wall. "Clyde? Hello?"

I heard a muffled call that might have been an answer, and I straightened my shoulders to keep my purse from slipping down my arm.

I only had to wait for half a minute before Clyde pushed past the rattling beads. He was a large man with a rough appearance. He was in his midforties, or so it appeared. He was really much older, though I wasn't sure how *much*. His thin black aura still made me a little uneasy, even though I knew this Demon wasn't my enemy.

His eyes brightened when he saw me, making the wrinkles on his face deepen. "Why, Kate Bennett. What a surprise!" His voice was a little too loud, but that was just his way.

I smiled despite myself. "Hello, Clyde. How are you doing?"

He leaned against the counter, offering me a dirty hand in greeting. I took it, trying to convince myself it was only dust ingrained in his skin. "I can't complain. Business has been picking up lately. Good thing too. Times are tough on the self-employed. But how are you doing?" Though his voice was coarse, I knew his question was sincere.

I nodded once, setting my folded arms on the edge of the counter. "I'm doing okay. Thanks again for being at the funeral."

He grunted. "'Course. I wouldn't have missed it. Henry's been my closest friend . . ." His words trailed off, and his eyes sharpened. "So! What is it I can do for you?" Before I could form an answer, his forehead furrowed deeply. "Where're your Guardians?"

I decided not to lie. "I came alone."

"You're not here to leave more insane messages with me, are ya? 'Cause I can tell ya right now, it ain't happening."

"No, no messages. Actually, I was hoping you might have some news for me."

He shifted his weight and placed his elbows against the glass, causing it to creak. "News?"

"About the Demons. Far Darrig. Selena Avalos. The Demon Lord—"

"Whoa, whoa, girl. Easy. I know what you meant. I was just surprised. You see, I was playing with the idea of coming to visit you."

"Really?"

He nodded. "Sure. I've been debating it, though, since I value my life. Obviously I was worrying for nothing—I mean,

I thought the Guardians would have practically locked you in your room to keep you safe, and yet here you are, wandering the streets alone."

"My Guardians wouldn't hurt you," I argued, avoiding his main point.

He grunted. "Maybe the ones that know me. But there have to be others. Seriously, how many guards do you have now?"

"Clyde, that's not really important."

"Not important? Kate, no one escapes the Demon Lord. No one."

I sighed. "I've heard that once or twice now."

He snorted. "And I can see it made an impression. Maybe you don't realize the danger you're in—"

"Maybe I don't. But I'd like to. What was it you wanted to tell me?"

He stared at me for a long moment, as if debating whether he really wanted to share this with me. His fingers slipped into his apron pocket, and he fingered something inside—probably a box of cigarettes he was struggling not to light in my presence. "You remember Philippe? You've never met him, but—"

"He owns a bar," I said. "He's one of your best sources."

Clyde nodded his agreement. "He certainly is. Many Demons and Seers frequent his place, along with some dangerous humans. He drove down here a few days ago, wanting to tell me in person to keep my guard up."

"Why?"

His expression was dark. "Seems he had some of the Demon Lord's inner circle come into his bar, sometime earlier this week. I don't know which ones you've heard of, but they're all dangerous. Selena Avalos was among them."

"Selena's in the state?" I felt a tingle rush down my spine.

"Seems to be. She and some rather intimidating companions. Maybe you met the Dmitriev brothers during your trip to Vegas?"

I swallowed hard, thinking of the thickly built Russians, Viktor and Yuri. "Yeah. I ran into them."

Clyde bit his lower lip and shook his head. "They're bad news, that's for sure. A few others were with them—the scariest was a Seer, apparently. A Japanese fellow. Tacky, or something like that."

"Takao Kiyota."

"Yep. That was his name. Very aloof but dangerous looking, so said Philippe."

"Yeah, he is." I fought a shiver. All four of them, so close to home . . . This couldn't be good. "Did Philippe hear anything?"

"Not a whole lot. He delivered their drinks himself, but they clammed up when he was near. Seems they didn't meet with anyone or anything. Just came in for some drinks, talking quietly amongst themselves. Before they left, the beautiful one—Avalos—she came up to the counter and asked Philippe if he would mind passing a word along to any Demons in the area." He paused, but only briefly. "Looks like the Demon Lord's put a bounty on your pretty head, honey. Selena was spreading the word."

I blinked. A bounty? The word hardly made sense. A reward attached to me? It seemed so weird—so terrifying. And so unlike the Demon Lord. He was a calculative man, a manipulative enemy. He did things cleanly or not at all. Putting up figurative wanted posters for me seemed a little ridiculous. He was too powerful for this. Why not come after me himself?

Was this somehow a decoy? Was he going to try and distract my Guardians and then bring in the real threat? What could be worse than setting loose a hundred Demons driven by a reward, all wanting to get their hands on me?

Clyde watched my face for several long seconds, then he instinctively reached out and patted my arm. "The Demon Lord has a most wanted list—his prioritized enemies. It just usually involves Demons who've offended him. So far as I know, a Seer's never quite made the cut. Demons squabble over 'em, hoping for the reward, and the Demon Lord sends Far Darrig after some—but that's the end of the story. I think you're the first Seer, Kate."

I blinked up at him. "That's supposed to make me feel better?"

"Philippe had to pass the word along," Clyde continued quickly, sounding apologetic. "If he didn't, he would be risking his life. But Selena gave him pictures of you and everything. I have one, if you'd like it."

Feeling a little disconnected, I nodded.

He pulled his hand out of his pocket and handed me a folded sheet of paper. I took it from him, slowly uncurling the edges until I held a full-size page, half of it taken up with a picture of me. It was my senior picture from school. I didn't even want to think about how they'd gotten it. The smile on the picture was small, and the words beneath seemed surreal.

> *Kate Bennett, Seer. Wanted alive. Believed to be under heavy Guardian protection. Two positively identified Guardians are Patrick O'Donnell and Antonio Alverez. Both are extremely dangerous. A reward of*—I choked—*one million US dollars will go to those who manage to secure her. Seer may or may not be in hiding.*

My home address was included on the bottom as a starting point for anyone interested in getting the reward, along with Selena's number, in case there were any questions.

Clyde's voice seemed really distant. "You haven't seen any of these bounty hunters yet because they're being cautious. They want that money. Badly, I would imagine. The Demon Lord doesn't usually offer quite so much. Philippe doesn't know you're Henry's granddaughter, but he knows I like to stay informed. Sharing this with me was his way of keeping me from running into these zealous killers."

"This isn't the Demon Lord's style," I argued weakly, still staring at the monetary amount I was apparently worth. I guess I could have felt honored or something. In reality, I only felt sick.

"If you want my honest opinion, Kate, I think you should leave here—the sooner the better. Maybe even leave the country."

"What? I can't leave. They have my address!"

"*That's* exactly why you need to leave—try to cover up your tracks." Clyde shrugged helplessly. "I don't know what to tell you. But you can't stay here, Kate. For that amount of money . . . Every Demon in the state is going to be trying his best to get at you. The Guardians can't protect you from that kind of attack. Your enemies are too many."

"But what can I do? My friends, my family . . . They're all in danger. Even if I leave, I can't bring everyone I love with me."

Clyde's face was calmly serious. "They're not going to rest until they have you, Kate. That's the Demon Lord's style."

three

Clyde and I talked for a while longer, but time wasn't on my side. Toni would be expecting me back any minute, and I was still a good fifteen minutes away—almost twenty. Clyde let me keep the wanted poster, and we exchanged cell phone numbers. He promised to call me if he learned anything else, though he wasn't optimistic, then we exchanged hurried good-byes. He patted my hand before I left, and the feel of his calloused hand brushing against my skin lingered as I got into my car and started the drive back home. As soon as I was driving, I called Toni to let him know I'd lost track of time and I'd be home soon. He sounded incredibly bored, but he didn't press me like I thought he would.

That done, I leaned back against my seat and tried to think.

If I told Patrick about this latest development, he'd know I'd gone to Clyde's. He'd be upset, but he'd get over it. He needed to know about the price on my head. Almost more important, he needed to know that a bunch of Demons knew where I lived. As much as I didn't like admitting my home may have lost all security, I needed to be smart about this.

Still, I didn't want to ruin our date tonight, because we both needed it so badly. We both needed a break, but that wasn't going to happen if he knew a bunch of Demons were plotting to come after me. I felt like that piece of news could wait for several hours. Clyde had agreed it would take a bit longer for the bounty-hunting Demons to organize themselves. We still had some time, I finally decided.

In the end, all my fragmented thoughts brought me back to a single question. What was I going to do? I couldn't just run to another country with my Guardians. That would leave my family and friends unprotected. They were targets, almost as much as I was. But I couldn't uproot them all and take them with me. Clyde was fairly certain bounty hunters wouldn't concern themselves with my family, if I wasn't around, but I wasn't willing to take the risk.

A small part of me wondered if I should tell my Guardians at all. What if I didn't get a choice? What if Terence brought in his private plane and they whisked me away without asking my opinion? I couldn't lose my family and friends. I needed them, and they needed me.

At the same time, I couldn't leave my Guardians unwarned. They needed to know about the danger. They needed to protect themselves, though Clyde was fairly certain there wouldn't be one massive strike. Demons were selfish and greedy. They wouldn't form a large band, because they'd want the biggest share of the money possible. The biggest group might hold four Demons, Clyde assumed. They were logical assumptions. But the whole situation was so illogical, so unlike the Demon Lord.

I pulled into the driveway, turned off the car, and climbed out. Stepping inside the house, I could hear the muffled sounds of the TV in the family room, and I could see Jenna playing the piano in the front room. I assumed Grandma was in the kitchen when I heard one of the low cupboards banging closed. Toni was lying on the puffy couch opposite the piano. He was presumably invisible, though for how much concentration Jenna was pouring into practicing, even I was practically invisible to her. She didn't move at all when I closed the door, though Toni—who was flipping idly through a large book—did. He gave me a small wave but hardly looked up from the pages. I'd never seen him reading before, but I was too overwhelmed with my own thoughts to figure out what he was looking at.

I moved up the stairs, heading to the sanctuary of my room. There I looked at the piece of paper one last time before folding it up and pushing it back into my purse. It could wait while I showered and got ready for tonight. It might be one of the last peaceful nights I could enjoy with Patrick for a long time.

Just this morning I'd been regretting how the Demon Lord hadn't attempted anything. Strange how an opinion could change so quickly. My bravado from this morning was completely gone, and I was back to wishing the Demon Lord had remained silent.

Once out of the shower, I hurried to get dressed in a nicer outfit than I'd worn to school. I wasn't sure what Patrick was planning on doing, so I stuck to a pair of light jeans and a red blouse. I'd discarded the blue top I'd been thinking of wearing, because it was the same shirt I'd worn in my senior picture; the one that adorned my wanted poster. I was thinking about it enough, without the help of wearing the same outfit.

Patrick was a little early, but I was more than ready to go. We didn't linger at the house. We were both anxious to get away from the invisible Toni, who wouldn't stop talking even when we were trying to carry on a conversation with my family.

Jack and Patrick shook hands, pretending to have a casual knowledge of each other, since the twins were present. They'd met at the funeral and a few times since, so they weren't exactly strangers in the eyes of my sisters.

Toni told us not to be out too late, and finally Patrick was able to close the door on him. Once we were alone on the porch, Patrick placed his hands on either side of my face and pulled me gently forward. I kissed him deeply, my own fingers brushing over his chest, then sinking to curve around his waist. When I eventually pulled my mouth back, his eyes were closed and his smooth face was almost vacant. His lips pressed together and his eyes cracked open to regard me. "Wow, Kate," he breathed.

I blushed a little. "I'm excited for tonight."

"I can tell." He chuckled. "You've been holding out on me, all this time."

"We haven't had an evening alone together since—"

"Since you kidnapped me, I think."

"It's been a while," I admitted.

His lips twitched into a half smile, eyes shining brightly. "I should get you excited about things more often."

I think we would have kissed again if I hadn't noticed Toni's face in the living room window, watching us. I tugged on Patrick's wrist, and after he stuck his tongue out at his partner he followed me to his car, which was waiting at the curb. He opened the passenger door for me, and I slipped into the midnight blue Altima. It was the most expensive thing my Guardians owned, hands down. They wouldn't even have this nice of a ride, if Terence didn't have connections in the car world.

I set my purse on the floor by my feet while Patrick walked around the car. I was just pulling my seat belt on when he opened his door and settled behind the wheel. He shot me a smile that needed no interpretation, then started the car and we pulled away from my house.

"So," I said, reaching out to turn down the radio, "what's on the agenda for tonight?"

He was focused on the road, but he took a second to glance at me. "Well, I thought we'd start this very normal date off by going out to eat. You still like pizza?"

I nodded approvingly. "A very normal choice."

"I can be incredibly normal," he assured me, a small grin dominating his otherwise smooth face.

My heart started to pound. "I'm not so sure about that," I said, faking an ease I didn't really feel.

His eyes shined toward mine, his tone lightly teasing. "You think me abnormal?"

"Just incredible, actually."

His eyes rolled. "At least I've got you fooled."

"You're doing an excellent job," I agreed with a smile.

He might have blushed, just a little. "All right, so for this perfectly normal evening we're about to have, are there any subjects to be avoided? Toni, for instance?"

I shrugged. "Honestly, I don't care—I just wanted to be alone with you."

"And here I am, completely alone and in your power." He braked at a stop sign and I reached for his hand, which he'd dropped to the armrest. Our palms pressed tightly together, and he gave me a fast look before starting forward again. "You really are in a good mood, aren't you?"

I squeezed his fingers. "So far so good."

He seemed pleased, and I knew I'd made the right choice to keep my visit to Clyde a secret. Patrick needed tonight just as badly as I did.

He took me to a popular pizza place downtown, crowded with families and young couples on dates. It took several minutes, but soon our pizza was ordered and we were seated in the corner near a front window. The atmosphere was still loud, and the background rock music didn't help things, but since we were on the edge of the crowd we could at least hear each other without raising our voices too much.

Across the small round table from me, Patrick was nodding. "Oh yes, I feel like we're completely alone."

I smiled. "There's no Toni. Or Jack. Or Claire . . . How's that been going, anyway?"

He winced just a little. "She doesn't like speaking to me, but she's not going to leave unless Terence tells her to go."

"I don't understand her."

He shrugged. "She came from a different world. One where men dominated women. She didn't like it then, and she doesn't like it now. It's fairly simple."

"So she hates you just because you're a guy? I got the impression it had more to do with what happened in Vegas."

His face softened a little. "She doesn't regret helping us. She just—"

"She thinks I botched up her assassination. It's okay. You don't have to spare my feelings."

Patrick spoke quickly. "She doesn't blame you, Kate. If anything, she blames *me* for pushing her plans forward."

"You?" I couldn't hide my surprise.

He nodded simply. His eyes followed his index finger that surreptitiously brushed across the table's edge. "Claire feels I'm an inferior Guardian because I couldn't keep you out of trouble."

"But none of that was your fault," I protested. "It was all me. I took you to Vegas against your will!"

He shook his head, hand dropping back to his lap, his eyes coming back to mine. "No. I'm as guilty as you, if not more so. My weakness made it necessary for her to advance her plans, so she holds me personally responsible for every breath the Demon Lord continues to draw."

I shook my head. "She's such a cheerful person."

"Toni doesn't seem to see her flaws."

"He's still . . ." I hesitated, unable to find a delicate way to voice his more than obvious infatuation.

"Throwing himself ostentatiously at her feet?" Patrick supplied, before nodding once. "At every opportunity."

"You'd think he'd get the hint."

He shrugged. "Toni will be Toni. I don't think he's really invested at all. He just likes annoying her."

Our drinks arrived, and I took a quick sip of the sharp root beer. I waited until Patrick had lowered his own glass, then I spoke carefully. "I'm sorry I've been so . . . out of it lately. That wasn't fair to you."

"What are you talking about?" He honestly looked confused. "Kate, you've been going through an impossibly hard time."

I slid a finger over the rim of my glass, watching the drops of condensation slip down the frosted sides. "But I haven't been the only one suffering." I peered at him through my eyelashes, wondering even as I spoke if I was doing the right thing by bringing this up. "Seeing Sean again, realizing everything he's done . . ."

It was amazing how quickly his body stiffened. His whole bearing changed in an instant. In the second I mentioned Sean's name, Patrick turned his head and stared out the large window, watching as the cars darted past along the thin street. "You don't have to do this," he said, his voice low, knowing some words were required. "We don't have to talk about him."

"He's your brother, Patrick."

"No, he's not." I couldn't see his face, but his words were enough to stop my hand from reaching for him. "That monster, that Demon . . . he's *not* my brother."

I pursed my lips briefly and then forced myself to continue, despite the growing unease in the pit of my stomach. I'd known this would be a hard subject for him, but I trusted Lee's opinion that he wanted to talk about Sean. "I can't even begin to understand what this must be like for you—"

His eyes came back to mine in a rapid turn, and I was surprised to see how pale he was. His face was tight and his words were hard. "Stop. Please, Kate. Just stop. I can't do this . . . not with you."

I tried not to let the hurt leak into my voice. "I think it would help you to talk about him."

He shook his head. "Not after everything he's done to you."

I stretched my hand out, my fingers brushing the back of his loosely clenched fist before settling over it completely. My hand flexed around his, and our eyes remained firmly on each other. "I'm not the only one he's hurt," I said slowly, speaking just loud enough to be heard over the clamor of voices and music. "I love you, and I'm going to be here for you. You can talk to me about anything."

"Even your grandfather's murderer?" His words might have stung me, if he hadn't almost choked on them. His eyes were deeply pained. "Maybe you're strong enough for this, but I'm not."

"You aren't responsible for his actions."

He nearly snorted, his voice almost desperate. "Everything he's done is on my head. I'm the reason he's this way. The hate he feels for me justifies everything he's done, at least in his mind."

"He can blame you all he wants, but you're not accountable for any of it."

His head lowered, his eyes gazing firmly into his dark drink. "Maybe I could overlook the fact he's a Demon. The horrible things he had to do—that he must have *enjoyed* doing, to reach this point—they're haunting enough. But helping the Demon Lord and hurting you . . . My own brother tried to kill me. And you." I could feel his hand tremble beneath mine, and his words spilled quickly after that. "I gave up everything for him, and I only succeeded in destroying him. My brother isn't alive. Sean is dead. Only Far Darrig remains."

For a short moment, I wasn't sure what to say. I just stared at his ducked head, drawing a mental blank. When my mouth opened and words started to come out, I could have sworn the message came from someone else. "Maybe I can't help you understand that you're not responsible for Sean. Maybe that's because I don't know what you're going through, or maybe you won't listen to me because you think I'm incapable of understanding. But there is someone who knows *exactly* how you feel. The betrayal, the hurt, the guilt." His eyes lifted, but his expression was still guarded. He didn't press me to reveal a name—maybe he thought I was referring to deity. But no matter what he thought, he was surprised by the person I named. "Your father suffered through this too," I reminded him gently.

The song playing from the speakers was much too upbeat for this moment, but Patrick didn't seem to be aware of the noise. He was focused on me, on my words. "My father's gone," he whispered at last.

I nodded once, allowing that. "Now. But he wasn't always . . ."

I expected him to look relieved—maybe even excited. Instead, all I got was a rapid blink and a pale face. And he was stiffer than before. "No," he said firmly.

I waited for him to elaborate, but when he didn't I let my forehead crinkle. "No? What does that mean?"

His voice remained level, slightly clipped. "You're not . . . I'm not going to let you use your traveling abilities to go back and visit my father for me."

"Why not?"

"There's no need to risk it. I don't want you to travel ever again."

"But you could write a letter to him, get his advice—"

His eyes bored into mine, but he wasn't angry, just frustrated. "Kate, I don't want you experimenting with time. The past isn't supposed to be influenced by the present. It's unnatural and wrong. That makes it dangerous."

"I did it before."

"That was different. You were forced to do it. There's no reason to go back now."

I tried to be as persuasive as possible. "Your father would love to hear from you. After everything that's happened—everything you both went through—he needs this contact as much as you do."

"I'm your Guardian. Your safety is more important than my personal problems."

"I disagree. I love you. Nothing is more important to me than your happiness."

He looked a little taken aback. Maybe *stricken* was the better word. "Please, can we just drop this?" he pleaded. "What happened to that normal date we were supposed to be having?"

I ignored his last comment. "You're being unnecessarily difficult. What could be so dangerous about my going back to see your father?"

He didn't answer for a long minute. His clear eyes were hard to read. So many emotions were warring inside him that it was almost impossible to guess what he was thinking. The only thing clear to me was his pain. And above all, I wanted that to end.

Finally he spoke carefully. "If anything happened to you, Kate, I would never forgive myself. For as long as I existed, I wouldn't stop blaming myself. And I've never felt so helpless or useless as when you traveled to the past. I couldn't protect you there, because I couldn't follow you. Can you understand that? Letting you go—even for that split second—was the . . . the hardest thing I've ever had to go through. If something happened to you in the past . . . what if I lost you?"

I wasn't sure how to argue, so I made the first observation that came to mind. "Did it occur to you that I might be safer in the past? At least then I don't have the Demon Lord after me."

"He can travel too," Patrick pointed out evenly.

"Do you honestly think traveling is more dangerous than being here?"

"At least I'm with you when you're here. I can protect you here. As long as I'm with you, Kate, I *can* keep you safe."

His hand was no longer a fist beneath my palm. He was gripping my fingers on the table, as if he could hold me here forever. I understood his protectiveness. I just didn't understand why he thought my visiting his father was such a bad idea. I personally believed it was inspired. But how was I supposed to convince him of that?

Before I could come up with a good reply, our server stepped up to the table, invading the space between us.

Patrick released my hand and I drew back to make room for our pizza on the table. The server set out a plate for each of us, placing our napkin-wrapped silverware on the side. He told us to enjoy our meal, and then he retreated.

I pulled in a deep breath, meant to brace myself for the resuming of our disagreement. Instead, I got a giant mouth-watering whiff of the warm crust, melted cheese, and perfectly spiced sauce. My stomach growled without my permission. It wasn't loud, but loud enough.

Patrick's stiff shoulders relaxed and he forced a smile that was sincere except for the lingering tenseness in his eyes. "Perhaps we should put this discussion off until *after* our attempt at a normal date."

I nodded once, because I knew he was stubborn enough to hang on to his reservations all night. "If you'd like."

His lips pressed together a second before he spoke again. "I'm sorry. I don't mean to sound ungrateful for your offer. I just—"

I forced a smile. "It's okay. We can try being normal again. It lasted all of what, five minutes last time?"

"I'm not very good at normal, it seems."

"Neither am I, I guess." I hesitated then reached out for the spatula that had been slipped under one of the large slices. I lifted the piece up and waited for Patrick to hold out his plate.

Soon we were eating, both of us trying to avoid anything that would bring us back to the topics we'd already covered. We talked about school, which brought us to Lee. We both saw that would ultimately take us to Peter Keegan, so Patrick deftly steered over to what classes I was taking next semester. Before I knew it, we were discussing possible college options, almost like we were a normal couple. I hadn't really thought of what would happen after high school lately, because I'd been so focused on my more immediate fate. But the way Patrick talked about the future made it sound like life could continue, even if I was an enemy to the Demon Lord. I don't know how much I believed him, but it was nice to talk about different universities, possible cities to live in. The best part was knowing even if Terence somehow managed to fix things and I no longer needed several bodyguards, Patrick still planned on being with me. It was great to know that when Patrick said he would love me forever, he meant it. Even if the Demons were persuaded to believe I was unimportant, Patrick fully intended to stay with me.

The seriousness of our relationship didn't scare me, like I used to worry about me and Aaron. How I felt about Patrick was something that would never change; I would always love him, and he would always love me.

True, this came with problems. I was aging every second, while Patrick remained untouched by time. And though it didn't make sense that I wasn't afraid about what would happen when our time together ran out, I had complete faith in Pastor O'Donnell's promise that everything would work out in the end.

We were nearing the end of dinner. For the past fifteen minutes or so we'd been asking questions back and forth. We'd covered most embarrassing moments, favorite childhood memories, and Patrick's favorite decades to live in—all of the really obvious stuff.

It was back to my turn now. "Okay—did you ever know any grandparents?"

He pursed his lips, then slowly shook his head. "Not really. My father's mother lived the longest, but she barely saw Sean's first steps. I hardly remember her at all."

I was saddened at the thought because my grandparents had always been such an integral part of my life.

He took a small bite of his remaining pizza, hurried to

chew and swallow, then he cleared his throat. "The thing you miss most about being under ten years old?"

"Under ten? What kind of a question is that?"

"You have to answer it—the rules, remember?"

"What I miss most . . ." I was twisting the straw in my drink, forcing the melting ice to clink against the sides of the glass. "Bedtime stories," I finally decided. "My mom or dad would read with me almost every night. Saturday night was the best. We'd all sit on their big bed, and Dad would read a book of our choice."

His smile was gentle and full. "Most children hate bedtime," he pointed out, almost as an afterthought.

"Did you?"

"Does that count as your question?" he joked. He shook his head. "No, I didn't hate it. I liked the time to think. But sometimes I would have preferred staying up all night. I hated stopping when I was in the middle of a project."

"Can I ask how old you were when you started to paint?"

"If that's your question . . ."

I hesitated. "I had another one I wanted to ask."

He rolled his eyes. "You're getting a lot more out of me than I am out of you." He blew out his breath, letting himself think back over two hundred years. "I was painting before I learned to read. I wasn't quite three when my mother took me out to her garden with her. I used the mud and smeared it over a large rock, and somehow she recognized it was a flower. I had a few scattered lessons, but most I picked up on my own."

"I've still never seen you paint," I mused regretfully.

"Don't you dare complain—I've never seen any of your work, and you've already seen my terrible sketches."

"Maybe that's why I'm nervous about sharing," I hinted. "Your terrible is really pretty amazing."

He smiled ruefully but didn't verbally reply. He was waiting for my next question. It was one I'd wanted to ask since we'd begun this question game, but the time had never seemed right.

Not that right now felt perfect, but the meal was wrapping up and I was intensely curious.

I made myself meet his eyes, though even before I opened my mouth I could feel the blush starting on my cheeks. "Okay, here's my question: I was wondering if . . . Did you ever kiss Sarah McKenna?"

He didn't laugh, but his mouth twisted and his eyes glowed. "Are you jealous?" The thought obviously amused him.

"No." But I'd answered too quickly, and he clearly didn't believe me. I tried to explain. "I'm not jealous, and I'm not worried—I was just curious. She was incredibly beautiful, and she obviously had a crush on you."

"A crush on me, huh?" He leaned back in his chair, reaching to scratch the back of his neck. "Are you sure you're not jealous? Because you're getting a little red there."

"Are you enjoying this or something?"

"Something." He nodded with a half grin. "Maybe now you'll have some sympathy for me. Watching you with Aaron was never easy."

"Did you . . . love her?"

He watched me for several seconds before responding. "No."

"No?"

"No. I didn't ever love her. I was quite fond of her, and she had similar fascinations, but I never loved her. I've only ever loved one girl."

My blush deepened. "But did you ever kiss her?" I pressed.

His head bobbed. "Once. A few days before Sean and I left to join the United Irishmen. I went to her house, because I knew it was something I had to do. I didn't go over there thinking I would kiss her—she kissed me, on her doorstep. It was a first kiss for both of us."

It was easy to imagine the scene. Moonlight, picturesque Ireland, their hands unsure of where to rest. It sounded like the perfect first kiss. "But you never loved her?"

"She was my friend. Aside from my family, she understood me the most. But I was never in love with her. I was taken with her, but she never stole my heart."

"Are you calling me a thief?"

His blue eyes were bright. "Maybe Toni was right when he said everyone's a thief at heart." He leaned forward suddenly, balancing his hands on the edge of the table. "Do I get one last question? It only seems fair, after you got so many in a row."

"All right," I agreed.

His arm slipped around the almost empty pizza pan, his fingers seeking mine. I surrendered my hand, and, for some reason, my heart started to pound.

His voice was steady and calm. "Do you love me, Kate Bennett?"

I stared at him, wondering where this was coming from. "Yes. Of course I do."

He smiled thinly, his beautiful eyes devoted solely to me. "Thank you." It looked like he might have expounded on that, but instead he settled for a quick, "Do you like bowling?"

I gave him a strange look but squeezed his hand affectionately. "Um, yeah. Do you?"

He shrugged a single shoulder. "I haven't gone bowling for fifteen years or so, but I enjoyed it last time."

I chuckled. "I might actually beat you on this one."

He grinned. "We'll see."

It took him several minutes to relearn the art of bowling, once we reached the alley, but he was good enough that even my head start barely saved me. I was able to win the game, though it was close. Amid the light teasing, high fives, and some pretty intense victory dances, it was almost easy to forget Demons even existed. I couldn't speak for Patrick, but this was one of the first times our relationship had ever felt completely normal. We were young, full of life, and deeply in love.

When the game was over I entrusted him with my purse

so I could run to the bathroom. I offered to meet him at the car, but he assured me he'd wait by the front double doors. I wandered to the back of the crowded building, surprised when I pushed into the bathroom to find only one other girl inside. She was washing her hands and our eyes met in the mirror for a brief second. I gave a timid smile, which she returned a little awkwardly. I hurried into the first available stall, wondering if I was the cause of the green cloud of unease in her aura.

I heard the water at the sink turn off, some paper towels were cranked out, and then a half minute later the door thumped closed. I was alone.

It wasn't until I was washing my hands in the empty bathroom that my phone rang. I shut off the water and quickly moved to the towel dispenser. As soon as my hands could pass for semidry, I pulled the phone out of my pocket to look at the display.

Terence.

I flipped it open and set it against my ear. "Hello?"

"Kate, I hope this isn't a bad time."

"Uh, no. Not really." My voice rang out around the tiled room and I hoped he wouldn't be able to guess where I was; that would be infinitely more embarrassing than meeting eyes with a stranger in the bathroom.

"Good. I'm calling to let you know I'll be in town tomorrow, and I was hoping we could meet somewhere around noon."

"Tomorrow?"

"Yes. I know it's short notice. I can't say much over the phone, but I would appreciate it if you and Patrick could both meet me at the malt shop. It looked like a charming place when I drove past it on my last visit."

"Just me and Patrick?"

"Yes, if that's possible. I wasn't able to get a hold of him, but I assume you can pass the word along?"

"You couldn't get a hold of him?" I asked.

He heard the note of surprise in my voice. "No, he didn't

answer his phone. I assumed he was off duty and sleeping. Is something wrong?"

"Uh, no. Maybe he left it in the car."

"You're together?"

"Yeah. We went out."

"I see." Sometimes I wondered what Terence thought of our relationship, but I didn't think I'd ever get up the courage to ask him. He always seemed pleasant about it, but it was the same kind of acceptance one might feel toward a mosquito bite—a fact of life and unavoidable. At least he wasn't openly against our being together. He was too kind for that. I got the feeling he believed our relationship wasn't worth the stress or distractions, but he probably assumed it would pass soon enough.

He was speaking again, breaking into my thoughts. "Well, I can't stay on the line long. There are a few things I need to take care of before I leave town. But I'll see you tomorrow?"

"At noon," I assured him.

"Good, good. I'll see you then."

We exchanged quick good-byes and then I shut my phone, moving for the bathroom door. I wasn't worried about Patrick ignoring Terence's call. Yet. But I was anxious to get back to him. Walking into the main room of the bowling alley made me realize how much quieter it had been inside the bathroom, and I found my step quickening in an effort to escape the rush of noise.

I stepped through a large group of teenagers who were waiting in line to rent their shoes, and then I was facing the front doors. I glanced around, but I didn't see Patrick. Maybe he'd decided to go out to the car? That made more sense than him moving back into the crowded bowling alley. The first real strings of worry wrapped around my insides as I pushed through the doors into the cool night air.

Although it was dark, the neon lights from the bowling alley kept the parking lot lit. This wasn't the most popular bowling alley in town, but the parking lot was still quite full. Several distant voices punctuated the night, though I couldn't see anyone.

I started moving along the building, heading toward the far end of the row where Patrick had parked. I was still a couple cars away from the Altima when I realized the car was empty, and he wasn't standing anywhere around it.

That was when I started to really worry.

four

Patrick O'Donnell

I stood just inside the front doors of the bowling alley, my trained eyes flitting carefully around the room while I waited for Kate to return. To an outsider I may have appeared relaxed, but part of being a Guardian meant never being completely at ease. Her purse dangled at the end of one slack arm, but my fingers were unconsciously tight. Though I didn't enjoy being apart from her, I was content to have a few minutes to myself.

All things considered, the night had been a good one. Perhaps *amazing* might be the better word. I had not yet reached the point where I took Kate's love for granted. Maybe I never would. Every moment I had with her was a miracle, every smile she spared on me a blessing. Getting the chance to learn more about her over the course of the evening had been everything I could have imagined. It was the rocky beginning that haunted me, that made me almost relieved to have a moment alone, almost desperate for the night to be over, despite the other wonderful moments we'd shared.

She was the last person on earth I wanted to discuss Sean with. She was the last person that deserved to know how much

I still cared for that monster. Despite everything he'd done, full-on hatred for him had yet to come. I'd felt glimpses of it, especially during Henry Bennett's funeral and the days immediately following. But the predominant and overwhelming emotion was simple pain. Sometimes I would wake in the night with tears in my eyes. Tears of hurt and betrayal. I'd given everything so Sean could live, and yet he'd tried to kill me—would have killed me, if not for Kate's saving efforts. Perhaps the thing that angered me most about the entire situation was the fact I wasn't sure I'd be able to do the necessary thing. I feared that when the time came, I might not be able to end his life. The thought of killing my own brother—no matter how evil he'd become—made me sick inside. And what if, in that moment of hesitation, Kate was brought to harm? I'd never forgive myself.

This complicated issue wasn't the only one brought up tonight, though, and it certainly wasn't the worst. I understood she believed she was doing me a favor by volunteering to go back in time and see my father. But she didn't know the things I knew. She hadn't seen our fate, like I had.

Kate didn't know I'd witnessed her ultimate death. She had no idea I'd held a future version of her in my arms while she tried to give me a senseless message. Though I'd had a month to ponder and dread that unreal visit, it still produced more questions than answers. The future Kate was clearly dying, her stomach and chest covered in blood from gunshot wounds. Even without that sure source of death, her coming to her own past was suicidal. But she'd overlooked all that.

Why would she do that? What event in the future could possibly drive her to such desperate extremes? Could the future be so grim that sacrificing her life seemed the only option? Her continued words seemed to indicate it was.

She'd told me that everything we tried failed, but that I was supposed to somehow change the outcome of those future events with the help of her warnings. I was supposed to save the twins and keep them safe. I was supposed to let Kate go, because she was as good as dead already. How could I do that? Abandoning her when she needed me most—it was unthinkable. I couldn't let it happen. I was determined to stop this nightmare future from ever occurring. Because there was no way I could survive losing her. Before I'd seen this horrible vision—before I'd first been infected by the Demon virus—I'd spent time contemplating what my life would be like when she died, as all mortals must. The grief I'd feel, the emptiness that would accompany her loss, the madness that would take over inside me . . . The thought of losing her had disturbed me ever since I'd discovered how much I loved her. But the thought of losing her so soon, so suddenly, and so violently—I was completely terrified.

At first I believed it would be possible to keep that future from happening. Simple, almost. For her to have come back, she would need to find access to that specific memory; it was how the special ability worked.

Easy. I would simply refuse to give it to her, if she ever asked for a doorway into my past.

But then I realized my fatal mistake. I'd yelled for Toni to come in, so the memory was not mine alone. She could get access to the deadly moment through Toni just as easily as through me. After further reflection on her words, I realized he probably *was* the one that served as her gateway through time, because in the future she'd mentioned I wasn't with her. *Why would I not be with her?*

Besides, her last fractured words had been about Toni. Perhaps she was trying to tell me he was the one who helped her make the eventual journey back in time. Naturally, I'd sworn Toni to secrecy about the future Kate's visit, and as far as I knew he hadn't told a soul. It was paramount that I kept this from Kate.

I'd thought about warning her; if she knew, maybe she wouldn't make the choice to go back, even when things started falling apart. But somewhere inside of me I knew telling her would only make things worse. It would only give her ideas. If there was one thing I'd learned about Kate, it was that she could become very self-sacrificing when it came to saving the people she loved. If something ever happened to the twins . . . A lone threat from our enemies would be enough to send her searching for a way—*any* way—to save them, regardless of the cost.

I just had to make sure no threat of harm came to the twins. I *would* keep Kate safe, especially from herself. I fully intended to change her destiny, because I couldn't face losing her.

Despite my deep thoughts, my face was still smooth and I was aware of my surroundings. A rowdy group of teenagers pushed into the bowling alley and I stepped easily to the side to avoid getting in their way. The room was loud, between the crashing of knocked over bowling pins, the cheers and jeers of the players, the pounding music, and the endless banter that filled every available space in between. Even so, my practiced ear picked up the sound of a pain-filled gasp. I turned instinctively toward the sound, craning my neck so I could peer around a tall man's bulky shoulder.

I saw the girl first. Her cringing face was easy to pick out. She was fairly pretty and quite small, and she was blinking rapidly, as if to force back tears. One arm was stretched out in front of her, captured in the tight grip of a large teenager. He was pulling her toward the doors—nearly dragging her. It was beyond obvious she didn't wish to go with him, yet she wasn't putting up much of a struggle. Reluctant footsteps and that thin whimper. That was all. Though his ducked head hid his identity from me, I knew there was something familiar about this guy. I knew him. I just couldn't recall . . .

They'd reached the doors, a couple feet away from me, and as his elbow pushed into the door to force it open he lifted his head a fraction. My eyes narrowed immediately and my already tensed body prepared to move. It was Micah Grimshaw, the arrogant quarterback from the school's football team.

In truth, I was surprised our paths hadn't crossed sooner. Over a month ago—back when I was just beginning to realize I was sick—we'd gotten in a fight. Even as I'd hobbled away after that incident, he promised me that I hadn't seen the last of him. I hadn't forgotten about his threat; it just hadn't been in the forefront of my mind. It wasn't like I didn't have other worries to focus on. Still, seeing him here, and now. . .

Just like the last time I'd attacked him, I felt the undeniable urge to pound out my frustrations on him. That was the problem with inner battles—they left you with nothing to physically fight. But if anyone deserved a strong dose of humility, it was him. And this time, there would be no doubt of my winning. I'd been fighting Demons, the worst kind of scum, for two centuries. One arrogant jock wasn't going to be a problem. I'd just need to keep myself in check. There was no reason to harm him permanently, after all.

He'd already pulled the girl outside. The door was swinging closed. I moved without thought. In the back of my mind I wondered if I was doing the right thing by giving in to this thirst for violence. But I knew this went beyond personal battles. I was a Guardian, and that girl needed my help. There was really nothing to debate. I pushed through the door before it could close completely, my eyes peeled despite the sudden darkness.

I paused on the sidewalk, willing my eyes to adjust. The girl's whimper and scuffing footsteps directed my gaze. They were walking along the side of the building, moving in the direction of my parked car. That's when I remembered I was still holding Kate's purse—that she would come looking for me in the next couple minutes. Would she panic if I wasn't there?

No. When Kate didn't see me by the doors, she would be left to assume I was at the car. I didn't intend to disappoint her, so my movements became quicker. I moved after the girl and ultimately Grimshaw, who had succeeded in almost reaching the end of the building.

Her thin voice carried on the slight breeze, destroying any doubts I may have had about her fear. "I want to go home."

He grunted something unintelligible, but continued to drag her forward. They reached the corner—she began to whine something and he jerked her painfully around the edge of the bowling alley, which cut off the sound of her complaint. Ducked around the corner, I lost sight of them; I lengthened my stride in the same instant. I was moving at not quite a run, but beyond a fast walk.

I felt my phone vibrate suddenly in my pocket, but I didn't have time to answer it because I was just rounding the corner of the building. Grimshaw had pushed the girl up against the brick wall, his palms forcing her shoulders to grind against the unyielding barrier. "Just shut up, beautiful," he growled menacingly, his blond head inclined toward her.

She gasped in pain.

Without thought I let Kate's purse slip through my fingers, leaving it to sag against the warm cement. The muted thump brought four eyes to me, and my tensed body became even stiffer when Micah's stare became understanding.

"O'Donnell," he grunted, his lips curling derisively. His eyes were angry slits, but they didn't alarm me. I'd faced much worse.

I gestured toward the girl with my chin. "Let go of her."

Micah's whole face twisted in a sneer. "Back off. She's my girl." His eyes brightened with an arrogant light. "Unless you're willing to trade, of course."

The young woman whimpered, her head angled toward me. "Please," she whispered, hope and pain making her voice crack.

"Shut up!" Grimshaw snapped. He turned to look at her for the briefest moment, and that's when I moved.

I took the couple necessary steps to stand beside them, one hand already crushing his arm before he saw me in his peripheral vision. He started at my sudden appearance and his grip on the girl loosened—she was no longer being forced harshly against the building. But he didn't take his hands away from her. Instead he turned his glower on me.

"That's it," he rasped, breathing more heavily as hot adrenaline rushed through his body. "You're dead."

I smiled grimly at the irony he wouldn't see in that statement. "Really? I don't feel very dead."

He shoved away from the girl and I was forced to release my hold on him so I could steady her. I gripped her elbow until she was firm on her feet, then I let my hand fall and my attention shifted.

The quarterback had taken a couple steps back. He was flexing his fingers into fists, rising up and down on the balls of his feet, preparing for a fight I was all too happy to supply him with. I lowered into a defensive crouch, raising my arms into a ready position. I almost felt bad for him, because he had no way of knowing how much training I'd had in hand-to-hand combat.

He was about to be rudely awakened.

I assumed he would try to tackle me, like he had in our last attempt at a fight. I assumed correctly. I could hear the girl behind me gasp and stagger back a couple steps when Micah lunged for me. It was an impressive show of his bulk, but it was a weak move. I leaned the upper part of my body to the side, caught one of his wrists and slammed my free fist into his unguarded stomach. He groaned and doubled over, which made it easy to finish throwing him over one of my bent legs. He slammed into the pavement, landing heavily on his side.

I didn't straighten out of my crouch, but I did pivot so I could keep a full gaze on him. I couldn't see the girl's expression, but she was standing silent and motionless behind me.

Micah Grimshaw rolled slowly off his side, pushing up from the ground to regard me through smoldering eyes, his back to the wall. He was angrier than before but more cautious too. He realized I knew what I was doing, so he would have to be more calculative with his next attack. "Not bad for a sicko," he panted. "Did Kate teach you how to stick up for yourself?"

I allowed a small mirthless grin to twist my face, and that silent reply was enough to resume the fight. He didn't try to tackle me again but instead decided that a calmer, circling approach would be better. He was eyeing my arms with new appreciation, seeing the subtly bulging muscles he'd underestimated before. He still had the advantage of size and brute strength, but it was obvious in his motions that he wondered if they would be a match for my obvious skill.

We paced around each other, and I noticed that in each round he inched a little closer. He was going to try and limit my reaction time. It was a worthy goal but a wasted effort. When his fist flew suddenly toward my left temple, I was able to flinch back and slam one hard arm against his wrist, batting it harmlessly away from me. His other fist moved to smash against the right side of my face, and his knuckles managed to graze my skin before I swatted his blow away.

He was angry now—frustrated that he couldn't hit me. He lashed out with more agility but less purpose. I continued to dodge and deflect his attacks, until the perfect opportunity to strike him arrived. His face was unguarded, and I made use of that by delivering a solid punch to his cheekbone. His head snapped around from the force of the blow, but the pain only seemed to make him more desperate to hit me.

He got his chance a few seconds later when his leg, which had been rooted to the ground up until this point, suddenly swung into the back of my ankles. I had no idea he knew how to use his feet in a fight, so the unexpected swipe served its purpose beautifully. My arms swung instinctively to help retain my balance, and his fist caught my jaw in a harsh uppercut. My neck strained back from the fierce punch and the girl let out a cry as the quarterback shoved me up against the wall.

By the time my head hit the wall, I was already gripping his arms, trying to pry him off me. He thrust his knee up, catching me in the gut. I grunted grudgingly, then curled one of my arms and sent my elbow into his chest. That propelled him backward, but he was still holding my arm, so I was dragged along with him.

I delivered a few staggering punches, and then I had *him* pinned against the wall, his nose bleeding. We were both breathing heavily, our hot faces mere centimeters apart. I was clutching a fistful of his shirt, bunched up harshly near his throat. He was gripping my wrists, trying to scratch the skin from my bones. He was having little success, though I don't think he could see the fact that my body was healing itself after every scratch he managed to create.

I kept my eyes wide and my words calm, so he wouldn't misunderstand. "You are never to harass Kate again. If I see you mistreating *anyone* in the future, you will receive more than a simple warning. Am I clear?"

In answer, he spat in my face. I let the spittle run down my cheek, unwilling to show weakness by brushing it away. I tightened my grip near his throat, making him gasp. Our noses were nearly touching now.

Ironically enough, that's when Kate found us.

She'd rounded the corner slowly, her face pale and her eyes wary—maybe a little fearful. They widened at what she saw: me forcing Grimshaw up against the wall. Only slightly less alarming would have been the young woman standing off to the side, hugging herself in an effort to stop her steady tears.

"Patrick?" Kate asked, unable to form any more of a question. Her eyes darted between us, trying to make sense of the scene. The way her eyes hovered on the girl made me think she'd seen her before. Maybe from school?

I wasn't sure how to answer her largely unspoken question, so for the moment I turned my attention back to the football player in my grasp. I lowered my voice, trying to keep the animosity between us. "You should leave," I said.

He stared at me for a long moment, the blood still dripping from his nose. When he finally spoke, it was a low whisper. "You'll regret this, O'Donnell. I swear you will."

I gave one of my tense smiles for an answer before straightening my fingers abruptly and twisting away from him. I reached down to grab Kate's purse, and by the time I'd turned back around, Grimshaw was stalking away, moving toward his black jeep.

I watched him until he was inside and the engine roared to life. The lights flashed on, blinding us momentarily. He started forward, peeling out of the parking lot with a reckless jerk of the wheel. His tires screeched past us and the jeep whipped around the corner. The sounds of his mad retreat gradually died, leaving silence to settle around us.

I knew Kate's eyes were firmly on my face, but I chose to look instead at the other young woman, who was looking at me with a small degree of awe.

"Are you all right?" I asked.

She nodded, slowly at first and then more rapidly. "Yes. Thank you, for . . . that. I'd heard stories from other girls at school, but . . . I thought they were just stories." She was almost blushing, and a quick flick of my eyes showed that Kate was watching the girl's aura. The girl continued to talk quickly, almost babble, really. "He was a little too touchy at dinner, and then when I asked to go home, he took me here. He convinced me it would be fun. After the game, he wanted to take me to his house, but I knew I didn't want that. I went in the bathroom to call my brother." Her eyes flitted to Kate. "He told me to wait in there, that he'd call me when he got here, but I felt rude just leaving Micah out there. I told him I'd called my brother, and he dragged me outside. I didn't want to make a scene inside, but—"

"It's okay," Kate broke in suddenly, reaching out a hand to place on the other girl's arm. I would never quite understand the care—almost love—a woman could feel so quickly for another woman. They were strangers, yet they were strangely bonded together by a single shared incident. Kate brushed her hand up and down, rubbing gently. "He's a jerk. He doesn't have any right to treat you like that."

The girl nodded quickly, barely holding back tears. "I know. I just didn't know what to do. I've never gone through anything like that. I wasn't thinking clearly. I didn't know how to react." Loud music began to play, and the girl dug into her pocket quickly, sniffling loudly. She pressed a button that ended the rather annoying ringtone, and then she held the flat phone to her ear. "Derek? Yeah, I'm okay. Where are you? . . . I'm just around the building. No, I'll be right there."

She closed the phone, ending the call. "My brother," she told us. She pursed her lips and then spoke quickly, focusing almost exclusively on me. "I'm not sure how to thank you."

I shook my head quickly. "No thanks is necessary. I've been wanting to do that for a while now."

She cracked a thin smile, as if my words were perfectly sane, then glanced toward Kate. "Maybe I'll see you guys around." She gave me a last timid smile before turning and walking back toward the front of the bowling alley.

As soon as her footsteps faded Kate swiveled to look at me, her eyes wide. "Well. That was a perfectly normal end to the evening."

"I'm sorry," I responded, though my heart wasn't in the apology.

She tilted her head at me in a way that was uniquely hers. "You don't look very sorry."

I shrugged a single shoulder. "I might have enjoyed teaching him a lesson."

"Yeah. I'm getting that vibe." Her eyebrows drew together in sudden worry. "Are you all right?"

The corner of my mouth lifted and I stepped toward her, fingers tightening around her purse. "As a matter of fact, I'm quite capable of handling a high school jock. A Guardian doesn't always need his Seer, you know." *But I'll always need you,* I finished mentally.

She gave an expansive nod. "Uh-*huh*. Is this a macho side to you I didn't know existed?" she asked rather rhetorically.

I held out her bag. "Sorry. I may have gotten some dirt on it."

She took it slowly, gaze still locked with me. "You're in a funny mood tonight."

"Funny?"

"Well . . . different. Are you sure you're okay?"

I decided to be truthful. I habitually shoved my hands into my pockets, keeping my tone light despite the seriousness my words inflected. "It just feels really good to finally do something, after a month of absolutely nothing but worrying. Even if it was only giving that Grimshaw a taste of humble pie."

"I don't know how effective that is when it's forcefully fed, . . . but I'm glad you were around to help her out. She looked pretty green in the bathroom."

"Green?" I could hear the low alarm in my voice. "She was ill?"

"Oh, no. No, I meant her aura," she was quick to clarify. "It had a lot of green in it. She was uneasy. I kind of feel bad I didn't ask her what was wrong. We might have avoided this whole thing . . ."

I reached for her hand, which she surrendered at once. We walked directly beside each other, the short walk to the waiting car giving me just enough time to dig out the keys from my pocket. I pressed the button, which released the power locks, then I moved to get the door for her.

I picked up the conversation then, my voice sounding highly

philosophical, even to me. "You can't talk to everyone who has an uneasy aura, Kate. There's no way you can help every person you come in contact with."

She tossed me an easy smile. "Probably not. But there's this story I heard once, about an old man on a beach. He was walking the length of the ocean, tossing starfish back into the water that had been beached. You know, when the tide went out."

She paused her narrative while she lowered herself into the car, and I took the opportunity to make an irrelevant comment, my fingers drumming lightly on the roof of the car. "I love how we went from talking about green auras to men on beaches. This really is the best date I've ever been on." She sent me a wry look over her shoulder, but I just grinned and closed the door.

As soon as I was settled into the driver's seat, Kate resumed her story; her passion for a simple parable was almost comical. "So this man walked the beach, throwing these starfish back into the ocean so they wouldn't die. And this other guy, a younger guy, comes along, and he sees this beach is practically covered in starfish. And he says to the old man trying to save the starfish, 'There are so many, you can't possibly make a difference.'" She hesitated for dramatic effect, her face glowing from the lights on the dash. "And do you know what the old man said?"

"'Mind your own business?'" I guessed.

She actually slapped my arm, but the familiarity that small action attested to warmed my heart, so it wasn't really a viable reprimand. She was fighting to keep a straight face. "No, that's not what he said at all. He just picked up another starfish and chucked it in the water. Then he turned to the other man and said, 'It made a difference to that one.'"

I nodded slowly. "So . . . are you saying you want to chuck starfish on our next date?"

She rolled her eyes and reached for her seat belt. "Patrick O'Donnell, you are completely—"

"Hopeless?"

Her mouth twitched. "Close. I was going to say *wonderful*."

"You were not."

"Maybe I was."

I blinked. "Really?"

Her words appeared sincere, but her expression was teasing. "You'll never know, because you interrupted me."

I let my eyes carefully caress her beautiful face, before turning my attention to driving her safely home.

We didn't talk much while I drove, but the quiet wasn't empty. Silence could be peaceful, when shared with someone you care about. Kate reached for my fingers, and I helped balance our hands on the middle armrest while I navigated carefully through the traffic. Her house wasn't far, but I almost wished it was.

The radio played softly, and occasionally Kate would start humming unconsciously along with the music—sometimes making up her own harmonies. A part of me wanted to join her, but I was afraid that if I drew attention to the instinctive counterpart she might stop the impromptu performance. I contented myself with just listening to her voice, trying to commit it to memory, though I had every intention of hearing her voice every day of our time together. I may not get her forever, but I wasn't going to waste a moment of the time we had.

And I certainly wasn't going to let fate rob us of the precious amount of time allotted to us. I would see Kate grow old, no matter what it took. I would protect her so her hair could become gray with age, keep her safe so I could smooth the wrinkles on her face. I may not be able to grow old with her—destiny had stolen that from us already, though I knew I had no right to complain. Without my immortality, we never would have met. Still—I was going to live every second I could with her. Every second she would give me, I was going to take as greedily as a starving man gropes for food. Gorge myself now, before the famine came and stripped me of everything that mattered.

I twisted my fingers with hers and her thumb caressed the back of my hand in response. I don't know that I'd ever lived a better moment than this. But then, that's what I thought every time I was with her.

five

Kate Bennett

I fought the invading sunlight by closing my eyes more tightly. I tried to cling to the sleep that was leisurely slipping from my body, but my efforts were in vain. I was awake now, though still extremely tired. I rolled onto my back, stretched my legs out, and reluctantly blinked until my eyes were wide open against the morning light. The night had been way too short. I still felt stiff and my mind remained cloudy. Scattered fragments of dreams—including one involving Far Darrig—slowly disappeared, and soon the only thing I could remember from my night was the look on Sean's face when I stabbed him in the heart.

I stared at my ceiling, twisting my arms out and above my head to take the kinks out. I yawned in a huge, unladylike fashion, then burrowed back under my sheets, turning on my side and curling into a ball. I stared at my closed door, mentally going over what today promised to hold.

After Patrick had walked me to the porch last night, just before he'd stolen my breath with one of his deep and amazing kisses, I'd remembered to tell him about the missed call he'd had from Terence. He'd seemed a little surprised by the late notice, but there was a new tension to the set of his shoulders that made me worry Terence's visit might concern some bad news. I don't know what I thought of his visit, but I knew from past experience that a Guardian overseer only came around if there was something serious going on. Did he know about the wanted poster?

For some reason, the thought of Terence knowing I had a reward on my head made me wince. It wasn't that I didn't trust Terence, but I was worried about how he'd react to the revelation that a bunch of Demons knew where I lived. I mean, obviously they hadn't been too worried about that possibility, because they hadn't relocated me after the funeral even though Selena, Far Darrig, and pretty much any other dangerous servant of the Demon Lord knew where my house was. So either they thought moving me would do no good—they'd just find me again—or the Guardians believed they could protect me. Would that change if Terence knew about the bounty hunting Demons, though?

I decided it was better not to speculate. For one thing, it hurt my head. For the other, Patrick had lifted his hand to my cheek at that moment to gently stroke my skin with his attentive fingertips.

He'd offered to pick me up around eleven thirty for the meeting, but I asked him if he wanted to come over earlier and hang out at the house. My arguments were simple. "The twins will be home, and I don't want to suffer alone with Toni."

He'd smiled and nodded once. "I would love to."

In my room, I glanced up at my alarm clock on the nightstand. It was almost nine. Patrick would be over around ten, so I couldn't really procrastinate getting out of bed for much longer. But before I left my room, I decided to set up a game plan.

Since I'd intended to tell Patrick about the wanted poster today, and since Terence might be coming about that very thing, I decided to wait and bring up the reward later. If Terence knew about the danger, then he could warn us and I wouldn't have to tell Patrick I'd gone to Clyde's the other day. A win-win, unless Terence insisted on relocating my family. The twins had gone through enough already—they didn't need to lose all their friends, their home, and reality as they knew it. I understood that someday they would have to learn the truth about Guardians and Seers; it was inevitable, since Patrick didn't age. They were bound to learn there was something weird with us, but I wanted them to remain as sheltered as possible for as long as possible. Ignorance really was bliss, as long as you didn't know things were being kept from you.

So I would keep quiet about the wanted poster until I heard what Terence had come to say. That plan was good enough for me—I slipped out of bed and started getting ready for the day.

The twins were already done with breakfast by the time I came down, and Grandma was out grocery shopping. The twins didn't know it, but she hadn't gone alone. Making some silent observations, it was easy to conclude that Toni had accompanied her, since Jack had been on night duty and Claire was currently in the kitchen.

She was most likely invisible, though the twins were upstairs, and she was sitting at the table, thumbing casually through a small paperback. She had the silver aura that marked her as a Guardian, and it only enhanced her ethereal beauty. She was the prettiest person I'd ever seen in my life—a different kind of beautiful compared to Selena Avalos. While Selena was mature and exotic, Clair was small and pixie-like. She had a thin but muscular body, and she was barely five feet tall—if that. Every feature was perfect and miniature, her nose, her chin, her cheekbones. She had long golden-blonde hair that she usually wore up in some way. She was very fairy-tale-princesslike, and her voice was beautiful with its rich French accent. While Patrick and Toni's accents had seemed to fade a little over time, hers seemed unerringly strong.

I didn't know much about her life, only that she'd been born in France in 1430 and apparently didn't really care for men. She seemed to like nice clothes, because I often saw her wearing a dress or an especially classy blouse. She wasn't talkative, and I hadn't had many opportunities to be left alone with her, thank heavens. I was grateful for everything she'd done for me and everything she was doing still. But her cool eyes had a way of biting into me, and I got the feeling that even when I wasn't speaking, I was somehow annoying her.

Claire glanced up from her book when I opened a cupboard in search of a bowl. "Good morning," she said, her tone making it clear she was just trying to keep it polite.

I gave her a thankful smile. "Have you been here long?"

"My shift started at seven." She watched me as I crossed the room to the pantry, where I started searching for cereal. Nothing sounded great, but I finally settled on some Cheerios.

After I'd gotten my spoon and taken my seat across from her, Claire spoke again, her voice easy and her light brown eyes still firmly on me. "What do you hope to get from your relationship with Patrick?"

The milk I was pouring splashed onto the table, and I quickly ended the flow by jerking the gallon back. I blinked at the Guardian sitting opposite me, a little surprised to see she wasn't blushing. In fact, she didn't seem to find her question rude or invasive at all.

"Uh . . . what do you mean?" I asked at last, hesitating a second too long.

She straightened in her chair, her beautiful nails drumming absently on the closed book cover. "I'm just curious. Obviously there are some large issues you'll face, and I was wondering what you intend to get from him."

"*Get* from him?"

My less than graceful reaction didn't seem to affect her. "Yes. Before you end things."

I didn't care what my expression looked like—I was too shocked by her words to keep my surprise in check. "End things? You mean, when I die?" It felt a little weird, being blamed for dying, like it was a dumb accident I could avoid with a little smarts.

Her slim eyebrows drew together. "No. I mean when you leave him."

"What do you mean, leave him? I'm not going to leave him."

She looked genuinely confused. "Surely you can't be serious. No Seer stays in this world for long. Some make it ten years, but those are the strong ones." She saw my shoulders stiffen, and she inclined her head respectfully. "I mean no offense. But you've already lost so much. You want a normal life, Kate. A steady life. Patrick cannot give you that."

I bristled, but tried to keep my tone conversationally polite because I knew she wasn't trying to be antagonistic. At least, I didn't think she was. "I love Patrick. He's everything I've ever wanted."

"The words of a love-struck romantic who's had no taste of reality," Claire interrupted, her voice smoothly accented. "You will mature and age—he will not. You will see friends and family grow, see them with nice houses and jobs. They will not live in constant fear of Demons. They will have children—eventually grandchildren—and you will not. With Patrick, these things are not possible. Those around you will lead normal lives, and you will long for that. It's only natural. And you will look on at their happiness, knowing that theirs can go on forever, while death will eternally separate you from Patrick."

I swallowed hard. Mostly because she'd touched on some sore topics. I hadn't actually gotten up the nerve to ask Patrick about the possibility of, well . . . having a family together. And here was perhaps my least-favorite Guardian dashing my hopes with a few short words and without any real explanation of *how*. Still, I didn't want her to see my hurt. I tried to keep my voice even. "I know. I've considered those things—"

A single eyebrow rose, stopping my words. "Have you? Your eyes tell a different story, Kate."

I felt my gaze narrow. "Look, I know you're trying to be thoughtful, but this really isn't—"

"I'm not doing this for you alone," she overrode my protest, her eyes almost flashing with the intensity of her emotions. "This is for Patrick's sake as well. It will be easy for you to move on, but it is infinitely harder for an immortal to forget." She cocked her head at me, her small face open and honest. Her words felt so cold. "Are you simply looking for someone to hold you during your period of weakness and mourning? Someone to kiss you when you feel afraid? Someone to whisper loving words in your self-doubting ear? Because if that's all you require, it would be best for Patrick if you were to seek comfort elsewhere."

My face was flushed with a mix of embarrassment and anger. My voice was low, but it wavered with the rush of emotion I was feeling. "I don't know where this is coming from, but you have no right to judge me like that."

"Judge you? I aim to help you. To show you what your infatuation entails, so you can stop this before you and Patrick become even more enamored with each other."

"I love him. And I'm going to spend the rest of my life with him. No matter what I have to sacrifice."

She actually sighed. "Even if this isn't just a passing fancy, you're not thinking about what's best for Patrick. If by some miracle you are able to live a long and happy life together, you will die. There's no stopping that. And where will that leave him? Alone and aching. *Forever.* Surely you don't want that for him?"

"So you think I should just break up with him and start the separation now? Great idea, thanks."

My sarcasm wasn't lost on her. Her mouth twitched. "I don't want you to torture him needlessly. Not only that, but—you don't deserve to be stuck in this world. You didn't make that choice."

"Maybe I didn't choose to be a Seer. But I've made my choice where Patrick's concerned. And no matter how good intentioned you are, you can't change my mind."

She was silent for a moment—I thought maybe I'd convinced her to keep her mouth shut—but then she spoke steadily. "I know from personal experience that you are making a terrible mistake."

That stopped me. I couldn't just toss out a reflexive, "Oh yeah?" Instead I simply waited for her to continue.

She did, slowly. "I was once in love with a mortal—a Seer. He promised to stay with me. He was . . ." She straightened in her chair. "I let my guard fall, put down my defenses. We were together for almost two years before he moved on."

I knew her hurt was genuine, so I tried to soften my firm words. "Claire, I'm sorry. But you're not Patrick. And I would never leave him."

Her chin lifted a fraction, her abrupt smile fake and chilling. "Every story is different, it's true. But each one has an ending. Don't forget that, Kate." She stood suddenly, tossing a nod toward my cereal. "Enjoy your breakfast," she said quickly, turning and treading lithely from the room.

***

I forced myself to eat, though I hated soggy cereal, and, for the record, I really wasn't all that hungry anymore. I was more bothered by Claire's attempt at conversation than any secure person should be, but I knew that wasn't because I believed she had a point.

Okay, so maybe I could see where she was coming from. Mostly I was just annoyed that she'd think so lowly of me. It seemed wrong that she'd even attempt to judge me, because she hardly knew me. I was also bugged that she'd brought up some things I'd been carefully avoiding up until this point. Suddenly my head was filled with all these new things I'd never thought deeply about—most important, Patrick's feelings. I mean, I knew he loved me. But what if Claire was right and our relationship only hurt him in the end? What if he ended up as lonely and crabby as her? It wasn't something I'd considered thoroughly before, but now it was all I could think about.

So much for a relaxing Saturday. *Thanks a lot, Claire.*

I rinsed out my dish and placed it in the dishwasher, wiping my hands on a nearby towel before moving to put the milk away. That's when the doorbell rang, signaling Patrick's arrival. I closed the fridge and crossed the kitchen, quickly moving through the entryway. I reached for the door and managed to pull it open before the twins started crashing down the stairs.

The sunlight did amazing things to Patrick's hair. It highlighted the dark brown strands while making some parts look decidedly blond. It was a good look for him. The scattered freckles on his smooth face were even more obvious in the sun, and his beautiful eyes seemed to glow when they met mine. His hands were in his pockets, but he was already drawing them back out to wrap me in an embrace, right there in the doorway.

"Good morning," he whispered near my ear, despite the twins yelling a chorus of "gross" in the background. His encircling arms around my shoulders were tight yet gentle. Setting the side of my face against his firm chest was the natural, easy thing to do. My own arms flexed around his waist, my hands rubbing against his lower back as I attempted to draw him closer. As I embraced him, I listened to the sound of his heart beneath my cheek, felt the deep breaths he took, smelled the scent of lingering soap on his skin. The fears Claire had awakened—even the ones I hadn't before acknowledged—receded, and I tilted my head up so I could place my lips to his strong jaw.

"Good morning," I breathed in answer, sliding my mouth along his skin with closed eyes.

I felt him shiver, and I inwardly thrilled at the thought that I could affect him in the same way he affected me.

His head shifted and our cheeks brushed together briefly before he pressed his lips to my left temple. His voice was barely audible. "I need to take you out more often."

My mouth twisted into a smile, my eyes cracking open so I could find his lips with my own. They slid together, fitting with a perfection I doubted could be improved with time. His kiss tightened my stomach and made my heart thump and my lungs constrict. His fingertips on my shoulders seemed to be filled with warm electricity. Everywhere he touched began to tingle, and when one hand lifted to cup my jaw, my knees weakened dramatically.

"Yo, Kate!" Josie griped at the base of the stairs. "Are you going to let him in or not?"

"At least go up to your room," Jenna groaned, sounding completely disgusted.

Patrick smiled against my mouth and then leaned away to face the twins, one supporting arm still wrapped around my waist. "And how are you two?" he asked easily. I wondered how he managed to sound so normal—I was still pretty breathless, and my cheeks were warm, knowing I'd forgotten my sisters were present.

Josie's nose wrinkled. "I'm scarred for life."

"Me too," Jenna agreed, pretending to be sick over the banister.

I rolled my eyes at them but didn't dare speak. I didn't want my sisters to hear how my voice would surely waver.

I don't know if Patrick knew my thoughts, but he spoke quickly anyway, drawing attention back to him. "So, what have you girls been doing this morning?"

"Being bored."

"Want to join us?" Jenna asked, hopeful.

He hesitated. "Well, I don't really like being bored. Do you have any other ideas?"

In a minute, he regretted asking. Josie proposed we have a Guitar Hero tournament—a game Patrick had somehow avoided playing until now. If the twins thought it was odd that he'd never played before, they didn't reveal it. Or maybe their excitement managed to hide it. But in a few minutes, we were all in the family room, and Josie and Patrick were battling each other while Jenna and I waited on the couch for our turns. Josie did a lot of showing off, which was to be expected. She played on the "expert" setting, complete with dance moves and occasional bursts of singing.

At least Patrick was familiar with many of the more popular songs. Probably thanks to Toni for that one. His quick reflexes also came in handy, though it was obvious he wasn't much of a gamer. He had hand-eye coordination, but he was used to using those skills in a fight, not for fun. Still, his ability to adapt quickly to new things saved him from losing too badly.

When the song was over, Patrick pulled the guitar strap over his head, handing the thing gingerly to Jenna. "Good luck," he told her simply.

She just laughed, her long hair wavering as she stood up from the couch. "You were even on easy," she told him. She fiddled with the strap, trying to make it smaller. The guitar started to slip from her grasp, but Patrick was quick to hold it for her. Once it was the right size for her eleven-year-old body, Jenna slung the guitar over her head, and soon the twins were playing the hardest song on the game.

Patrick lowered himself next to me, his eyes wide on the colorful screen. "Holy. Cow." His voice grew more pinched. "How do you even hit all those notes?"

"Pure luck," I muttered.

"Practice," Jenna grunted, jerking the guitar up harshly.

"Talent," Josie disagreed with a shake of her head. Her fingers flitted quickly, but her stance was easy—almost lazy.

I slid my fingers into Patrick's hand and we watched my sisters play without saying another word.

When the song was over, Josie surrendered her guitar to me. I shrugged it on and Jenna and I had a turn together. I wasn't great, but I was able to hit most of the notes on the "medium" setting. While I was still holding out the last chord Josie urged Patrick to take Jenna's guitar.

"Come on! You can beat Kate!"

"That I doubt." But that didn't stop him from taking his place beside me. As we started to play I was struck once again by the normalcy of the moment. Just like last night, I felt like we were a normal couple. Only this time I had Claire's words running through my head the whole time. Wherever Claire was hiding in the house, I mentally thanked her—very sarcastically—then tried to focus back on the game.

Grandma came home just as the song was ending and she asked for all of us to help carry in the groceries. It took a few trips to haul all the bags inside, and an invisible Toni sat at the table the whole time, smug in the knowledge that he didn't have to share in the work.

Once the groceries were in, Jenna dragged Patrick back to the family room so she could have her turn to "beat Kate's boyfriend." They were such little sisters.

I wandered in behind them, with Toni following near my elbow. "So you're teaching him how to play? Sweet. Maybe he'll get addicted and let me steal one."

I shot him a look since Patrick couldn't—the song had started—and spoke softly. "You're a lost cause."

"And proud of it." He watched Patrick, then began to cluck his tongue sadly. "Man, he sucks." He raised his voice. "You hear that Patrick? You suck!" He turned back to me, his voice normal once more. "So where's Claire?"

"In the living room, I think," I said, hanging back so the twins wouldn't have a chance of hearing me.

"Sweet." Toni grinned. "I swear I'm going to teach that girl how to flirt, even if it takes a hundred years." He turned to leave, but something made me reach out and grab his arm.

"Toni," I hesitated, then kept my voice below a whisper. "I have something I want to ask you. It's a little . . . awkward."

"Now, now, things are only awkward if you believe them to be," he chimed happily. At least he followed my lead and kept his voice lowered. I didn't think Patrick could hear us.

I still wasn't sure if I wanted to be asking this, but I was seizing the moment. "Come here," I whispered, reaching for his wrist.

"Gracious, Kate!" Toni burst out loudly, making Patrick practically whirl around. "I can't *believe* you'd ask me that—how incredibly awkward!"

"Shut up," I growled, my cheeks warming with color.

The twins yelled for Patrick to pay attention, and though his eyes met mine quickly in question, he turned back to the game. I hoped the twins would keep him busy for a couple more songs.

I glared at Toni, yanking on his wrist to drag him from the room. I pulled him through the kitchen and down the entryway, pausing when I realized I'd have to take him upstairs to avoid anyone hearing this conversation. Especially Claire, who was reading in a large armchair in the living room

"Come on," I muttered ruefully, releasing his arm at the same time. I started up the stairs but turned around when I didn't hear him following. I questioned him with my eyes.

"The stair rule," he reminded me pointedly.

I sighed loudly, and he got the message. He jogged lightly up the steps, passing me up about halfway. He waited in the hall, pointing toward my bedroom. "Eh?" he asked suggestively.

I led the way inside, closing the door carefully before

turning to see him stretched out on my bed. "Comfy," he complimented.

"Could you knock it off for one second?" I asked, my back against the door.

"Probably not. So! What's this horribly embarrassing thing you want to ask me?" He reached for my old teddy bear and set it up on his stomach, making it clap its paws together.

My already pink cheeks turned red. "I think I've changed my mind."

The game of pat-a-cake stopped, and Toni looked at me with sincerity for the first time today. "Wow. You're really blushing. What's up?"

I pursed my lips, knowing I wouldn't have long before Patrick would be up here, yet unable to form the words I wanted. "Look, Claire was talking to me this morning. She mentioned something, and . . . I'm curious."

He nodded once. "Curiosity's good. Except for its annoying tendency to kill cats." He rolled his eyes at my lack of reaction. "Sheesh, relax! I'm kidding. Sorry I've got a sense of humor." He suddenly lifted his chin. "What're you curious about? I'm guessing it's Guardian related."

"Sort of." I didn't think my face had ever been this red. I kept my body against the door, hoping it would keep me from running. "Okay, so . . . I was wondering . . . can Guardians, um . . . I mean are they able to . . ."

"Reproduce?" he guessed, then chuckled. "Goodness, let's not be embarrassed of our bodies here! God created them, you know. At least, that's what Patrick's always telling me."

My face flushed. "How'd you guess?"

"You're redder than a tomato—not the green ones, of course, but ripe ones—you're in a relationship with a Guardian and unable to finish sentences. I'd say it was pretty obvious." He tossed my bear aside and swung his legs out, so his feet were on the floor. His face was perfectly smooth and his arms were balanced on his knees. "Now, Kate, when you reach a certain age your body will start to undergo some changes—"

"Toni!" I hissed.

"All right, all right! Yes, Guardians can have kids."

I blinked. "Really?"

"Sure. I mean, we're immortal and we live on an entirely different plane of existence, but we still have all the necessary pieces to play the game."

"Toni, please don't try to gross me out."

"Why the heck would you ask me of all people, then? My way or the highway, girl." He waited, but when I didn't leave, he continued. "I'm assuming this isn't just you asking on the FYI basis, so I'll get right to the point. Immortals can create life with other immortals, because they exist on the same plane. They have little immortal babies who age until they reach their midtwenties, and then they become completely immortal."

I considered his words. "Is it common for Guardians to . . . do that?"

"Make babies? Let's keep our questions clear, so we can avoid misunderstandings. Frankly, no. Most Guardians chose this life because they didn't want serious responsibilities or relationships." He pointed to himself as an example. "There *are* some who get married to other Guardians, but it's rare. It's more common for Demons to have kids. And I guess I don't have to explain that one to you—Demons enjoy breaking those ten guidelines religious people always go on and on about. Anyway, most Guardians feel pretty complete with themselves. They don't need a significant other. That's sort of why they chose this instead of heaven. You with me?"

"I think so." I wasn't surprised by his answer. I mean, Claire had revealed as much downstairs, that Patrick and I weren't . . . compatible. Still, it was hard to hear. Especially since I'd been secretly hoping she'd been lying out of spite.

So Patrick and I couldn't be parents together, because he was immortal and I was human. We didn't live on the same plane. We never would.

"Is there a reason you asked me instead of him?" Toni asked, and for the first time his tone was calm, bordering on sympathetic. I almost preferred his joking.

I shrugged, folding my arms over my stomach. "I guess I didn't want him knowing I was thinking about that."

"About babies, or . . . *that?*"

I rolled my eyes. "Kids."

He blinked. "You're afraid of scaring him off with your serious plans for the future? I thought you guys were already to the I-can't-live-without-you stage."

"I don't want him thinking I have any doubts or regrets."

"*Do* you have any doubts or regrets?"

"Nope."

"Liar. Your pants are *definitely* on fire."

"Claire just gave me some things to think about. I guess I've been so focused on the moment and my own fantasies, I didn't really stop to consider what Patrick might want."

"Um, I'm guessing he wants *you*."

"I know, I just . . . I'm trying to make sense of the future."

"Well, that takes the surprise out of it."

There was a knock on the door. "Kate?" Patrick called curiously. I gave Toni a warning look. He pretended not to understand at first, then he sighed and locked his lips. He even tossed away the invisible key, but as I turned to open the door I saw him snatch it back and push it into his pocket.

I pulled the door open, and Patrick's eyes flickered over me to rest on Toni, sitting on my bed. "Is anything wrong?" he asked, turning back to me.

"Of course not," I lied quickly. "I just wanted to beat it into his head that he's not allowed up here anymore."

"She dragged me up!" Toni defended himself quickly. "She

pushed me onto the bed and everything. She's abusive! Get out of the relationship while you still can, bro!"

I shook my head at him, but Patrick didn't even bother to do that. "So you brought him up here, to tell him not to come up here anymore?"

"Talk about mixed signals," Toni agreed. He stood quickly, brushing his hands together. "Right! Well, Kate, consider the message delivered. I'm going to go bug Claire now." He slipped around us and started down the stairs without another word.

Patrick watched Toni's retreat from his position at the doorway, and then he turned to look at me. I think he might have been preparing to question me, but he spotted the painting on my wall. "Yours?" he asked softly, thoughts of Toni gone in an instant.

It was an abstract starry sky with an especially bright shooting star. It wasn't even close to realistic, and it wasn't good at all.

I followed his gaze. "Um, yeah. Back when I was ten." I'd been so proud of it at the time, I begged my parents to buy a frame for it. Their condition was that it would have to hang up forever, because they were afraid the expensive frame I wanted would just end up in the closet.

Their prediction came true—a couple weeks later I had a new masterpiece that I thought was better than the shooting star, but I was never allowed to take it down. I was feeling a little self-conscious to have Patrick see this first, of all things, but as he crossed my room for the first time to get a closer look at the canvas, I decided embarrassment was a small price to pay.

I moved to stand beside him as he silently made his observations.

"I'm extremely jealous," he finally breathed.

I may have snorted. "Of this?"

His eyes remained on the painting. "Your ability to create from the imagination," he clarified. "I could only paint the things I'd seen. You . . . you can paint anything."

"Anything except a masterpiece. I'm much better at drawing, trust me."

Patrick's eyes came to mine, a half smile on his face. "May I be the judge of that?"

A minute later we were sitting on my bed, one of my large sketch pads in his hands. He flipped haltingly through my art, his words few but his open admiration more satisfying than anything he could have said. He complimented only the especially impressive ones. He was fascinated with a sketch I'd made of a small girl in worn suspenders, taking her picture in a mirror. He praised my creativity, the angle I'd chosen, and my shading. "It's flawless," he finally managed, attention riveted on the page. "Now I feel inferior."

I rubbed his knee. "Don't. You're many things, Patrick O'Donnell, but never inferior."

He didn't reply, only turned to the next drawing.

I hadn't shared my soul like this for so long, it almost felt wrong to let him thumb through my work. But at the same time, it felt so good. It was another bond we were creating together, and I wished I'd taken the time to invite him in weeks ago.

I became so absorbed in watching his profile as he examined each curve of my pencil stroke, I almost forgot to look at what he was currently seeing. I didn't need to look at my drawings; seeing his face was more satisfying than anything I might have sketched.

He flipped yet another page, but his reaction was different this time. The skin around his eyes tightened. His lips pressed together, dropping the absent smile he'd been carrying for several minutes now.

I found myself glancing away from his almost grimacing face so I could see what had upset him. My breath caught in my throat, making it impossible for me to swallow.

It was a sketch I'd forgotten. I'd started it the day I returned home from the hospital, after my parents' funeral. It was the last thing I'd sketched.

It was overwhelming how much emotion and anger I'd managed to pour into that single drawing. The girl was me, though she looked so consumed with pain and grief she was hardly recognizable. Fingers clawed uselessly at her face. Her eyes were bloodshot and filled with an agony not many people lived to feel in their lives. Her elbows were balanced shakily on her unsteady knees. She was sitting on a porch, though the background was wispy and almost unreal looking. Very indistinct. The only stark thing was the girl, and her suffering. Hair fell over her shoulders and framed her small face. It almost looked like her shoulders were shuddering, and tears slipped from the corners of her eyes.

A caption under her feet read simply, "I should have died."

Patrick wasn't breathing. Maybe he now thought I was a lunatic, or at least disturbed. I peeled my eyes away from the page so I could see his face, morbidly curious to see his disgust.

There was nothing like that in his pale expression. His jaw was clenched and his posture stiff. But it was the moisture in his eyes that assured me he didn't think me insane.

"Kate," he croaked at last. But he couldn't continue. The sketch pad shook in his grip.

I laid my hand over one of his. "It was after I got back from the hospital, after my parents died," I whispered, trying to keep my voice from cracking. "I came home, and . . . I needed to draw. It was the only way I knew how to cope. It was the last thing I ever drew. I should have died in that accident. Died with them. But I didn't. At the time, I . . ." I didn't really need to finish. The picture spoke for itself. Quite loudly.

He swallowed laboriously, blinking quickly. His mouth cracked open thinly. "I've never seen anything like this."

I watched as a tear escaped his eye, dashing down the cheek

turned toward me. I reached up to brush at the wet trail the tear left behind and his head slowly twisted to face me.

I was able to produce a thin smile, and I tried to keep my voice reassuring as my thumb traced light soothing trails against his skin. "That's not me anymore, Patrick. Anything that remained of that girl . . . she died when I met you."

He let the sketch pad sink against the bed, and in a swift motion he was suddenly cradling my face delicately in his hands. "I will never let anything happen to you," he promised. "You will never go through that again."

I followed my instincts and a second later we were kissing gently, his hands supporting my easy movements while my fingers smoothed over his face. I felt like we were sealing an unspoken promise, but I didn't bother to stop and ask him if he felt the same. I just basked in his warmth and overpowering love, completely at peace with the world in that moment.

SIX

Terence looked like a respectable state senator or, at the very least, a prominent businessman. He had silver hair, a warm gaze, and noticeably weathered features. I still had no idea how old he really was, but Toni had mentioned that the man had changed his name at least twice over the course of his existence. The rumor was he had to change it to keep it modern. I wondered how long he'd been using the name *Terence,* and how soon he planned to change his name again.

He was a comforting sort of person. Easy to be around, calming with every word he spoke. He was also prompt; he was already sitting in a corner booth at the malt shop by the time Patrick and I walked in. Terence saw us immediately and waved us over, indicating he'd already purchased lunch for us. Patrick set a palm at the small of my back, guiding me carefully around the lunch crowd.

Terence stood, like proper gentlemen do in old-fashioned movies, and he gave us both a smile and a nod. "Kate, Patrick—I'm sorry if I've ruined any of your plans for the day."

"No, not at all," I was quick to assure him.

Patrick didn't bother to keep his voice low—no one was

close enough to be paying us any attention, and the room was pretty loud with the distracted lunch crowd. "What news do you have about the Demon Lord?"

Terence shook his head minutely. "All in good time. I thought we'd eat first. Pleasure before business, as the saying goes."

"I think you've got that backward," I warned him lightly.

He smiled and gestured to the food on the table. "A serving of cheesy fries and a cheeseburger might change your mind."

He was right. Patrick and I slid onto the bench opposite the older Guardian, and we followed his lead as he reached for a heavenly-smelling cheeseburger.

While we ate, Terence asked how things were going, how my grandmother was faring, what the twins were up to, if I was looking forward to fall break. He worded the question tactfully, but he asked Patrick if Claire was driving him insane. He asked after the other Guardians and Seers—especially Maddy, Claire's Seer. "She's so young," Terence sighed. "But I'm sure she's perfectly safe. Claire is protective of her."

He also asked how things were going between us. I know he was genuinely curious, but I was sure he shared Claire's opinion about our relationship: not so much that our love wasn't right, but that it had no way of lasting.

Though we answered him politely, Terence rushed to change the subject, and we didn't stop him.

We learned the antidote for the Guardian-killing virus was completely perfected now and had been successfully administered to all infected Guardians. That was about the only thing we learned from Terence. He seemed to be saving the rest for later—after the milkshakes. Patrick and I shared a look when we got those, because we knew he must be bracing us for something really big and most likely bad.

We were just finishing up our milkshakes at a quarter to one when Terence finally straightened in his seat. "I'm sure you've already guessed that I'm not here to tell you all is well. I'm afraid the Demon Lord is still wreaking havoc, and he is still interested in you, Kate, though his inactivity suggests otherwise. The Guardian Council has been hard at work trying to find the best solution to our problems. Demons are controllable enough when they're divided, but if the Demon Lord can finish uniting the majority of them, we're in terrible trouble."

"Guardian Council?" I asked, hating to interrupt him now that he was finally starting to talk.

Patrick answered for me, hoping to keep it short and simple. "A group of senior Guardians who serve as our organizers. Terence—along with other district leaders—are members."

I nodded once, and Terence continued. "We've tried to think of everything and anything. Another assassination attempt would be fruitless, we fear, now that the Demon Lord's guard is up. Some members of the Council feel we should try and bribe the more powerful Demons to resist him, at least for the time being. Anything to give us an advantage. But he's just too powerful. He has too many followers, too much influence. We considered many alternatives, but no option we could come up with was viable."

"You're using past tense," Patrick noted. "You've come up with a plan?"

Terence hesitated. "Yes."

"That didn't seem very confident," I pointed out.

Terence smiled just a little. "*Wary* might be the better term. It's not my first choice, but it has been voted the best option by the council. And really, after all this stalling, I must get right to the point. Kate, I was sent here to enlist your help, if you'll give it."

I blinked. "My help? What can I do?"

Beside me, I could feel Patrick's arm tense.

Terence spoke quickly, his eyes locked on mine. "The Demon Lord is far too powerful. We've been driven by the need to find a weakness. It's our only hope. The Council believes his only weaknesses lie in the past. We would like you to lead a group of Special Seers into the Demon Lord's past and exploit a particular weakness that's been brought to our attention by a Special Seer, a Dr. Radcliffe. If you do this, we may perhaps even stop the Demon Lord before he has a chance to become a Seer."

"You want me to lead an assault team into the past?" I asked slowly for clarification's sake. The words seemed even more ridiculous when I said them.

He nodded once. "Yes. If you're willing. The Guardians have little knowledge of this special ability you have, and so we have little or no information to pass along to our Special Seers. Long ago, it was decided that meddling in the past was too dangerous—certainly not worth dying over. But you have been trained by the Demon Lord himself—the master at this art, if there is such a person. You know more about traveling through emotions than anyone else on our side. I won't lie to you; we need you, Kate."

I wasn't sure what to say to that, so I said nothing. But my mind was working overtime.

Patrick wasn't saying anything either.

Terence waited for some kind of reply, but when one wasn't forthcoming, he dared to glance at Patrick—someone he'd been avoiding through the entire exchange. "I felt the need to ask you both at the same time, because of your unique relationship. Obviously this is something you will have to discuss together. But I'm afraid we're running out of time. We know the Demon Lord is preparing to make a deal with a powerful Demon who reins in Romania. If our sources are correct, they'll have a treaty finalized soon after Christmas. Once that's done, the Demon Lord will have enough allies in Europe to distribute various strains of the virus in the States as well as overseas, simultaneously. He plans to annihilate the larger part of the Guardian population in one swift stroke, so we won't have time to organize ourselves or combat the mutated infection with antidotes. We will continue to fight—it's the Guardian way—but winning seems quite hopeless against such odds. There seems no way to stop him. He's too heavily guarded. But in the past? . . . It might be possible to stop this all from happening."

I could hardly believe he'd just done that. The old "of course it's up to you, but if you don't help us, we're all going to die" trick. How was I supposed to refuse when he put it like that?

I wished Patrick would say something. *I* certainly didn't know what to say. But Terence was obviously waiting for some sort of answer.

I cleared my throat. "What would you want me to do exactly?"

A spark of hope lit up his countenance. "That depends on how deeply you wish to be involved, of course, but we mostly need you to teach a handful of other Seers how to travel. We have volunteers who are willing to go back and attack the Demon Lord's past. It would be up to you if you wish to join them for the actual mission, but we're only asking that you help get them there. The Council recognizes you have already gone through more than most Seers, especially where the Demon Lord is concerned." He leaned forward against the table, his eyes bright. "As for me personally, I wouldn't ask this of you unless the need was urgent. I hope you realize that, Kate."

Patrick spoke suddenly, his words uttered with almost no inflection. "Terence, could I speak with you privately?"

Terence's expression seemed to waver, but he offered a thin smile at my Guardian. "Of course, Patrick."

Patrick stood swiftly, indicating that the private conversation would be happening *now*, and Terence followed his lead with only the slightest hesitation.

"Patrick," I started, but he interrupted me gently.

"Please, Kate. We'll be right back."

I bit my lower lip as I watched them walk away from the table. They moved for the front door, wandering between tables and people with ease. Patrick was in the lead but only just. I wondered what he was thinking, but then I figured I could probably hazard a pretty safe guess.

Patrick held the door for Terence, inviting him to leave the restaurant first. Luckily the whole front of the building was glass, so I could watch them through the windows. They stood on the sidewalk, the sweeping breeze rustling Patrick's thick brown hair. His back was to me, so I had to watch Terence's face to try and catch the gist of the conversation.

Surprisingly, they didn't appear to be arguing. Terence was adept at keeping his emotions in check, so his face remained very smooth. His features weren't distinct at this distance, but he might have been frowning.

Patrick's back wasn't completely stiff. His shoulders shifted with movement as a result of unhelpful hand gestures. Terence didn't say anything for a while, just listened as Patrick tried to convey his message. Or maybe a story of some kind? He was certainly talking for a long time without interruption or input . . .

Since they weren't trying to keep a low profile I assumed they'd shifted to invisible. Probably a good idea, since talk of time travel and Demons might scare a human innocently passing by.

Finally Terence said something, his face still calm.

Patrick shook his head in response, but Terence didn't stop talking. His eyes were filled with understanding, but the set of his mouth was firm. Whatever Patrick had shared, Terence wasn't moved.

They continued to debate, and I was left to watch them, my mind wandering to Terence's plea.

If I did this, helped these Special Seers . . . I wouldn't actually have to do anything risky. Teach them how to travel, that was all. If that could somehow stop the Demon Lord and save the Guardians, what was there to argue? It wasn't like Terence was asking me to take on the Demon Lord personally. Why was Patrick so adamant I stay away from this?

The more I thought about it, the more I realized how little Terence was asking of me. A bit of my time. An afternoon to teach the Seers who'd volunteered for this. I was almost embarrassed by my hesitation. If he thought me too delicate to handle that, what must he really think of me? All I had to do was show a group of people how to travel to the past. They'd take care of the rest. Simple. Not only would I be stopping the Demon revolution and possibly the Guardians' extinction, but I'd also be securing the safety of my family.

I'd become so absorbed in my own thoughts I didn't see that the Guardians were on their way inside until they were almost back at the table. Patrick's mouth was tight, but Terence was offering me a small smile. As soon as they stood beside me Terence spoke. "I'm afraid I must be going, Kate. I'm to meet with another Council member this evening, and I mustn't be late. But I urge you to think seriously about this. We would be greatly indebted to you if—"

"I'll do it," I interrupted easily. "I'll just be teaching them what the Demon Lord taught me. It won't be dangerous."

Patrick looked like he wanted to say something, but the words wouldn't come. Maybe he was reluctant to argue with me in front of Terence.

Terence glanced between us, his voice kind. "Why don't I let you two talk it out? If you're still willing to help after that, a simple phone call will do just fine. I can arrange for the Seers to come to you, for your convenience."

I nodded. "Okay. How soon could you get them here?"

Patrick's jaw flexed, and neither Terence nor I missed his restrained reaction, though we both ignored his obvious annoyance.

The older Guardian didn't answer my question exactly. "They could be assembled rather quickly. But I'll be waiting for your phone call, either way. Until then, take care." He reached out to shake my hand and I tried to make my grip firm. He gave me a nod, as if to let me know he got the message.

He inclined his head to my stoic Guardian, who was not bothering to meet anyone's eye. "Patrick," he murmured in casual farewell, before slipping around us and heading back toward the door.

I turned my attention to Patrick, since he was moving at last. He stepped closer to the table, snatching up our garbage and stacking it onto one of the two trays our food had arrived on. "Are you ready to leave?" he asked mildly, not looking directly at me.

I nodded once and began to help him clean up the table without a word.

We didn't speak until we were in his car, driving back toward my house. I finally opened my mouth to free the words desperate to escape. "It's not going to be dangerous. I'm not going to go with them."

"I know."

I glanced over at him, surprised at his quiet admission. He was focused purely on the road, so he didn't meet my look. "Then . . . you'll let me help?"

He braked at a red light, let all the breath ease out of his tense body in a slow sigh, and then he turned to match my stare. "You're going to do it anyway, regardless of what I say—we both know that." He quickly added the last part, when I opened my mouth to offer a weak rebuttal. One brown eyebrow raised on his face until I closed my mouth and nodded once. He was right—I'd already made my decision.

Patrick shook his head slightly, eyes lingering on the windshield before coming back to me. "I just . . . I don't want you to do anything else. I don't want you involved with the mission. After you've taught them how to travel, that's the end. Can you promise me that?"

"Wow."

His forehead wrinkled at my unexpected answer. "What?"

I shook my head. "Just wow. I thought you'd put up a fight or something."

He snorted deep in his throat and then looked back out the windshield. The light was still red. He didn't look back at me. "Believe me, I tried. Terence didn't think my concerns were very . . . relevant."

I bit my lower lip, studying the side of his stern face. "Are you mad at me?" I whispered at last.

His fingers were wrapped tightly around the steering wheel, his eyes focused straight ahead. But though outwardly he seemed upset, his voice was gentle. "Of course not. You want to do your part. I can respect that. It's just . . ." His eyes slid over to me, almost of their own accord. "You know how I feel about you going back in time. The reasons why I think it's a bad idea."

"I know. I can understand that. But if this is what it takes to stop the Demon Lord, so he never comes after us again . . . isn't it worth it?"

He swallowed hard. "Yes," he agreed reluctantly. "I just wish it was a risk you didn't have to be the one to take. I wish . . ." He hesitated and then disregarded whatever he'd been ready to add.

I stretched out my hand, and though his fingers continued to grip the wheel, I sensed the muscles in the back of his hand relaxing at my touch. "I'm going to be fine."

He met my thin smile but was quick to look away, in time to see the car in front of us start to shift forward, and then we were driving again.

I think we both realized at the same time that I hadn't agreed to his terms. I hadn't promised to limit my involvement to just teaching the Seers what I knew. But he wasn't about to press me into an oath, thus rendering it empty, and for some reason I couldn't make myself utter the words I knew he wanted to hear.

***

"Hey, Kate! You have a second?"

I turned around to see Aaron walking behind me, a small grin on his face. His bright aura was not quite as glowing outside as it would have been indoors, but his happiness and excitement were still undeniable.

"Yeah, sure," I replied quickly, stopping on the sidewalk to face him fully. "What's up?"

His grin widened, though he tried to keep it in check by biting his lower lip. His bag hung casually from one shoulder, and it swung a little when he drew to a stop in front of me. Students continued to file past us, oblivious to our partial obstruction of the sidewalk. "I was sort of wondering what you were doing after school tomorrow. Patrick too," he added.

My eyebrows scrunched up in thought. The first of the Special Seers would be arriving tomorrow, and Patrick was hoping to give me a couple more training lessons, which had been infrequent at best these past few weeks. Other than that, I was pretty open. "Nothing important that I know of. Why?"

He tilted his head faintly from side to side, as if hesitating. But his words were controversially confident. "If you guys aren't too busy, I was wondering if you'd like to do a group date thing tomorrow night at my house. I've already invited Jaxon and Maria, and I was hoping Lee and Rodney might be interested."

"Um. Yeah. That sounds like fun."

His eyes twinkled. "Good. I thought it would be a great chance for you to meet Alyssa."

"Alyssa?"

The yellow in his aura throbbed. "Alyssa Meadows. She's homeschooled, but she does a few extracurricular things here."

The name wasn't familiar, but at least I now understood Aaron's new happiness. He'd found a girl. Inwardly, I was cheering. "That's great. And of course I want to meet her." By mutual and silent consent, we were walking again, moving side-by-side toward the front doors of the school.

There was relief in his voice, though he tried to hide it—it was especially obvious in his aura. "Good. I mean, I was hoping you'd want to. She's really awesome."

"Have you been dating long?"

"Almost three weeks. For my part, it's been exclusive, but I don't know about her."

"You haven't asked her?"

"She's really . . . She's taking things slow. She barely let me hold her hand last weekend."

I smiled, because his tone was so adoring. "So you don't want to scare her off?"

He nodded once. "Something like that."

"So you're not official yet?"

He shrugged, a small grin fighting to free itself. "She hasn't told me to get lost yet . . ."

"I'm really happy for you, Aaron." And I was. More than I thought I'd be.

His eyes were almost shining. "Thanks, Kate. That means a lot."

We walked up the stairs in silence, but it wasn't awkward at all. When we reached the top, Aaron stepped ahead so he could pull the door open for me, and once we were inside he asked, "I was hoping to start the movie around seven or eight. Is there a time that works better for you guys?"

"Either time sounds great to me."

"Sweet. Well, I guess I'll talk to Lee and then let you know."

"Right." I heard a familiar voice, and I turned quickly to see Trent, one of the special-needs kids, standing halfway down a side hall, waving to every student who filed past. "Hello!" he said brightly, a huge grin splitting his face even though hardly anyone glanced his way. "Hello!"

Before I could step completely past the hallway, I hesitated.

Aaron walked on another step without me, before realizing I was no longer with him. He sent me a questioning look, but then he heard Trent and understanding dawned. "Is he supposed to be away from the others?" Aaron asked.

I shook my head, feeling my ponytail sway. "No. I bet he slipped away and some aide somewhere is going crazy." I was already stepping away from him. "I better help him out. See you in class?"

"You're going to be late," Aaron warned, but it was more of a playful taunt. He knew I hated being late to anything.

I tried to ignore his teasing. "Tell Patrick I'll be there soon, okay?" As soon as I was done speaking I turned, not bothering to wait and get his answer.

I thought I heard his footsteps move away from me, but so many other people were walking the halls it was impossible to know for sure. I wasn't the tallest person in the surrounding area, but Trent's booming voice couldn't be missed, so I just followed the sound whenever my view was obstructed.

"Hello!" Trent called out to someone.

I thought I heard someone in the crowd mutter, "freak," but I don't think Trent heard. His smile didn't waver, in any case. I slid past a larger girl, and then Trent and I were finally face to face.

"Hello!" he burst out when he saw me, looking excited. "Kay!" It was how he pronounced my name.

A smile tugged my lips at his sheer enthusiasm. "Hey, Trent. Aren't you supposed to be in class?"

"Hello!"

"Hi." I reached for his hand, knowing he paid better attention when physical contact was involved. His eyes actually met mine, though they rolled away just as quickly. "Come on. I'll take you to Mr. Thompson's office."

"Tom-son?" he asked eagerly.

"Yeah. Mr. Thompson." He was the teacher over the

special-needs kids; he'd know where Trent should be. I kept a firm grip on his long fingers, since I had to practically drag him the first couple of steps. But soon he fell into the rhythm of things. He just called out his hellos while we walked.

The warning bell rang just before I turned Trent over to a thankful Mr. Thompson. I told Trent good-bye, and that I'd see him at lunch. He gave me yet another big hello, and then I started back toward American Lit.

The hallways became less crowded as I made my way to the other side of the school, but in all honesty I wasn't paying a lot of attention to the students around me. My mind was occupied with other things. More specifically, the one thought that had been in the back of my mind for days now—ever since Terrence's visit.

I hadn't told Patrick about the wanted poster yet. In the beginning that was just because there were other things to focus on, and I had expected Terence to mention it. When he hadn't . . . I guess the opportunity to bring it up just hadn't arrived yet. I mean, how was that conversation supposed to start? *By the way Patrick, I'm worth one million dollars to the Demon Lord. How do I know this? Oh, I went and visited a Demon about a week ago, and he warned me that a bunch of rogue Demons are going to be after me. I have the poster and everything, but I didn't tell you because I didn't want you to worry. How was your day?*

Basically, I knew that telling him out of the blue would be a big mistake. He'd freak out that I hadn't told him sooner, and then he'd want to lock me in my room 24/7. In the end, it was easier not to tell him at all. He was anxious enough about me teaching the Special Seers how to travel. What would he do if he found out about the other, more real danger I was in?

I'd decided last night that I just needed to put the whole thing out of my mind. Just forget I knew anything about it. After all, I had multiple bodyguards for a reason. They didn't have to necessarily know about the threat to take care of it.

That was my current reasoning, but it was easier to convince myself of the logic when I wasn't staring into Patrick's pale face. He looked so worried and tense these days. Especially since I'd called Terence to let him know I was willing to do whatever was required of me. It was almost like Patrick could see something I couldn't—feared some horrible outcome I didn't even anticipate.

I needed to stop thinking so much. It made me jumpy.

I turned a corner, just as the starting bell rang. I quickened my step when I saw the corridor I walked was deserted. Classes were beginning. I hated walking in late . . .

And then I wasn't alone in the hall anymore. A man rounded the corner ahead of me, his eyes going immediately to me—almost like he knew I'd be standing exactly there. Like he was expecting me.

There were still several paces between us, and I stopped moving the instant I saw him. Despite the distance between us I didn't relax. Partly because he was smiling in a triumphant, creepy way, but mostly because his black aura and unfamiliar face marked him as just the thing I'd been telling myself there was no reason to fear—a Demon bounty hunter.

Seven

My heart barely had time to pound before I was glancing wildly to the side, searching for an escape. There was a door leading to a random classroom a couple steps behind me and to the right. It might be embarrassing to dive into the wrong classroom—late—but it was better than staying out here with a Demon.

Before I could even tense to move he was speaking slowly, his brown eyes wide. "Oh dear, I wouldn't do that if I were you. Your sisters wouldn't thank you for it."

He'd said possibly the only thing that would make me pause. And so I wavered, half inclined to turn and run as my eyes slid over the Demon in front of me.

He was big, his muscles thick and bulging under his tight black T-shirt. He appeared to be in his thirties, and his longish hair was black and unkempt. He looked extremely powerful and dangerous, but somehow I was able to speak without sounding too frightened.

In fact, I almost managed to sound annoyed. "What are you talking about? My sisters are perfectly safe."

"They have a Guardian and a Seer looking after them," he said, allowing my words with a thin smile. "But my partner could handle a pretty blonde—even if she's got a knife."

Claire. He knew about Claire. Meaning . . . he really *did* have someone watching my sisters.

I swallowed hard.

He started to tread closer, and I couldn't make my taut muscles move me back to maintain the distance. His voice was deep but horribly cheerful. "You must have really rattled the Demon Lord's cage, Miss Bennett. He doesn't usually pay this handsomely—and never for a Seer. But I must ask—am I the first you've seen? It's an issue of pride, you see."

I decided to play dumb, for the sake of stalling. "The first? Pay—?" I choked on the word, tried to make the cut-off sound intentional. "What are you talking about?" I added quickly.

He grinned—only three steps from me now. "Good. I love being first." He stopped directly in front of me, our toes nearly touching. I cringed back from his nearness, but my feet were frozen to the floor.

"Are you invisible?" I asked, my voice tenuous because I'd come to the realization that stalling wasn't going to do a bit of good. Any unease Patrick might feel at my tardiness, Aaron would have annulled when he told him I'd gone to help Trent. He wouldn't realize anything was wrong until it was too late.

The Demon didn't miss the waver in my voice. His smile became even more confident. "Of course. I've been following you for a couple of days now—Friday was the start of it. I never imagined it would be this easy, though, to get you isolated. I mean, I'm good, but . . ." He shrugged. "Then again, luck was with me today."

"So what now?" I asked, my stomach so tight I felt like it might constrict to the point of disappearing.

"My truck's in the parking lot," he said simply, extending a hand. "Come quietly and your sisters won't be harmed. It's really that simple."

I stared at his hand, his large and tanned fingers laid out easily in front of me. Simple? Not even . . .

He sighed suddenly but was somehow able to keep the smile on his face. "We're wasting time. If I don't call my partner in the next five minutes, he kills one of your sisters. Do you really want to stand around waiting for that?"

Without thought my hand lifted, a purely reflexive action. He was waiting for me to touch him, because the defensive mechanism that kept him unable to touch me could only be broken by me touching him first. My fingertips brushed his palm and in a flash his hand was strangling my wrist.

"Much better," he said happily.

I refused to show how much his grip hurt me. My face went absolutely expressionless; it was that or flinch uncontrollably. A split second later he was pulling me down the hall, back the way he'd come. Closer to Patrick . . .

"So you're a bounty hunter?" My question was so sudden, it startled even me.

He only chuckled, continuing his advance. "Sure. And I must say you've got the heaviest price on your head out of anyone I've ever taken care of—that includes some really important people I targeted in my last life too. Though that was awhile ago, and money's lost some value since then . . ."

There went any hope of pleading with him. He was probably as hardened as you could get.

I tried another tactic. "My Guardian is here. When he realizes I'm not where I'm supposed to be, he'll find you."

"The Irish guy? Yeah, I watched him beat up that guy at the bowling alley. I wasn't impressed."

I got chills thinking about him being so close to us without my realizing it. I mean, I was a Seer, for crying out loud! I needed to be more observant.

We passed one emo student, but he didn't even look up from the floor. He was listening to his iPod, earphones firmly in place, shoulders slouched inside his black hoodie, and completely oblivious to the fact that I was being kidnapped by an invisible Demon.

It was amazing how empty the school seemed when I knew it was really so full.

I couldn't think of a single thing to do. Maybe I should have tried running earlier. I might have reached Patrick. A phone call could have warned Claire to round up the twins, and in less than five minutes Patrick and I could have been at the elementary school. Why hadn't I done that? One thing was sure—I shouldn't have let the Demon touch me. I didn't think I could pull away from his grip without losing my whole arm.

We turned into the main hall and the Demon jerked me toward the front doors. We passed the front office, where no one seemed to notice me and my plight, and then we were pushing out of the front doors. He pulled me down the stairs toward the wide sidewalk. There were a few scattered people around, but the Demon didn't release me. He didn't care if I looked like a weirdo, walking with one arm stuck out in front of me.

If I'd been panicking inside the school, now that we were walking toward the parking lot I was starting to shake. Was this really happening? I was so close to Patrick it seemed almost impossible for me to be in danger of being taken back to the Demon Lord. I could feel my phone in my pocket, but I worried he'd see me reaching for it. Maybe if I didn't try to get it, he wouldn't realize I had it. I could text Patrick from the trunk or wherever he planned to dump me.

As if the Demon could sense my urge to fight, he threw a look over his shoulder, still walking fast. "Think of your sisters, Miss Bennett. Or do you prefer Kate? Katie?"

I decided not to answer his question. I'd given up trying to talk to him, period. Obviously it wasn't going to do me any good.

We stepped off the curb and into the parking lot. My heart was hammering, but my thoughts were strangely clear. I needed to slip away. Somehow. As long as I could get a message to keep the twins safe, there was nothing he could threaten me with. It was an incomplete plan, but it was the best I had at the moment.

He'd parked far away—almost the farthest corner of the crowded lot. But all too soon he was pulling me up to a silver pickup. It was large and appeared to be relatively new. Almost as intimidating as its owner.

I tried to keep my breathing even. I tried not to think about what I intended to do until . . .

His grip loosened subtly as he reached in his pocket for the keys. I made my move at that moment, anticipating this would be my best chance. I slammed my heel into the top of his foot, almost grinding down. He gasped in surprised pain, but before he could tighten his fingers around my arm, I was jerking through his weak point—where his thumb met with the other fingers. I ducked and started to run. I heard him yell behind me and curse loudly, then he was coming after me. Clumsily at first, but picking up speed.

"You've just killed one of your brat sisters!" he cried out harshly.

But I didn't stop. I dived between two parked cars in one of the middle rows. I weaved between some, but he was sliding across hoods and moving a lot faster than I was now. He was going to overtake me in seconds, unless something turned the tables.

My backpack slapped against my back annoyingly, but I didn't dare spare the second it would take to shrug out of it. My head was ducked, watching my feet so I wouldn't trip over them or anything else. I almost skidded into one of the parked cars in front of me, but I was able to catch myself with two well-placed palms. At my rocking touch the car shivered and a responding alarm rent the air.

There was another panted curse behind me—closer than I wanted to realize. A car away? Maybe two? I gasped evenly for air and continued to dart madly toward the school. What other choice did I have? My legs pumped furiously, but I knew it wasn't going to be enough. No way could I continue to outrun him—even with his hurt foot, he was going to catch me.

For the first time, I worried about what he would do when he had me in his power again. That fear was enough to propel me forward, but it wouldn't last for long.

I felt his fingers grope at my bag. I tried to put on a last burst of speed, but it was no good. He clutched my backpack and the resulting tug was enough to jerk me back against his chest, making us both stagger to an awkward stop. My shoulders felt like they'd been yanked out of their sockets, and I knew I'd have the burning welts for days to come. If I lived that long.

I cried out, simply because there was no way to hold it in. He'd regained his balance. In a sweeping motion that was graceful in its simplicity, he had one hand around my throat, the other slamming my shoulder against the side of a nearby car. I was already struggling to breathe after my futile run, but his choke hold had me straining for the thinnest tendril of air. My lungs were on fire in seconds, and my bulging eyes watered.

A terrible sneer twisted his face, which was pushed right up to mine. "Try that again, Katie," he grated out with muted fury, "and the Demon Lord's going to have himself a dead Seer."

His hand was still forcing my bruised shoulder against one of the car windows. I expected the glass to buckle at any moment, because surely it wasn't designed to withstand this kind of sustained pressure. My bones were groaning, and if I'd had the air I would have screamed. Instead, all I could produce was a pitiful rasp that might have been a wordless plea.

My vision seemed to rattle, and then my eyes focused on some movement beyond his hulking shoulder. I could barely believe what I was seeing. It was too wonderful to possibly be true.

Patrick was coming toward me at full speed, a knife gripped

tightly in one fast pumping fist. He was several long yards away but closing the distance inhumanly fast.

But I'd made the kind of dumb mistake so many damsels in distress do. By staring at him, allowing my eyes to widen revealingly, the Demon was aware that something was coming from behind. He glanced over his shoulder—surprised to see how quickly Patrick was coming—and then he was moving too. Or rather, he was moving *me*.

One second I was looking at Patrick—watching his eyes as they flashed with fear—then I was being shoved aside. I didn't really understand that he was knocking my head against the side mirror of the car until after the fact. All I felt was the horrific crack my head made as it connected forcefully with the plastic top of the mirror, and then his strangling fingers were gone and I was falling to the ground. I couldn't see anything but black, but I could feel everything—the sting of loose pebbles grinding into my uselessly extended arms, the thump that drove the lingering air from my lungs when I slammed into the asphalt. My hip took a lot of my initial weight, and my already beaten head pounded firmly against the pavement. I rolled partially onto my stomach, my twisted limbs unresponsive for the moment. I felt broken glass from the mirror, shattered into a thousand fragments, rain down on me.

The pain in my head exploded in a horrible throb. I knew I was bleeding. But had the impact cracked my skull? I had no way of knowing. My body shuddered for breath, my lungs uncaring about the condition of my head because suddenly they could fill with air. I gasped convulsively, but that was the only sound I could come up with.

I was distantly aware of the Demon tensing in front of me, but I couldn't see anything. When I tried opening my eyes there were too many shapes and shadows to see anything real. He might have taken a step away from me.

I heard the slam of bodies coming much too harshly together.

The hood of a nearby car buckled under sudden weight. I heard some gasps amid the sounds of heavy scuffling—a grunt—and then a body crumpled into a pile at the victor's feet. The fight was fierce but rapid, and it was impossible for me to know who'd won. I couldn't see anything.

Shaking footsteps came toward me. I was blinking profusely, but I was literally seeing stars. Someone knelt hard in front of me. Trembling fingers slipped into my hair, touching the sorest part of my very sore body. Pieces of glass slipped out of my hair and off my shoulder, raining to the ground.

My limbs jerked in response and a whimper escaped me at his touch.

"Kate?" Patrick's voice broke painfully. His weight shifted in front of me and then he gently maneuvered me onto my back—my head cradled on his shaking legs. "Kate, stay with me," he begged, parting my hair to assess the damage.

There was a sharp intake of breath; his thumb rubbed under my eye. "Kate, look at me. Please, I need you to look at me."

My eyes narrowed, trying to follow his orders, and I could almost make out his pale face with squinting. But that only caused my pounding head more pain. "Patrick?" I gasped.

"I'm here. It's all right. You're going to be all right." One hand remained on my face, smoothing my skin with motions too quick to be assuring, and the other flipped open a phone. Seconds later he was fairly barking into the speaker. "Toni, get down to the high school. Kate's been attacked. I'm taking her to the emergency room, but I need you to take care of a body. . . . Take the van then!"

"Wait," I pleaded blearily. "The twins. He wasn't alone . . ."

Patrick just shook his head at me. "It's okay, Kate—they're safe."

I think I lost consciousness for a moment, because the next thing I knew my cheek was rubbing against his crisp shirt, his rolling footsteps rocking me gently except for the steady jolt that accented each footfall. One of his arms supported my back and the other clung around my knees. I could feel every muscle in his body straining to hold me steady; even his chin was taut upon the top of my head, striving to hold me motionless. The side of my head that felt completely dented was getting a lot of air as we walked, but it was strangely calming against the warm blood I could feel already congealing in my hair.

"What about the body?" I whispered suddenly, the words partially slurred. "You can't leave him for someone to find."

If Patrick was surprised to hear me talking, it didn't show in his clipped words. "It doesn't matter. He's invisible. Toni will come for him, then meet us at the hospital when he's done."

I struggled to swallow. I closed my eyes and focused on breathing. The clean scent coming off his skin helped center my thoughts. "I'm sorry," I breathed.

He didn't reply. Maybe he hadn't heard me or maybe he was too upset to speak.

We must have reached his car because he stopped walking. He lowered my legs to the ground, careful to have at least one supporting arm around me at all times. That was a good idea, because I was still unsteady. I swayed against him at the same time one large hand tipped my head back so he could stare critically into my eyes.

I took this opportunity to do a little inventory for myself. My vision was already almost back to normal. That had to be a good sign. My body throbbed with pain—especially my neck, hip, and shoulder—but the pain in my head was so sharp it made the rest seem like minor discomforts.

"Pupils look good," he finally muttered to himself. Then, to me: "Are you feeling dizzy? Nauseated?"

"Um . . ."

"Kate?"

I frowned at him. "Can you give me a second to think?" I

didn't know where my sassy tone was coming from, but I hoped Patrick would read it as a good sign.

I pulled in a slow breath, trying to center my thoughts. "I felt a little dizzy at first, but now my head just hurts. I don't feel nauseated. That's good, right?"

He didn't really reply. He just reached for the keys in his pocket and I allowed my forehead to dip and rest against his strong shoulder. "Hold on, Kate," he whispered hoarsely, mouth at my ear. "Just stay conscious."

The locks disengaged with a whir and a signaling chirp. He opened the passenger door and lowered me inside, carefully sweeping my legs in because I couldn't seem to move them myself. I leaned my head gratefully against the seat, pursing my lips together to help keep things from spinning.

For the record, it didn't really help.

The glove box opened in front of me and Patrick searched inside for the first-aid kit. He practically tore the plastic lid off in an effort to get it open sooner, and he didn't seem to care that items were spilling out to bounce against the floor around my feet. Finally he found some squares of gauze. He pressed these to the side of my head an instant later and I hissed in pain.

"I know, I know," he fairly groaned, his other hand reaching for mine. He settled my fingers against the gauze beside his own, instructing me to hold it as tightly as I could.

"It hurts," I protested thinly.

His voice was incredibly tight. "It will help. I promise."

I pressed my fingers firmly against the wound until he trusted my efforts enough that he drew back. But as soon as his hand was gone and the door was closed I let up on the pressure. I felt like it was the perfect trick, because he wouldn't be able to see my slack fingers from the driver's seat. Brilliant.

A distant part of me knew I was thinking pathetic thoughts, but it didn't stop them from coming.

The driver's door opened seconds later. He was closing his

door and shoving the key into the ignition in the same instant, tossing me a concerned look. "Keep up the pressure, Kate."

"I am," I lied.

As an afterthought he reached over and slipped my seat belt on. It took him three tries before he was able to fit the end of the belt into the receiving buckle, since his hands wouldn't stop shaking. That was funny to me because when he'd held me, he'd been completely steady.

Once I was secure he shifted into reverse, not bothering with his own seat belt as the car rolled back quickly. Seconds later we were out of the parking lot and speeding toward the ER.

"How did you know?" I asked, though I didn't shift my head to look at him. It wasn't worth the risk of throwing up.

"Know what?" he asked, his voice a strange balance of distraction and concentration. Distraction because he was paying strict attention to the road, concentration because he was carefully attuned to my every shaking breath.

"Where I was. That I needed you." My voice couldn't seem to inflect the words into questions.

The lump in his throat bobbed when he swallowed. "Peter spotted a Demon at the elementary school and alerted Claire and Maddy. Claire went in pursuit, and Maddy called me because they thought I should know. I came to find you immediately. Aaron said you were with Trent, but once I was in the hall my feet took me outside instead. I don't know why. And then I heard the car alarm and I guessed . . ." He switched lanes briskly, but I think he was using the light traffic as an excuse to stop talking. The emotion was thick in his voice, and he was obviously trying to stay strong for me.

"You can slow down," I said after a tense moment. "I'm feeling better now."

It was actually the truth. I was feeling less out of it, more in control. I was still in pain, but I wasn't fighting the impulse to laugh anymore. That had to be good.

But he didn't react to my words. Not even a weak protest or a simple grunt. If anything, he more firmly planted his foot on the accelerator.

I sighed and delicately peeled the gauze away from my head so I could look at the blood. There was less than I thought there would be, which gave me hope that I might not need too many stitches.

"Keep it on, please," he mumbled distractedly, his eyes already sliding back to the road.

"Patrick, you can breathe. Really, I was just dazed before. I'm okay now."

"I'm going to let a doctor decide that."

I sighed, but I put the gauze back to cover the gash. "What am I supposed to tell them?" I murmured, able to form a real question this time. "That I was attacked by a Demon?"

"No. Just . . . Pretend you don't remember. I'll take care of the rest." His voice was heavy enough that I decided to stop talking to him. My words only seemed to be increasing his distress.

I wouldn't let him carry me into the emergency room, but I was grateful for his steadying arms as he helped guide me inside. He led me up to the nurses' window where a middle-aged woman calmly asked me what had happened. Where I hesitated to speak, Patrick quickly filled in the blanks. In less than a minute the basic story was out—he'd found me in the high school parking lot, head knocked against a side mirror. Pretty simple, and she didn't seem to care for further details. At least not yet. She suggested I keep pressure on the wound, handed us a clipboard, and told us to fill out the paperwork while we waited.

Patrick was still extremely tense as we took our seats in the corner, near a young girl who was hiccupping through her tears and clutching her arm while her mother bent over her clipboard. I insisted I was well enough to fill out the forms, and Patrick didn't fight me.

He crouched on the edge of his seat, head ducked, legs bouncing as he tapped his feet, jaw rigid, eyes slicing up whenever anyone walked past or a patient was called back.

I tried to focus on the meticulous task of writing out my address, but his jittery movements were hard to ignore. Finally I sighed and lowered the pen.

"Patrick."

His head twisted toward me, his body otherwise freezing. I rolled my eyes at him. "Calm down. Okay? The nurse wasn't worried; I'm not worried; you shouldn't be worried."

His lips parted, compressed, then thinned. He just shook his head and glanced away.

"What?" I asked, exasperated.

"Nothing," he muttered.

Though of course I didn't believe him, I returned to my paperwork, and he returned to his nervous tics.

When everything was filled out, I stood and Patrick practically leapt to his feet behind me, taking hold of my arm even when I told him I was perfectly steady. We returned the clipboard to the nurse and soon she buzzed us through to another room where she had me take a seat. She took my vitals, asked me to rate my pain level on a scale of one to ten—I chose four, because I really was feeling much better—and she also questioned me about my medical history. Patrick stood anxiously beside me the whole time. After she was done, the nurse led us to a curtained-off bed and asked me to lie down and wait for the doctor, leaving us with the sounds of low adult voices and the whimpering cries of children surrounding us.

I sat on the bed, but Patrick wouldn't sit beside me. He paced the length of the bed for the next fifteen minutes or so, refusing to meet my eye.

And then the doctor was shaking my hand while a male nurse encouraged Patrick to take a seat as the doctor worked. The doctor examined the wound against the side of my head, cleaned it, and commented that it really wasn't too bad—not that Patrick seemed to relax after the pronouncement. Six stitches later the doctor offered to prescribe me some heavy painkillers, but assured me that Tylenol could just as easily do the trick. I opted for the Tylenol, having had past experience with prescription painkillers after the car accident. The memories weren't good.

The doctor swept out but the male nurse lingered, looking to Patrick. "She'll need someone to stay with her for the next twenty-four hours or so." His eyes moved between us. "Make sure you come back right away if you lose consciousness, begin to have seizures, experience bleeding from nose or ears, or if symptoms increase in severity or persist."

"Can I go home and sleep?" I asked, desperately ready to take a nap.

"Soon. The police were alerted of the assault, and they're on their way. They just need to ask you a few questions." He glanced back at Patrick, who was as rigid as ever. "Both of you."

"Of course," Patrick cut in, speaking for the first time in over a half hour.

I almost jumped at the abrupt sound of his voice, and the male nurse seemed to notice my reaction. He tipped his head toward Patrick. "Sir, if you don't mind, I've got a few more questions I need to ask Miss Bennett before the police arrive. Privately. Would you please step out?"

Though we weren't touching I could feel Patrick bristling. "I need to stay with her," he countered at once.

I stretched out a hand and touched his stiff arm, and he glanced over at me, eyes grim. "It's all right," I assured him.

His eyes narrowed, but he nodded curtly, met the eye of the nurse one last time, then slipped around the curtain.

The male nurse began to question me for more specifics about how I'd incurred my injuries, including the bruises. I kept my answers short and admittedly hazy.

"It definitely seems like it was a deliberate attack," he said sympathetically, after I'd finished speaking. "Especially because of that bruising," he added, nodding toward my neck.

My hand lifted to finger the large bruise at my throat. I could still feel the Demon's fist crushing around my neck, pinching out my breath, draining my life . . .

"There's bruising on your wrists as well. The police will want to know if you can remember seeing an attacker. Even a partial description will be helpful."

My gaze wavered when I saw Patrick standing behind the nurse, eyes firm on mine. I frowned at him, belatedly realizing he must be invisible because the nurse hadn't noticed his return.

"Miss Bennett?" the nurse prompted, drawing my attention back. "Did you know your attacker? Was it the guy who brought you in? Your boyfriend?"

Patrick's head fell forward, braced tightly in one hand while his shoulders curled inward.

"What?" I choked, hand dropping to my lap, feeling sick at the very implication. "No!"

"Are you sure?" the nurse persisted. "This sort of thing happens . . ."

"I'm sure," I insisted.

I don't think he believed me entirely, but he leaned forward to more carefully examine the bruises along my neck. It was during that quiet moment that a middle-aged police officer poked his head inside. He smiled kindly at me, then focused on the nurse. "Is she ready for some questions?"

"Sure."

"Great. She was brought in by someone?"

My eyes flickered to Patrick, who met my gaze quickly.

"Uh, yeah," the nurse said haltingly. "He was going to wait right outside. Maybe he moved to the lobby."

"Maybe you could point him out to my partner? We'd like to ask him some questions too."

Patrick spoke lowly, though of course I was the only one who could hear him. "Remember, Kate—you didn't see anyone. Neither did I. All right?"

"Miss Bennett?" The officer took a step forward and the nurse moved around him, greeting the other officer who must have been on the other side of the curtain.

I nodded, and the officer smiled. Patrick bowed out, moving fast—he needed to beat the others to the lobby.

The officer pulled out a notepad and the polite but insistent questioning began.

I retold the sketchy story for the officer, who scribbled notes in his palm-sized notebook. He would often ask me to clarify points, making the whole process even more repetitive. *Yes, I'd gone out to the parking lot alone. Yes, I was headed to my car. No, I didn't see anyone come up behind me . . .*

"And that's it," I summed up with forced concentration. "I was on the ground, and then I saw Patrick running toward me. He brought me here. Everything else is pretty blurry."

"Patrick's your . . . ?"

"Boyfriend," I reconfirmed.

"He drove you here?"

"Yes."

"Did he mention seeing anyone?" the officer persisted.

"No. I . . . no."

"Do you have any enemies, Miss Bennett? Anyone who would be interested in attacking you?"

Only most of the Demon population, which you don't know exists . . . "No. No one."

After a few more minutes of questions the officer declared us "nearly done." "I've got to confer with my partner, but we can go out to the lobby and wait for them. We'll just need a couple of minutes."

"And then I can go home?" I asked.

He half smiled. "Sure. Once we've got this cleared up." It

was beyond obvious he thought Patrick's guilt had been assured in the other room.

I nodded my thanks to him anyway and slipped off the bed, following him out. Pushing the curtain aside we found ourselves face-to-face with the nurse, who reminded me to take some medication for the headache as soon as I got home. He also suggested rest, and I wasn't about to disagree.

Patrick and the other officer—a younger man—were waiting in the corner of the lobby. Patrick silently took my hand and we stood together while we watched the policemen a few paces away, heads bent together, notebooks out.

I was almost surprised when, a minute later, the younger officer closed his notebook, pocketing it. The older officer frowned, but the younger officer merely shrugged, hands on hips.

Patrick leaned closer, lips at my ear. "I made sure he believed me."

"How?"

Patrick nearly chuckled—a miracle, considering everything we'd been through today. "I can be persuasive . . . I convinced you once that I wasn't dangerous, remember?"

It took me a second to recall the single event he was referring to—one of the first times we'd met, at school; he'd opened the door for me and stared down at me, his eyes so wide and innocent. The moment had inspired an irrational but undeniable trust in him, which he'd later explained as a perk of being a Guardian. I suppose all humans were susceptible to the powerful influence, then, and not just Seers.

The officers told us we were free to go, assuring us that if they learned anything, they'd let us know.

Patrick didn't speak to me again until we were outside, standing next to the Altima.

He turned toward me and laid his hands gently on either side of my face. His clear blue eyes were riveted on mine. "Kate,

I am *so* sorry. This is completely my fault. This never should have happened."

"Patrick, you can't blame yourself for this."

My dubious words faltered when his lips touched gingerly against mine. I leaned closer to him, my own lips just as eager as his. He kissed me slowly, careful to hold my head in place as our mouths moved easily together. The ball of his thumb trembled against my cheek and his other palm slid to support the back of my neck. His breath was thin against my face when he pulled back, but he remained bent over me so he could get a better look at my throat. His shaking hand shifted from my cheek to lightly finger the bruises on my skin—the large handprint almost identical to his.

His voice was hardly audible. "If anything happened to you, I would be completely lost. When I saw him . . . He could have killed you so easily, Kate, and I couldn't have stopped him. I was too far away. Too slow."

"Patrick." I spoke his name firmly. His eyes flitted up to mine, and I could see how shaken he really was. "You're an amazing Guardian. It's not your fault the Demon Lord wants me so badly."

The skin around his eyes tightened. "That doesn't give me an excuse to slip up. I've been taking your safety for granted."

"No, you haven't," I protested.

He overrode me. "Kate, he's just been waiting for me to lower my guard. Nothing like this will happen again. I promise." I opened my mouth but he slid a thumb over my lips, halting the words. "I need you to tell me anything you can about him," he said gently. "Anything he said. If Claire didn't succeed in catching his accomplice, we won't know how many might still be out there."

"He only mentioned one partner."

"Did he admit to being sent by the Demon Lord?"

Sort of . . . But if Patrick learned about the price on my head, he would never relax again.

"I don't know. I would assume so. He made a comment—something about how surprised he was by the Demon Lord's interest in a Seer. That was all." *Mostly.*

Patrick nodded slowly, almost to himself.

The screech of tires burning rubber caused both our heads to jerk up, and I watched open-mouthed as my grandma swerved the minivan into the parking lot, grating to a stop in a parking spot two down from where we were standing. The engine cut off sharply and the driver's door snapped open as Grandma pushed out.

Her aura was redder than I'd ever seen it. The brown pain was hardly visible among all the anger billowing out from her. She slammed the door and lurched up onto the sidewalk, stalking toward us, her eyes furious. I instinctively grabbed Patrick's hand, hoping to keep him firmly at my side so we could face her wrath together.

She didn't even look at me. She stopped short in front of us, jabbed a long finger into Patrick's chest. "*Where* in the world *were* you?" Her voice throbbed with fury. Her hand slashed the air in front of his face, vehement gestures to accentuate her low but passionate words. "Where *were* you? *Where. Were. You?* That Demon could have—if she hadn't run—if you'd just done your—*you* made her face that *Demon* on her *own!* What is the *point* of you?"

A rather pale Toni was inching away from the minivan, eyeing Grandma like he'd never really seen her before today. He glanced between Patrick and me with alternating pity and compassion.

Patrick wasn't breathing beside me.

Grandma continued. "If you can't keep her safe then *why* are you still *here?* Do you think that I—Kate, you be quiet!" At last her voice shot up into a yell, cutting off my weak attempt to stop her flow of words. "I'm talking right now, and I've been waiting *too* long to say my piece."

Grandma was panting, cheeks flushed, aura flaring as she glared again at Patrick. "Do you think I like having all you Guardians hanging about?" she hissed. "Do you think I *like* watching you surround my granddaughters day in, day out? You're the constant reminder that they're in horrific danger! Jenna and Josie don't deserve this. *Kate* doesn't deserve this! Do you think I like being reminded it was *your world* that stole my husband from me? You serve as a *constant* reminder that he's dead and I don't know enough about Demons and Guardians to protect my *family*!" She slammed a palm against Patrick's unmoving chest, and though the blow wasn't physically impressive, I flinched, squeezing his hand in comfort.

Tears burned in her eyes as she slapped his body again. "Do you think I *enjoy* looking at *you* every day, thinking of your *Demon* brother *killing* my Henry? Don't you know I imagine it's *you?* That he looks *just like you*!"

"Grandma!"

I was shaking. I dropped Patrick's limp hand and inserted myself between them, grabbing her hand that hung in midair.

"That's *enough*," I croaked, equal parts mortified and wounded. "Patrick's the reason I'm alive!" I couldn't continue. Emotions were too high, clogging my throat.

Grandma seemed to be suffering from the same problem.

Toni coughed loudly. "Hate to draw attention to myself in this *highly* awkward moment, but I feel the need to remind everyone that this isn't a freaking soap opera, and that we aren't exactly in a private place."

Grandma's jaw locked. She looked purposefully away from Patrick and clutched my hand tightly. "Come on, Kate. I'm taking you home."

"But—"

She tugged, grip tightening. "*Now* Kate."

I craned around so I could see Patrick. His eyes were

hooded, his skin tinged with gray. He didn't hold my gaze, and his voice sounded oddly parched. "It's all right. Go. I'll be right behind you."

"Yes," Grandma snapped before I could form an answer. "*Behind*. Sounds like your usual place lately."

"Stop it, please," I whimpered.

Patrick's voice wavered but had a bit more power than before. "Charlotte, let's get Kate home. Once she's resting, we can continue this."

They'd carry this conversation on later? Without me there to referee? No *way* was I letting that go down. "But—"

Grandma's head bobbed. "Agreed," she told him.

"*What?*" I spluttered.

Patrick's hand was on my shoulder. He was finally meeting my eye. "Kate. Go. Really. You need to rest."

"You'll come to the house?" I asked for reassurance.

He nodded. "I promise." He looked over my head, past Grandma. "Toni, come on."

Grandma pulled on my arm, and I slowly followed her to the van. As Toni slunk past us I could just pick up his whisper to Patrick.

"I'm sorry, man. She wouldn't let me take the van alone. And I'm never letting her drive me again—just because I'm immortal doesn't mean I can't get scared to death . . ."

Grandma released her grip on me and I rounded the hood, glancing over my shoulder to see Patrick watching me, clearly ignoring his partner. I sighed and climbed into the van.

As soon as my seat belt was on Grandma spoke. "Are you all right? Did they give you stitches? I saw that crushed mirror at the school, and . . ."

"Six stitches. I'm fine."

"Do we need to stop somewhere and pick up a prescription?"

"No." I suddenly felt exhausted.

We didn't speak again until we'd pulled into the garage, but the gentle hum of the drive had almost lulled me to sleep by the time she shut off the van. I straightened in my seat and watched Patrick in the side mirror as he eased the Altima into the driveway behind us.

"Grandma, please don't yell at him," I whispered.

"Don't worry about that," she replied gruffly, opening her door.

I pushed open my own door and Patrick was there to catch it. He helped lower me out, one arm flexed firmly around my waist for support. He helped me into the house, Grandma just in front of us, Toni trailing behind. Grandma opened doors and led the way up to my bedroom; she even pulled down my blankets for me. "I'll get you some Tylenol," she murmured roughly.

She trod out of the room toward the bathroom, and Patrick held my arm protectively as I sat down. I noticed Toni hadn't followed us up.

I reached toward my head with one scraped-up hand, searching for the elastic that held my somewhat askew ponytail. My arm was heavier than I thought, though, and I could barely lift it past my shoulder.

"What do you need?" he whispered, concerned with my feeble movements.

"My ponytail," I muttered, allowing my hand to fall to my lap. "It's driving me crazy."

He responded immediately, his fingertips brushing fleetingly against my scalp as he carefully uncurled the elastic from my hair. He was just running his fingers against the freed locks when Grandma came back inside carrying a glass of water and a couple small tablets. She handed them to me and then turned to face Patrick.

"Would you please wait for me in the family room?" Her deep voice brooked no arguments.

He bowed his head respectfully. "Of course." He waited

until I finished swallowing my pills, then he bent to press his lips to my forehead. "I'll be right downstairs," he breathed.

I reached for his hand, and once it was in my grip I gently kissed his fingertips. I spoke against his skin, my voice tired but sincere. "Thank you."

Grandma cleared her throat and Patrick obediently pulled free of my hand. He glanced over at my grandmother, and then he moved for the door. He was in the doorway when I called softly, "Patrick?"

He paused, looking over his shoulder with one hand caught on the door's frame. "Yes?"

I had so many things I wanted to say. I settled for a simple, "I love you."

He swallowed hard, returned the sentiment quietly, then he was gone.

Grandma closed the door behind him, emotions fighting for dominance in her eyes and aura. It was easy to see she was trying to force back any compassion so she could maintain her strict anger. She helped me change into something more comfortable and then tucked me carefully into my bed. "Call if you need me," she said gruffly. "I'll be up to check on you in a while."

"Thanks, Grandma."

She almost seemed surprised by my words, after our silent drive. "Just get some sleep, all right?" she said at last.

I blinked heavily. It was amazing how tired I was. Still, there was something important I needed to convey before I slipped into unconsciousness. "Please don't yell at him anymore. Please don't blame him for things he didn't even do."

She patted my quilt around me. "Never mind about that."

"He's already blaming himself more than enough. For everything. Even for what happened to Grandpa . . ."

"Don't worry about it, Kate," she repeated firmly.

She closed the door when she left, and that's when I knew without a doubt that she was on her way to chew him out. I wanted more than anything to get up and defend him, but now that I was lying in my cool bedroom—feeling completely safe, the world no longer spinning, the adrenaline no longer pumping, no longer forced to keep my eyes open—I didn't have the energy to move.

Sleep came fast.

eight

I woke up to a throbbing headache. The medicine had worn off, which told me I'd been asleep for a couple hours at least, though it felt like I'd hardly slept at all. I squinted at the clock on my bedside, finding it was already 2:07 p.m. Later than I'd first realized.

"Ah! You're not dead, then," a cheerful voice called from across the room.

I stared past my feet to see Toni, watching me from the chair at my desk. He'd been doing something on my laptop, but now that he saw I was awake he was plucking out his earbuds and swiveling around to face me.

My voice was dry. "Toni? What are you doing in my room?"

He shrugged. "Watching you sleep. I *enjoy* watching you sleep . . . Isn't that what that one vampire dude says in that one book about that one girl?"

"Huh?"

He went back to answering my original question. "I'm making sure you don't slip into a coma or stop breathing. I know—talk about overprotective. But you've been asleep for a long time. You were making some people anxious." He suddenly grinned. "And can I just say, I had no idea your head was such a weapon. That dude's mirror was completely smashed! We should have trained you with some nice head-butting to work up your skill set."

I rubbed at my eyes, more grateful for his humor than I let on. It was a lot better than the serious edge everyone else seemed to be using today. "Do you think you could go get me some more Tylenol?"

He stood at once. "Sure. But you probably should eat something too. Anything sound good?"

"Not really."

"Sweet. I'll bring you something random, and you can't be disappointed."

He walked toward my door, but before he could make it there I called him back. "Is Patrick still downstairs?"

He hesitated. "Will you be mad if I say no?"

"Only if you're lying." But the disappointment was clear in my tone.

He gave me a sympathetic smile. "He's actually at the warehouse, packing."

"Packing!" I immediately regretted my raised voice, and the instinctive lurch of my pained head as I pushed myself up into a weak sitting position.

He held out his hands, palms out, urging me to stay calm and remain leaning up against the headboard. "Whoa! Let's not blow a single word out of proportion. He's not packing, *packing*, he's *packing*, packing. As in, he's moving, not leaving."

"Moving? Where?" Surely Grandma wouldn't have said anything that would drive him to something this drastic?

"You know your dad's old den? That's where he's moving."

My heart skipped a beat. "Patrick's moving into my house?"

He nodded easily. "Your house, our house . . . which happens to be in the middle of the street . . ."

"*Why* is he moving in?" I overrode his attempt at humor.

"Seriously? You didn't get that line? You know, from that song—?"

"Toni, please!"

I must have looked really pathetic, because he actually listened to me. "Well, you were there for the parking lot scene, and the home version was marginally worse. I mean, like, *really* worse. I now know where Josie gets her impressive set of lungs. Wow, your grandmother freaks me out sometimes."

I cringed. "Was it that bad?"

Toni grimaced. "You saw the preview—just envision that but more intense. Your Grandma was obviously letting a lot of pent-up emotions explode out of her and rip into him, poor guy. He was taking it in that really humble way of his too. Up until the point she started accusing him of not really caring about you."

"She *what?*" I gasped.

He nodded sincerely. "You better believe it. I'm probably not supposed to be telling you this . . ." He shrugged and continued. "But anyway, she accused him of caring more about his own feelings than worrying about you and yours. That's when he found his voice. And—honestly, I can't believe you slept through all this!—they've reached a pretty delicate understanding, but I wouldn't recommend being alone in a room with them for a while. Tylenol?"

I groaned. "If she's so mad at him, why is she letting him move in?"

"Because in the end they both want the same thing: your safety. Patrick's convinced Demons are going to start jumping out of thin air now. He wants to be as close as possible."

"What about the twins?"

"They never go in your dad's den. That's what dear Grandma said." He shrugged. "I spend most my days there without a problem."

"But you're invisible."

"As Patrick will be," he reminded me, his tone carrying the

opinion that maybe my head had been damaged more extensively than previously thought.

I frowned. "I'm used to having you invisible. But Patrick . . . how can I pretend he's not there?"

"Are you saying I'm easy to ignore?" He actually looked offended.

"It's different," I hedged.

"That was a cop-out if I ever heard one." He grunted once. "Right, well, I'm going to go get your drugs—I used to be pretty good at that, once upon a time . . ."

I rolled my eyes as he left and put a steadying hand to my forehead. After watching Grandma verbally beat Patrick at the hospital, it was far too easy to imagine the escalated argument she'd carried on at home. But Patrick raising his voice at her? Inconceivable. Sure, they'd both been under a considerable amount of stress, but . . . I couldn't imagine him yelling at her. Couldn't imagine him yelling, period.

Grandma was the one to bring in a tray with some applesauce, a glass of water, and my medicine. She set it on the end table, pushing back the clock and clutter that dominated the surface before finally meeting my gaze. "Are you feeling any better?" she asked meaningfully.

I answered honestly. "My head hurts. But I feel more alert."

"Good. Toni said you're not very hungry."

"Not really," I admitted. "Nothing sounds very good."

"Well, I want you to eat this. I'm making some homemade chicken noodle soup—none of that wimpy canned stuff. It should be done soon, and I'll bring some up."

"Thank you, Grandma."

The skin around her eyes relaxed a little. "You're welcome, dear." She picked up the bowl of applesauce and an accompanying spoon, handing them to me with simple instructions: "Eat."

She wouldn't let me take the medicine until I had something in my stomach, so that alone encouraged me to swallow some applesauce. When she was finally satisfied, she handed me the pills, which I took gratefully with some water. Once they were washed down Grandma took the glass and set it aside.

I wasn't sure how to broach the subject of their argument, but I needed to know the things she'd said to him—if for no other reason than to help belay any doubts she may have instilled in him.

I decided to start with something simple. "Toni said Patrick's moving in."

She brushed a hand over my blankets, trying to get rid of imaginary lint. "Yes. He seems to think it's the safest thing for you."

"I already have a nightly guard," I said cautiously, seeing in her aura that these emotions were still dangerously close to the surface.

"I'm well aware of that," she fairly sniffed, still more interested in my bed than me. "But he doesn't seem to feel that's good enough."

I kept my voice quiet. "Grandma, did you really yell at him?"

Her eyes flashed up to mine, then narrowed. "Toni. Of course. That annoying little tattle . . ." She sighed. "I don't want you worrying about that."

"What did you say to him?" I asked softly.

The muscles in her jaw worked briefly. Her voice was rough. "Things I probably shouldn't have. But what's done is done. I just don't understand how your grandfather managed to . . ." She swallowed hard. "Well, I just don't know how to handle all of this strange, supernatural business."

I reached for her hand, squeezing her weathered fingers gently. "You've been doing a great job," I assured her.

"I don't know about that, but . . . I've been trying." She hesitated shortly, shame filtering into her aura. "I should probably tell you I said some pretty harsh things to him. I didn't really mean to speak the words; they just sort of . . . came out. Well, you saw. I was just so frightened . . ." She pulled her hand away suddenly. "Then again, you've been talking to Toni. You probably got the play by play."

"Not exactly."

She straightened. "It's just as well. It's in the past."

"Your aura doesn't agree with that."

She blinked but recovered firmly. "Kate Bennett, I order you to stop looking at my aura."

I forced a smile, but my eyes remained steady and uncompromising. "I love him, Grandma. And he loves me."

For a long minute she didn't say anything. Then she patted my leg. "I know. It may not be easy for me to accept or even understand. But I know." She reached for my glass before I could question her further. "I'll get you a refill. You finish that applesauce, young lady."

***

Lee drove the twins home in my car and they all came right up to see me. As far as the twins knew, I'd mysteriously fainted, knocking my head against one of the school lockers. I made sure my T-shirt collar was up enough to hide the worst of the bruising. Hopefully the visible discolorations would look like harmless shadows.

I shouldn't have been so worried. They didn't linger. Josie stayed only long enough to make a few jokes, and Jenna just wanted to make sure I really was okay. Once they were reassured they slipped out, moving to the kitchen to get something to eat.

Lee sat on the edge of my bed, her face pale and her aura flushed with worry. Monday brought her new fashion phase, so she'd already given us a few days to get used to her new look. Rainbow Days was over, and the fifties had begun in full swing. She'd taken out her nose ring a couple weeks before, and in that time the small hole had mostly mended. She was wearing a blue poodle skirt and plain white tennis shoes. She'd cut her hair before Rainbow Days, but in the seven weeks it had grown to almost her shoulders. Though her ponytail was a little short for the style, the long and thick ribbon she wore helped sell the illusion of a true fifties haircut. Her hair was actually dyed back to something resembling her natural color—a simple brown. It was weird not seeing all the bright-colored makeup on her face. Some lipstick, a little mascara . . . that was really all she had on. She looked really pretty—almost full-blown beautiful.

"You scared the living daylights out of me," she confided. "Toni called, but . . . what all happened?"

And so I told my story for what felt like the millionth time. The only good thing about rehashing it with Lee was that I didn't care if some of my fear leaked through. I didn't feel the strict need to hide my emotions from her, like I did to keep from further worrying Patrick and my grandma.

When I was done catching her up she just shook her head. "This is weird. I mean, the Demon Lord hasn't done anything for so long. This seems so random." She paused, and I was *this* close to telling her about the reward he'd put out for me. But then she was speaking again, and the desire to tell her faded. "Toni said that Peter was the one that tipped them off?"

I nodded slowly. "That's what I've been told. He saw a Demon hanging out at the school and figured it probably had something to do with me."

"I honestly don't know how to feel about that," Lee admitted. "I mean, I'm glad he helped and all, but it's weird to think that he might choose to help that creep Selena at any time. You know?"

"Yeah."

"So where's Patrick?" she asked suddenly, peering around the room like she might have just missed him before.

"Packing at the warehouse," I muttered.

"Huh?"

"He's moving in, I guess."

"Moving in? As in, *here*?"

"Into my dad's den, apparently."

"Seriously? And your Grandma's okay with this?"

"She isn't stopping him. I don't think she's happy about it, though."

"Oh my Oreos, Kate—your boyfriend's moving in with you!"

My face was red. "It's not like that, and you know it."

"Maybe not, but it's still fun to say those words together like that."

I rolled my eyes, but Lee was already changing the subject. "So Aaron talked to me at lunch, wondering if I'd be interested in a movie night tomorrow at his house. He said he'd already talked to you?"

"Oh yeah." I'd completely forgotten.

"So, are you guys going?"

"I don't know—I haven't talked to Patrick."

She winced. "Well, I hope you do."

"Why?"

"Because Rodney has work, so I don't think I'll be able to go. I'd feel bad if we all bailed on Aaron."

"So are you two officially a thing now?" Toni asked a little too loudly from the doorway. We turned to watch him amble into the room, thumbs snagged in his pockets. His expression was open and unassuming. He looked too innocent to be believable, though; Toni never looked innocent, unless he was hiding something.

Lee actually squirmed. "Um, sort of. I mean, we aren't actually together yet, but . . ." I'd never seen her looking so awkward. Her aura was . . . Was she *excited* to have Toni walk in on us? Embarrassment was there too. Was she regretting that Toni had heard her talking about Rodney? I knew she'd had a crush on Toni from the beginning, but she'd been moving on. Especially after finding out about him being an immortal Guardian.

But if she was over him, why was there a slight blush warming her cheeks?

Toni wandered closer, his voice even, looking straight at her. "So I could ask you out, if I wanted to?"

Lee's eyes widened. "Are you asking this rhetorically?"

He shrugged. "I can be rhetorical if you want me to be. But I *was* genuinely curious."

There was no doubt about her blush now. "Um . . . Yeah, I guess you could."

He nodded once. "Good. So tomorrow night then? For Aaron's shindig?"

I spoke before Lee could. "Toni, what about my sisters? You're supposed to be invisible at all times. You'll freak them out if they see you in here!"

He hardly spared me a glance. "Just a second, Kate. This is important. So, Kellee, is it a date?"

She just stared at him for a moment, completely taken aback by his seriousness. When she realized she was being silent for too long, she settled for a quick answer. "Sure."

Toni nodded, his face still smooth and his brown eyes intense. "Great."

He might have said more, but the doorbell rang. The twins could be heard running through the entryway, and Toni gave Lee a polite nod before fading from her sight. I knew he was invisible because he suddenly turned to look at me, his breath coming out in a huge burst. "Wow. Do you think that was the wrong approach? Never mind, don't answer that. And stop looking at me like that. For heaven's sake, she's going to think I'm saying something about her!"

"What's he saying?" Lee asked, eyeing the place he'd been standing just a second ago. "Toni, what are you doing?"

Toni rolled his eyes at me. "Thanks a lot, Kate. Remind me to dislike you later."

"What did I do?" I grumbled at him.

But he was already leaving the room. Lee was looking at me questioningly, but she didn't have time to form a question because the twins were coming up the stairs, catching Patrick up on how dumb I was for falling into a locker.

They all entered the room at seemingly the same time, but my eyes went right to his. He looked tired. Like he'd been working constantly for days on end, only to realize that his sacrifices meant nothing. He'd managed to create a small smile for the sake of the twins, but it was probably the worst lie he'd ever told in his long life.

Lee followed my gaze, and it was obvious that she could read the same things I was. She stood quickly, offering him a short greeting before turning to the twins. "What did you guys find to eat?"

"Grandma made homemade chicken noodle soup," Josie said.

Lee frowned. "In my day, an after school snack was an apple. A cookie, if you were lucky. You're so spoiled."

"Do you want some?" Jenna asked.

"Absolutely I do." They shuffled back out into the hall, and Lee was considerate enough to close the door behind them.

Patrick was still standing a couple feet from my bed. One hand was in his pocket, the other was rubbing the back of his neck. The smile he'd managed to get for the twins had faded, solemnity taking its place.

"How are you feeling?" he asked, seconds after the door closed.

"Better." I bent my legs under the sheet, pulling them closer to me. I patted the bed beside me, closer than Lee had been sitting. "So, I hear you've been packing."

His hand dropped away from his neck as he stepped forward. He sank onto the bed, careful not to bounce me. "Is that all right?" he whispered.

"It'll be different . . ."

His lips pressed together. "I'm sorry."

"For what?"

"For making your life so unusual."

I stretched out my hand, watching as his fingers wrapped almost eagerly around mine. "You're the best part of my life right now," I told him truthfully.

"Even with all the bad that comes with me?"

"You make it sound like you're the one trying to off me."

He closed his eyes deliberately. "Kate, please don't joke about that."

I'd struck a real chord, which only made me more anxious to know the details of this afternoon. "Patrick, what on earth did she say to you?"

He offered a half smile that held no mirth, his sad eyes only accentuating the pain he so obviously felt. "Nothing I didn't deserve."

"I don't believe that."

He peered up at me through his lashes. "Maybe there wasn't truth to everything she said. But I *do* have a job, Kate, and I failed to do it today. I failed to protect you."

"I'm alive—I'm here."

He shook his head partially. "You're making me feel worse."

"What? How?"

"I'm feeling guilty about how quickly you're driving *away* my guilt."

"Patrick . . ." I decided to try a different approach. "Did that Demon hurt you?"

He lifted a single shoulder in a partial shrug. "Nothing that didn't heal."

I tightened my grip on his fingers. "Same here. It just takes me a bit longer than you, that's all."

He sighed. "I should have been paying more attention. If Peter Keegan hadn't seen the Demon, if I hadn't acted immediately . . . That's why I need to be closer to you. The warehouse is close, but not close enough. Not if we suffered another surprise attack like this one. I can't . . . I can't be helpless again."

He grimaced suddenly. "Also, um . . . I'm afraid I may have hurt your grandmother's feelings. I'm definitely not on her good side right now. I thought I should warn you."

"Toni hinted at that. So did my grandma."

"I promise I didn't mean to hurt her in any way."

I shook my head, halting his stilted apology. "She can be a little rough. Especially when she's upset about other things." I trailed my thumb over the back of his hand, keeping my voice soft. "So are *you* going to tell me what she said? No one's dared to give me any specifics."

He watched my thumb move for a silent moment, then quietly spoke. "She said several thought-provoking things. The most prominent in my mind is . . . She believes that I'm using our relationship for my own gratification, and in so doing I'm ruining your life."

"Ruining my life? She said that?"

He didn't meet my stare. "Exactly that."

"Patrick, you know that's not true."

He looked up at me at last. "Of course it's not true. I love you more than anything, Kate. I would never do anything to intentionally hurt you. But I can't give you the things your family wants for you, and they resent that." He swallowed hard. "Your grandfather felt the same way. Even Terence realizes how unhealthy this relationship is for you. He's just too polite to say anything."

"My grandpa respected you," I argued.

Patrick nodded. "Yes. But he didn't appreciate my feelings for you."

"What about how I feel? Doesn't that mean anything?"

His eyes traced my adamant face, his lips pursing tightly at what he saw. "Of course. It means everything to me. But I can't be the best choice for you, Kate. You have to realize that—see their point of view. I can't give you the simplest of things. Normalcy, stability, a family—" His voice almost cracked, though he continued quickly to hide the slight break. "Even something as simple as aging alongside you; it's beyond my capabilities. I can love you forever, but something as trivial as death will divide us in the end. We're a tragedy waiting to happen."

I blinked. "That's a really positive view of things. The cup's half empty for you, isn't it?"

He almost smiled naturally for the first time today. "Yet another of my failings. Chronic pessimism."

I shook my head. "Luckily I take a different perspective. I happen to think the glass is half full."

"What glass are you looking at?"

I chuckled. "It sounds like we've each got half a cup," I argued lightly. "So logically, if we put our cups together . . ."

"We'll be whole." He nodded, conceding my point.

I pushed carefully away from the headboard, leaning toward him encouragingly. "So, how much more gloom and doom did you want to do today?"

"I've probably had my fill," he admitted, watching me with a look that could only be described as charged.

"Good. Because I can think of better ways to spend our time . . ."

He grinned at last, though it was small, then he leaned in and met me with a tender kiss.

nine

Grandma refused to let me go to school in the morning, and in all honesty I didn't really try to resist. My head was still hurting pretty badly, and staying in bed was just too easy. I slept off and on in the morning, but once I got the medication going I was able to get up and move around. I didn't shower, because I didn't want to risk getting the stitches wet. I tried to put on a little makeup though, layering on some foundation a little too thickly around my throat. It didn't cover the bruises perfectly, but it helped.

Downstairs I ate a late breakfast while Patrick sat at the table, watching me. We didn't say a lot at first, since Grandma was in the other room folding laundry, but the need to break the strained silence overwhelmed the awkward knowledge that she'd hear every word.

"So the first Special Seer comes in today, right?"

Patrick nodded from across the table, but his thumb and forefinger continued to spin the green lid from the milk like a top. "Sometime around noon, probably."

"Will he be going straight to the warehouse?"

"Yes. Jack will be there to meet him."

"Will you go over there too?"

"I go where you go."

Grandma may have snorted. Or maybe it was just an innocent sneeze. Regardless, we both glanced toward the open doorway that led to the family room. I settled back on him. "So am I allowed to go see him?"

He shrugged. "If you feel up to it."

It took a bit of convincing, but my grandma finally agreed that I was probably okay to go. So just after 11:30 a.m., we walked out to my car. I almost asked if he knew how to drive a stick. Then I remembered who I was talking to—he'd probably driven a Model T.

I felt a little uneasy leaving my grandma alone at the house without a protector, but since she was planning to leave in the next few minutes for the grocery store, I decided she'd most likely be okay. She loved to cook, so Thanksgiving was really her favorite holiday. The money she spent on the appetizers alone . . . Grandpa had always teased her about her habit to overdo things. This holiday was definitely on the top of the list.

While we drove, I remembered to tell Patrick about Aaron's party. I told him that Toni and Lee would be going, as well as Jaxon and Maria. Just like earlier, he assured me that he would go if I was. He didn't sound overly thrilled about the prospective date, but I knew that was only because he didn't want everyone asking about my injuries, not because he resented my ex-boyfriend at all. The mutual respect Aaron and Patrick had for each other was both unusual and refreshing. They didn't treat each other with undertones of jealousy or bitterness anymore. In fact, they'd been almost friends since they'd teamed up to fight half the football team several weeks ago. That of course came as a great relief to me because I loved them both—in different ways, of course.

At the warehouse, Jack spent the first few minutes teasing me about head-butting a car. I took his jokes in good humor, knowing that deep down he was just relieved I was okay. Patrick didn't seem to appreciate his jokes though, so we moved off that topic pretty quickly. By the time we'd covered cursory topics, Jack decided to go wait out in the dirt-covered yard for the expected arrival of the Seer. Patrick and I followed him because we had nothing better to do. We held hands as we walked, listening to Jack tell us about the fourth floor they'd been clearing up for the visiting Seers.

"They have the nicer spot, no doubt about it," Jack said, accent thick. "That floor hardly looks like it belongs in this bodgy place. It just goes to show how much more Terence cares about them, I guess."

"So they didn't get their mattresses from the dump?" I asked glibly.

Patrick elbowed me gently. "Be nice. I have tender feelings."

It was hot outside, but there was more airflow outdoors, so the change didn't seem drastic. Patrick and I stood near the open doors, while Jack continued to wander forward without us, heading toward the narrow alley. I sent Patrick a queer look, and he answered my unspoken question at once. "This Seer wouldn't be the first person to miss the turnoff."

I nodded in understanding, and we stood together in silence, watching as Jack ambled from sight.

Mere minutes later, a gold Altima swept through the alley and up toward the building where we stood. Jack was in the passenger seat, talking to the driver. With the sun's glare on the glass it was almost impossible to tell much about the new Seer. He looked a bit older, though—late forties or so.

The car rolled to a stop in front of us, the gentle purr of the engine dying as it was shut off. Jack opened his door and the driver was only a beat behind him.

He wasn't very tall—about my height. He was balding and had dull brown eyes. He wore a pair of khaki pants and a simple red polo shirt. He had scuffed brown shoes and an old gold watch on his wrist. He had some thinly rimmed glasses pushed high on his nose, making him look like a smart but absentminded professor. His aura was simple, as most auras go. His life—despite being filled with the supernatural—seemed to be quite ordinary, at least in his mind.

His face was meaty and round, but his smile was wide and full. His eyes went right to me, his thick British accent unmistakable. "You must be Kate Bennett. What a pleasure to meet you!" He stepped forward at once, leaving his door ajar in the process. I extended my free hand, which he clasped eagerly in both of his. "I must say I was delighted at the opportunity to come and learn more about our amazing abilities. I'm a physics professor at University of London, you see, and I'm quite interested in learning the science involved in time travel. Since I was a boy, I've dreamed of these very possibilities, and as soon as I learned about our unique abilities—well, obviously I was more than anxious to learn as much as possible!" He was still shaking my hand, and his eyes were right on mine so I couldn't look away. "It's just fascinating, isn't it? I was wondering if you've taken the time to document your experiences yet? You *have* traveled, haven't you? I was made to believe that you had. I can hardly believe I'm even having this conversation with another human being. I'm talking to someone who's actually ridden the space-time continuum! I do apologize if I'm overwhelming you—I'm afraid it's in my nature to let my mouth do a good amount of my thinking. It's not always a bad attribute, I suppose . . ."

My smile by now felt completely fake, but he wasn't blinking, and I felt rude pulling away.

Luckily, Patrick recognized my plight. He stuck out a hand, which was hard for the new Seer to ignore. "I'm Patrick O'Donnell."

The Seer's words faltered, but his smile didn't. He was quick to shake Patrick's hand, again using both of his. "Ah! A pleasure to meet you, Guardian O'Donnell. I'm afraid I've been awfully rude. Allow me to introduce myself. I am Dr. Winston Radcliffe."

Patrick nodded. "Dr. Radcliffe." He somehow managed to slip his hand away. "How was your flight?"

"The flight from London was wonderful! But it was bloody inconvenient driving in from Colorado. Terence assured me it would be unsafe to fly right into the state, and since he supplied me with a car, I suppose I can't complain too strenuously. Besides, it gave me more time to think about the most interesting part of this time traveling puzzle—why can we travel when others can't? Is it a physical difference, and if so, is it a natural step in human evolution? That seems a little unlikely, but of course it's something to consider."

Jack was standing behind Dr. Radcliffe, giving the back of his head an almost wary look. I understood Jack's feelings completely—*this* was the guy who'd come up with the assault plan? The Guardian Council must have believed in him, or they never would have set the plan into motion, but I was becoming just a little doubtful.

I glanced to Patrick, seeing that his face was frozen in a polite stare. I didn't want to be the one to interrupt the doctor, but luckily I didn't have to say anything—he was stopping himself.

"I *am* sorry if I'm overwhelming you. I assure you, I'm trying to keep myself in check. It's just that it's all so fascinating! But more of that to come, I suppose. Here, here! Would you men give me a hand with my bags? I'm afraid I've never been one to pack lightly. It gets rather expensive, I must say!"

Patrick squeezed my hand, then released it to follow Jack to the back of the car. Dr. Radcliffe pressed a button on his remote, popping the trunk open. They each grabbed a bag, Jack grunting heavily. The strap creaked as he drew it up over his shoulder, and Dr. Radcliffe urged him, saying, "Do be careful! My encyclopedias are in that one!"

"What sort of doddering fool travels with his whole library? Hasn't he heard of the Internet?" Jack grumbled under his breath. I caught the words easily on the breeze, but the Englishman didn't seem to hear anything. He was snatching up a briefcase from the front of the car.

He then pulled himself out and shut the door, walking back toward me with a smile. "Not exactly a five-star hotel, is it?"

I didn't have much to say to that, so I only smiled. There was a lot of dialogue as we tried to get him settled, but finally Dr. Radcliffe—or Winston, as he was perfectly fine with being called—told us he'd like to catch some rest.

Back on the main floor of the factory, Jack was shaking his head. "Asking that dill over here might have been a blue. If that bloke doesn't drive me crazy . . ."

Patrick shrugged a little. "It takes all kinds."

"Yes, well, I can see why his Guardian was fine with just putting him on a plane. I certainly wouldn't want to go to another country with the good doctor. "

"How many others are coming?" I dared ask.

Jack's words were spoken in an exhale. "Four. Blimey, I think it's almost time I retired from the Demon hunting gig. About time I got myself a job and just donated some of my moolah to the cause."

Patrick looked to me. "We might as well head back to your house, if you're done here."

"Gee, thanks for bailing out on me, mates," Jack grumbled before I could respond. "I'll love you forever for that one."

***

That night, Lee and Toni were in the backseat of the Altima, with me and Patrick in front. Toni and Lee weren't saying much, but they really hadn't communicated much since Toni had rather abruptly asked her out. It wasn't awkward between them—just different. Lee's aura was more confusing than ever.

Her emotions were so jumbled it was almost impossible for me to figure out what she was feeling at the moment. Things had been going so well with Rodney, I hadn't been worried about her crush on Toni for weeks. Now it seemed like everything was back to how it had been in the first place. I had mixed feelings about this because as much as I loved Toni, I didn't really want my best friend stuck in the same sort of impossible situation that I was.

Patrick was quiet too, though his silence seemed reflective more than anything else. It made me anxious to know what he was thinking.

Aaron's little brother Tim invited us in, giving me an extra wide smile. I tousled his six-year-old hair with old familiarity, which made him squirm away with a laugh. My own mouth was twisted into a wide grin. I'd missed the little guy.

Lee and Toni had walked past me toward the sound of Jaxon's booming laugh, but Patrick was still behind me, watching me closely. His expression made me hesitate to ask about his thoughts. He looked grave. Almost sorrowful. Then the moment passed and he was forcing a smile. But in his eyes the sadness lingered, even when he took my hand and we walked together in the direction of Aaron's muffled call.

"Come on down! We're in the basement!"

We wandered downstairs where I saw Lee—wearing white pedal-pushers and a wispy pink scarf around her neck—shaking hands with a pretty girl with rich brown hair that fell around her shoulders. This must be Alyssa Meadows, Aaron's girlfriend. She was tall and slender, and she matched Aaron in a natural way. More important, her aura seemed to be an extension of his; both were billowing with blue contentment, yellow happiness, and sparks of pink excitement.

Aaron stood at Alyssa's side, shaking Toni's hand while offering a basic nod of greeting.

Lee was already past introductions with Alyssa and deep in

conversation—as if they'd been friends forever. "I'm so jealous. Aaron said you're homeschooled?"

She nodded, her smile easy. "Since first grade." Her voice was a beautiful alto, and she spoke with a smooth grace that hinted at quiet intelligence.

"Wow. That's really cool. You're lucky."

"There were days I wasn't so sure, but . . . I'm really grateful to my parents now."

"You're a senior?"

"Yep."

Patrick and I had paused at the base of the stairs, lingering just outside the edge of the conversation. Jaxon was standing near a bookshelf full of DVDs, his girlfriend, Maria, arguing good-naturedly about what to watch.

"Kate, Patrick!" Aaron had spotted us. "Welcome." He winced at my head. "Lee told me about your fall. Are you feeling okay?"

"I'm feeling a lot better, thanks." I extended a hand, which Alyssa took quickly. "It's a pleasure to meet you."

"Same." She smiled easily. "Aaron's told me so much about you. I'm really glad you could make it tonight."

"Me too." I gestured to my Guardian with one hand. "This is Patrick."

He reached around me, shaking Alyssa's with a gentle firmness. "Hello."

"Hi. It's good to meet you, Patrick."

"The pleasure is mine."

Once initial greetings were out of the way, Aaron tried to shoo his brothers out of the room. Tim wouldn't go until he showed me his tooth, which he'd lost earlier that day. Aaron's mom came down carrying two deep bowls of popcorn. Toni took one from her right away and moved to claim the edge of the sofa, with Jaxon only a second behind him for nabbing the second bowl of popcorn.

Aaron's mom promised to keep the boys out, and then she came over to embrace me quickly.

"It's good to see you, Kate," she murmured softly. "How're you and your sisters doing? What about your grandma?"

"They're good. We're all fine."

Her arms flexed comfortingly around my shoulders. "Well, you let me know if you need anything, okay? Pass that along to your grandma."

"I will. Thanks."

She gave me a smile that bordered on sympathetic before herding Aaron's two young brothers back up the stairs.

Jaxon and Maria couldn't agree on a movie to save their lives, so Lee and Alyssa wandered over to the shelves. Jaxon took his bowl of popcorn and he and Maria crashed down into the giant beanbag that dominated the floor space. Patrick tugged gently on my hand, pulling the two of us to sit on the long sofa, taking the end Toni hadn't sprawled on.

"Oh, I love this one!" Alyssa said over the sound of crunching popcorn—Toni wasn't exactly quiet.

Lee glanced at the movie Alyssa had plucked from the shelf and let out a happy cry. "Oh my Oreos, I haven't seen that in ages!"

"What is it?" Aaron asked, standing in front of the love seat.

Alyssa brandished the case, which I recognized it easily. It had been my mom's favorite movie.

"*Somewhere in Time,*" Alyssa said.

Lee was grinning happily. "It's horribly romantic."

"Ew," Toni muttered through his mouthful of popcorn. Everyone ignored him.

"Jane Seymour is absolutely gorgeous!" Alyssa said, playing off of Lee's enthusiasm perfectly.

"Oh, I know—and Christopher Reeve without tights!" They both giggled.

Jaxon grunted. "Sounds dumb."

Maria elbowed him pointedly.

Patrick whispered lowly beside me, curious. "Have you seen it?"

I nodded, unable to form words at the moment. I had no idea how many times I'd seen the heartbreaking romance played out, but I'd taken my mom's copy off the shelf soon after the funeral. It was probably boxed up in the garage out of sight, where I didn't have to be reminded of her. The two of us would watch it whenever my dad was out late or when she was sick. I'd curl up with her, crying a little bit more each time I watched it. Her eyes would always be red and puffy afterward, and dad would only have to take one look before he smiled, knowing exactly what had made her cry. "You're a hopeless romantic," he'd tell her, the eyes behind his glasses full of love.

The wash of memories made me both warm and cold. I swallowed, hoping Toni and Jaxon would protest more loudly so they'd pick something else—anything else.

But no one was about to argue with Lee, and Aaron was more than willing to please Alyssa. Before I could decide if I could handle this, the projector was on, the lights were switched off, and the movie was starting.

Jaxon and Maria cuddled closely—they could have been the same person, for all the space they were taking. They were in sharp contrast to Aaron and Alyssa, who held hands chastely on the love seat. Lee pushed Toni's feet away so she could sit beside him, and she dug her hand into the popcorn bowl before turning her whole attention to the large screen.

Patrick leaned back into the couch, angling his body so he was leaning partially against the armrest. He wrapped his strong arms around me and I allowed myself to rest against his hard chest, my head tucked under his chin. I tried to relax so Patrick wouldn't realize how scared I was. I honestly didn't know if I could watch this, but I certainly didn't want to cause a scene by leaving.

Surprisingly, the movie became easier for me to watch as it progressed. I watched the characters fight to be together—fight the very fabric of time—and I felt a closeness to my mother that I hadn't known for so long. Even though my tears flowed easily, I found myself smiling as well.

Patrick's hold on me never wavered. I knew he was paying strict attention to my fluctuating emotions, perhaps thinking my tears came only from the drama on screen—still, the story managed to hold his attention. He'd never seen the movie, obviously, and he'd been completely sucked in—despite Toni's occasional muttering. It still surprised me that immortal people didn't take the time to watch movies. I mean, when you had forever, it seemed like you could manage to spare a couple hours here and there, but, according to Patrick, Toni was probably the closest a Guardian had ever come to becoming a couch potato. I wasn't about to admit that immortals might have their priorities straight, compared to us mortals, but I'd definitely enjoyed introducing Patrick to my favorite films. I mean, he hadn't even seen *Star Wars*—how out of touch could you get?

I was toying with Patrick's leather bracelet when Christopher Reeve pulled out the stupid penny and disappeared from the past, and that was when I realized Patrick wasn't breathing.

I angled my head and caught a glimpse of his face. He was pale, whiter than I'd seen him since his horrible sickness. I didn't dare say anything, with the room so quiet, but I took this moment to step out of my own thoughts and quickly see this movie through his eyes, to try and figure out what could have possibly triggered his adverse reaction.

The story of a man who traveled through time to find the woman he loved, only to have fate rip him from her side. Though our story was quite different, many of the elements remained the same—too many. Someday we'd be separated, and even though it wouldn't be because of something as trivial as what happened to these two lovers, there was nothing we could do to stop it. Sooner or later Patrick would be left here, and I would be forced to another plane of existence. I was confident that a mistake of Patrick's wouldn't lead to our end, but even if he didn't have to blame himself, I knew he wouldn't respond well to my death.

And I feared that *I* would struggle with this movie.

All I could do was grip his hand, a stranglehold too desperate to be comforting.

The credits finally rolled, but no one moved. The girls were sniffling, and the guys were sporting various expressions; Aaron's arm was around Alyssa's trembling shoulders, Jaxon was yawning and patting Maria's arm, and Toni was rolling his eyes even as he squeezed Lee's fingers.

Patrick's breath was rattling slowly from his lungs, his whole body stiff around me. Neither of us spoke, though I knew a similar weight lay heavily on our minds.

When Aaron flipped on the light, the room seemed brighter than it had been before the movie. Patrick released me so I could stoop over and retrieve my flip-flops which I'd kicked to the floor earlier, and I knew by the firm set of his jaw that he didn't want to talk about what had happened so silently between us.

Toni and Lee were already standing when I looked up, their hands carefully at their sides despite the cuddling that had been taking place moments earlier. Jaxon was pulling Maria to her feet.

I pushed up from the couch, Patrick right behind me. He stepped away, preparing to lift one of the partially emptied bowls of popcorn, but Aaron assured him the cleanup could happen later. It was almost eleven, and I was feeling the late hour. After some fast but sincere thank-yous and good-byes we were walking out the front door, each toward our separate cars. Jaxon offered to give Alyssa a ride home, and Aaron followed us out to the porch to make sure we all got on our way safely.

After silently opening my door Patrick went around and slipped into the driver's seat. He started the car, waiting to flip on the lights until Toni and Lee joined us. Lee was talking to Aaron, Toni standing firmly behind her.

I took this moment of privacy to look at Patrick through the dimness of the car, opening my mouth to speak the words I hadn't yet formed in my mind.

He beat me to it. "Kate, don't worry about me. I'm fine." His voice was precisely measured, but he couldn't fool me. He was extremely bothered.

My mouth twisted, revealing my doubt. "I'm sorry. I should have warned you at the beginning, I just didn't realize . . ."

His eyes still carried a haunted look, but a carefully structured smile lifted his lips. "Really, Kate, it's okay. It was just a movie."

Before I could answer Toni pulled the back door open, and Lee climbed in behind me. I waved to Aaron as we pulled away from the curb, starting down the quiet residential street behind Jaxon's car.

"Well, that was the dumbest movie I've ever seen," Toni declared loudly.

Lee's slap against his arm was even louder. "Knock it off! It was beautiful."

"A penny? The obsessive freak forgot to check his pennies? I mean, really! He was driven mad by his obsession with a picture, but he didn't recheck his change? How stupid can you get?"

I glanced at Patrick's mutedly glowing profile, but the dash lights didn't reveal much—just a blank, hard expression.

Lee snorted. "It's tragic, not stupid."

Toni continued to rave, as if he hadn't heard her. "He lets one dumb mistake ruin everything. And then he just gives up and dies? How's that not stupid?"

Lee wasn't convinced. "He did try to go back, but there was nothing he could do. It was too late. She was already gone."

"I still think it was dumb."

Lee was silent—I knew my friend well enough to know

without seeing that she was scowling deeply, refusing to engage in a debate when she knew the opposition could not be swayed.

Patrick changed the subject firmly. "Toni, are you on duty tonight?"

"Nope. It's my night off."

Patrick nodded, almost to himself. "We'll stop at Kate's house, then you can drop Lee off on your way back to the warehouse."

"Sounds good," he replied easily.

We drove in near silence for another minute or so. We were nearing my house when Patrick suddenly slammed on the brakes. I grabbed the dash as it came sailing toward my face, a gasp escaping me as my seat belt locked into place. Adrenaline rushed through my body, but Patrick was already apologizing heavily. "There was a dog—I'm sorry."

I glanced out the windshield and saw a small beagle staring up at us, just in front of the hood. But seeing the reason for the abrupt stop didn't calm my actively racing heart.

Lee blew out her breath shortly. "Oreos, that was close."

"Gee, Patrick," Toni grunted. "Do you think you could stop a little harder next time? My head didn't get yanked off this time around."

"Are you okay?" Patrick's words were for everyone, but his eyes were on me. I nodded quickly, mostly because I couldn't speak.

Toni's voice was faintly sick. "I think my stomach's in Canada."

Patrick honked the horn briefly and the dog responded by loping over to the sidewalk. The car rolled forward once the way was clear, though Patrick drove more cautiously than before.

He pulled carefully into my driveway and released his seat belt. The back doors opened, and I reached down for my purse, only to find that the contents had been dumped all over the floor. Receipts, pens, wallet, sunglasses, hand sanitizer—the purse was pretty much empty now. Patrick saw the mess and immediately leaned over to help me clean it up. I shoved things in quickly, conscious of the fact Lee was standing just outside my door, waiting to get in. I picked up a tube of lip gloss and Patrick snatched up a handful of receipts.

Once everything was off the floor I opened my door and stepped out, shoving the odds and ends that filled one hand into the open purse. Lee gave me a half hug, whispering that she'd talk to me tomorrow.

I walked around the front of the car, offering a quick wave to Toni as he backed out. He nodded in response, and then they were driving down the street. The porch light was on, keeping us from total darkness. Patrick walked easily beside me, unfolding the different receipts while we moved. He shook his head after rifling through a few. "Kate, some of these are months old. Why keep them?"

I grabbed the ones he'd already looked at. "I hate cleaning my purse out, that's why."

He smiled, a fond edge to the gesture, then he went back to looking at the receipts he still held. We stepped onto the porch and I moved in front of him, pulling out my key from inside my purse. It was near the bottom, though, so it took a little longer to dig it out than normal. I heard Patrick's steady breathing behind me, heard the rustle of unfolding paper—silence.

I turned instinctively, hand still buried in my purse, fingers still wriggling around. They stopped moving when I saw his pale face. He was staring at a wrinkled sheet of paper—one that I'd completely forgotten about. It had been mixed in with the receipts, and I hadn't noticed it before. Now it was open. His intensely furrowed brow was trying to make sense of the words, my picture.

My stomach dropped. All I could do was watch his eyebrows draw together and see his mouth twist into an uncomprehending frown as he read.

"Kate," he finally breathed, eyes riveted on the page. "What is this?"

I swallowed hard, my voice bare and halting. "I . . . I meant to tell you . . ."

"Kate, what *is* this?" he repeated more urgently, wounded eyes flickering up to mine. He was reading the words, but they didn't make sense.

I pursed my lips, meeting his stare even though it was difficult. I wasn't sure what to say, how to make this moment less alarming for him. I settled for the truth. "It's a wanted poster." I winced as soon as the words were out. Poor word choice—I couldn't have made that sound any more dramatic, had I tried. I fought quickly to repair the damage. "Selena's been distributing them, for the Demon Lord."

His eyes were still on mine, his face frozen. "Why do you have it?" he whispered. "How on earth do you . . . ?"

I grimaced. This wasn't going to be good. "Clyde gave it to me."

"Clyde?" He blinked. It was almost like he was in shock.

"Clyde—my grandpa's friend. I went to visit him last week."

"Last *week*?" His voice rose just a little. The paper was shaking in his hands.

I let a sigh escape. I wasn't handling this well at all. I pulled my hand out of my purse, taking a slow step toward him. "Why don't we go inside. I'll tell you everything, I promise."

He glanced back at the page, blanching at the sight of my face smiling back up at him. "How did they get this picture, Kate?"

I shook my head. "I don't know."

His eyes widened suddenly, and I knew he'd seen the reward money for the first time. A second later his eyes ran over the most disturbing thing. His tone was sick. "They know where you live."

I wrapped my fingers around one of his wrists, but even

then he didn't look up at me. "Patrick, let's go inside. We can talk in there, okay?"

His eyes slowly rose. His voice was choked. "Why didn't you tell me? Why didn't you show me this?"

I gently rubbed his arm; the action didn't seem to soothe him. "I didn't want to worry you. I didn't see the point in making a big deal—"

He was overcoming his speechlessness. In fact, he was getting loud. I hoped he'd had the presence of mind to go invisible first. "The point? The *point?* Kate, I'm your Guardian! It's my job to keep you safe, and I can't do that if I don't have all the information!" Understanding flashed across his face. "That Demon at the school—he was hunting you because of this. Wasn't he? And you knew! Why didn't you tell me?"

His accusations hurt, but it was the helpless tone ringing in his voice that hurt the most. "Patrick, please, just listen to me—"

The front door opened, interrupting my explanation mixed with apology, and Jack's head poked out. "Hey, you two, I don't mean to be clucky, but you've got school tomorrow. Your grandmother's already gone to . . . Patrick? Is something wrong?"

I spoke before Patrick could. "Nothing's wrong. Why would you think something's wrong?"

Jack gave me a strange look. "Well, I don't know. You don't have to be a knocker, though—I just thought I'd ask."

I expected Patrick to say something, but he didn't. He'd lapsed back into his blistering silence. Still gripping his wrist, I pulled him into the house, wanting to herd him up to my bedroom as quickly as possible.

Jack held the door for us, flipping off the porch light with the quick flick of a finger. He didn't seem to notice the page Patrick was holding, even though he wasn't trying to cover it up at all. "Can I ask how your date went?" Jack ventured carefully, obviously sensing the tension.

I nodded once. "It was good. Thanks for waiting up."

"Um . . . I'm on duty."

"Right—well, thanks anyway."

He rolled his eyes. "I won't tell your grandma."

"Huh?"

"You two can go upstairs if you want. I'm no whistle blower."

Though it would definitely give him the wrong idea, I thanked him concisely before steering Patrick up the stairs. My bedroom door was open, and once the light was on and we were both inside, I shut it before turning back to face my agitated Guardian.

He was watching me from a few short steps away. His words were low but uncompromising. "Kate, you were wrong to keep this to yourself. We needed to know this."

We? Was he trying to keep this fight from becoming overly personal? It was obvious that he was in full Guardian mode, and I wasn't sure if that was better or worse. It felt less accusing than if he'd said *I*, but the *we* certainly made me feel stupider.

"What's the big deal?" I asked suddenly. "It's not like it's a surprise or anything. So what if the Demon Lord spread some flyers?"

He jerked the paper, accidentally flinging some receipts to the floor. "They have your address," he snapped.

"So? The Demon Lord's always known where I lived. That's why I have you guys, all this extra protection—"

"This is different."

"How?" I found myself almost hissing. It was infuriating that he could rave and be as loud as he wanted—Jack was the only other person in the house with the ability to hear him—but I had to keep my own voice moderate or fear waking my sisters.

His finger jabbed low on the page. "One million dollars. Do you have *any* idea how that's going to stir up the local Demon population?"

"It's a lot, I know—"

"It's not just the reward that will attract them. It's the *idea* of the reward, the chance to capture someone worth so much. They like the high danger gives them, and an absurd reward like this promises them just that."

I succeeded in shrugging, though the motion was stiff. "So you'll protect me."

He groaned as the page slapped against his right leg, dropping out of sight. "Like I protected you last time? Kate, I'm trying—*believe me*, I'm trying for all I'm worth—but I can't be everywhere. As much as I hate to admit it, I can't keep you safe from everything the Demon Lord is capable of throwing."

"I know—that's why I have Toni, Jack, Claire—everyone!"

He swallowed convulsively, shaking his head. "You're no longer safe here. This house has been compromised."

"*Compromised?*" The word twisted my mouth in an unfamiliar way. "What about Jenna and Josie? What about my grandma? We can't just leave. I can't do that to them. And if Terence finds out, he'll make us go and you know it."

"Better to have you upset with me than *dead*." His voice cracked on the last word, losing the power he'd held earlier.

I pulled in a deep breath, trying to steady my nerves and subdue my flaring temper. I didn't want to do this with him. I peeled away from the door, crossing the short distance to stand in front of him. He was watching me warily, unwilling to relax. I reached up and placed a hand on either side of his tight face.

I kept my voice soft. "I don't want to argue. But I can't go. I can't lose my home. Can you understand that? In the past six months I've lost three of the most important people in my life. I can't lose anymore. I'll go crazy if I do."

He stared at me, his penetrating gaze revealing nothing. His lips parted. "Kate. I. Can't. Lose. You."

I pulled closer to him, my arms pressing against his hard chest, my fingers tensing on his face. "You won't. I promise."

He let out a weak, mirthless laugh. "You can't promise that."

"Patrick, please. Please . . ."

He studied my face, but I saw no sign of surrender in his firm expression.

I closed my eyes and ducked my head against his stiff collar, my nose brushing the bare skin of his pulsing throat. My hands slipped from his face and my arms wound around his shoulders, his neck. "Please," I breathed. "Patrick, please don't make me leave my home."

The room was silent aside from our steadily lengthening breaths. I heard his heart beating beneath my cheek, and I felt his exhale stir my hair. A minute passed. My thoughts were jumbled, unable to organize, only *hope*. Finally there was movement. His clenched fist—the one holding the flyer—pressed against the small of my back, his other hand spread over the back of my head, keeping me pressed up against him.

His words came out, low but surprisingly strong. "I won't tell Terence. Or any of the others. Because you're right. He would make you leave, despite the fact that the Demon Lord already knows where to find you."

My arms flexed around him, my eyes pinching more tightly closed. "Thank you—"

His movement cut me off as his hand on my head slipped abruptly to my shoulder. I lifted my head and opened my eyes so I could catch a glimpse of his serious expression—the firm set of his jaw. "You have to promise me something in return," he said, his gaze unwavering. "And I mean this, Kate."

I tried not to let his intensity intimidate me. "Of course—whatever you want."

The papers in his hands dropped to the floor and he cradled my head with his large hands, his fingers tracing my face as he leaned closer. His nose brushed mine, and then our foreheads were resting against each other. His eyes were closed tightly. "I want you to promise that you won't go anywhere without telling me first. No more vigilante visits to Clyde, and absolutely no more secrets. I need all the information. I need you to be completely honest with me. Can you promise me that?"

His lips were too close to ignore. I pressed my mouth to his. His fingers trailed into my hair, mindful of the stitches. One hand eventually dropped to cup my waist and shift me closer up along the length of his body.

When I finally pulled away—my breath shaky and my hands buried in his hair—I answered him without reservation. "I promise."

ten

The evening before Thanksgiving found me in the kitchen with my grandma. She was regretting the fact that we only had one oven in our kitchen, because she was used to the two at her old house. She had to alter her dinner plans accordingly, so we were baking a batch of pies tonight in order to get ahead for the big feast tomorrow. The twins were in the other room, watching TV with Jack and Patrick. I was somewhat grateful for the chance to be alone with her, doing something as simple as cooking.

I worked on the apple pie while she cut up strips of crust for the top. We worked largely in silence until she suddenly cleared her throat. "I was wondering . . . what all these Guardians and Seers were planning to do for tomorrow."

I glanced up at her. "What do you mean?"

She wasn't looking at me, just continued to drag the knife through the thin dough. "I'm assuming they aren't planning to spend the holiday with relatives, since they've been flying in here from who knows where?"

"Um . . . Yeah, I doubt they have plans."

She nodded once. "I was thinking we should invite them over here."

"To our house?" Having Guardians over would be one thing—they could eat in the other room, invisible. But what about the Seers? "What about the twins?" I asked.

She shrugged, her rough voice carrying a somewhat defensive edge. "We can tell them it's a new charity project for the church, or something of the like. Inviting people into our home when they don't have any family nearby." She looked over at me, eyes casually narrowed. "A person can't spend Thanksgiving up in a warehouse."

I gave her a small smile, touched by this show of kindness from her. "You're right."

She grunted. "I'm always right. How many can I expect?"

I ran over the names in my head, speaking them subconsciously. "Well, there's Patrick, Jack, and Toni." She nodded, revealing she'd already considered them. "Maddy and Claire. Jason is spending the holiday with his new girlfriend and her family, so . . . then it's just the new Seers. Dr. Radcliffe, and Alex Perry; he came in this morning, along with Ashley Grey."

"Alex is the Marine, isn't he?"

I nodded. "I don't know much about him. He seemed pretty quiet. I know he's been on extended leave for the past several months, though. He was suffering from post-traumatic stress. At least, that's what the doctors put on his record."

"How else would you expect them to explain seeing auras? So what about the girl?"

"I know even less about her. She's a few years older than me. She's from back East, I think."

"How many more are you waiting for?" she asked.

"Just one. He should be coming in Friday morning."

She bobbed her head, watching as I finished smoothing the pie filling inside the crust. When I was done, she started taking up the strips she'd cut to make a crisscross top. While she did that, I started preparing the cherry pie.

Once again, her words were unexpected. "I know I haven't

asked too many questions. I'd rather not know about a lot that goes on these days. But these Seers . . . are they all Special?"

I wasn't going to lie to her. "Yes. They're Special. And they've all volunteered to do something for the Guardians."

"And does this 'something' have to do with the Demon Lord?"

I bit my lower lip before answering. "Yes. But before you start worrying, I'm not getting myself into anything dangerous." I almost grunted, thinking about the possibility of me doing something dangerous with Patrick hovering around me—it wouldn't ever happen. If he had his way, I'd always be safe.

"So how are you involved?" Grandma asked.

"I'm going to teach them to travel. That's it."

"So . . . they've volunteered to do something in the past?"

"And they need me to teach them how to do it. *And,*" I cast her a sure look, "I promise, my job is completely safe."

"Mind the filling, dear—it's terribly sticky."

I tipped the jar carefully and we went back to working quietly, though the fact we'd had the conversation at all made my heart feel lighter.

***

Sort of surprising me, Jenna and Josie believed Grandma's simple explanation about the church charity without question. I watched them open the door for the tall Alex Perry, wearing his dress uniform for the occasion. I watched as Dr. Radcliffe shook their small hands, giving them each a warm smile. Jenna thought she recognized Maddy from school, but that didn't stop her from welcoming the Texan Seer. Claire, Toni, and Ashley Grey were all invited in warmly as well. With Jack, Patrick, Peter Keegan, Lee and her mother, the house was definitely full. Jeanette Pearson was a little confused by all the new faces, but Grandma's "church charity" cover was enough to keep Lee's mom from being too questioning.

Everyone was wearing nice clothes, marking the day as special. Claire was wearing her short white dress, the one she'd worn in Las Vegas. Lee was in a poodle skirt, of course, with her hair hanging loose around the silk scarf tied at her neck. Maddy was wearing nice jeans and a classy top, following Ashley Grey's example. Grandma was in a dark blue dress that flowed around her legs. I was wearing a dress with a plaid theme that reached to my knees. A maroon shrug clung to my shoulders, accenting the lines on the dress and bringing out the darker strands in my blonde hair. Toni was in a white shirt and was even wearing a loose red tie. Jack, Peter, and Patrick had all worn suits. Patrick's didn't look exactly new, and maybe it was a little out of style, but at this point I was convinced he could pull off pretty much anything.

The house was warm and the air was heavy with delicious scents. Mouthwatering turkey, thick mashed potatoes, buttery rolls, seasoned stuffing, spicy pumpkin pie—all the best smells in the world. Grandma was preoccupied, trying to get everything in order before noon. Everyone with sense tried to steer clear of her and her obsessive tendencies.

The Guardians and Seers weren't allowed to bring up anything abnormal, and for the most part they succeeded. I only heard a few slipups, but luckily no one was around to catch them.

Peter looked a little uncomfortable with the present company. Jeanette had abandoned him to help set the table, and Lee was off somewhere—probably with Toni—leaving Peter in a room with Guardians. Before he could slip away I made my way around Claire and Jack, who were discussing the pros and cons of having turkey instead of ham.

"Turkey makes you tucker out, so you can't eat as much."

Claire snorted, the sound startlingly stark compared to her fluidly spoken words. "Weak excuse. At least with turkey you can make those delicious sandwiches for days afterward."

"Turkey sandwiches? What about *ham* sandwiches? They're

ace! Besides, you can have so many flavorful options when you use ham. Bake it with pineapple, or honey . . ."

Peter was fiddling with his glasses beside the china closet in the living room, but he returned my smile tentatively as I came to stand in front of him. "Kate," he said, "I hope you're feeling better."

"Much better. Thank you." My stitches were out now, and I was feeling good as new.

He gave me a quick nod, his fingers tightening around the tall glass of apple cider he'd poured for himself. "I'm glad to hear it."

I reached out to touch his arm, continuing in a softer voice. "Thank you, Mr. Keegan. For looking out for Jenna and Josie. You saved them and me the other day. I owe you."

His cheeks flushed dimly. "Well, I . . . it was the least I could do."

I let my hand drop back to my side. "I just wanted you to know how much I appreciate what you did. You didn't have to stick up for them."

His eyes flickered away from mine, falling to look at his drink. He swirled the cider gently in the glass with one rotating hand, his words quiet and smooth. "I don't want to be your enemy, Kate. And I certainly don't mean any harm to come to the twins. It's just that . . ." He glanced up through narrowed eyes. "Selena's hold is powerful. Even if I didn't have Jeanette and Lee, I have my other friends to consider. She'll kill them if I ruin her plans."

"Has she contacted you recently?"

He pressed his lips tightly together, his eyes darting briefly around us to be sure no one else was listening. "Not for nearly three weeks. In truth, I'm getting anxious. I suppose it's too much to hope that some Guardian blade did her in at last."

I agreed with a sigh. "According to my latest sources, she's still out wreaking havoc."

His mouth twitched. "I'd love to kill her myself. I hate living like this."

"Mr. Keegan . . . can I ask what your last orders were?"

He didn't hesitate this time. "Nothing too diabolical. I'm just to keep tabs on you and your family, so I can alert her if you try to run."

I nodded to myself, unsurprised. "I guess it could be worse."

"Most definitely." His head tilted to the side. "May I ask a question of my own?"

I shrugged. "It only seems fair."

"I assure you, it's nothing terrible. I just . . . I was wondering if . . . that is to say . . ." He released his breath sharply, before beginning again. "One of my friends—one that Selena nearly killed, along with me—his phone was recently disconnected. He's just dropped off the face of the earth. But before that, we were exchanging letters. It was the safest way for us to communicate with any semblance of honesty. I'm sure the Demons listened to our phone calls."

I made a *hmm* sound, but I didn't know what else to add.

He continued quickly. "His name was Ken. Ken Bridges. I got his last letter two weeks ago, and I've been trying to contact him ever since. I think he found out something the Demons didn't want him to share."

"What do you mean?"

He shifted his weight, leaning closer to me as he did so. "In his last letter, Ken told me that he'd found out that he was different. That he didn't see things the same way other Seers did."

My eyebrows rose. "He was a Special Seer?"

Peter's eyes grew excited. "You know, then! You know what he was talking about?"

"Yeah. It's rare, but some Seers are able to see multiple emotions at once—a bunch of colors, instead of a single shade."

He blinked slowly. "It's rare?"

"Apparently. Demons and Guardians alike are always looking for those with Special abilities."

"Abilities?"

"Yes. There's more to them than increased Sight." I hesitated. "Peter, are you different too?"

He was staring past me. For a moment I didn't think he was going to answer. Then his mouth parted. "If I answer yes . . . if Selena finds out, will I disappear too?"

I reached for his hand instinctively, feeling a deep empathy for a fellow Seer. "You need to keep this a secret. If she finds out, you'll be sent to work for the Demon Lord. Like I was."

His eyes widened. "You're Special? That's why all this security—the Demon Lord himself wants you because you're different."

"Yes. And if they had any idea how many of us were here, in the city . . . I don't think he'd be so standoffish with me."

"So all of these Seers here today . . . are like us?"

"Most are," I admitted.

His mouth opened and then closed just as quickly. His eyes became intense. "I probably know enough. More than enough." He pulled his fingers away, straightening in the same motion. "I should go see if they need help in the kitchen. I'm glad you're feeling better, Kate." He turned on his heel, nearly sweeping into Patrick, who'd come up silently beside us.

"Mr. Keegan," my Guardian said, his tone moderate.

Peter swallowed hard, face defensive. "Yes?"

Patrick's eyes ran over the guarded expression, the mildly flushed face. I thought he was going to start interrogating the Demon Seer, but in the end he just stuck out his hand. "I didn't get the opportunity to thank you for your help. Your actions saved Kate's life. I'm in your debt."

Peter just stared at the extended hand for a breathless second. Then he lifted his own hand, their fingers flexed around each other. "I was happy for the chance to help," he managed to say, not quite sure how to take Patrick's firm gaze.

Their hands fell away mutually and Peter once again excused himself. I watched him walk past Patrick, Jack, and Claire, sliding easily out of the room.

I didn't realize I was watching his retreat with a frown until Patrick's finger traced my lips lightly. "Are you all right?" he asked.

I met his questioning look with only the slightest hesitation. "I just feel so bad for him. I can't imagine what I would do if I were in his position. He's never had a Guardian to help him with all of this crazy stuff."

The back of Patrick's finger moved across my cheek. "I don't know about that. You seem to be keeping an eye out for him." He tucked some strands of hair gently behind my ear.

I gave him a wry look, accompanied by a reluctant smile. "Patrick O'Donnell, are you mocking me?"

"Of course not." His eyes sparkled. "No Demon would ever dare cross a fierce Guardian like you."

I rolled my eyes. "If only. Then our problems might be solved."

He shook his head. "Problems don't exist today. At least, that's what Jack's been telling me."

"Really? I'm excited for the day off."

"I wish we'd had more time to anticipate the break," he agreed, leaning in to kiss me. When he pulled back his expression was incredibly soft. "Have I told you that you look absolutely beautiful today?"

I smiled despite myself. "All this flattery. It makes me wonder what you want."

His hands rubbed my shoulders, his ducked head emphasizing his serious words. "What I want is you, Kate Bennett."

My palms moved to rest on his chest. "Then I guess you have what you want, huh?"

He gave me a half grin. "Can I ask you something?"

"Anything."

He seemed to think about his question, and something in his face made me wonder if he'd changed his mind at the last second. "What is it you're most grateful for? Right now, in this minute."

"This very minute? That would have to be you."

"Really?" He seemed extremely pleased.

"Hands down."

Before he could reply Grandma's voice boomed from the kitchen. "Everyone to the family room, before the turkey gets cold!"

Jack cheered. "Hah! Ham can be reheated *easily!* Just plop her in the micro, and kazooie!"

"So can turkey," Claire argued, her French accent clear and superior. "You just have to cut it up first. And there's no *kah-zoo-ee* necessary."

The long table looked a little haphazard, mostly because it was three different tables, all different sizes. Only the tablecloths held the makeshift banquet table together. There was the long outdoor picnic table, the regular table, and a card table tacked on at the far end. Food was laid out everywhere, and mine wasn't the only stomach to growl as we all filed into the room—no Guardian stomachs, though; they were exempt from that because they never got hungry. They also never got full, so I was adamant when I told Toni I wouldn't compete against him in a pie-eating contest.

Grandma sat at the head of the table, with the twins on her right side and me and Patrick on the left. Everyone else scrambled to find chairs, and once everyone was seated and Lee had slapped Toni's groping hand away from the potatoes, Grandma led us in a prayer.

While she thanked God for all our blessings, I let my eyes crack open to steal a glance at Patrick. My whole body warmed when I saw he was peeking at me. He gave me a smile. He reached under the table for my hand. Our fingers intertwined, and at his silent prompting I closed my eyes again. But I swear I could feel his gaze still running over my face. It was wonderful and maddening at the same time.

After a chorus of amens and a yell from Jack to "Bog in!" we started filling our plates. Conversations were plentiful, despite the huge feast. Most comments were about the food, of course, and Grandma looked pleased with the praise. I was glad—I knew not just from her aura that she'd been expecting today to be unbearably hard without Grandpa. I knew partly what she was going through. It was the first Thanksgiving I'd ever eaten in my house, without my parents, without Grandpa's easy laugh . . . Patrick's arm brushed against mine often while we ate, and I tried to focus on him—reality.

Soon enough we were eating pie, the twins offering to dish up some ice cream for anyone who wanted it on the side. I kept an eye on the new Seers, curious to see if they were overwhelmed by my family, but they were surprisingly at ease. Alex was answering some of Maddy's questions about his hometown in North Carolina, and Claire was deep in a discussion with Ashley. Dr. Radcliffe and Peter were debating about world politics, and Toni was talking to Lee's mom about the fake trials he was undergoing at the college he didn't attend.

A perfectly normal Thanksgiving.

We ran out of pumpkin pie and Grandma asked me to run to the kitchen to get the second one. I pushed my chair back, only half surprised when Lee followed my lead. After all, we hadn't had a chance to talk in private ever since our group date at Aaron's. Since she was sitting further down the table I reached the kitchen several seconds before her. I was able to locate the pie on the cluttered counter before I heard her step up behind me. "Kate, I need to ask you something," she fairly whispered.

The laughter and rumble of voices from the next room almost drowned her out. I felt my brow furrow at her seriousness. "Sure. What is it?"

Her clear fingernails were tapping almost nervously against her legs. "Do you think I'm completely odd?" she blurted out.

I decided to be honest. "You're wearing a fifties outfit, Lee."

She waved that aside. "Kate, please—be serious. Is there something wrong with me?"

"No, Lee. I don't think there's anything wrong with you. You're not odd."

"Then why did Rodney break up with me last night?"

"What? Why?"

"Shh! I don't want anyone else to know yet." She drew in a deep breath. "I made it sound more dramatic than it is. I mean, I sort of went to his house to break up with him. He just got the words out first."

"Lee, I . . . I'm confused."

She let a shaky laugh escape. "Join the club—we should get T-shirts! I feel like I've been living in the *Twilight Zone* or something, only it's not scary beyond all reason."

"Why did you want to break up with him? I thought things were going great between you two."

"They were. Sort of. Until . . ." Her whisper dropped further. "You know I had a crush on Toni from the beginning. We went on some dates, he kissed me, and it was the closest I'd ever felt to having a semi-serious relationship. But it was kind of weird. And then I learned the truth about you, about him . . . he stopped treating me the same way. So I stopped too. And things were going okay. Rodney was great. And then Toni asked me out again . . ."

"And?"

She sighed. "And I think I'm falling for him. Fallen, actually. As in, already happened. And you can't change something after it's already happened, no matter how much you want to."

I wasn't sure what to say, and in my short silence she groaned and grabbed my wrists. "Say something, please. I'm insane, right? Completely insane. I'm in love with an immortal who's probably crushed on a thousand other girls!"

"Lee, I don't think you're insane. I'm just not sure I understand. You and Rodney . . . He's liked you forever. Why did he want to break up with you?"

She shrugged. "Same reason I wanted to break up with him, I guess. We're still friends and all, but we didn't like each other in that way. You know? There's this flutist in band, and I think he's wanted to ask her out for a couple weeks now." She shook her head. "I know I'm a weird person. So I thought it was great that I could be myself around Rodney. But when I'm with Toni . . . It's more than just being myself. It's, like, completely natural. I don't have to *pretend* to be myself. Even with you and my mom, I wonder sometimes about what outrageous thing I should do next. With Toni, I don't, and . . ."

My lips formed a slow smile. "Then I guess I should just be happy for you. I'm not one to judge on insane relationships."

"*Happy* for me?" Her cheeks were pink with emotion. "I'm freaking out!"

"Just calm down. Take some deep breaths."

She didn't seem to hear the last part. "Kate, what on earth am I supposed to do? My mom doesn't know any of this immortal stuff—heck, Toni doesn't even know that I *like* him!"

"For what it's worth, I think Toni feels the same way."

She hesitated. "Seriously?"

"Seriously. Why else would he have asked you out? So are you going to talk to him about this?"

"Heck no! I'm not going to make a fool out of myself."

I stared at her. "Lee, you wore neon green for a week. Not to mention the eight-month hippie stunt, the yellow jumpsuit in fifth grade, the cardboard box hat in second grade, the twenties dresses, the week you were a tree, the plastic bubble in seventh grade—"

"Sheesh! Shut up already, will ya? And it wasn't a *plastic bubble*. It was a cocoon made with bendy straws and plastic wrap, and it was awesome."

"You wore it for a month."

"Best month of my life. Steven Coombs couldn't shoot spitwads in my face for four whole weeks."

"You couldn't *breathe* for four whole weeks."

"There were air holes," she protested.

"*Or* walk through doors without collapsing yourself first."

"We're getting off topic," she said.

I sighed. "So if you're not going to talk to him about it, what are you going to do?"

She shrugged. "Beats me. Maybe I should let him fess up first? If he really cares about me, he won't wait too long, right?"

Someone cleared his throat behind us and Lee turned aside at once, giving me a view of Alex Perry, his cheeks reddening slightly. "I'm sorry to interrupt. Jack wanted to make sure you weren't eating all the pie."

Lee grunted. "Think I might pitch it into his face for that." She reached past me, scooped up the pie and hurried from the room.

Alex was standing at attention in his stiff uniform, eyes drifting toward me.

I smiled, trying to make his stance ease up. "How was the food?"

"Excellent," he answered at once. "Your grandmother is a gifted cook. I haven't eaten that well in a long time."

"She is pretty amazing."

"Yes. I've thanked her already for inviting us, of course, but I should probably extend some thanks to you as well."

My lips twitched wider. "We Seers need to look out for each other."

His mouth bent upward in the beginning stages of a smile. "I suppose so." He paused and then continued more slowly. "Claire mentioned you're not going to be joining us on the mission."

I shook my head. "No, I won't be. It's . . . complicated."

"I understand. For a Special Seer, you still have a lot to live for."

I know I looked taken aback. "What do you mean, 'for a Special Seer'?"

"Haven't you heard Dr. Radcliffe's latest theories on why we're different? He believes we suffer more loss than regular Seers."

"I thought the reason was biological."

"That's one standing theory. It seems to make sense, but so does Dr. Radcliffe's. He believes Special Seers lose—or will lose—almost everyone they love. That's the case with most of us here, I think."

"You mean our extra Sight is like . . . a bad omen?"

His broad shoulders lifted a fraction. "Maybe, maybe not. It's all hypothetical. But it seems to be true, at least in my case. And Ashley's. And Dr. Radcliffe's." He glanced out the window beside me, overlooking the backyard. His eyes didn't seem focused on anything in particular. "I was fighting in the Middle East when a bomb exploded, taking out most of our vehicle." I saw his eyes flicker down and I instinctively followed his gaze. His hands wavered, as if he were fighting the urge to hide them. It was that slight action that drew my attention to the scarring on his hands—the burn marks that I hadn't been close enough to notice before. I could feel my face tighten into an expression of compassion, but his words kept me from speaking. "I nearly died in the explosion. All my buddies did. But I survived." He was back to staring out into the backyard, his hands rolled into fists. "I was shipped home as soon as I was stable. My . . . girlfriend, Cynthia . . . she died in a car accident a week after I got back. My mom discovered a fast-moving cancer a month after I was released from the hospital, and she died a month after that. I never knew my dad, and I didn't have any siblings. I found myself—abruptly—alone."

"I'm so sorry," I said, painfully aware of how inadequate the words were.

He tried to offer a slight smile, but his eyes remained cold. "My Guardian found me just after Cynthia's accident. He's convinced it was the Demons, trying to get to me." He blinked, glancing back at me. "Maybe I'll never know who was responsible, but I like blaming someone."

"The Demon Lord?" I guessed.

His chin dipped down, a subtle nod, the lump in his throat bobbing once. "I volunteered immediately, knowing this mission would be dangerous. I have nothing else to lose and everything to gain. If I die, I'll be with Cynthia and my mom. If I live to fight another day, I can continue to take down the remaining Demons."

I noticed a touch of color in his cheeks as he glanced around the kitchen, eyes settling on the counter. "Should we carry that apple pie in too? Just in case?"

I tried to compose my face, knowing he didn't need to see any more sympathy than he already had—my glistening eyes, my empathetic aura, they revealed enough. I moved to grab the pie, but he beat me to it with his scarred hands. "Allow me, ma'am." His accented drawl was enhanced by his word choice. "According to Toni, you've already done more than just about any other Seer alive."

"I just wish I had your bravery," I said honestly.

"Trust me—you've got something better." I cocked an eyebrow, and he actually gave me a smile before explaining himself. "You've got hope, Kate. And a lot of it."

He turned and headed back to the family room. I was slower to follow.

I had hope? I suppose I should trust his eyesight. He could See things about me that I couldn't. But if I had so much hope, why was I still so afraid of the future?

eleven

The TV was playing in the background. Toni, Lee, Maddy, Jenna, and Josie were playing a card game in the living room. They'd just managed to get Alex and Claire to join in, though Ashley politely declined their invitation. Patrick and Jack were on dish duty, while Grandma, Jeanette, and Peter attempted to cram leftovers into smaller storage containers. Ashley and I were folding up tablecloths and setting aside the random salt and pepper shakers that had been left behind in the initial cleaning sweep.

Ashley was a pretty girl in her early twenties. She had raven-black hair and clear skin. She hadn't said more than two words to me in the short time I'd known her, but she wasn't really unfriendly. Just quiet.

I was still running the conversation I'd had with Alex through my mind, and I was more than curious to know what made this girl's aura look do depressed. She didn't seem like she was about to open up about herself, though, and I wasn't going to ask her any prying questions. Instead we worked in silent companionship.

Once the tables were cleared I wandered into the kitchen, coming up behind Patrick and slipping my arms around his waist. He'd taken off his suit coat and hung it on the back door's knob, and his white sleeves were pushed up to his elbows to avoid the water. His hands were plunged in soapy water when he looked over his shoulder at me, a smile brightening his face. "Hey, you."

"Hey." I leaned closer, keeping my voice low. "I miss seeing you in a jacket already. You look great in a suit."

He glanced back at the bowl he was scrubbing, a grin pulling at his mouth. "Kate Bennett, are you flirting with me? You should keep your voice down—you don't want your grandma to hear you."

I set my chin on his shoulder, my arms flexing around him. "I think she already knows how I feel about you."

Jack stepped next to us so could rinse a platter Patrick had already washed, a towel slung over one shoulder. "Does she really?" He clucked, having obviously picked up the conversation. "Is that why she's been as edgy as a bunyip?"

"A what?" I laughed incredulously.

"A bunyip! They're strange buggers who thrive in the land Down Under."

"Bunyip?" I repeated doubtfully, pulling my head back so I could see him better.

"Sure! You've never heard of them?"

"Never."

"Well, now, that's a little surprising."

"Are they dangerous?" I asked.

He nodded. "Bloody yes." I must have looked disbelieving, because he rolled his eyes. "You Yanks—you got more kangaroos loose in the top paddock than any Aussie. Even the drunk ones."

"Aren't they all drunk?" Patrick asked smoothly, handing the dripping bowl to Jack.

"I'll ignore that racist comment," Jack said shortly, spraying water over the dish.

"What about your racist comment?" I asked.

He shrugged. "Fine, in the interest of being fair, I'll ignore that one too."

I leaned forward so my forehead was near Patrick's ear. "Is there really something called a bunyip?"

Jack overheard and chortled. "Of course not. I was just having a lend of you!"

"Huh?"

Patrick translated. "He's taking advantage of your gullibility."

I frowned at Jack. "Thanks a lot. I'm glad I have people I can trust."

"You can trust me to keep your mind quick." Jack winked. "It's a real mythical creature, though, if that counts."

I shook my head at him. "How long have you been a Guardian, Jack?"

"Since the mid 1800s. Why do you ask?"

"You'd think you would have found some time to mature a little."

"And be bored for the rest of eternity? Not bloody likely."

Grandma's foot stomped on the other side of the kitchen. "Whatever you're all blabbering on about, I'd appreciate it if *Uncle* Jack would stop using such language. If the twins pick it up, I swear—"

"Empty threats," he muttered, too low for her to hear over the running water.

Patrick passed off a soapy dish to Jack before turning partially in my arms, hands still in the sink. "I love you," he told me honestly—right before he drew out his soap-covered hands and pressed them against my face. I squealed and pushed away from him only to dive back toward the sink, succeeding in getting a handful of bubbles before he reached to stop me. I grabbed his wrist with my free hand and smothered my share of soap into his hair.

I could hear Grandma's light scolding but Patrick's easy laugh filled every other space, distracting me from everything else but him.

In the end, my dress was speckled wet and the shrug covering my shoulder was all but drenched, and his white shirt was covered in wet splotches. His hair looked darker, and mine was wet and stringy in places. He plucked up a strand, flipping it over between his thumb and forefinger. "It curls," he stated, amused.

"Parts," I admitted.

"I like it."

"I'd like it more if it all cooperated." I reached out to wipe his lips with my fingertips. "Did I get soap in your mouth?"

"More than a little." He nodded calmly.

"You've made a lake on our floor," Grandma scolded. "You two are on mop duty, I hope you know."

Patrick shook his head at me—as if I'd started the whole thing. He turned to go back to the dishes but Peter had already replaced him as a dishwasher, so I smugly told my Guardian where the mop was located.

He moved to the broom closet, which was next to the pantry. I struggled to wriggle out of the wet shrug, but I was still meeting with difficulty by the time Patrick came back over with the mop. He set it down, leaning it carefully against the counter before reaching to help me escape the sopping thing. I thanked him once I was free, then draped it over his hanging suit coat, hoping to transfer some of the water to it. He rolled his eyes, guessing my motivation, and grabbed for the mop.

While he took care of the puddles on the floor I got a towel and wiped off the cupboards that had received some good splashes. Grandma and Jeanette wandered into the front room to put their feet up, and Jack and Peter went to dismantle the ersatz banquet table, leaving us alone.

Patrick and I worked easily side-by-side in the ensuing quiet.

I would have been content with the continued silence, because it was so companionable, but Patrick's hesitating voice wasn't unwelcome by any means.

"The last Seer will arrive tomorrow," he started from somewhere behind me. "They'll probably be ready for you to teach them how to travel on Saturday morning."

I let the damp towel slide across the edge of the counter, sopping up errant bubbles. "That works. I don't really have any other urgent plans."

I heard the wet mop drag across the floor before he continued. "I was just wondering if you intended to travel with them for their first time?"

I glanced over my shoulder to see that he was watching me, his hands curled around the unmoving mop handle. I kept my voice cautious. "I was planning on it, just to help them with the disorientation. Why do you ask?"

He lifted a single shoulder, his chin rising imperceptibly. "I was curious about where you intended to go with them. That's all."

I pursed my lips briefly before lifting the towel, moving to stand in front of him. I twisted the material in my hands, but that was the only nervous action that might betray me; my eyes met his without pause. "I was hoping that . . . Well, the first place I went worked for me." I hurried to list my reasons. "It's far enough in the past that it shouldn't wipe them out for a day, especially if they don't stay long, like I did last time. And the area is so secluded we shouldn't stumble on anyone."

I was a little surprised to see him nodding. "You're right. It's a good place."

"So . . . you're willing to open a memory for us to use?"

His eyes dropped to watch my hands wrapping around the towel. "I would rather send you to somewhere I knew was safe than leave it up to someone else. I've been considering this for a few days now, and I think I have a good memory in mind."

"Is it after my last visit? Would your father know me?" I didn't bother to hide the eagerness in my words.

Patrick almost smiled at the sound of my excitement. "I'm not sure how long after, but yes—he would remember you."

I lifted one hand up to rest on his arm, fingers squeezing gently. "Since I'll be there anyway, do you want to write him a letter or something?"

He let out a low, short laugh. It held the sound of lost hopes, but somehow it wasn't entirely mournful. "I don't know the first thing I'd write to him. My last memories of him weren't exactly good."

"But he didn't mean any of that—anything he said was my fault—"

He let go of the mop with one hand so he could lay his fingertips across my open mouth, halting my apology before it could fully escape. "Kate, it's all right. Really. And you can send him my love. I just . . . I can't think of anything else I'd say to him."

He shifted his weight and my hand slipped from his arm. He returned to mopping and I moved slowly back to the counter, wishing there was something I could say to ease his pain.

***

"Traveling takes concentration, but, most important, it takes the emotion of another person. This emotion is a doorway to a memory, whether it's present, recent, or deep in the past. This could be one of the major reasons why only Special Seers can travel through memories. Regular Seers can only view one emotion—the present emotion."

My words halted as I saw Dr. Radcliffe scribbling down everything I was saying into a composition notebook. And just because the others in the room weren't taking notes didn't mean they weren't listening intently.

We were in the warehouse, standing on the main floor. It was a bright Saturday morning and the sunlight filtered through the boarded-up windows. I was feeling more than a little self-conscious, being the center of attention. All the mental notes I'd made over the past couple days seemed to fade now that it was time to speak. I'd never taught anyone how to do anything like this before, and I felt like I was a young kid again, pretending to be a schoolteacher for one of Jenna and Josie's games.

Alex was standing next to Ashley, who was standing next to Dr. Radcliffe, who was turned slightly away from Hanif Shenouda. Hanif had been the last Seer to arrive, coming in late last night. Even with the help of his Guardian Hanif had nearly gotten lost twice on his way from Egypt. It was his first time in America, but his English was good, possibly because his mother was British. He was lanky and his skin was deeply tanned. He was twenty years old and extremely cheerful and polite. He had a skinny face and an easy smile, but his Guardian—a worn-out woman named Hanna—warned us to keep a close eye on him. "He's not as innocent as he looks," she'd uttered. "His bad luck has caused his village to blame him for the latest drought."

"You're not staying, then?" Jack had asked quickly.

She shook her head. "As much as I'd love to, I need to get back to my other Seers. There aren't as many Guardians there as you'll see in America."

I could now see what she'd meant. Hanif had already started the warehouse on fire cooking some eggs this morning. Claire looked especially harried with him.

Standing behind the Special Seers were the Guardians not currently watching over my family: Patrick, Toni, and Claire. Everyone was watching me closely, but Patrick's gaze seemed especially heavy.

I cleared my throat and continued. "The farther back in the past you go, the easier it is to recover."

"What do you mean, recover?" Ashley asked, speaking directly to me for perhaps the first time.

"After you get back to the present, you'll be really tired. The more time you spend away, the longer you'll be wiped out. In my experience, passing out can be a side effect, and I was asleep for a few hours."

"How far back have you gone?" Alex asked curiously.

"The late 1700s. I spent over a half hour there."

"And did it take you long to recover?" Dr. Radcliffe asked, still scrawling in his notebook.

"A few hours."

Hanif whistled lowly. "That's it? Amazing. I've always dreamed of seeing the construction of the pyramids. All I have to do is find a Guardian who's old enough, and—"

Dr. Radcliffe interrupted him easily. "I'm afraid our own personal ambitions will have to wait for another time. Our mission will be taking place in the 1970s. That's one of the reasons you were each specifically approached—you're all young enough to be safe there, since we cannot travel into our own lifetimes without risking death."

Hanif's face fell with disappointment.

Alex looked confused. "May I ask why the 1970s, sir?"

Dr. Radcliffe flashed me an apologetic look before stepping forward to stand at my side. "I suppose now is as good a time as any to give you a quick briefing. I was contacted by the Guardian Council about a week ago and given a file of all the information they'd managed to gather about the Demon Lord. I was asked to help assess any possible weaknesses he might have, primarily in his past. I was, of course, extremely shocked when I realized that the Demon Lord and I were both in Chicago in the same year—the same night, in fact."

I felt my eyebrows rise at that, an action I could see repeated throughout the room. A memory the Demon Lord had told me himself stirred. Chicago, a Christmas Eve, back in the 1970s . . .

Dr. Radcliffe was still speaking. "But before I get ahead of myself, I should probably tell you that the Demon Lord is not a Demon. He's not even immortal."

"But he's been influencing evil for two hundred years or more!" Ashley protested.

Alex had figured it out. "He's a Seer," he stated. "A Special one, like us. Isn't he, sir?"

"Exactly right, Mr. Perry." The professor grinned at his quickness. "He is a Special Seer. He was the lead expert on time traveling, back when he worked for the Guardians. A long story cut short, he made alliances with Demons and now aspires to unite them all against Guardians and humans. Obviously, we can't let that happen.

"The council of Guardians asked me to help plan this attack against him, which will be taking place in the past, using my memory. I've done some extensive research and been aided by the Demon Lord's own written account of his early life, which he documented when he was with the Guardians. His brush with death occurred on Christmas Eve, 1971, when he was seven years old. That was the night his mother and sister were murdered by his mother's boyfriend, and the Demon Lord was also shot."

"So we're going back there to stop him from almost dying?" Ashley guessed. "We're going to save his life so he won't become a Seer?"

Dr. Radcliffe shook his head. "No. That won't be good enough. The Demon Lord might not be able to journey back to his past, if we caused him to lose his Seer abilities, but there's no telling what evil he still may have grown to do—or what if he nearly suffered death again later, and our mission accomplished nothing?"

"So what are we doing, then?" Hanif asked.

Alex answered before Dr. Radcliffe could. "This is an assassination."

"Indeed," the professor confirmed thinly, breaking the abrupt silence. "A horrible thing to resort to, but so many lives are in danger . . . His life is a necessary sacrifice."

Ashley spoke hesitantly. "Won't his death affect the past? So many events wouldn't have happened. It would untangle so many things. I thought that's why we couldn't ask Guardians in the past to help us out—it's why we'll be on our own."

My own thoughts were spiraling. If the Demon Lord didn't exist, then . . . would my grandpa somehow still be alive? Would Vegas have ever happened? And Sean . . . Sean had become a Demon, independent of the Demon Lord as far as I knew, but maybe he wouldn't be quite as evil—maybe he wouldn't be Far Darrig.

Could killing the Demon Lord in the past really solve all of these problems? It was too much to imagine. Not to mention a bit disturbing. Despite the necessity, despite the possibility of it solving all our problems, murder seemed extreme.

Dr. Radcliffe was still speaking. "I've thought this through, Miss Grey. Long and hard. And it's worth the possible risks. The Demon Lord must be stopped."

I swallowed hard, grateful I wouldn't have to worry about the actual assassination part. But I would want to ask Patrick about his ideas on the consequences of what the Seers and Guardians were going to bring about. The Demon Lord hadn't killed my grandpa, hadn't fully corrupted Sean—but if he was out of the picture, would those things change? I barely dared to hope.

Dr. Radcliffe waited for the next question, but when one wasn't forthcoming he spoke again. "I'll give you more specific details later. First, we need to learn how to travel and return to our own time. Then we can worry about the actual mission." He stepped back into the ranks, his pen poised and ready above the page, returning the spotlight to me.

I pulled in a short breath. "It's really quite easy. You shouldn't be nervous." I nodded toward Patrick. "I've asked my Guardian to supply a memory for us to practice with. We'll be traveling back to Ireland, to the year 1797. Patrick?" I held out a hand, gesturing for him to come stand beside me. He shouldered smoothly through the small knot of people, his eyes on mine. He stopped in front of me, and if our every move wasn't being closely monitored he might have said something. In the end, he just turned to look back at the group.

I continued hastily, disliking the fact that my words were almost exact copies of the instructions the Demon Lord had once given to me. "When the aura is revealed, Patrick will focus on the specific memory, isolating a single dominant emotion. All you do is look into that prominent emotion. Try to channel it into yourself. You'll be drawn to where you need to go. Getting back is even simpler. The longer you're away from your time, the more obvious the pull to come back will be. It will guide you back with little concentration to the exact second you left in. To those you leave behind, the whole thing is instantaneous."

"Incredible!" Dr. Radcliffe muttered to himself, still writing madly.

I looked to Patrick and he gave me a small nod, indicating he was ready. His silver aura was no longer alone; colors floated in a cloud around him, too many to take in at once. I'd seen his aura before, but it still took my breath away. Maybe all Guardians had complicated auras, due to the long lives they lived. But the wealth and depth of Patrick's emotions was incredible to observe.

While he worked to expand the single emotion that would lead us to the right moment in his past, I turned back to the Seers. "We'll go at the same time, but I'll hold back until I know you've all made it. So if you're ready . . ."

Alex Perry stepped forward immediately, coming to stand in front of Patrick. Ashley was right behind him. Hanif paused to elbow Dr. Radcliffe, who was still scribbling in his notes.

"Oh! Yes, of course!" He stumbled, closing his notebook with the pen still inside.

In seconds we were all gathered around Patrick, who had

his eyes closed as he concentrated on the distant memory. We all watched as a blue ribbon of color widened and grew around Patrick, until it was obviously the right one. Flecks of yellow marked the integrated happiness of the moment, and I could feel my heart beginning to pound in excitement. My eyes narrowed, trying to see it better . . .

From the corner of my eye I saw Seers begin to drop. First Ashley, then Alex, then Dr. Radcliffe. Hanif's body went suddenly limp beside me, and so I allowed my own body to begin to lighten. It was amazing—so different from last time. I was in control, because I knew what to expect now. It was an exhilarating sensation.

Just before I felt like I was going to fade at last, I felt Patrick's fingers wrap around mine, something thin and stiff pressing between our palms. "Please give this to him," he whispered urgently.

And then he was gone.

twelve

May 21, 1797
Kate Bennett
Wexford County, Ireland

I was first aware of the gentle wind billowing against my face, tugging at my hair. I was standing on the top of a rolling knoll, the long green grass almost familiar. Dim sunlight was filtered through the largely overcast sky. The sounds of bleating sheep punctuated the otherwise tranquil surroundings.

Finding the church was easy. It was resting in a lush pasture area, in a beautiful valley that dipped just lower than the surrounding hills. The white walls of the building were stark against all the green. A beautiful home was a short distance away from the church, and I knew I was looking at the house Patrick had been raised in.

I could hardly imagine growing up in such a peaceful place.

"By Jove, it really worked!" Dr. Radcliffe exhaled beside me.

The others were in similar states of awe. Hanif looked almost frightened by all the long weeds that were wrapping around his legs with the breeze. I lived in a desert too, so I could relate a bit.

Alex was standing with his feet spread apart, scanning the area with a soldier's grace. "If this was O'Donnell's memory, where is he?"

"From my past experience, he should be nearby," I said.

"So we're deposited on the *edge* of a memory. How fascinating!" The professor cracked open his notebook and made a notation.

Ashley was tapping the screen of her phone. "It doesn't work," she said.

Hanif nodded. "No cell towers, of course."

Alex glanced at his huge wristwatch. "The clock stopped. The whole display is blank."

"How extraordinary!" Dr. Radcliffe muttered. "It must be some kind of built-in defense that the space-time continuum possesses to keep things from unwinding completely. Oh well, it would have been too much to hope for. Imagine being able to come back and record the highlights of history! Of course, technology is a small thing to sacrifice for the chance to come back and witness all these splendid things. I say, I never dreamed I'd be traveling to past centuries. Just think of the books I could write! I may turn from the science world over to the historic branches. Only I'd be tempted to brag almost constantly, so that wouldn't do any good."

We'd all tuned him out at this point. We spread out instinctively, each of us wanting the opportunity to revel in this experience privately.

I looked toward the church, wondering if that's where I would once again find Patrick's father, Pastor O'Donnell. I could hardly wait to see him again. I was fingering the folded piece of paper Patrick had handed me at the last minute. I was intensely curious to read what he'd written, but I decided against peeking. If he'd wanted me to see the words, he would have given it to me sooner. I could study the paper, though.

It was a regular sheet of lined paper, torn from a notebook.

He'd folded it in half several times, and I could see a few lines and curves where he'd pressed too hard and indented the page. It wasn't enough to decipher into a clear message, but it revealed that he'd found more to say than he'd first let on.

I glanced up from the folded paper just in time to see a figure darting for the church from the direction of a wooden fence that lined the yard between the house and the church. He was running along the worn dirt path as if he'd done it a thousand times. I knew it was Patrick, even without seeing the black sketchbook tucked firmly under one arm.

The wind shifted and the distant sound of singing washed ethereally over the hill. I fought a grin. He was late to church? It seemed so . . . unlike Patrick. He'd been working on a drawing, no doubt. Sean would probably tease him for his tardiness, and though I'd never met his mother I imagined she might scold him lightly before asking to see his sketch.

He'd almost reached the one-room church. He was slowing down as he made it to the steps to avoid pounding them and making even more of a scene. He pulled the door open, peeked his head inside, then slipped in.

"Was that Patrick?" Hanif asked, following my gaze.

I just nodded, carefully curling my fingers around the slip of paper I held. I didn't want the others to see the note. It seemed too personal to share.

Ashley spoke suddenly from behind us. "This place is so beautiful. I've never seen anything like it."

Alex turned to Dr. Radcliffe, who was hardly taking the time to admire the sights around him because he was so busy documenting it. But Alex was a soldier, concentrating on the ultimate mission. "Sir, the night the Demon Lord got his Sight—won't that be a heavily guarded night in his past? The Demon Lord obviously knows he is vulnerable then, and he may have taken precautions. He may have asked Demons and Seers to keep a lookout."

Dr. Radcliffe was nodding. "It's a risk we must be willing to take. In my research I've found that his mother—a single woman—moved around a lot. Most of the time there's no record she had a place of her own. She lived with boyfriends, neighbors . . . The truth is, we wouldn't know where to find the Demon Lord before he got his Sight, except on the day the police showed up to arrest the boyfriend. After being released the Demon Lord was in orphanages for years. It would be almost impossible to find him until he was with the Guardians, and by then he would be less vulnerable."

Alex shook his head. "They'd still be in the same apartment a couple days before the shootings, right? I'd feel better if we could take them off guard."

"It's possible that wasn't their first day there, yes. But the moving boxes were still scattered all over the place, and the Demon Lord couldn't even tell the police the address. He just had to give them landmarks. According to his report, he and his family had moved in with the boyfriend only a couple days ago. Besides, the night of the shooting will be the best night to end all of this."

Ashley sighed. "So we're going to have to fight off who knows how many people, plus assassinate the most dangerous enemy the Guardians have ever had? With only four of us?"

"Four? No no, my dear girl—only three."

"What?" Hanif asked, glancing around and recounting each of us.

Radcliffe blinked. "Didn't you realize? I'm supplying the memory. I will be unable to assist you."

"What about her?" Ashley asked, pointing to me. "I meant her."

Alex shifted closer to me. "Kate's not going. She doesn't have to. I can lead this mission, and I can get us all out safely."

"Seriously? You, me, and Hanif?"

Dr. Radcliffe laid a hand on her arm. "You're the only ones

young enough and willing to volunteer. Your gifts are rarer than you realize."

She didn't shake his hand off, like I thought she might. But she was eyeing me with a look caught between disgust and envy. Unable to meet her stare, I opened my mouth to address everyone. "If that's all the time you need, we should be getting back. You don't want to be unconscious for too long."

I explained again how to feel the tug in their stomachs, instructed them to close their eyes for concentration's sake, and then I watched as each one successfully vanished back to the present. When I was the last one standing on the hill I turned and made my way down to the church.

I wasn't dressed for a Sunday service, but I wasn't planning on going inside—yet. The walk was long and leisurely, like stretching a tired body against a firm bed after a hard day. I angled toward the back of the church, where I could hopefully wait in safety for the church to empty. There was a small, peaceful cemetery on the side of the church, and around back was a gigantic tree. I leaned up against the rough bark and listened to the muffled end of the sermon.

Pastor O'Donnell's voice was soothing but powerful. I couldn't quite get the gist of the lesson, because I couldn't pick out many clear words. But just the sound of his confident tone made me feel warm and energized. The congregation concluded by singing a hymn of praise.

I heard feet scraping against the wooden floor, heard people on the steps outside, and knew the service was over. Cheerful Irish voices called out good-byes to friends and family, until hardly a crowd was left at all.

The sounds of wagons and horses faded, and I crept back around the side of the church, unwilling to be seen.

As I got nearer to the front of the church, I heard the unmistakable voice of Sean O'Donnell. Laughter undulated in every syllable he uttered. ". . . make him live in the church, then he won't be late. In addition to that, we'd be rid of him, mostly."

A kind woman's voice was gently reprimanding. "Now, Sean, that'll do. Besides, he feels bad enough. Don't you, Patrick?"

I pressed my shoulder against the church, my stomach clenching for some reason.

His voice was perfect, and it made my heart pound. "Of course, Mam. I promised it wouldn't happen again, and now I've broken that promise. It's just that . . . this inspiration comes at the worst of times. I can hardly stop mid-stroke."

Pastor O'Donnell's voice was heavy but not unkind. "Your talent is a gift. But the Lord expects us to divide our time wisely."

His wife cut in before he could launch into another sermon. I found myself smiling at her words. "The Lord also believes in Sunday dinner, Patrick, love—so why don't we save the lessons for later, hmm?"

"Oh, all right. But first I must gather my notes."

"Should we wait for you?" she asked.

"No, I'll be along."

The wooden steps rattled and then I spotted Patrick and Sean walking on either side of their mother, holding her arms like it was the most natural thing to do. Sean was whispering something to her, and she actually threw back her head and laughed. It was an angelic sound, and I wished more than ever before that I could step out and meet her too. But that would be unwise. I didn't want to mess up anything Patrick and I had in the future. He'd already seen me once in the past—I couldn't let it happen again.

Once they were nearly to the house, about a quarter mile away, I stepped around the corner and made my way up to the entrance of the church.

The one-room church was more dimly lit than the last time I'd been inside, but that was due to the coming storm that hindered the light outside. There were no lights or candles.

Several pews were in the center of the room, leaving an aisle along each wall. Simple windows lined the length of the building, and a wooden pulpit sat at the back end of the room. Dominating the space was a large wooden cross mounted onto the back wall. It wasn't really ornamented; some delicate etchings, and that was all. But it was still incredibly beautiful.

A middle-aged man stood at the pulpit, wearing a plain black robe with a white collar. His head was bowed over a sheaf of papers, which he was trying to shuffle into his thick Bible. He glanced up when he heard the floor creak beneath my feet, his penetrating blue eyes taking in my presence.

His aura was as I remembered it—peaceful, happy, and simple; much like the church he loved so much. There were more bits of gray than last time, and the green uneasiness had also lengthened. A dull brown also faded in and out of nearly every other color. It was a pain I'd put there; the pain of knowing the fate of his family, knowing what he would have to do to bring that future into play. But white was there too. Hope. I wondered if the hope Alex had seen in me was as prevalent as this. If so, I'd be amazed.

He had a lined face, but the effect was pleasant. Comforting. Real. His hair was thinning, especially on the top of his head. But his brown hair had managed to retain most of the color, despite the few silver hairs creeping in at the temples.

He breathed in deeply, a thin smile lifting his face. "Kate. You've returned."

My own mouth twisted up without prompting. "Pastor O'Donnell." I paused, but when he didn't say anything else, I added, "I hope this isn't a bad time."

His eyes widened, as if surprised at his own staring. "No! No, of course not!" He set his Bible down and hurried around the podium, coming to me quickly. I didn't expect him to throw his arms around me, but I didn't regret getting his powerful hug. "Oh, I'm so relieved! I've been praying every day for your safety.

How long has it been for you? Did you manage to escape from the Demon Lord? How is Patrick? Have you heard anything more about Sean?"

I chuckled, pulling back enough so I could look into his eyes—eyes that dimly matched Patrick's. They weren't quite as brilliant, but maybe I was prejudiced. "We got out all right. It's been over five weeks now."

"Five weeks?" he muttered, astounded. "Heavens."

"How long for you?"

"Eleven days," he replied at once, proof he'd been keeping a careful record. "Isn't it amazing? I can hardly wrap my mind around it. But if the Lord can, that's all that really matters. What of Patrick?"

I extended the note, unable to stop grinning. "It's from him," I added, when he simply stared at the proffered paper.

His eyes lit up; he took the folded paper with fingers that trembled with anticipation. He began to unwrap the message, belatedly asking me to sit, if I'd like. We sat together on the front pew and I tried to look at anything other than his face. I knew this was a private moment for him, but it was hard to keep my eyes from wandering back to take in his expression.

He scanned the message, and I saw his jaw clench once. His eyes were moist with emotion and his aura was constantly changing, shifting to brighter colors. The pain was still present, though, flaring occasionally.

He looked up at me, a thin smile cracking through. "Have you read this?"

I shook my head.

He handed it over immediately. "I think you should."

I tried not to look too eager as I focused on the small and neat script.

Dear Father,

I have so many things I would like to say. So many

things I wish to tell you. In the end, I am rendered thoughtless. If it weren't for Kate, I probably wouldn't say anything at all. But she's right—I have a miraculous opportunity, and it shouldn't be wasted.

Let me begin by reminding you of my love. Despite the things that transpired between us, you remain my moral compass. You will always be the one I look up to. The one I wish to emulate. I know that telling Mother about these things is impossible now. She doesn't deserve the burden. But someday, please convey my truest love to her. Let her know that I will never stop revering her, that she will always be my angel.

I wish more than ever that I had you with me. Times are so uncertain. I don't know what to do. Sean is not the same person. He is a Demon, in every sense of the word. He has done so much. So many terrible things. But if he is completely evil, why do I still love him? Why do I find the thought of killing him so sickening? If I don't do something, he will haunt me forever. He will haunt Kate. I can't allow that. I feel so lost. So afraid of what is to come. I can only hold on to your hope, trust in your faith.

Despite everything, I want you to know that I am happy. Happier than I have ever been. I love Kate with all my heart. With all my strength. With all my thoughts. With every breath I breathe. When you think of my death, I don't want you to think of pain and loss. I want you to think of Kate. For she is my happiness. She is my home. She is my heaven.

I love you, Father. I will for the rest of eternity.

Your son,

Patrick

I was blinking back tears. Pastor O'Donnell handed me a white handkerchief, which I took at once. While I wiped my eyes, his markedly rough voice filled the room. "He has always amazed me with his ability to express emotion, whether through art or the written word. He is an extremely talented young man."

"He is," I agreed quietly. I glanced up at him, gently brandishing the letter. "Thank you. For letting me see this."

"Of course. I'm sure he wanted you to know." He retrieved the precious letter and folded it care. "But I should be thanking *you*. For so many things. For convincing him to write this, for carrying it to me . . . for your very presence in his life."

I blushed. "It's not like it sounds. I mean—*he's* all those things to *me*."

"Are you calling him a liar?" he asked calmly.

"No, but . . . You know what I mean."

He nodded. "And I approve of your modesty. Humility is an important trait. But don't let it become self-deprecation." He leaned back against the hard bench. "But enough of my lectures for one day. What brings you here?"

I did my best to bring him up to speed. It was easier than I thought it would be—the story just sort of poured out. I cried as I talked about my grandfather's death, but he was patient with my rush of emotions. After the tears stopped falling, I felt amazingly refreshed. I told him about all the Guardians and Seers watching over me and my family, about the reward the Demon Lord had put out for me. I told him I'd come here to train some Seers so they could assassinate the Demon Lord and stop all of this from happening.

He wondered what that would do to us, if the Demon Lord never lived to force me back in time. He was especially anxious to know if it would save Sean from becoming Far Darrig. I didn't have any answers for him, but I think he could hear the doubts I harbored about the last one.

The only thing I didn't tell him about were the dreams I'd been having about Sean; the ones where I killed him. I didn't want Pastor O'Donnell to know about my weakness. He was trusting in me to make everything right, to save his youngest son; I couldn't do that if I killed him.

By the time I was finished he was shaking his bowed head. "These are indeed dangerous times, Kate. I understand Patrick's unease."

"He worries a lot."

"He worries about you. About all those he loves." He hesitated, raising his head to meet my gaze. "How much longer can you stay?"

I could already feel the uncomfortable pull in my stomach, beckoning me to come back to my own time. I ignored it. "However long you need me to."

"I would like to reply to his letter. I'll write quickly, I promise."

"Of course."

He stood at once. "I haven't anything to write with here. I'll need to return to the house. But I feel terribly rude asking you to stay here alone."

"Don't. I'll be fine."

"I will hurry," he assured me. He was already moving, walking briskly past the pews. I watched him until he disappeared behind the door. I heard his retreating footsteps, and then—aside from the growing stiffness in the wind—silence filled the steadily darkening church.

thirteen

May 21, 1797
Kate Bennett
Wexford County, Ireland

I didn't remain sitting for long. I wandered over to one of the near windows, watched as the clouds thickened for the coming storm. I took in the beautiful countryside until it began to rain; the effect was both relaxing and melancholy, and I could only stand to watch the raindrops sliding down the glass for a short time.

I moved to the pulpit, opening the Bible to expose Pastor O'Donnell's notes. I let my eyes run down the words he'd handwritten, skimming the markings and marginal notes without definite purpose. I'd read parts of the Bible, and though I was familiar with most of the popular stories, I'd never actually studied the words. My mother had read the New Testament daily, and I knew my father favored the Psalms and Proverbs. It seemed that Patrick's father did as well.

He'd circled some of his favorite verses and my eyes were immediately drawn to one of them—Psalm 33:22. "Let thy mercy, O Lord, be upon us, according as we hope in thee."

That seemed to fit perfectly with all this talk of trust and hope. I turned a small chunk of pages, almost excited when the next marked verse jumped out just as readily. "A soft answer turneth away wrath: but grievous words stir up anger" (Proverbs 15:1).

I had mixed feelings about this one. Sean's face leapt immediately to mind; was this some kind of divine intervention? Was I supposed to see this verse because this was the way to help him? Should I put away my anger and treat Sean with sympathy and love? I wondered if that was humanly possible. It was the age-old moral, to love your enemy. Could I do that after everything Sean had done to me personally? To those I loved?

I turned a single page, still feeling troubled. Proverbs 16:25 fell into view. The words were ominous and made my arms feel strangely heavy. "There is a way that seemeth right unto a man, but the end thereof are the ways of death."

Right on cue, the first boom of thunder shuddered nearby. I jumped, my hand jerking harshly against the edge of the podium, earning my palm a shallow scratch. But even without the theatrical emphasis of the thunder and the sting of pain, the verse was haunting. I don't know why the words seared into my mind so completely. They didn't seem to have anything I could relate to, unlike the other scriptures. And yet . . . It seemed eerily prophetic.

The mission to assassinate the Demon Lord seemed like the right thing to do. But it would lead to death. Maybe one day he would be a horrible enemy of good, but when the Demon Lord was killed, he would be a frightened little kid. Could that possibly be the right path to take? Ensuring the death of an innocent child? And what of all the repercussions? Would his death lead to other deaths? Or would the people he killed come back to life? Would my grandpa come back?

The door to the church opened—a gust of wind blew in, whipping some of the pages closed. I looked up to see Pastor O'Donnell, dripping wet and still in his black robe. His was breathless from running. "My family believes me to be insane . . . I'm sorry for how dark it is."

"It's fine." I stepped away from the Bible, away from the words that kept playing over in my mind.

We met in front of the first row of pews and he handed me a sealed envelope. There was something small and heavier than paper inside, but my fingers didn't investigate the curiosity because he was speaking. "I apologize for keeping you so long. There was so much to say . . ."

"I understand. And it wasn't any trouble. No one will be missing me."

"Really?" he asked, water dripping from the tip of his chin. "How do you mean?"

"It's instantaneous for them. I'm gone and back in the same second."

"How amazing." He exhaled loudly, trying to slow the low panting as he reached to take my free hand. His rough palm rubbed against my smoother fingers. "I'm grateful for you, Kate. I will continue to pray for you."

An unbidden smile twitched the corner of my mouth. "Actually, I was hoping you might say one of those prayers with me now."

He bowed his head. "As you wish."

We didn't bother to sit down, and he didn't release my hand. Our eyes squeezed closed. He began to pray.

Unlike last time, when I'd been so overwhelmed by so many emotions, I tried to listen to every word Pastor O'Donnell said. He began by addressing God as if He were a dear friend he respected greatly. His words were comforting and warm, as deep and meaningful as I remembered. His tone of voice changed as his words became especially personal. "Bless thy daughter Kate as she goes through these horrible trials. Let her know of thy love and the love of her departed loved ones. Let her know her strengths, her wonderful potential." He paused briefly, nearly overcome with emotion. "Please, dear Father, be with my sons. Bless and watch over them. Let them know how fortunate they are to have Kate in their lives. Help Patrick as he protects her, and bless Sean in his darkest night to see hope again."

He was quiet for at least a full minute. His hand was shaking. I tried to steady him by flexing my fingers around his. I don't know if I helped or not, but he was speaking again—not as surely as before, as if he wasn't positive of the words. As if they came from somewhere else. "Bless Kate in her coming trials. Let her have the courage she will need. Keep her faith strong as it is tested. When she sees death next—no matter how many times—let her understand that thy ways are higher than our ways. Bless her to make wise choices, for she will be influencing so many lives." Another pause. "And bless Patrick that he will not blame himself for the things to come. Let him know, as Kate knows, that all will be resolved in the end."

I didn't like the sound of this. The things he was saying, the blessings he was imparting . . . They were as ominous as the scripture I'd read. At the same time, there was comfort; I was beginning to feel less frightened of the future. More prepared to face whatever was coming. The only thing that had me aching was the thought of more deaths. *Please,* I prayed silently. *I can't lose anyone else. Please . . .*

Pastor O'Donnell finished his prayer. I'd missed the end, but I didn't mind. I don't think I could have taken much more foreshadowing. His grip on my hand tightened, and then he impulsively pulled me into a firm embrace. His strong arms reminded me so much of my father, my breath was stolen.

"I love you, Kate. I thank God for the chance I had to know you."

Had? I thought mentally, a second too late. I could feel myself beginning to fade. I was being pulled back. I willed myself to stay, but it took a lot of concentration. "I have to go," I said into his shoulder.

He nodded against me. "I know. Godspeed, Kate."

"Thank you for everything. I love you too . . . Dad." I don't know what possessed me to add the last part. But his aura showed me that he was pleased. It was the last thing I saw. His arms evaporated around me, and I was falling. The sounds of the storm vanished. My eyes were already rolling back into my head.

Patrick grunted as he caught me, his words already trailing away into my dreams. "I've got you, Kate. I've got you . . ."

***

Present Day
Kate Bennett
New Mexico, United States

I knew I was in the warehouse long before I opened my eyes. I could hear the echo that filled the spacious room, ringing off the ceiling and walls as Toni talked easily.

"I mean, come on man, just once. You can watch me the whole time!"

"You're fast, Toni. Too fast." Patrick sounded amused but adamant. He was also right beside me; that was the most important thing.

"I wouldn't steal from my best friend, all right? I want to see what it looks like on me!"

"Don't you have anyone else you can bother?"

"There's no one else I'd rather bother."

"That's supposed to make me feel loved?"

"Definitely. So! How much longer, do you think? She's already been out . . . three hours longer than the others."

"She'll be awake soon," Patrick assured him, unworried.

"You sound a bit chipper about the whole thing."

"This is a lot better than last time."

"I can imagine . . . When's she going to wake up?"

"Toni—"

"I'm awake," I groaned, peeling my eyes open to stare blearily up at Toni, who was sitting near my feet.

He grinned. "Kate! Welcome back."

Patrick's hand brushed my arm. I rolled my head to meet his stare. "Are you feeling all right?"

"Yeah. I think my body knew what to expect this time." I pushed up into a sitting position, grateful for Patrick's supporting hand against my back. I glanced around the room, noting we were the only ones present. "All the others made it back?" I asked.

Toni nodded. "Yep. They were only out for about an hour and a half."

Apparently they'd already cleaned up their mattresses too; we'd laid them out before the lesson began, knowing we'd need a place to rest and readjust to our proper time.

Patrick was rubbing my back absently. "How long did you stay?"

"Almost an hour this time, I think."

Toni whistled lowly. "It's almost creepy, you know that? Knowing you could go back and watch my death or something. Eerie."

"Toni?"

"Patty, you need to learn some new words."

"Like, 'go away, Toni'?"

"I think you mastered those too."

"Please?" I put in. "Can you call my grandma and let her know everything went okay?"

He sighed deeply before standing. "If I must, I must."

"You must," Patrick said.

Toni stuck his tongue out at his partner before spinning on his heel and marching toward the double doors.

I twisted around and Patrick's hand fell from my back. I sat with crossed legs, facing Patrick where he sat. I immediately noticed the envelope from his father, the flap lifted partially. "You read it?"

His head dipped once. "Yes. Have you?"

"No. He wrote it in the house." I hesitated. "He let me read yours, though," I admitted at last.

He almost smiled. "I knew he would."

"You're not upset?"

An eyebrow rose. "Should I be?"

"No, of course not." My fingers wandered to his and he scooped them up easily. "The things you said . . . they were beautiful. Thank you."

His cheeks glowed with color. "They were still inadequate." He released his breath and lifted the envelope, passing it to me.

"Are you sure?" I asked.

He nodded. "Very."

I had to pull my fingers away from his to take the envelope, and the action applied pressure to the thin cut on my palm. I winced, fingers flinching back from the discomfort reflexively.

"What?" Patrick asked, brow furrowed.

"It's just a scratch," I assured him, bringing my palm up for closer inspection. The cut was pink and thin, curved at the end, like a sharp hook.

Patrick leaned in, his hand gently reaching to curl carefully around my wrist. I let him get a good look at the light graze, but my tone was dismissive. "It's not bad. I'd just forgotten about it. I got it from your dad's podium."

He shook his head slightly, but he wasn't disagreeing with my analysis—he was just marveling. "It's so strange. I know you were there, but . . . this is physical evidence. It's almost absurd." He frowned, perhaps bothered that injury was possible in the past.

I spoke to pull him away from that line of thought, before he could get lost in needless worry. "Your dad's letter wasn't evidence enough?" I asked him.

Patrick released his grip on my hand. "It's just weird for me. To picture you there, where I was all along. In a church that was probably destroyed over a hundred years ago."

"You don't know that."

He shrugged a little but didn't bother to voice his opinion.

Duly prompted, I turned my attention back to the envelope. I slipped out the letter, my fingertips knowing instantly that this paper was special. From a different age. An object was pulled out along with the folded page. It was golden and would have fallen to the floor if Patrick's hand hadn't flashed out to catch it. I set aside the envelope and he dropped the object onto my palm.

It was an intricately decorated ring. The metal was scratched, indicating its considerable age. It was in impressive condition, notwithstanding it had just jumped two centuries.

"The family ring," Patrick told me. "In the family since the late 1500s. One of my regrets was never knowing what happened to it. I understood why he didn't give it to me before the war, but I never saw him give it to Sean, during the time I spent with him as a Guardian. Now I know why I never saw it—he'd already given it to you."

"To you," I disagreed. I lowered the letter to my bent leg and wriggled my free fingers, urging him to give me his hand. He rolled his bright eyes, allowing me to slip ring onto his middle finger. "It's a little big," I stated unnecessarily.

"The O'Donnells used to be sturdier men, I guess."

"Is that a cross on it?" I asked, focusing on the design beyond the scuff marks.

He nodded. "It's a family tradition to be religious." He tossed his chin toward the letter. "Are you going to read it?"

I gave him a frown for rushing this special moment but obediently picked it up, sensing he'd suffered enough attention for the moment. I pulled back the stiff folds and started to read. I sensed Patrick shift over to sit beside me on the mattress, his arm coming around to support me as he read over my shoulder.

My Dearest Patrick,

I will follow your example by first reminding you of my ever-present love. My heart is full of many emotions, but my love is most prominent of all. I am still unsure of all the things I will eventually say to you, to succeed in driving you away. I want you to know without a doubt that I didn't mean any of them. From what Kate tells me, the words will be strong and hard to forgive. But I hope you will find it in your heart to do so.

Kate is a marvelous young woman. Treasure her always. When you said she was your heaven, I believe you were absolutely right. I am comforted to know you have someone so wonderful, so full of love, to share your life with. Though it pains me to know I shall never again see you in person, I feel a measure of the joy you must feel, being in her world. I am forever grateful for that, as I know your mother will be when I eventually share these things with her.

The news of Sean's fate troubles me deeply. I am at a loss for what I should say to you about this issue. Though I know you have every right to hate him, after all he has done to you, Kate, and so many others, I feel urged to remind you that he is your brother. You cannot hate what you love. I know these words seem foolish, but there is truth therein. Instead of hate, I would have you choose to love him. Nurture that love until only love remains. Perhaps I am preaching again—it is Sunday. But you knew that. You were late again. Maybe that's why today stuck out in your mind. For all I know, you may have remembered my strange behavior. Running in from the church after being in there for near a half hour—only to dash upstairs to my study and then eventually run back out into the pouring rain.

I cannot seem to focus my thoughts. I would apologize,

but you know it happens to me frequently. I hope you will allow me my dose of senility. I do not wish to keep Kate waiting for long. So I will suffice myself by once again expressing my love, and I appreciate all of the choices and sacrifices you will make. I hope you are remembering to pray. There is One who understands all your needs. I would hope that I taught you enough that you would go to Him. You have many worries on your shoulders, and though I wish I could meet with you face-to-face, help is never far. Remember that.

My family has always been my greatest earthly treasure, and I am comforted to know you understand the worth of love.

I would love to hear from you again, Patrick. Until such a time as that is possible, I will rest in the knowledge that you are well, happy, and loved. And not just by Kate.

My deepest love forever,

Da

I lowered the letter, glancing over at Patrick. Tears were in his eyes, but he met my smile. I lifted a hand to his knee, rubbing gently. And in that perfect moment, nothing needed to be said.

fourteen

Jack was waiting for us in the driveway after school on Wednesday. The twins were so used to seeing him by now that they weren't the least bit fazed by the sight of him. But I was instantly on my guard.

Though he had a smile on his face when he urged the twins to hurry inside for some cookies, I could read between the lines. He was afraid. Nervous? Something was definitely wrong. I waited until I heard the twins disappeared into the house before popping the trunk. While Toni struggled to hop out, Jack caught and held my door as I dragged my backpack free of the car. Toni was straightening behind the car, forcing the lid of the trunk back down.

As soon as I was clear Jack closed my door. He grabbed my arm and pulled me toward the house. Jack was already pulling me toward the house, but he didn't start explaining until Toni was at my heels and close enough to listen in.

His words were clipped. "Jason came over after his classes. He saw a Demon parked on the street a few houses back, just watching the house." My stomach clenched. I tried to get a look at the road, but Jack was shielding me too well. Jack continued in a rush. "As soon as Jason made eye contact, the Demon drove off."

"Was he alone?" Toni asked, coldly professional. I hated it when he got serious—it scared me.

Jack nodded once. "But that doesn't mean he doesn't have friends. The Demon Lord would never send just one."

Unless it's a Demon hoping to make a million dollars. I swallowed stiffly.

We were to the porch now. "What are we going to do?" I asked in a whisper. I hoped they wouldn't hear the tremble it held.

"Not much we *can* do," Jack muttered ruefully. "Your grandma doesn't want to scare the twins by moving back to Bourke in a single afternoon. She's going to see if she can take them somewhere to spend the night—a friend's house or something of the sort."

"Have you called Patrick?" Toni asked, already whipping out his phone.

Jack shook his head. "Haven't had the time. This happened about five minutes ago." He jerked the door open, releasing me only to wave me inside. I stepped into the entryway, heard the twins clamoring for the cookies in the kitchen. Everything seemed normal. Only it wasn't. Everything had changed.

Toni was invisible, already murmuring quickly into his phone. I tried to tune into the words he was saying. "Patrick, we have a possibly problematic situation. Jason saw a Demon outside Kate's house . . . Just a couple minutes ago. No, he's not there now . . . She's okay. She's inside. Jack's here." He walked into the living room and the excited voices of the twins drowned him out easily.

I wanted to follow him, but Jack was speaking to me again. "I tried to get your grandma to relax a little, but it wasn't working. Maybe you want to give it a try?"

I nodded once. "Where's Jason?"

Jack looked toward the kitchen. "In there. I'm calling him

my godson for now. You go on in—I'm going to give a call to Claire, see if she can come over too."

I took a steadying breath and followed his instructions. I walked to the back of the house, stepping into the warm kitchen with a fake smile on my face. Jason was sitting at the table, talking with the twins, but he was distracted. He glanced up at my entrance, and Grandma pretended to introduce us. Her voice shook minutely, but the twins didn't seem to notice.

Introductions past, Grandma focused on the twins. "How would you two like to spend the night at a friend's house?"

Josie blinked. "Seriously? In the middle of the week?"

Grandma forced a shrug. "Why not?"

"Because it's a school night," Jenna pointed out.

"So? Your friends go to school too, don't they?"

"Can we really?" Josie nearly gasped.

"Make some calls. See if anyone will take you two ruffians." Her voice was rough, and she wasn't meeting my eye. Her aura was overwhelming, impossible to decipher.

Things happened in a blur. The twins spent ten minutes arguing about who they could go stay with. Jack wandered back into the kitchen, offering Grandma a slight nod that told her the twins could be split up. That problem solved, the twins eagerly left to pack their bags. Grandma followed them without a word.

I sat at the table, my bag slumped against one of the legs. I had an uneaten cookie sitting in front of me, but I couldn't make myself touch it. I stared at the wall, stung by Grandma's blatant silent treatment.

Jason offered me a sympathetic look before returning to guard duty at the front of the house. Jack soon joined him, but I wasn't alone for long. Toni walked into the kitchen, snatching up a cookie on his way to the table. He sat beside me, watching my blank face while he chewed.

He swallowed the bite of cookie. "Are you okay?" he asked.

I sent him a look that needed no translation.

He grunted, then took another bite. He spoke through the crumbs. "It's not that bad, you know. It was only one Demon."

"What if he comes back?"

He shrugged. "Then we'll be ready for him. Kate, this is what we do. A little faith, please." He gestured with his chin at my cookie. "You going to eat that? No? Mind if I do?" He grabbed it up before I could open my mouth, finishing the entire thing in one bite.

Jack returned abruptly. "Toni, when will Patrick get here?"

Toni struggled to speak around the gooey mouthful. "Any second, I guess. He was almost to the warehouse to check in with Dr. Radcliffe and the other Seers. I doubt he's following the speed limit, either. Or any other laws of the road, for that matter."

Jack was thoughtful. "Claire is on her way too, and she's bringing Maddy."

"So what's the plan?" Toni asked. "The twins are going somewhere . . ."

"To stay with friends for the rest of the night," I supplied, hoping that the action of speech would make me feel more proactive.

"And the way your grandmother packs, they'll be ready any minute," Jack added.

"Separate houses?" Toni clarified.

Jack nodded. "I figured you and me could each take one."

The invisible Guardian pulled a face. "Just what I always wanted—to attend a little girls' sleepover."

"Are we blowing this out of proportion?" I had to ask.

They both turned to look at me but didn't bother to reply.

Patrick arrived just in time to see the twins off. Grandma was herding them out to the van, Jack and Toni right behind them, both completely invisible.

Patrick conferred with Jason by the front door, their voices loud in the deserted house. Jason caught Patrick up on all the details we knew, also informing him that Claire was on her way with more backup.

I remained at the table, my head balanced in my hands. I heard Patrick's shoes scuff as he stepped into the kitchen behind me. He hung back for a few long seconds.

He spoke quietly from the doorway. "Kate, everything's going to be okay."

I didn't move. I didn't visibly react at all.

His already stressed voice grew more worried. "Kate?"

Reluctantly I lifted my head, but I didn't turn to him. I just continued to stare at the wall, "I don't know why I'm so surprised. I mean, we knew this would happen. You knew it would. I just didn't think . . . my own house . . ."

He came up behind me, his hands settling over my tense shoulders. "Nothing has happened yet. We're just taking added precautions."

"Should we tell them?" I asked softly. "About the reward?"

He didn't answer right away. "I'm not sure. I don't think it makes a real difference at this point."

There was a knock on the door, and Jason was quick to answer it. We heard the murmur of voices, then Maddy's thick Texan accent overrode the rest. "I'll keep watch with you out here."

Seconds later my protectors were filing into the kitchen. Claire was in the lead, with Alex, Ashley, and Hanif right behind.

"Thank you for coming," Patrick said quickly, still gripping my shoulders. "I realize you're busy training—"

Alex cut him off. "We can run through our plans here."

"It'll be a nice change, not having Radcliffe's constant droning," Ashley added.

Hanif offered me a small smile, as if he understood what I was going through.

Claire was speaking to Patrick. "Should we move her?"

He shook his head. "I don't know where we'd go."

"A hotel?" she pressed.

I cringed at the thought of abandoning my home to the Demons, but I didn't have to voice my thoughts before Patrick was speaking again.

"No point. If the Demons are watching the house, they'll only follow us. If they aren't watching, they still know this is her home—they'd be patient. They'd wait until we came back, when we weren't as prepared. At least here we have an advantage. There are more variables in a public area. If it comes to a fight, we've got a better chance here."

"Maybe we should relocate her permanently, then," Claire offered without pause.

I couldn't keep my head from jerking around to look at her.

Patrick's voice was firm behind me. "That's not an option. We don't have the time to move them, their belongings—"

"Time? Belongings? You don't grab your things in a fire—in an emergency. It doesn't take long to drive away. We could be out of the state—"

Alex broke in. "Patrick's right—the Demons are going to keep coming. But today they lost their element of surprise. Strategically, it's better for us to remain here. At least for tonight. Maybe in the morning we can come up with something better."

"Hopefully the danger is minimal," Hanif commented.

No one said anything for the length of a few heartbeats, then Alex turned to Patrick.

"Do you think it was a scout?" he asked.

"I'm not sure," my Guardian returned easily. "But the twins have been relocated for the night. Toni and Jack are with them now."

"And the grandmother?" Ashley asked.

"With the twins, for now," Patrick said.

Claire was shaking her head. "I don't like it. We shouldn't all stay here. Patrick and Maddy should take Kate to a motel for the night, just to be safe, and the rest of us could stay here and ambush them."

Alex disagreed. "We can't keep dividing ourselves up. We'll become weaker."

"If it was a scout," Hanif said slowly, "does that mean the Demon Lord is planning an all-out attack? We wouldn't be able to withstand that, would we?"

The kitchen was silent. No one had a positive answer for his question, so none was offered.

That's when my phone started to ring. I pulled it out of my pocket quickly, conscious that I was the center of attention. I looked at the display and saw it was Lee. I flipped the phone open and pushed back from the table in the same motion.

"Hey, Lee," I said, trying to sound like everything was fine. "What's up?"

She didn't even say hello. "Toni texted me about the Demon. Are you okay?"

"Yeah. Yeah, I'm fine." I felt Patrick move away from me as I walked from the room. I wanted some privacy, mostly because that would make it easier to have an honest conversation.

"Don't lie to me," Lee warned. "Look, my mom's out of town. You're coming to my house."

"I am?"

"Heck yes you are. Bring along any of the bodyguards you want. Your grandma can come too."

I set my hand on the banister, looking up the tall staircase. "Lee, thanks for the offer, but I don't want to compromise you."

"What sort of freak military talk is that? Just get your fanny over here!"

"Seriously, Lee. I might need to fall back on that later, but I'll be fine tonight. I've got plenty of protection right now."

"Should I have called Patrick?"

"No. Really, I'm fine."

"Okay . . . I'll be over in about ten minutes."

"What?"

"You think I'm going to abandon you in your time of need? I can bring my mom's car."

"Lee—"

"See you soon!"

Before I could start another protest she hung up. I peeled the phone away from my ear, shaking my head at her flashing name.

"Is Lee all right?" Patrick asked, directly behind me.

I whirled around; he was instantly apologetic. "No, it's not you," I overrode him, palm rubbing against my forehead. "I'm just jumpy." I blew out my breath. "She's coming over."

He frowned. "That's probably not the best idea."

"Yeah. I tried telling her that."

***

Lee had fallen asleep on my bed a long time ago. I was lying next to her, but I honestly didn't understand how she'd managed to find sleep. Claire was sitting at my desk, and though she wasn't exactly staring at us, it was still really weird.

Lee and Grandma were probably the only people asleep in the house. I knew Patrick and the others would be wide awake. Jason, Maddy, Ashley, Alex—they were all keeping watch around the house. It had already been one of the longest nights of my life, and it was barely one in the morning. Lee had brought over *Anne of Green Gables,* and we'd watched well into the second movie before she'd finally announced she was ready for bed. She'd fallen asleep almost instantly, leaving me and Claire alone in a dark room.

I wasn't able to stay there for long. I finally sat up, and Claire glanced over at me.

I explained in a whisper. "I need a drink. I'll just be downstairs."

She nodded once but stayed where she was. I slipped out

of the sheets, straightening my pajamas as I stepped into the dark hall. My hand slid over the banister as I moved downstairs. When I neared the bottom a figure stepped out of the front room to meet me.

Patrick's expression was hard to make out in the darkness. "Are you all right?" he whispered as soon as he realized who I was.

I paused on the last step, directly in front of him. "I can't sleep."

"Does Lee snore?" he asked, trying to joke.

I cracked a smile. "Only when she's asleep." I hesitated. "Have you checked in with Jack and Toni?"

Patrick nodded at once. "Jack just texted me about Jenna. She's perfectly safe. Toni says Josie's been asleep since ten."

"That's good." I bit my lower lip, desperate to avoid going back upstairs, but drawing a blank on any intelligent questions to ask.

He sensed my internal dilemma. "Jason keeps nodding off. We could use another Seer, if you feel up to it."

I agreed at once.

He almost smiled, but the action carried a regretful edge. Or maybe just tired. I wished I could see his aura to know for sure.

We wandered into the front room, which was filled with silver moonlight mingled with yellow light from the streetlamp across the street. Jason was sitting on the couch, rubbing his eyes behind his glasses. He looked up when we entered, his aura flashing with guilty colors. "Sorry, Kate—studying for finals has been killing me."

"Don't worry about it. I can take over."

"Are you sure?" he asked.

"Of course. One of us should get some sleep."

He stood stiffly. "Thanks. I appreciate it."

I told him he could find a quilt in the family room, and he

shuffled out, unbuckling a sheathed knife from his belt as he went.

A quick glance to Patrick's waist showed me that he had at least two blades of his own. Seeing the leather hilt on his largest dagger brought back images of my dream. Sean had continued to haunt me every night, though I was almost getting used to it. We talked, he killed my grandpa, my grandpa asked me to save him, and I killed Sean; it was sickeningly simple.

"Kate?" Patrick sounded concerned.

My eyes flickered up to his. "It's nothing." I moved to sit on the couch where Jason had been, grateful that the back was low so I didn't have to crane my neck to see out the large window.

Patrick lowered himself down on the opposite end, letting the plush arm support his back.

"Patrick, can I ask a stupid question?"

He half smiled. "I doubt it. No stupid questions, right?"

I smiled briefly in return. "I was just curious . . . Why don't Guardians carry guns? I mean, I know that a knife is the only thing that can pierce the Demon's heart and kill him, but . . . *They* carry guns. Wouldn't it even the playing field for you to have them?"

Patrick was nodding. "Certainly not a stupid question. But easy enough to answer. Guns equal stray bullets, and Guardians refuse to increase a human's danger. Demons don't care about harming an innocent, so they use guns freely. In fact, most prefer guns over a knife, simply because, well, why bring to a fight the one weapon with the power to end them?"

"Makes sense. But you know how to use a gun?"

"Of course. We practice with them; we just don't carry them."

He waited, but when I didn't persist in questioning him, he turned his gaze out to the quiet street. I followed his example a short second later, and we stared outside for a couple minutes in silence. I thought about going back upstairs to tell Claire where I'd gone, but I was too comfortable to move. She'd probably realize I was with Patrick and not worry about my prolonged absence.

"Where are the others?" I asked.

Patrick waited to answer until after a slow-moving car had ambled past. Even then, he didn't look at me. "Alex and Maddy are making rounds around the house. Ashley is in the laundry room, keeping an eye on the garage, and Hanif is in the kitchen, watching the back door." He glanced my way. "He's probably eating you out of house and home too. For being such a skinny kid . . ." His words drifted to silence, gaze locked outside.

"Are you tired?" I asked.

He shook his head minutely, eyes unwavering. "No."

I curled my legs up on the couch, pulling my knees to my chest. My shoulder dug into the back of the couch, and I admit it—I was watching him a lot more than I was watching for Demons.

"You're wearing your ring," I commented suddenly.

His eyes dipped down, brushing over his right hand. His fingers tightened into a fist. "I debated wearing it at all, until I can get it sized. But . . ."

"It looks good on you."

"Thank you."

I sighed loudly, lowering my chin onto my knees. "I'm sorry."

He turned toward me again. "For what?"

"I can't be quiet for more than two minutes."

The corner of his mouth twitched. "More like *one* minute."

I grinned in the semi darkness, and it felt good. "I'd be horrible on a stakeout."

"I'll keep that in mind."

He went back to staring out the window.

I kept staring at him.

His strong jaw and serious eyes were in conflict with his untidy hair, which hinted at an easiness he certainly wasn't feeling. One arm was poised on the back edge of the couch, the other slightly bent and resting against one leg. I wanted more than anything to be wrapped in those arms, but I sensed that he wouldn't feel now was an appropriate time for something frivolous like that. The light from outside highlighted his somewhat stern features, but even in stoic stillness, he was the most heart-stopping figure I'd ever laid eyes on.

"You're so incredible." I'd whispered the words without thought. Amazingly, I didn't blush when he turned his head to look at me.

He could have said so many things, but in the end he settled for, "Kate, that barely broke a minute."

I smiled, and we both turned back to the window.

Still, it wasn't long before I voiced my newest thoughts—a subject I'd wanted to broach but hadn't been able to form into words. I kept my eyes focused outside, unable to keep the hope out of my voice. "Patrick, what happens to Sean if the Demon Lord is killed in the past? If he never became a Seer, would it change Sean's fate? Would he—?" The weight of Patrick's stare forced me to glance his way, effectively cutting off my words.

His expression was somber, his eyes dark on mine. "The Demon Lord didn't turn Sean into a Demon. My . . . brother did that all on his own." Patrick bit his bottom lip, inclining his upper body toward me, lowering his voice even further. I felt his warm fingers curl around mine below my line of vision, our hands balanced together on my lap.

Patrick continued honestly. "I don't know how it will affect your grandfather's death—if he'll still be alive. Or if killing the Demon Lord will bring back countless others he's killed over the years. I don't pretend to understand something as convoluted as changing the past. Sean will still be a Demon, though. I'm sure of that. And there's a good chance that once the Demon Lord's gone . . ." His eyes flickered away, his jaw stiffening. "I won't even know Sean became a Demon. I won't know where he is in the world, and he won't know where I am. I won't know I failed him . . ."

I squeezed his hand and our eyes met again. My voice was quiet but firm. "Patrick, you're right about one thing: no one forced Sean to become a Demon. Not the Demon Lord, and definitely not you. You can't keep blaming yourself for his mistakes."

I frowned, thoughts switching to a new level. "But how can you be so sure Sean *won't* change? That he won't become a Demon? The Demon Lord is the one who forced me to go back and convince your father to force you both to war, so Sean *could* become a Demon. If the Demon Lord hadn't done that . . ."

I felt my face go pale in an instant, a new thought occurring to me. A horrifying thought. Patrick watched the sudden change in my mood with concern. "Patrick, if I don't journey back and convince your father to send you both away, you won't join the United Irishmen. Neither of you will. And if you don't, you would never choose to be a Guardian. You said yourself you only did it to protect Sean." My panic was rising, entering my voice and speeding up my words. "You never would have chosen this life, because you wouldn't have had to protect Sean in the war. We would never meet. I'll never know you.

"But I'd still become a Seer. The Demon Lord didn't cause the accident with my parents. But Romero and Selena never would have come after me because the Demon Lord wouldn't have been around to care about me. I never would have become such a focus for the Demons, but . . . I wouldn't have you. If they succeed, I'm going to lose you."

Everything was unraveling. My whole life, it seemed, would become completely altered if the Demon Lord was killed.

That's when I felt Patrick's free hand—the one not clinging to my now cold fingers—come gently against the side of my face, thumb stroking earnestly along my jaw. His blue eyes were bright and fierce, his voice throbbing. "Kate Bennett, I'm not going to lose you. I refuse to believe we could be separated in such a way. It doesn't make sense. Things can't change that drastically—that thoroughly."

I blinked quickly. "But there are consequences, Patrick. Always. To every action. If they kill the Demon Lord, things *will* change."

Patrick's forehead tipped against mine, his hand slipping around the back of my neck to hold me in place. "*This* won't change," he whispered fervently. "The love I feel for you is too real to just disappear, no matter what happens with the Demon Lord. *We* control our fate. I will never believe anything else. Some things are too complicated for comprehension, but this I know: I love you. And whether or not the Demon Lord is killed, whether or not Sean becomes a Demon, I will find you. I *will* become a Guardian. I know it. Because becoming a Guardian is my only path to you, and so it is the only path I can take."

My heart was hammering. Tears were clouding my vision. But as much as his words warmed me, I wasn't completely comforted. "So you believe we're born with our stories already written? You believe everything is set in stone?"

I felt his head shift against mine and shake in the negative. His voice grew firm. "Not set in stone. I'll never believe destiny can't be dictated by us, by our desires and actions. The future isn't set in stone, and for people like you, even the past is alterable. But if for some reason things change, and we're not together . . . I would change my destiny, Kate, if it keeps you in my life. I would do anything—sacrifice anything—to have you. Even become a Guardian."

I fought to keep my low voice from cracking. "But you won't remember me. If the Demon Lord's death really triggers all of this . . . you'll have no memory of me. How will you know to become a Guardian? How will you find me if you don't know I exist?"

Patrick's two hands slid to cup my face, his thumbs brushing at the tears that leaked from my blurry eyes.

His eyes were narrowed, locked on mine. "Because I am meant to find you, Kate. And you're meant to find me. The Demon Lord can't change that. A distance of two hundred years can't change that. If we are somehow separated by all this—by the Demon Lord's death, or whatever else comes at us—I'll find you. You have my word."

His words were spoken too sincerely to doubt. He was completely confident, and it would have been impossible for me to distrust both his love and faith that we would be together in the end—even if my thoughts were still spinning in unanswerable questions, unending circles of actions and reactions, choices and consequences.

I closed my eyes briefly, relishing his touch. Then I opened my eyes to stare him down, my hands wrapping around his wrists to keep him close. "You better not leave me, Patrick O'Donnell. Because I swear I would come after you." His lips quirked into a half grin at my firmly spoken threat, and I hurried to finish. "I don't know why you picked me to love, out of everyone out there, but I'm *not* going to give you up. Even if I lose my memory of you, I promise I'll never lose my love. I'll find you too."

"Then how can we lose?" He continued to grin freely, and that's when I leaned in and kissed him.

We passed a quiet minute that way, until he groaned and pulled away from me, hands still cradling my face. "You're a terrible distraction, Kate. It's final. I'm never bringing you on a stakeout. How am I supposed to be an alert Guardian when you keep doing that?"

"What?" I asked, smiling widely. "This?"

My lips barely brushed his before he pushed my shoulders back. "Yes, *that*. Now, would you please let me get back to protecting you?"

"Sure. Want me to leave?" I teased lightly.

His eyes darkened. "Don't you dare."

And so I stayed beside him, our fingers entwined as we looked out the bay window.

It was almost two in the morning when Patrick's phone vibrated. My eyes flickered away from the empty street to watch him read the incoming text. The light from his phone lit up his face for a moment as he took in the words, then he made a fast reply. He lowered the phone and returned to watching out the window.

"That was Toni," he murmured without prompting. "He just wanted to make sure we were still all right."

"Is Josie okay?"

"She's fine."

We sat in silence for several minutes—we hadn't seen a car for over a half hour now. My eyelids were beginning to get heavy, but I wasn't going to leave Patrick.

His phone went off again. He glanced down and I closed my eyes, hoping to quench the stinging while he was distracted; I didn't want him to pressure me into going back to bed.

"What . . . ?" he muttered distractedly.

I opened my eyes and looked to him. His forehead was wrinkled in confusion.

"What's wrong?" I asked softly.

He didn't answer—just handed me his phone. I scanned the text, noting it was from Alex.

Looks good in back. What about

It cut off there, an unfinished question. I looked up at Patrick, who was looking between me and our somewhat limited view of the front yard. "Maybe he sent it on accident?" I offered.

"Maybe . . ." Patrick reached for the phone and I handed it back.

We waited in silence, expecting another text to follow the first.

It didn't.

After two minutes Patrick rose to his feet. "Stay here. I'm going to check the back." He glanced back at me. "Do you have your phone?"

I shook my head. It was on the nightstand in my bedroom, charging.

Judging by the expression on his face he'd already guessed the answer. He kept his voice assuring. "I'll be right back."

I kept an eye on him as he wandered out of the room into the darkened entryway. Some light flickered in through the slim window beside the front door, but even with that he was just a silhouette. A shadow. I lost sight of him when he moved around the corner, headed for the kitchen.

I looked back out the window, trying to tell my heart that it had no reason to be beating like it was. Nothing was wrong. *He wouldn't have left you if he thought something was wrong.*

I heard Patrick's voice, unintelligible but unmistakable, and Hanif whispered something back. A door opened and closed—silence. My heart continued to ignore me; it was pounding now.

I tried to focus on the empty front yard, on the street beyond it. I needed to keep watch. Not only was I protecting myself, my grandma, and my home, but I was also protecting Lee, Patrick, Claire, and all the Seers who were willing to sacrifice so much for me.

The feeling came suddenly—completely overwhelming: I needed to get behind the couch.

I'd never experienced anything as poignant as that single, overruling impression. I needed to hide. I didn't stop to question; the feeling was too powerful to ignore. I pushed off the couch, only to sink to my knees on the carpet. I slithered into the small space between the wall and the sofa, succeeding in getting all my limbs in behind me. Curled up on the floor in this awkward position, I allowed myself one moment to feel ridiculous. I might have even convinced myself to climb back out, especially when I heard the footsteps coming toward me.

It was probably Patrick. That was the logical assumption. He was coming back. If he found me crouched back here, he'd probably think I was insane. And even if it wasn't him, it was probably only Hanif, Jason, or Ashley. Or maybe it was Claire, and I'd missed her coming down the stairs. Heck, it could have been my grandma.

I heard a muffled whine, followed by a low growl. "Where is she? Where's her room?"

It wasn't a voice I recognized. I swallowed hard, my stomach dropping as I realized how close that deep voice was. In the doorway?

A second voice, even deeper than the first, spoke quickly. "Upstairs, you fool. I tell you, we don't need him."

"Insurance is never a bad thing," the first argued.

"That didn't stop you from killing the others," the second voice pointed out.

A woman's voice, high yet dark came next. "Oh, just bring him."

The first man almost chuckled. "I haven't tortured a Seer for so long. I've missed it. They're always so pathetic."

"I prefer the Guardians myself," the woman said. "You can kill them again and again, and they never die."

"Well, she has plenty of both," the deepest voice said. "So get moving!"

I heard them on the stairs. I paled. They were going to find Lee!

Though it was beyond tempting to stay here against the wall, I knew that wasn't possible. Not when my best friend was about to be surrounded by at least three Demons. Demons who'd already killed. Was that possible? I felt sick at the thought. Had they really killed someone tonight—here, at my house, because of me? And they had a hostage. Who?

I squeezed out from behind the couch, my body shaking as I stepped toward the entryway. Just as I placed my first foot carefully against the wooden floor a hand shot out from the darkness, slapping over my mouth.

fifteen

I was too breathless to scream, which turned out to be a good thing. It was Jason—I could tell by the glint off his glasses. He had one finger against his lips, urging me to be silent. He retracted his hand the moment he knew I'd understood the message.

He mouthed the words, not daring to whisper. *Go hide.*

I shook my head. *Lee!*

He frowned, pointing to himself. *I'll help her.*

I didn't get the chance to form a reply. There was a shout upstairs, followed by a scream—Lee. I bolted away from Jason's side, ignoring his groping fingers. I darted up the stairs, taking them two at a time despite the darkness. He didn't follow me. I hoped he was going for help.

I almost tripped on a body at the top of the stairs. I couldn't see who it was, but he had short hair and he was long and skinny. He was moaning, clutching his forehead. Hanif? I didn't wait around to find out. I jumped over him and gripped my door frame, almost swinging into my room. I'd never seen it so chaotic.

My window let in limited light, but it was enough to see the fights going on. Lee was on the bed, being crushed by a large

Demon, who was trying to wrap his arms around her wriggling form. She was screaming and cursing, trying to get free.

Claire was in front of my closet, grappling with the Demon woman while another Demon came at her from the side. Even as I watched he used a knife to slash at her face, forcing a shriek out of her and causing her fists to falter.

What surprised me most of all was the presence of a fourth person—one who had been silent downstairs. He was standing in the middle of the room, unsure of where he was needed most. He was wearing a cowboy hat, and he had an aura. I assumed he was a Seer.

He saw me.

I was running for the bed before the Seers could decide to come after me. I crouched on the mattress and shoved uselessly at the Demon on top of Lee. "Get off of her!" I yelled, not that I expected him to obey the command.

Lee managed to poke her head out of the sheets. Her eyes widened in fear as she got her first look at her large attacker.

The man in the cowboy hat was suddenly shouting, his voice almost squeaky. "It was a decoy! That's not Kate Bennett. *That's* her!"

Suddenly I wasn't in a position to help anyone. The Demon struggling with Lee backhanded her harshly, ceasing her efforts as she reeled in pain. He turned on me, and that's when I realized I'd made a huge mistake in attacking him. I'd broken the barrier that protected a human from a Demon. He could touch me now.

Though I tried to backpedal he was already grabbing my arm, yanking me into his cage-like arms.

I saw Hanif in the doorway, stumbling to his feet at last. He looked dazed. He slumped against the wall next to the bathroom, shaking his head. He almost fell over when Jason flew past him, overshooting my room in his haste to get up here. Jason was still clutching his phone when he made it back to my room. I assumed he'd texted or called for help. He lunged into the fight by going for the cowboy, who was pulling out a handgun.

The two Seers slammed together and I heard the gun drop to the carpet. They were knocked out of my line of sight, so I looked to Claire, who was being overpowered by the two Demons. The man was holding her arms and the woman was spinning a slim knife in each hand. "If only we had more time," she mourned huskily. She shoved one blade into Claire's heart, the other into her stomach. The Guardian cried out before falling to her knees, released only so she could fall onto the floor with the knives still inside her.

The Demons each took a turn kicking her into the corner before they turned to look at me. They didn't seem to care about the fight between their Seer and Jason. The woman smiled at me from across the room, her eyes full of evil. The man didn't look any better.

I clawed at the arms around me, but the Demon's grip didn't loosen. He dragged us both to our feet, forcing me to face his friends.

"One million dollars," the one holding me muttered triumphantly.

It was the last thing he would ever say. Lee screamed for me to duck, and I listened. I felt the hiss of a blade sent sailing through the air, and it stuck into his windpipe above me. His arms relaxed and I almost lost my balance as I lurched away from him.

I whirled around to see Patrick in the doorway, arm just falling, menace in his eyes as he watched the Demon grabbing for the knife in his throat. He didn't get it out on his own—Patrick dived around me and grabbed the hilt, ripping it out of the Demon only to plunge it into his heart, killing him instantly.

As the Demon crumbled to the floor, Patrick grabbed for

my arm, jerking me out of my frozen state and throwing me toward the door.

"Go!" he yelled sharply. "Get out of here!"

His fingers slipped away from my arm and I heard him grunt. The momentum of his shove slammed me against the wall near the door. A streak of color flashed by me the split second after my painful impact, darting from the doorway. I turned to see who it was, but her voice gave her identity away before my eyes could focus.

"Claire!" Maddy cried, going instantly for her Guardian in the corner, everything else forgotten. My eyes followed her briefly but were already flickering to see what was happening to Patrick.

The second male Demon had crashed into Patrick, knocking them both back against my nightstand and the wall behind it. My bedside lamp smashed against the floor, glass shattering against the carpet. The Demon was slamming Patrick's head against the wall, one large hand on his shoulder, the other gripping a fistful of his hair.

Lee was off the bed. She'd picked up a large hardcover book and had darted over to the cowboy Seer, and was whacking it over his head. I thought I saw his knees give out under the impressive blow, but before I could see its full effectiveness the Demon woman was in front of me, up close and personal. The shock of having her near made me jump and reflexively—stupidly—I tried to push away from her. My hands brushed her arms, and she could touch me. Her long nails dug into my cheek and jaw in a split second, while her other hand snaked around my wrist.

She pulled me away from the wall, releasing her agonizing grip on my face only once her arm was tucked firmly around my waist, pinning my hands down at my sides. I tried to squirm away from her, grunting angrily as I struggled. I was facing Patrick now, but he couldn't see me. He probably thought I'd listened to him, that I was already out of the house by now.

He was no longer losing the battle against the Demon. He had traded places with the bigger man, his hands clutched around the Demon's throat as he levered him off the floor, sliding him up against the wall, strangling him. It wouldn't kill him, but it would weaken him—hopefully long enough that Patrick could draw a blade and stab him.

I felt the Demon woman's arm weaken—I was almost free.

And then I felt her knife against my face, slanted across my cheek. It didn't break skin—only hovered less than a breath away, ready to slice me open if I moved. I stilled instantly in her grasp, breathing hard.

"Guardian!" she snapped loudly, her mouth right beside me. "Stop or I'll kill her!"

Patrick's tensed body hardened impossibly further at her words. He looked over his shoulder, his pale face becoming enraged in a split second. But his arms didn't fall.

She threw a glance to Jason and Lee, who I couldn't quite see. "You two as well. Let go of him."

Patrick continued to choke the Demon. "You wouldn't," he hissed between his teeth. "You want the money."

"Drop him!" she commanded again. "I may not kill her, but I swear you won't recognize her when I'm done."

His straining arms wavered, his narrowed eyes locked on us.

Her fingers tightened. I gasped as the point of her blade drew blood from my cheek.

Patrick reacted at once. He released the Demon with a shove, sending him to the floor in a heap. He landed in the broken glass, gasping for breath on his side as he groped at his bruised neck. Though I couldn't see Lee or Jason, I imagined they followed Patrick's lead.

Patrick's whole body trembled as he faced us fully. He held his hands out at his sides, palms exposed. "I'm unarmed," he growled, furious, pointedly not meeting my eye. "Get that away from her."

She didn't reply for a moment. And then her voice was sickly sweet. "I must say, I've never seen *quite* this level of devotion in a Guardian before. You go through Seers so quickly, after all. Why get needlessly attached?" Her fingers flexed again—the tip of the knife went deeper inside me. I whimpered but didn't allow myself to shift away; I didn't want to worsen the damage.

Patrick's hands were balled into fists. "Stop," he ordered darkly.

The quivering emotion in his voice goaded her on. "You like this dog more than your others?" she questioned happily. She was obviously psychotic. The blade began to skirt across my face, never retracting yet never cutting. There was something practiced about her movements, which only deepened my feeling of nausea. The patterns grew more intricate, ghosting around my eyes, across my forehead, over my nose, under my chin. "How wonderfully thrilling," she murmured. So she was sadistic too.

Patrick's teeth were clenched to the breaking point. He was rolling onto the balls of his feet, helpless to move closer for fear of forcing her hand. His eyes were burning with rage. "If you hurt her, I swear, I'll tear you apart."

"Really?" She sounded excited.

"Sandra," the Demon on the floor grunted. "We don't have time for this." He pushed up to his feet, mindful that Patrick was still nearby.

"We can make time," she disagreed. "No one will interrupt us now. Besides, she doesn't really need to be pretty for the Demon Lord to exact his revenge, does she?"

I closed my eyes tightly, unwilling to let Patrick see how close to tears I was. I waited to feel the bite of her blade again, but the haunting whisper continued to explore my face.

Patrick made a guttural sound in his throat.

And then I heard Sandra cry out in distress. My eyes

whipped open and I saw Hanif behind Patrick, forcing a dagger into the male's Demon's heart. I felt the knife falter and slice into my forehead, near my hairline, and then we were both jolted from behind. She released me as she stumbled. Patrick caught my waist and yanked me hard against his body.

I glimpsed Claire standing over the Demon woman; Maddy stood behind them, holding the one of the knives that had been inside her Guardian moments before. Claire gripped the other.

Claire's eyes were ablaze, her front covered in blood. "For that, you die," she spat at the Demon. Maddy pinched her eyes closed and I followed her lead, though Patrick was already twisting me fiercely away.

Sandra screamed feebly, and then she was silent.

I heard pounding footsteps and Jason yelling for Hanif to stop someone. The footsteps banged down the stairs, but before they could have reached the bottom, there was an unexpected thump. It could have only been caused by a body crumpling to the ground.

Patrick's arms were tight around me, one hand pressing my head to rest against his heaving chest, not caring about the blood that would surely transfer to his shirt. He shuddered around me, his voice rasping my name in a mixture of horror and relief.

The cut on my face was stinging, but I didn't want to pull away from him. Not until Lee spoke from beside me. "Geez Louise," she muttered in shock.

I opened my eyes and squirmed in Patrick's grip, until I saw my grandma in her long blue nightgown, standing in the doorway with my grandpa's old handgun. She'd even managed to attach the silencer.

Her face was grim. "Do I dare ask who I just shot?" she asked any of us.

***

I leaned against the edge of the bathroom counter, watching as Patrick washed his hands after bandaging my cut. Thin streams of blood washed down the drain in hypnotic swirls. Lee stood on my other side, gripping my hand tightly. Her aura was surprisingly calm despite everything she'd been through a mere half hour ago. The whole side of her face was either bruised or inflamed from where she'd been struck, but she hardly seemed aware of the pain. It was a small thread in her aura, hardly noticeable as she worried for me.

"Kate, are you sure you're okay? You're still really pale."

Patrick glanced up to catch my reply.

"I'm fine," I whispered dully.

Claire, Jason, and Hanif were gone taking care of the Demon bodies and that of their Seer. The bodies they hadn't taken remained in the garage. I could barely think of them without being overwhelmed with shame and regret. Because they had died for me.

Patrick had found Alex's body in the backyard. He and Maddy had both discovered the side door to the garage, suspiciously ajar. Ashley's body was lying just inside.

Dr. Radcliffe was on his way to collect them, though I wasn't sure what he intended to do with them. Send them back to family? I knew Alex had no relatives left. I hardly knew anything about Ashley, but I doubted she would have come here over the holidays if she had loved ones. The only comfort I had was that—at least in Alex's case—he was with his loved ones now. I could only assume that Ashley was with someone now too.

I let out a shaky breath as Lee rubbed my arm. "Hey, can I get you something to eat? Something with salt, or sugar?"

I shook my head. "I think I'd just throw it back up."

She gave me an understanding look. Patrick shut off the water, gripped the edge of the sink, and spoke in a worn-out whisper. "Lee, you should call Toni. Tell him what happened." He was watching as his knuckles turned white from the strain of his grip. It felt like he was choosing to focus on anything but me.

Lee nodded once while squeezing my hand, before leaving us alone.

I continued to stare at the shower curtain across from me, resisting the urge to dissolve into tears. Being in shock helped hold that sort of thing back, luckily.

Patrick was silent beside me. I expected him to break it eventually, but not in the way he finally did. I heard something that resembled a croak but was more like a gasp. My eyes slid to see him hunched over the sink, his shoulders quaking with dry sobs.

I was so shocked by the sight of his anguish, I hardly knew what to do. I'd never seen him break down before. That was usually my prerogative.

I moved slowly, peeling away from the counter to hesitate at his side. I placed a hand on his back and he shivered at my touch, still panting heavily. "Shh," I whispered soothingly. "Patrick, what's wrong?"

He didn't answer. Maybe he couldn't. His throat sounded tight, the air he managed to get inside his lungs exhaling just as quickly. He was going to hyperventilate. Could Guardians do that?

My fingers stroked his back, my other hand coming to run up and down his arm. "Are you hurt?" I asked, deeply concerned. "What's wrong?"

I swear I heard the counter crack under his weight; the pressure of his crushing hold threatened to rip it from the wall. "I don't know what to do," he finally gasped. "I don't know how to stop this. I don't—"

"Shh," I repeated, trying to gather him into my arms. I laid my head against his shoulder, pushing myself up against him. "Patrick, it's okay. It's over."

"It's not over," he rasped, almost choking on what could have been a hard laugh. "It will never be over. Not until you're gone. And then there won't be a point to it. To anything."

My eyes burned, but I didn't know what to say or how to comfort him. I pressed my lips to his shoulder, moved my hand down his tense arm. His grip on the sink faltered. I took advantage of the momentary lapse by sliding my fingers around his elbow. For a second I thought he would fight me, intent on keeping me shut out. But then his body sagged and he let me get in front of him, my back to the counter. He buried his head in my shoulder, wrapping me in his arms so tightly I could barely breathe. I tried to hold him just as strongly, but I'm sure my feeble arms didn't succeed. I just wanted to calm him down—bring him back to being the Patrick he'd been just a few hours ago. Had we really been flirting in the living room only hours ago? So much had happened since then.

"Why?" He shuddered into me, moaning deeply and breaking up my thoughts. "Why do I have to lose you?"

My whole face scrunched in confusion, pulling uncomfortably against the bandage on my face. My grip on him tightened. "Patrick, what are you talking about? You haven't lost me—I'm right here."

"Now. But not forever. Kate, please don't leave me here alone." His voice sounded so lost, so broken.

My eyes pricked with tears and I pulled him impossibly closer, my arms coming around his bent neck. "I'm not going to leave you, Patrick. I'm *never* going to leave you. Remember? I promised."

He didn't reply right away. He just continued to shake with the energy of his grief—a grief I hardly understood. Why was he falling apart like this? I'd been through worse. We both had.

He whispered so softly I barely heard his words. "Yes, you will."

I frowned. "What?"

"You're going to leave me."

I tangled my fingers in the hair at the back of his head, hoping the feel of my fingers against his skin would help soothe him—assure him of my presence. "Patrick, I'm not going anywhere. I'm not leaving you."

I felt his lips graze my neck, his forehead brushing back into my hair. "But you do. I've seen it."

I tried to pull away from him, to look at his face, but he held me firmly in place. I nearly growled in frustration. "What are you talking about? Seen it? Seen what?"

"The night of your grandfather's funeral," he spoke huskily against my skin. "You came to me. From the future. You told me to change the past. To keep the twins from dying. You said I needed to let you go so I could protect them. You asked me to let you die. How could you ask me to—?" A harsh breath was expelled, his question unspoken, haunting the space between us.

I stopped trying to pull away from him. I tried to wrap my mind around this new information. The fact that he'd seen our future and hadn't told me. He'd seen me basically commit suicide but hadn't bothered to tell me. And the twins? They were going to die? My mind shied away from the very implication. They couldn't die—I wouldn't allow it.

Patrick was still speaking, almost mumbling now. "You said that everything we try fails. That *I'm* going to fail. That I'm not strong enough to protect you. You were covered in blood." His arms flexed around me. "And when you disappeared from my arms, I knew you were dead. I—I can't let you die, Kate." He gulped back a fresh sob. "But it will happen. I know it will—I watched it happen . . ."

My lips parted. It took a full minute before I could force words out, and when I did they were incredibly weak. "Why didn't you tell me this? It's been weeks, Patrick. *Weeks*."

His breath snorted weakly. "I couldn't tell you. I didn't want you to know. I didn't want to give you any ideas. I thought I could change things—save you. Keep you from traveling back . . ."

He didn't have to add the last part. *But it's impossible to change what's already happened.*

But, no. Patrick couldn't believe this was over. He'd said it himself, downstairs. He'd said our fates weren't set in stone. We could control our destinies.

And if he really believed that, I realized, *he wouldn't be in such despair now. He would have told you about your future visit sooner. He was lying to you before. Things* are *set in stone. You're going to die.*

He seemed to notice for the first time how still I'd become. He pulled back swiftly and I saw his tear-streaked face at last. It was contorted into a look of pure torture, his eyes horrified at what he'd done. "Kate, please. Please forgive me. For keeping this from you. For telling you. For letting it happen, I—"

I reached up to touch his face—trace the trails left by his tears. I couldn't explain the calm that had come over me. "There's nothing to forgive. You were doing what you thought was right."

His breathing came even faster now, as if my easy acceptance frightened him more than screams and denials. "I didn't mean to tell you. Let alone like this."

"It's okay," I whispered.

He groaned. "No, it's not. Kate, you shouldn't have to carry this burden."

I shook my head. The few facts I knew kept running through my mind: I was going to die. Patrick had seen it. He didn't think my fate could be changed. I was going to die.

"Kate," Patrick groaned.

"Let's not worry about this right now," I interrupted unhurriedly, my eyes on his. "Tonight's been . . . We're both here, and we're both alive. I can't . . . I can't be freaking out about the twins right now. I . . . I can't worry about this right now. Please?"

He didn't answer right away. It was obvious he wanted to talk it out—flush out my true feelings and convince me there was nothing to worry about. But I knew better than that.

Patrick knew that this—my death—was inevitable.

My steady gaze must have convinced him I was stable, though. At least emotionally sound enough to discuss all the implications later. The night had been long enough already; it had changed everything.

He bowed his head to escape my steady stare. "All right," he breathed shakily, agreeing to put off the discussion—for now.

But as we held each other tightly, I knew the conversation was still going on in our minds.

sixteen

The cleanup of the house took the rest of the night and into the morning. The twins went straight to school from their respective sleeping places, so at least I didn't have to worry about them seeing a bullet hole in the wall by the front door, let alone the blood both inside and outside of the house. I didn't want to go to school myself, but in the interest of convincing Patrick that the news of my imminent death hadn't completely disturbed me, I went.

I was distracted and distant in class. Patrick was silent as well, though he asked me every now and again if I wanted to go home. I shook my head every time, because I knew going home would just make me think of the six lives lost there last night, most poignant being those of Alex and Ashley. Trudging through school was nothing compared to the torture of being in my own home.

I didn't hear a word any teacher spoke. I was concentrating on everything Patrick had told me last night.

He'd seen me die. Weeks ago he'd listened to my last words, held me in his arms while I bled out . . . While I died. I was going to die.

I was going to die.

Death was something every living thing had to come to terms with. But usually one didn't get this much warning, this kind of detailed information. Thinking of my fate didn't make for a cheerful morning or afternoon. And to think that Patrick had been dealing with this since Grandpa's funeral . . . Every time he'd looked into my eyes, held my hand, he'd been thinking of my death. He had to have been—something like this was impossible to ignore. It was why he'd been so adamant I not go back to his father, why he didn't want me helping Terence with the mission to stop the Demon Lord . . . He'd known all along that we were going to fail, that I was going to die. And he hadn't told me.

I tried to be angry, but really I was only hurt. Hurt that he'd been dealing with this on his own. Hurt that I couldn't comfort him. Hurt because I couldn't be strong for him when I was so terrified myself.

And then I had my most immediate fears.

The safety of the twins had me freaking out even more than my imminent death. Why hadn't I given Patrick more specifics when I'd traveled to warn him? How exactly could he save them? Would his presence be enough to stop what was going to threaten them? When were they going to be in the worst danger? How would I know? How could I help protect them?

Everything we try fails. That phrase could mean a lot of things, but I found myself figuring out a reasonable explanation.

When Dr. Radcliffe came to get the bodies of Alex and Ashley last night, he just shook his head. "I'll have to call Terence. This pushes our plans back—perhaps indefinitely. Already we were short on help. No one was willing to possibly sacrifice his life for this mission. And to find Special Seers young enough . . . I don't know what we'll do now."

In my mind, it was all beginning to make sense. Two Seers had been lost last night. But I happened to know two Special Seers who could serve as replacements. It was beyond obvious

I needed to help now. If I didn't volunteer, the Demon Lord might never be stopped. The twins would never be safe. And if my attempt was due to fail, at least I could die with the knowledge that I'd tried to make things right.

The words of the scripture in Proverbs kept running through my mind: "There is a way that seemeth right unto a man, but the end thereof are the ways of death."

Maybe I was wrong to try—doomed to failure. But I couldn't stop trying to protect those I loved just because I might fail. Living like that would drive me crazy.

Now I just needed to tell Terence and, of course, Patrick. I wasn't looking forward to the latter conversation, but I knew I couldn't put off the first any longer.

During lunch I escaped to the bathroom. Patrick stood to follow me out of the cafeteria, but Lee must have sensed my need to be alone because she stood, latching onto my arm. Patrick probably also realized my need for privacy, but he wavered a moment before allowing us to go without him. He gave me a hard look, as if trying to judge if I was really coping as well as I kept assuring him I was. But in the end he stayed behind. So maybe I was getting the hang of lying.

I didn't want to tell Lee about my fate. She'd definitely freak out, and I was already putting her through so much. She was my best friend. I knew she would want to know, would gladly take on the extra weight and concern in order to help me cope. But I was already having a hard time convincing Patrick I was okay—I didn't want to lie to Lee as well. And so when we reached the bathroom, I told her I needed to make a phone call to Terence, alone. She nodded, though she looked curious. As the door swung closed behind me, I heard Lee tell a girl that someone was throwing up violently inside and to find another bathroom.

I made sure the stalls were all empty before dialing Terence.

He interrupted me as soon as I told him I was volunteering to help on the mission, urging me to talk to Patrick before making any rash decisions. I could pick up the keywords; it was obvious Patrick had told him about seeing the future me; probably that day at the malt shop, when they'd gone outside. Terence knew all about my destiny, and it was time he knew I knew about it too.

I took a deep breath and assured him I knew everything and was still prepared to help stop the Demon Lord.

I was prepared for a fight, but fortunately he agreed with me. He believed that trying to take out the Demon Lord was worth any risk. He only wished we had more eligible Seers.

It was then I told him I could get another Special Seer to join our ranks. At least, I was fairly certain I could. Peter Keegan might not be entirely willing at first, but I was pretty confident I could convince him to help. And I was pretty sure he was young enough.

Terence promised to call Dr. Radcliffe and let him know of my help immediately, before he and Hanif decided to go home. He also added that Alex and Ashley would be buried in their hometowns, according to their wishes.

All of this was happening in a fog. I hardly felt like the moment was real until he voiced the question I'd dreaded most. "Kate, have you told Patrick of your plans to help on the mission?"

I turned where I stood, facing my pale face in the mirror. "No. Not yet."

"Don't put it off. He deserves to know. Considering everything . . . He should know."

I felt a tear slide down my cheek—the first real tear I'd shed since learning I was going to die in the near future. "Terence . . . you'll help him out, after . . ." I tried again. "He's going to need people around him, if things play out like he saw."

"Kate, the future is never certain. But, if it will ease your mind, he won't be alone. Do you honestly think his friends would abandon him?" He cleared his throat roughly, trying to push past the sudden emotion. "Now, Kate, since the Demon

Lord doesn't know about the warehouse, I think you should relocate there until the mission is complete. You'll have Guardians around you. You won't be alone."

But Patrick won't be with me when I die—when I go back. The future me said as much to him . . . I might as well be alone.

Emotion leaked into my voice as I ended the call. Terence told me one last time how brave I was, but I didn't feel brave. I felt disconnected, alone, and afraid.

***

Grandma was stacking a suitcase on the porch when I got home. Lee was still with me, sensing my need to have her around. She had nothing better to do at home, she said. Surprisingly, she hadn't questioned me point blank about what was wrong. I figured she would, eventually. But for now, she was willing to follow my timetable.

The twins hopped out of the car, rushing up to Grandma, who was just stepping back into the house.

"Are you going somewhere?" Jenna asked as she stepped through the open doorway.

"*We* are going on a little trip," Grandma said, loud enough for me to hear from the driveway. "You remember my friend, Lilly Gibbs?"

"The one who broke her leg?" Josie asked.

Grandma nodded as she stepped back onto the porch, dragging a rolling suitcase that bulged with luggage. "I thought it would be nice of us to spend a week with her. Maybe more."

"What about school?" Jenna asked, perceptibly appalled. "We can't just leave!"

"I've already called Mr. Keegan."

"Yes!" Josie punched the air.

Grandma continued quickly. "He can give me the necessary homework, and you can do it there."

"No!" Josie groaned.

Jenna looked appeased—perhaps even excited.

Grandma pushed them toward the front door. "Hurry upstairs and go pack a couple bags. I want to leave within the hour."

Once they were inside I popped the trunk, and Lee—who was already standing back there—helped push it open to let out the invisible Toni.

It startled me when I realized Toni *wasn't* invisible. As soon as he was free of the trunk he stepped up to Lee, cradling her bruised face delicately in his hands. "Do you need some more Tylenol?" he murmured, deeply concerned.

Lee shook her head. "I'm fine. It looks a lot worse than it feels."

He grunted. "I doubt that."

She gave him a quick hug, her large poodle skirt melting around his legs from the cool breeze. "You worry too much. You should have seen me smack that guy. I haven't picked up *Harry Potter* for years, but he sure served me well last night."

He began to kiss her, as if he couldn't wait another moment to touch her lips, and I turned around to give them some privacy. I knew Patrick would be only a couple minutes or so behind us, so I decided to figure out what Grandma was planning before he arrived.

She was still on the porch, waiting for me. Her arms were folded stiffly, her eyes tight with worry. She got right to the point as soon as I stepped up to her, her words quiet. "I can't keep the twins here, Kate. It's not fair to them. And I . . . I can't go through something like last night again."

I nodded. I understood completely.

"I want you to come with us," Grandma said slowly. "It's far enough away—we should be safe there until the Guardians can sort everything out."

"I can't. I have to stay here."

She pulled in a deep breath. "Kate Bennett, I'd take you

over my knee if I thought it would do any good. But I just have this feeling . . ." Her eyes filled with sudden tears. "It's like your grandfather is right here. Right next to me, whispering that everything is going to be all right. That you're old enough and wise enough to make your own decisions. You just have to promise me you'll be safe."

Though it was not something I could promise, I did so anyway.

"Is Jack inside?" I asked, quick to escape her before emotion overwhelmed me.

She nodded.

I gave her a brief hug and then slipped around her to find Jack in the kitchen. He was standing at the sink, staring out the window into the backyard. He turned when he heard me come in.

He took in my resolute expression, bobbing his head when he understood I had no intention of leaving. "I'll go with them, if you'd like," he offered.

"Please? They need you more than I do."

He swallowed hard. "Holy dooley, girl—don't look so morose."

"I look morose?"

"You look . . . resigned."

"I guess I am."

"To what?"

I didn't answer his question. "I might need your help, Jack. I want Patrick to go too."

His eyebrows shot up. "Don't be a galah. He'd never leave you. Especially not now."

"I can't tell you why, but . . . He needs to be with the twins now."

He pursed his lips. "I already called Claire—she wants Maddy away from here. She's not going to be happy, that's for sure. But maybe Claire's got a point."

I moved closer, sticking out my hand. "Thank you, Jack. For everything you've done. For me and my family."

He tried to smile as he shook my hand. "No worries, Kate. It was always my pleasure."

I heard the front door open and I knew Patrick had arrived. I dropped Jack's hand, but before I could move away he embraced me. "It'll be all right, Kate. It'll *all* be right."

"Thanks, Jack," I whispered against him.

By the time we pulled back, Patrick was standing in the kitchen, watching us. He looked to Jack. "Are you going, then?" he asked.

Jack answered smoothly. "Sure am. I think the young'uns will be glad to have me along."

Patrick nodded once. He was avoiding my gaze. "I'm glad you'll be with them. I think I might send Claire and Maddy, just in case. That should leave enough of us here for Kate's protection, until we can figure out another way to stop the Demon Lord."

"Patrick?" I asked suddenly. "Can I talk to you?"

It was obvious he didn't want to look at me, but his head moved fractionally until our eyes locked. His were wary. "Of course," he said with false ease.

I led the way into the family room, sensing him following right behind me. I tried to pull in steadying breaths, low and full. I didn't stop until we stood in front of the dark TV, and when I turned around we stood facing each other for a long moment.

His breath was coming faster. His jaw was tightening with every second I hesitated.

I cracked my mouth open. "I'm staying here, but I want you to go with them."

He stopped breathing altogether. He gripped both of my hands, squeezing tightly as he tugged me closer to him. "Kate," he whispered thickly, hoping to keep our conversation muted in the quiet house. "Please, just hear me out. I know you're terrified—*I'm* terrified. But I've been thinking this through all day. I have another option—a better option."

I sighed, rolling my eyes toward the ceiling because it was too hard to look at him, to see the desperate hope in his gaze. "Patrick, I don't want to argue—"

"Kate, I want you to come with me."

I closed my eyes, ducking my head. "I can't. I called Terence. I'm helping Hanif with the mission."

He froze before me. "No," he breathed at last. "You can't do that. Without Alex's military experience, you don't stand a chance—"

"Peter Keegan is a Special Seer. I'm sure if he's aware of what happened to Lee, he'll help us out. We'll have enough people to get the job done."

His words were urgent—lined with desperation. "You can't trust him. And even if you could, he's only a schoolteacher. Kate, you can't do this. You *cannot* lead these Seers in an assassination attempt. It's not in you, and we both know it. You need to come with me."

"I can't go with the twins. It will only endanger them—"

"Not with the twins," he interrupted, impatient I wasn't following his line of thought. "Just you and me. We'll go somewhere, where even the Guardians can't find us. Somewhere with no ties to the Demon Lord."

"What about the twins? My grandma?"

"It will only be for a few years. Until all of this has died down. Until Terence and the Council find another way to kill the Demon Lord. They will if we just give them time."

I shook my head. "Patrick, this is insane."

"No, it's not. I can work, provide for you. I can protect you, keep you alive. It doesn't matter where we go. I don't care. As long as I'm with you and I know you're safe."

Tears blurred my eyes, and I knew he noticed because his grip on me tightened. More than anything, I wanted to do exactly what he was describing. Just me and him. I trusted him perfectly—he'd keep me safe. After so much pain and fear, I'd finally feel safe.

The idea was intoxicating. But I couldn't lose my focus. "Toni? Lee?" I questioned, voice tight with emotion.

Patrick slid closer to me, voice turning soothing in an instant, sure he was winning me over. "He'll protect her, Kate. They'll be safe. Probably safer without us around."

I shook my head slowly. "Patrick, you're not thinking clearly."

"This is all I've been thinking about since last night," he argued. "We have to stay together. If I stay with you, that future can't happen. As long as we're together, things won't play out that way."

I blew out my breath. He was jumping to irrational conclusions. Didn't he understand that this was going to happen whether he was with me or not? I don't know how I knew, I just did. I was going to die, and we both needed to come to terms with it so we could focus on protecting the twins. "Patrick . . ."

His hands moved up to my shoulders, his long fingers flexing their hold, as if somehow he could force me to agree. "Kate, I'm *begging* you to come with me."

"What if I did?" I whispered, staring at a point past his shoulder. "What if that's what we did before? I came with you, and we were safe. For a while. And then everyone we left behind died because we weren't there to stop it? What if this is exactly what we tried and it failed? What if the twins died because we were selfish and didn't—"

"I don't care," he interrupted stubbornly. "I have to try. *You* have to try. For me. Kate, please, just do this for me."

It would be easy to say *yes*. Yet it was impossible. Maybe he sensed that. And so he did something I never imagined he would.

He sank to one knee, his brilliant blue eyes running across

my face before settling on mine. He spoke without further preamble. "Kate Bennett, will you marry me?"

I blinked down at him, completely shocked by the sudden shift in conversation.

His lips pressed together as he shifted to both knees, still clinging to my hands. His voice was uncommonly rough—throbbing with emotion. "I'm not afraid to beg, if that's what it takes. I love you more than any man could ever love you, Kate, and I promise to always love you, to always care for you. For every day of forever. I won't rest until I find a way to give you everything you deserve. I *swear* I will make you happy. Please, *please* say you'll marry me."

My mouth hung partially open. I was completely speechless. I'd often thought of how great it would be to love him for the rest of my life, but I hadn't actually thought the word *marriage*. But to know he had . . . I was distracted by the thought of becoming his wife. Thinking about the possibility of marrying him, being his completely . . . It caused my heart to almost dissolve with pleasure. Even if we never had children, if he never grew old . . . Life would be great with him. More than great. It would be a miracle. It would be a type of heaven.

But no matter how much I wanted him, he was the one thing I couldn't have. Because when I died, I would never see him again. I couldn't be his. Not in the way he wanted. Not in the way I was desperate to have him.

I reached down and took hold of his hands, tugging weakly. Pain crossed his face at my apparent rejection, but he followed my gentle prompt and rose to his feet, unable to meet my gaze, his shoulders slumped in defeat.

I slipped one of my hands free to stroke his tight jaw. "Patrick O'Donnell," I whispered, my voice trembling. "I want to say yes. More than anything I want to say yes. But I can't."

He pulled in a shivering breath. "Why?" he demanded.

I attempted to smile, failing miserably in the process.

"Because I don't know what's going to happen. I don't want to hurt you any more than I already will."

He bowed his head, forcing my fingers up into his hair. "Kate," he mumbled into the space between us. "I don't care if our time together is a lifetime or just one more day. I need to know that you love me like I love you."

I shook my head at him. Did he honestly doubt my feelings? "I do. Patrick, I love you so much."

He peeked up through his eyelashes, his tone pleading. "Then say you'll marry me."

I stared at him, waiting for someone—anyone—to tell me what to do. When no answer was forthcoming, I had to improvise. I leaned closer, seeking his lips. He realized what I wanted and his mouth eagerly found mine. He was willing to set any weapon upon me if somehow it could persuade me to say *yes* and come with him. My hand knotted in his hair, our joined hands interlocked and his free fingers framed my face. Our lips melted together, blurring our emotions until they were thoroughly mixed. We held each other tightly, forgetting that we were in my family room, forgetting the Demon Lord, and all the dangers that faced us. I forgot I was tied to the earth at all. In that wonderful moment, nothing could touch us. Nothing could pull us away from each other.

But it had to end. I had to keep this from happening. I needed to stay, and he needed to go. Somehow, it was the only way to save the ones I loved.

I ended the kiss, keeping my forehead against his. "You need to go."

His body shuddered and he swallowed convulsively, fingers curling around the back of my neck. "Kate, please . . ."

I laid my hands on his wrists and tried to pull his hands away. They only tightened against my skin in response. I sighed, tipping my head to rest against his forehead. I was losing strength, if not my resolve, to push him away. Couldn't he realize I was trying to be strong for him?

"I said that everything we try fails," I breathed. "I'm not going to take a chance with the lives of my sisters."

"Kate . . ."

I pretended to ignore the wonderful sensations his fingertips pressing against my skin inspired, and I cut into his plea. "If I died to tell you this, it must have been the only way to save them." I heaved in a short breath. "Patrick, I don't want you to go." My voice broke on the last word, and I could feel the muscles in his face waver and fight the urge to contort. I pulled in a breath, blinked back stinging tears that threatened to fall. "I made my parents a promise after they died: that I would look after Jenna and Josie. It's a promise I made to myself when all of this started in the first place. You're supposed to be with them, now. Not me. You're the only one I can trust to keep Jenna and Josie safe."

"Please, please don't make me leave you," he croaked.

My mouth compressed, my tears finally slipping free. He didn't pull away from the moisture, just pulled me in until my head was cradled between his neck and shoulder. His fingers stroked my hair, hooked it behind my ears, and my whole body shook.

"Please, Kate?" His lips were at my ear, his head ducked above mine. He held me tenderly, filled me with the confidence that I needed him with me.

"Patrick, I want—" I stopped the desperate words before they could betray me, before he could understand just how much I wanted to disregard everything and stay with him. But I had to give him up. It was the hardest sacrifice I could ever imagine, but if it saved my sisters . . .

I may have kept him from hearing the words, but they still ran through my mind, further wearing me down. *Patrick, I want you with me more than anything. I'm terrified. I don't want to die. I don't want to do this alone. I want you close so I won't be as scared. I've never been so scared. I want you, Patrick, forever. And I can't have you.*

I pinched my eyes closed against his shoulder and tried again. "Patrick, I need you to save the twins. Promise me that after I'm gone, you'll—"

He simultaneously jerked back and pushed me away, hands firm around my upper arms. His blue eyes were stormy, flashing with a fierceness that made my stomach drop. His low voice was bitter, his words brittle and snapping between us. "You've given up. Already. Since the moment I told you. Haven't you? You don't expect to survive this. You never did. You agreed to help Terence because in your mind, you don't stand a chance. You think you're going to die, and you've decided to stop fighting." His fingers curled more tightly. I'd never seen him so impassioned—so upset. "You're not going to die. Not now. *Not* like this." A tear streaked down his face, but his eyes remained hard on mine. "Do you understand me? Destiny can only control you if you let it. If *you* choose. You can't give up. Kate, please, you *can't* give up."

I swallowed, determined to stop his frantic words. I cupped his face in my too-small hands, fingers brushing against the moisture. I leveled him with my firmest stare, glad the emotions rushing through me had been stopped at the sight of his tears.

I could be strong now. I had to be. He needed me to be. It was the only way I could let him go.

"Patrick, you listen to me," I said evenly. "I haven't stopped fighting. I'm going to keep fighting, do you understand? I'm not going to quit. And neither are you. We've made it this far. I'm not about to give you up. Not even close."

He tried to say something, but I shifted my hand to cover his mouth.

"Patrick, I won't stop fighting," I repeated. "I promise."

His eyes squeezed closed at my words, his shoulders falling in defeat.

He knew I wasn't going to budge. I was still going to send him away, despite everything. I was still going through with the mission to the Demon Lord's past.

In his mind, I'd given up, despite my assurances that I hadn't. Or maybe he'd listened closer, heard that I'd only promised to keep fighting. Maybe he'd heard the undertones of defeat in my voice—the words I hadn't dared to voice.

I knew my end was coming. Just as he did.

And as if the knowledge wasn't painful enough to him . . . In his eyes, I was asking him to give up too.

***

I was sitting on my front room couch watching the sunset. My mind felt almost blank after the afternoon's strong emotions. I could hardly believe that Patrick was gone. That my family was gone.

Patrick had called a couple hours ago to let me know that they'd arrived safely. He was invisible, but Jack and Maddy were not. The twins didn't question Maddy's presence—Jack was weird enough that anything he did or anyone he brought along on an adventure didn't raise suspicions. They were safe. That was what I tried to focus on. My family was safe. That didn't mean they were entirely out of danger, but Patrick would be there to protect them.

Patrick . . .

I knew Patrick wasn't happy with me. He wasn't even accepting. But he followed my wishes just the same, packing his bags and then sneaking them into the back of the van without anyone seeing. He'd reentered the house before I could follow him, and watching him stand in the entryway, open door behind him, brought back memories of our first kiss.

He'd moved quickly, knowing time was limited. He'd stepped up to me and slipped off his leather bracelet—the black one Toni had stolen so long ago. He wrapped it around my wrist with sure fingers, whispering shortly, "You need to give it back to me, because I have to return it to the poor fool who lost it."

Though we knew it was a shaky promise at best, I told him I would.

He didn't kiss me on the lips when he left. Just a quick brush of his mouth along my cheek, as if he couldn't bear to be around me for another second. I tried not to let it get to me. After all, he had reason to be upset.

Saying good-bye to the twins was just as bad. They thought I was spending the week with Lee, and they barely took the time to hug me because they were so intent on rubbing in the fact that they got to spend a week on a farm. Jenna gave me a hug, but it was distracted. "Lilly Gibbs has horses!" she kept saying excitedly.

I patted her head. "Don't break your neck."

It had been the last thing I'd said to her.

Josie hadn't given me a hug good-bye, and I wasn't about to drag her back out of the van to give her one. I'd stood in the driveway and watched them back out. Watched them leave me. Just like I'd wanted.

Why didn't I feel a sense of victory?

Toni and Lee were in the kitchen with Claire, trying to pack up anything we could take over to the warehouse, where I would be living for at least the next week.

So wrapped up in my thoughts, I didn't hear Toni until he spoke from behind me. "Are you one of those freaks who like sunsets more than TV?"

I glanced up at him, my smile extremely halfhearted. It was the only answer I had energy to give.

He plopped down next to me on the couch, his khaki shorts exposing his knobby knees. "So, are you all packed?"

I nodded vaguely, staring out the window again. "Yeah, I think so."

"The warehouse isn't *that* bad, you know."

We sat in silence for a short moment, and I played absently with the bracelet on my arm. "Toni?"

"Yeah?"

"Patrick told me everything. About my . . . death."

I felt him nodding next to me. "Yeah. I know. He told me he told you."

I looked to him. "What did he say?"

Toni was squinting at the sun. "That I'm not allowed to let you use my memory, no matter how you threaten me. He'll kill me a million times over if I do."

"He didn't say that."

"Fine, not the last part. But he probably would. If I gave him the idea."

I continued to stare at him until he looked at me. "How does it happen?" I asked. "How do I die?"

"Geez, Kate." He looked away quickly, shaking his head. "Are you morbid or what?"

"Patrick said I was covered in blood. He didn't tell me how, though."

"Probably for good reasons."

I continued to stare at him until finally he rolled his eyes. "You should probably stay away from guns," he muttered.

I swallowed.

He saw the nervous action and groaned. "Man, Patrick's going to kill me."

"I won't say anything if you don't," I said, trying not to picture what it would be like to die from a gunshot wound. Unfortunately, I'd had too many experiences with gunshots. Grandpa's life had been stolen by a bullet. Quick, probably almost painless. But I'd seen Patrick suffer from a gunshot wound. It had been anything but painless. And since the future me had had the time to travel through a memory and have a conversation, I could expect my death wouldn't be quick and easy.

Toni patting my knee brought me out of my thoughts. I blinked and faced his narrowed eyes. "Kate, really. You shouldn't be thinking about this. It totally can't be healthy."

"What's it like?" I asked in a small whisper, ignoring his words. "Dying? You were shot, weren't you?"

He frowned. "Yeah. So?"

"What does it feel like?"

"What do you think it feels like?" he huffed. "It hurts. And then you're dead. I was shot in the head, though, so . . ."

"Where was I shot?"

"Sheesh! I don't know. There was a lot of blood . . ." He looked beyond uneasy. "I really don't think you should be worrying about this."

"Honestly, Toni? How can I not? Wouldn't you be if it were you?"

He thought about that briefly. "Fair point," he finally agreed.

I pressed my lips together. "What's dying really like? What happens after you die?"

He shrugged a single shoulder, still not comfortable with the conversation. "I can only tell you my own experience. I felt pain and fear. Lots of fear. Romero made me kneel on the ground, in front of his manor. Selena was there, watching everything without pity. Romero pointed his gun at me. And then he pulled the trigger." Toni shook his head, dispelling the awful memory. "It was like waking up. I was lying on a really soft bed in a white room."

"It was white?" I'd always imagined death to be dark, despite all that talk of light and tunnels. Death had to be dark, empty; that's how it felt every time I'd lost someone I loved.

Toni was still talking. "Yep. Completely white. And it was really empty, but not in a creepy way. The space was . . . almost calming. There was a little girl sitting at the foot of my bed. She was probably only six or seven."

"A little girl?" I raised an eyebrow at him.

"Yeah. I'm not making this up. She gave me this really nice smile and asked how I was feeling. I said something like, 'I'm dead, so it can't be good, right?' She didn't think that was very funny. She told me that I should feel perfectly normal. Surprisingly, I did. Better than normal, actually."

"And then?" I prompted, after he paused.

"She said she was my sister. That when we die, our last relative to reach Heaven comes to greet us, to present us with the choice."

"She was from Heaven?"

"Yeah, with some special pass or something, so she could meet me on this half-plane. She gave me the choice, and I chose to return to earth. To be a Guardian. We talked for hours, though, before I finally decided."

"I'm sorry, Toni. I thought you were an orphan; I didn't realize you had family."

"I didn't think I did. We never knew each other in life. She was my older sister, actually. She died at that age, so that's how she appeared to me. Apparently, she's twenty-five in Heaven."

"I'm glad you got to meet some family, Toni."

"Yeah . . ."

"What happened next?" I prompted, sensing he didn't want to linger on this moment.

"She gave me a hug. I got really sleepy. I woke up in a regular old hotel room, a really dingy one. I knew I was back in Mexico, so I almost thought I'd imagined the whole thing. I started looking for the things I'd managed to steal from Quin Romero—the things I must have stolen, if I were alive—but I couldn't find them. Then this guy named Pablo came in. He was a Guardian, and he let me know that dying hadn't been a dream. I started working for them right away. The rest is history, I guess."

"I wonder if Seers go to that room?" I speculated aloud.

"Ella, my sister—she said the room was a way station. A place to adjust to death without having to rush. I bet you'd still go there, when you eventually kick the bucket. And I mean eventually. As in, don't start buying funeral flowers and complimentary cookies, because you're going to live a long life, Kate."

I sighed but gave him a weak smile. "You don't have to lie to me, Toni. I know how this is going to end, just as well as you do."

His brow furrowed. "Yeah, maybe. But not if I can help it. And despite what you think, Kate, you don't know everything."

I hoped he was right. But I still had my doubts.

seventeen

I decided to skip school. I didn't feel like getting up when morning rolled around. I was too comfortable to move, too focused on the future to stand the thought of going to class. I was sick of pretending.

Though Claire had offered the use of Maddy's now-empty room upstairs, I'd chosen to stay in Patrick's instead. He hadn't been here for a while now; he'd stripped it of most of his things when he'd moved into my dad's den. Still, the room managed to smell like him. Even the bare mattress seemed covered in his comforting scent. I hadn't actually made his bed; I'd just slept on the mattress with a couple blankets on top. I texted Lee, letting her know I wasn't going to be able to pick her up for school. She promised to come by and see me afterward.

I could hear Toni moving around in his bedroom, which was next to Patrick's. I figured Toni was planning on following Lee around today, just in case she'd become a target for the Demons. A few minutes later, I heard him close the outer door, and I knew he was gone. Like Patrick was gone.

I firmly told myself to get a grip. I'd gotten my way. I'd been the one to send Patrick away with the twins. I needed to get past my own depression so I could fulfill my promise to him.

To keep fighting. To try my best to get rid of the Demon Lord, once and for all. I owed it to Patrick, my sisters, my friends, and myself.

When I finally stepped out of bed, I dressed slowly. I really needed to talk with Hanif and Dr. Radcliffe so they could fill me in on the mission details they'd been learning for the past week. But I wasn't the only one behind—I needed to get Peter Keegan on board so we could learn together. Looking at the clock beside Patrick's bed, I saw it was just past ten. I frowned, debating the best course of action. I'd been planning to approach Peter with Lee at my side, but she was in school. And the sooner I could talk to Peter, the sooner we could get started on the mission. The sooner I could put all this behind me.

I wondered if Patrick was right to believe I'd survive this. If I lived through the mission, if I could stop the Demon Lord, I would get Patrick back. Somehow. That's what I needed to focus on.

I wanted to call him, hear his voice. Apologize for the way I'd treated him yesterday. I fingered the phone in my hand, but the memory of his stiff kiss on my cheek, the way he hadn't even said a real good-bye . . . I pocketed my phone. I would face him later.

I left his bedroom behind and entered the living room/kitchen area. The run-down furniture and dusty space seemed even more desolate without Patrick and Toni around. I decided I wasn't hungry enough to linger in the oppressive room, so I hurried to the outer door.

Claire must have heard me climbing up to the fourth floor, because she was just stepping out of her room when I rounded the corner. "You're not at school? I thought I heard Toni leave with you."

"I decided it wasn't worth it," I said quickly, hoping she wouldn't see the depression in my eyes. I didn't want her to gloat that she'd been right all along, that my relationship with Patrick wasn't a positive thing for either of us. I cleared my throat, still heavy with disuse. "I was wondering if you'd come with me to the elementary school, actually. There's someone I need to talk to about the mission."

Her lips pressed together. "Terence told me you'd volunteered. He mentioned you had another Special Seer in mind, but he failed to say it was a child."

"A child? . . . Oh, no. He teaches at the elementary school."

She frowned. "The Demon Seer? Are you sure that's wise?"

"We really don't have another choice. Besides, he cares about Lee, and whether he wants to admit it or not, helping the Demons is only hurting her now."

Claire's blonde head bobbed. "Perhaps the mission will work. I hope your attempt at assassinating the Demon Lord goes more smoothly than mine did."

I had the distinct feeling she was blaming me personally for her failure, but before I could call her on it she was turning on her stiletto heel. "I'll tell Dr. Radcliffe where we're going and join you downstairs."

I rolled my eyes at her attitude as I made my own retreat.

She reached my car a minute behind me, and then we were pulling out onto the street. The silence was beyond awkward. I knew she didn't like me, but . . . something felt really off. She actually looked uncomfortable.

Finally, she broke the still air. "I know you think I dislike you, Kate. But that's not true."

"Um, sure. Okay. What's up?"

Her lips drew into a tight line. "I don't want to get hostile."

"Hostile? Who's getting hostile?"

She took a deep breath, her next words completely unexpected. "Joan of Arc was killed a couple short years before my birth."

I glanced over at her. "Claire . . . ?"

She sighed deeply, head turned away from me. She let

out a hard laugh. "I wanted to be just as she was. Noble, holy, and courageous. In the end, that's why I became a Guardian. It seemed like my divine mission. A chance to make the sort of difference I'd always dreamed about making in my past life." She glanced at me, but I kept my eyes on the road, afraid if I met her gaze she'd stop opening up to me. I couldn't explain exactly why I was so interested in the inner workings of her mind. But I'd never understood why such a grumpy person would choose to become a Guardian.

Claire continued. "I've worked so hard to become a warrior that I've forgotten the most important traits Joan of Arc possessed. Compassion. Bravery. Faith. I simply wanted to tell you . . . Your courage has put me to shame, Kate."

I had to look at her then, though I had no idea what to say when I realized just how serious she was. Her delicate face was more serious than I'd ever seen it. Yet, a vulnerability was there I'd never seen before.

She sighed and looked away from me. "Those are all traits I see in you, Kate. Goodness. Love. Sacrifice. You have these things, and they make you great. I . . . I wanted you to know you have my respect."

She'd just compared me to her lifelong hero. I'd never felt so accepted by her. It was probably the closest to reconciling we would ever get, and I was grateful for the resolution. Still, I had no idea what to say. I settled for a lame, "Thanks, Claire. I really appreciate all you've done for me and my family."

She didn't respond verbally, but I felt my shoulders relax as the tension between us gradually dissipated.

Claire was invisible when we entered the school. Since I couldn't do that neat trick, I tried to walk the empty halls as calmly as possible, hoping no one would appear to question my presence. I could say I was here for my sisters, but what would happen when it was realized they weren't here?

Fortunately I knew right where I was going, and when I

stepped through the open door, I found the classroom empty of everyone but the man I'd come to see.

Peter Keegan was wearing his usual brown suit, hunched over his desk and grading papers. The children must have been out at recess, and he was using the break to try and get ahead. He glanced up when he saw me, but he wasn't smiling because he saw Claire. He gave her a nod and asked me to close the door. I did and then stepped up to his desk.

"We need to talk."

My phone vibrated, distracting me. I knew without looking it would be Patrick. My heart started pounding in a mix of excitement and trepidation. But he'd have to wait. I needed to focus on convincing Peter to help us.

Peter didn't seem to hear my phone. He brushed a nervous hand down his tie, which was already straight. His aura was anxious, uneasy. "Kate, this isn't the best time."

"Have you told Selena about my sisters leaving?"

He looked down at his desk. "No. But I need to. And I'm sorry, but there's nothing you can say that can change my mind."

"Have you seen Lee's face?"

Peter looked up, grimacing. "Yes."

"Did she tell you what happened?"

"Yes." The word was a whisper.

"Then you know she's in danger too. We're all in the same boat now. We have to stop the Demon Lord, or we're going to be living in fear for the rest of our lives."

"Kate, it's not that simple. I can't just oppose the Demon population."

"Why not?" My phone stopped trembling in my pocket. I hoped Patrick would forgive me for ignoring him.

Peter was shaking his head. "I understand you're desperate; you've been living in constant fear for months now. But you can't just throw away your life like this."

"Peter, I need you. You're Special. We have the power to

stop him. And there are others. We have a plan. It can work. It *will* work. The Demon Lord will be stopped before he ever has a chance to begin. If we can alter the past, we might be able to stop you from ever becoming a Seer."

He stood, walking over to the wall of windows. He looked out at the parking lot, his hands in his jacket pockets.

I continued unassumingly, trying to keep the desperation out of my voice. "Think of Lee. Think of Jeanette. Think of someone other than yourself."

I worried I'd gone too far. I was almost ready to recall the words when Peter suddenly turned. His aura was fixed, decided. "What is this foolproof plan?"

I tried not to look too relieved. "We'll get to that. But first, what year were you born?"

He frowned. "1972. Why?"

I nodded once. "It cuts it a little close, but . . . how would you like to visit 1971?"

***

I pulled out my phone, balancing it on my palm. Sitting in Patrick's room, I knew I needed to call him back. But such a thing was easier said than done.

Claire and I had just returned from talking to Peter, and the whole drive back I'd struggled to figure out what I might say to him. He hadn't tried calling me again, so what if he thought I was angry with him? I couldn't stand that.

I blew out my breath, flipping the phone open. Facing his anger was better than this awful silence between us. If he was mad at me, he had reasonable cause. But he needed to know that I missed him. That I loved him. And that I was confident I'd done the right thing in sending him away.

He answered on the third ring. I tried to ignore the pull in my gut that told me he'd hesitated, unsure if he wanted to talk with me.

"Kate, I called earlier." His voice was soft, but the fact he'd skipped a greeting made me wince. He was definitely upset.

"I know. I was talking to Peter Keegan."

A brief pause. "How did that go?"

"Good. He's agreed to help us."

"Are you sure you can trust him?"

I nodded, though of course he couldn't see me. "Yes. I know I can. He wants to keep Lee safe, and he knows helping us is the only way to protect her."

"Are you going to teach him to travel?"

"I thought I'd ask Toni for a memory." I winced as soon as the words were out. "A safe one, of course. Not . . ."

"Kate . . ." He sighed heavily over the line. I could easily imagine him rubbing a long hand over his eyes. "I'm sorry. I'm sorry for the way I treated you."

"Patrick . . . what are you talking about?"

"When I left yesterday. I was rude and extremely unfair to you. I wish you were a bit less selfless sometimes, but . . . I lacked the courage and trust you deserve from me. I'm sorry that I disappointed you, and I hope you haven't lost all faith in me."

I blinked in shock. "You couldn't disappoint me. *I'm* sorry that I hurt *you*."

"You didn't."

I knew his words were a lie—especially considering his proposal, which I wasn't quite ready to discuss with him yet. "But you didn't really say good-bye. I thought you were upset . . ."

He sighed heavily. "I was a fool. I shouldn't have given up that chance to kiss you again."

My lips tugged into a slight smile even as my cheeks warmed. "So you don't hate me?"

"Never. Not for a second. I was merely upset with myself. I apologize that I caused you to doubt me."

I pursed my lips together. "I wish you were here," I breathed.

He groaned. "Kate, don't you dare. You've got to stay strong. Because all you have to do is ask, and I'll be in the car. I could be there within the hour." He paused. "In fact, I don't think you'd even have to ask . . ."

"How are the twins?"

"Fine. They're loving the farm, the horses."

"And how are you?"

"Coping. What about you?" He hurried to turn the conversation away from himself. "Where are you right now?"

I almost blushed. It felt good—normal. And I needed normal. "Your room. I moved in. I hope you don't mind."

"I only wish I was there too. You skipped school then?"

"Yes. Meeting with Peter seemed more important."

"You took someone with you?"

"Claire."

"Good. I don't want you going anywhere alone. What are your plans for the rest of the day?"

"Teaching Peter how to travel. Learning everything we can from Radcliffe and Hanif, and figuring out all the details of Alex's strategy."

"You'll call back? Keep me informed?"

"Of course. And I can text you before I travel in Toni's past."

"Please do. And be cautious. Toni's memories can lead to dangerous places. Make sure he keeps it out of Mexico. And Canada, for that matter."

"Sounds like a story . . ."

"One for another day," he assured me.

"I love you, you know."

"I love you, Kate. Call me later, and I'll tell you again."

My arms ached to hold him, and I knew he felt the same.

***

"I can't believe I'm doing this," Peter muttered one hour after school.

"Come on. You'll be great," Lee argued. "Mom would be so proud—if she knew about all of this. And if she wasn't out of state right now."

Toni was shaking his head, standing across from them on the bottom floor of the warehouse. "This is weird. I just . . . think of a memory?"

I nodded. "And then focus on the emotions it inspired. Try to break it down to one, but if you can't, that's okay—we should still be able to find it."

"I think I'm going to be sick," Peter admitted.

Hanif patted his arm. "That's natural, I think."

It was late afternoon, and we were ready to let Peter have his first experience with traveling. Hanif was coming along for extra practice. Dr. Radcliffe wanted to stay and see what it looked like from this side—the collapse and unconsciousness that always followed a traveling experience. He had his notebook and pen at the ready.

My phone buzzed in my hand. I opened it at once, anxious to see Patrick's reply to my text.

Be safe. Call me when you wake up. I love you.

I tapped back, *I will. Love you.*

"Kate, I think I'm ready," Toni said, breaking into my thoughts.

I sent my message and shut the phone, pushing it into my pocket. "It's in the States?" I asked again, just to be safe.

Toni rolled his eyes. "No, I'm taking you to meet my Mexican drug buddies in the 1800s. Of course it's in the States! New York, actually. And while you're there, do me a favor."

"Yeah?"

He looked a little sheepish. "Find out who I stole that bracelet from, okay? I always told Patrick that I knew, just to goad him. But I really have no idea."

I frowned. "You told me you were taking us to a safe memory! Not one where you stole something."

"Apples and oranges, Kate. Besides, I don't think I *have* a memory where I wasn't stealing something. Candy from babies, kisses from beautiful girls—"

"Hey!" Lee protested.

"Named Lee," Toni clarified. "Only the ones named Lee, I swear."

I rolled my eyes. "Okay, Toni. Can you show us the aura, please?"

"Sheesh. Let's be impatient, never mind that Toni's doing us a favor . . ."

"I'll find the bracelet owner, then we're even. How about that?"

"I'll go for that."

His aura was already being dominated by a single color—yellow happiness.

Hanif, Peter, and I gathered around Toni, concentrating on the growing color.

"Try to get at least a name and gender," Toni told me. "An address would be great. But if it doesn't come naturally, don't worry about it . . ."

Toni's voice faded as I dropped.

I was standing on a crowded street in New York City.

This was nothing like my trips to Ireland where we were out of the way, on the edge of thought. Maybe we were still on the edge of Toni's memory, but we were in the middle of the sidewalk. We were shoved and jostled, and I grabbed Hanif's slim wrist before he could be dragged away. Peter was already pressed up against a store front, looking more than a little overwhelmed.

"It worked," he muttered. "It really worked."

Hanif and I pushed up next to him. "And it's that simple," I said, feigning nonchalance. This was the most disconcerting traveling experience I'd ever had; no time to really adjust to new surroundings, just elbows and faces all around.

"I can feel the pull," Peter said. "It's either that, or me getting ready to vomit."

"That's the one," Hanif congratulated him. "It'll pull you straight back to your own time, when you're ready."

I was scanning the sidewalk, taking in the huge buildings and bustling humanity. I couldn't tell exactly what year it was, but my guess would have been somewhere in the fifties. That made me mentally roll my eyes at Toni. He'd stolen the bracelet a long time ago, unlike he'd told Patrick. The poor person he'd nabbed it from was probably already dead in the present, and Patrick was saving it for nothing. So much for Toni's story about stealing it especially for Patrick. For crying out loud, Toni wouldn't even meet Patrick until the late eighties!

Someone stepped on my foot but didn't apologize, just kept walking. A second later someone knocked into me. I felt Hanif buckle beside me, his small form not able to take my weight. Before I could fall completely someone grabbed my swinging arm. I thought it was Peter, but then I found myself staring into Toni's beaming face, his silver aura completely familiar.

"Whoa there!" Toni chuckled, hand on my arm. "Sorry about that. New York will be New York, I guess."

"Yeah." I stumbled out, shocked to come face-to-face with him so suddenly. "Thank you."

He steadied me before releasing his grip. "No problem. Watch yourself, all right?"

"Thanks," I repeated. He nodded and slipped back into the crowd. I lost sight of him almost instantly.

"Should we follow him?" Hanif asked. "To find that person he steals from?"

Peter grunted suddenly. "I don't think that will be necessary."

We both looked up at him. He pointed to my wrist in answer.

The bracelet was gone.

***

"It's just so crazy," I repeated, still disbelieving. "Toni got that bracelet from me, and then he gave it to you. But I got it from you in the first place!"

"I can barely wrap my mind around it," Patrick agreed, the line cracking subtly.

Toni was shaking his head beside me, speaking loudly so Patrick could hear him through my phone's speaker. "Yeah, yeah, it's an interesting conundrum. But what about tomorrow? Do you really think this is such a great idea? To do this so soon?"

I waved him away in irritation, but Patrick had heard. "Kate, maybe he's right. Maybe you should wait for another week or so. Terence may be able to find some more Seers to help you, and you can get better prepared. Toni can teach you some more fighting techniques."

"I thought you said I shouldn't fight—if there was trouble, I should just come back to the present."

"That's plan A, certainly. But the more you know, the safer you'll be."

"Terence doesn't seem hopeful about finding more Seers," I said. "It was everything the Council could do to find the ones they did. We'd be waiting for weeks, and that's out of the question."

"The twins are perfectly safe, Kate. You don't have to rush for their sakes."

But I do. "There's no reason to wait. We can get all this behind us tomorrow morning."

I could just make out his sigh. "It sounds like you've got everything figured out."

"Hopefully. Dr. Radcliffe and Alex put a lot of thought into this, and Peter and I have been going over their plans. Things will run smoothly. You'll see."

I hurried to distract him. "I *am* sorry about your bracelet."

There was a hint of a smile in his voice. "It's not your fault."

Toni was rolling his eyes. "If I *hadn't* stolen it from you,

Patrick would never even *get* it, remember? So actually you and I were doing him a favor . . ."

I shook my head at him but didn't respond because Patrick was speaking. "Toni, promise me that you or Lee will call me the second Kate loses consciousness. I want to be informed."

"Sure, I'll give you the play-by-play."

"I'll be careful, Patrick," I broke in. "Everything's going to be fine."

"Of course. I just . . . Call me in the morning?"

"Definitely," I said.

"Ew," Toni griped. "Don't turn all lovey-dovey on me."

"Good night, Toni," Patrick said firmly.

"Love you," I said toward the phone.

"And I love you," he returned.

When I looked over at Toni after closing the phone, I caught his mischievous grin.

"Oh, you *love* him. How *sweet.*"

I shook my head. "You've stooped to basic teasing? That seems beneath your usual style."

His eyes flashed brightly. "When it gets a reaction, heck yes I will. You love him." I set my phone aside and reached for my pillow, punching it to fluff it up.

Toni's words became annoyingly sing-song. "Kate and Patrick, sitting in a tree, k-i-s-s-i—"

I threw the pillow right into his face, hitting him a little harder than I meant to. He lost his balance and reeled back, slipping off the edge of Patrick's bed to land painfully on the floor.

"Ouch," he stated.

"I'd say I'm sorry, but—" I shrugged.

He came to his feet, handing me my pillow with a sour look. "I don't think I'm wanted here."

"How astute of you."

He muttered a rueful good night, closing the door behind him. I punched my pillow a few more times before sliding it into its proper position at the head of the bed. I moved my phone up onto Patrick's desk, then slipped under my blankets, finally leaning over to flip off the bedside lamp.

I settled down in the darkness, falling asleep in minutes, thoughts drifting into black emptiness . . .

It didn't feel like I was asleep for long, but when I jerked awake and looked wildly at the clock I saw that four hours had gone by.

I could still feel the dagger in my hand, fresh from my nightmare. Sean's face was emblazoned on my memory. Patrick's scream was still ringing in my ears. Trembling hands covered my eyes, forcing them shut as I willed the dream to die.

This dream had been different. The beginning, the middle—they were familiar. The conversation, my grandpa's murder, seeing the knife in my hand—nothing had surprised me there. It was the end—the horrific final scene—that caused me to shake.

I'd stabbed Sean. Only it wasn't Sean who died. I'd killed Patrick. Somehow, the blade was able to claim his immortal life. He fell to the ground, eyes wide, mouth gaping. Sean had disappeared, and in my anger I'd killed Patrick.

Still delirious with sleep, and shivering from a combination of fright and sudden awakening, I grasped for my phone. Seconds later it was ringing dully in my ear.

He answered on the third. "Kate? Is something wrong?" His voice was weak with sleep.

I couldn't answer right away. The guilt and fear clogged my throat.

I didn't realize I was choking on tears until he drew attention to the fact. "Kate, you're crying. What's going on?" His voice cracked, and he quickly cleared his throat.

"I'm sorry," I mumbled between my tears. "I'm sorry if I woke you up."

"Don't be ridiculous," he said quickly, voice more firm and alert. "Are you all right? Are you hurt?"

"No. I just—I just had a really, really bad dream." Distantly, I realized how ridiculous it was to call him like this; he couldn't do anything. But I'd needed to hear his voice. To know that he was okay. That he was alive. That the dream wasn't real.

"A dream?" A mix of relief and confusion colored his words. Frustration was present as well. I could understand that emotion—I was frustrated at the distance between us too. "What kind of dream?" he pressed.

I closed my eyes and let one sweaty palm support my forehead. "A nightmare."

"Do you want to tell me about it?"

"It was about Sean."

A short silence. Then he swallowed hard. "What happened?"

A fresh wave of grief hit me, washing over me until I thought I would drown. I cringed against the pain. "He killed him. He killed my grandpa." I sniffed loudly, my voice turning into a high whimper as the words came pouring out. Distantly, I realized I wasn't making much sense. "He killed him, and then I killed *him*. There was this knife in my hand—he told me to bring him back, but I couldn't. And so I killed him. But it wasn't him. It was you. I killed you. I'm so sorry!" I sobbed, unable to speak anymore.

His voice was low and comforting in my ear. "Kate, shh, it's all right. Hey, I'm right here. It was a dream. You have nothing to apologize for. Nothing to feel guilty about."

"But this wasn't the first time," I hiccupped. If I was aware of how pathetic I sounded, I would have been mortified. "I've killed him lots of times. But never you. I've heard you scream before, but never this."

"Kate. Please—it's all right. I promise, I'm fine. *You're* fine."

He continued to try and calm me for several minutes, breathing words of comfort and love, and eventually my heart stopped pounding. My tears stopped falling and my breathing steadied. My throat felt raw and my head was sore, but I was calming down. I was thinking rationally again.

"I'm sorry," I whispered at last, my throat constricted. "I shouldn't have called—it was stupid."

"No. I'm glad you did. You were upset." I could tell from his voice he was relieved I'd stopped crying, but another emotion dominated his tone now. He was aching, and so was I.

"I miss you," I murmured into the phone. Words I'd been too strong, too proud, to utter during daylight hours.

He didn't answer right away. Maybe he couldn't. "I miss you too," he said at last.

"Patrick?"

"Yes?"

"I . . . I love you. So much."

He struggled to speak, his voice cracking thinly. "Kate . . . If something happens tomorrow . . . if—" He blew out his breath, unable to finish. "You should go back to sleep. You need the rest."

"Okay," I whispered, too weak to protest.

He waited for me to end the call. I mumbled a last good night, then closed my phone. I lay back down, still clutching the small device in one hand, tucking it up under my chin. I couldn't make myself let go. Letting go meant losing my connection with him, as thin as it was.

eighteen

Dr. Radcliffe had run over the plan more times than I wanted to remember. He was sure he'd missed something, yet he talked with the confidence of a man who knew everything. He kept assuring us that nothing could go wrong, but Hanif didn't seem reassured—and watching Hanif wring his hands and pace was making me all the more jittery. I wished I was with Jason in a safe library somewhere, doing homework.

It was Friday morning, just after nine. I'd skipped school again, but this time Lee ditched with me. With Patrick gone, she was my greatest support. She stood beside me while we made our final preparations. Toni stood behind her, one hand resting on her slim waist. She was wearing a pink poodle skirt and a light pink blouse. A white scarf was wrapped around her neck, and her hair was in a short ponytail. Her face was still bruised but no longer swollen. Her presence alone infused me with confidence.

"Things are going to go great," she whispered, urging me to stop frowning. "You go in, follow the plan, then you hop back out. Easy!"

I forced a smile, but there was nothing real about it. Up to this point it was easy to focus on the details of the mission, not the actual objective. So many things could go wrong, especially if this date was as guarded as we suspected it could be. Demons, Seers—who knew what forces we would have to reckon with? Hanif had some training, and that was lucky for us. I'd been in fights, but I'd always had someone to rescue me when I got in over my head. Peter Keegan hadn't been in a fight once in his life; he'd confessed as much to me the other day.

And we were supposed to succeed?

But though I had all of that to worry about, it was impossible not to think about the reason behind all this stress and hard work—ending the life of a small boy who would one day become one of the most evil men to ever live. The thought still made me sick.

At least Radcliffe's plan wasn't too direct. None of us were actually expected to *do* anything to that little boy. Rather, we were supposed to make sure *no* one did anything. Hanif would cut the phone line, making it impossible for the young Demon Lord to call for an ambulance. Peter and I would watch from the sidelines, making sure no one interfered. Making sure the small boy bled to death.

I needed to concentrate on the Demon Lord's face. On all his horrible followers: the Dmitriev brothers, Mei Li, Takao Kiyota. And of course, Far Darrig. I needed to think of the twins—what would happen if I didn't succeed.

"I think I'm nearly ready," Dr. Radcliffe said to the room, his British accent pronounced.

I glanced up to see Hanif straighten. Peter's eyes closed tightly—he started muttering to himself. The words seemed too hurried to be a prayer, but I didn't know what else it could be.

Dr. Radcliffe scanned us all, then he smiled at me, his silver hair shining as he bobbed his head. "It's all right to be nervous. But I assure you, things will go brilliantly."

"That's what I'm afraid of," Hanif mumbled.

I silently agreed. I was glad I wasn't the only one with regrets about what had to be done.

Lee squeezed my hand. "You can do this, Kate. I know you can."

"I think you need to stop overthinking things," Toni commented.

Lee cast him a look before handing me a pair of some serious looking winter gloves. I was already wearing a thick parka—military-grade arctic camo, outfits that Alex had ordered the Guardians to supply for the mission into the past. I was sweating under the thick layers, having never worn anything so padded and stuffy. But since Radcliffe's memory would be depositing us in Chicago in December, I'd been assured that I'd need the protection from the cold. The winter gear I was wearing had been supplied for Ashley, whose place I was taking on the mission. We were close to the same size, so it worked. Peter was shrugging on Alex's coat, and it was obviously a bit too big. Hanif's fit perfectly, but he appeared uncomfortable, his face covered in a sheen of sweat.

Toni stepped up to me and whistled lowly. "Holy heavens, Kate. Would you look at all those pockets? You could steal all sorts of things and stash them in there."

"Thanks, Toni," I said wryly. "That was totally my first thought."

"Really?"

"Not even."

"You look like a cloudy marshmallow," he stated.

Lee slugged his arm. "Hey, what if I was wearing it?"

"You'd look adorable as a cloudy marshmallow."

"I'm dying of heat in here," I complained. "Can you flirt on your own time?"

Toni shook his head, but Lee waved her hand toward the gloves I held. "Now, put those on. If you get frostbite, Patrick won't ever speak to me again."

I rolled my eyes but obediently tugged them up to my wrists. They were surprisingly soft. And incredibly warm. I glanced over at Hanif, who was just pulling a similarly camouflaged wool hat over his dark hair.

Dr. Radcliffe cleared his throat. "Are you nearly ready?"

Lee handed me a hat, which I tugged over my head, pulling it low enough to cover my ears. She gave me a confident smile and Toni took hold of her hand. I moved to stand in front of Radcliffe, Hanif following my lead; Peter followed more slowly, but soon he stood at my other elbow.

Together we focused on Radcliffe's aura, gradually becoming dominated by a single color—a muted shade of purple I instinctively identified as frustration.

"Remember—catch a taxi as soon as possible," Radcliffe advised us. "You'll need all the time you can get in the past since the Demon Lord will be a good fifteen minutes from where I'll be dropping you off. You remember the address?"

I nodded, along with Hanif. Peter's head haltingly jerked forward. I brushed my fingers over my forehead, tucking some strands of hair under the hat. Beside me, I could feel Hanif shifting on his feet, uncomfortable in the heavy winter gear.

Dr. Radcliffe chuckled at us, guessing our source of discomfort. "Pull faces now—you'll thank me quite profusely in a minute. Come now—I think the memory is ready for you."

His aura was indeed almost fully a single color. I'd never seen a person isolate a memory so well. Peter was uneasily fingering the sheathed knife inside his coat pocket—one identical to mine, hidden in my pocket. I wished I could help him calm down, but since I wasn't in a much better state, he would have to get through this on his own.

I tried to concentrate on the wide color and the result was surprisingly quick—I was getting better at this. I felt myself falling, heard Lee let out a gasp of surprise . . .

And then it was freezing.

The wind was ripping through me, and everywhere the parka didn't cover was stinging with the harsh cold. The streets were covered in white, the snow capping everything in sight. Icicles hung from the nearby buildings, and when I tried to step further back on the sidewalk, away from the honking cars in the street, I slipped on some ice and slammed to the ground.

I'd never actually seen snow. When I was little, I thought it would be fun to build a snowman, go sledding, or have a snowball fight. At the moment, I'd never hated anything more than this cold, stinging stuff all around me. I couldn't breathe—I felt like I was being smothered by the cold. This was a worse sensation than New Mexico's most stifling summer day. My nose was running like I'd just eaten one of the spicy burritos my parents had often brought home for their in-house date nights.

Hanif was coughing, but since his breath was stolen by the raw wind he ended up merely gasping, his gloved hands fumbling to jerk his parka's hood down to better cover his face.

Peter Keegan appeared beside us, shuffling quickly back from the edge of the sidewalk. His shoes hit a patch of ice, but the tread must have been better than mine—or maybe he'd stepped on ice before and knew how to handle it, unlike me.

I pushed up from the ground, shaking as I tried to follow Hanif's example and pull up my own hood.

"Holy *crap*," Hanif shivered, his voice muffled by the high collar.

I thrust my hands into my pockets, wincing when my face was further exposed to the elements. I dropped my head into my own collar, trying to hunch in on myself for better protection. I was pretty sure I was about to freeze to death. Surely the body wasn't meant to get this cold, this stiff? I couldn't imagine not having the army-grade parka—I silently thanked Alex and Radcliffe for their foresight in realizing our need for the cold weather gear.

We might have just stood there, frozen and unsure, until

we did catch our deaths. But luckily we heard a familiar English accent further up the sidewalk, his words thrown toward us by the incessant wind that funneled between the buildings.

"Taxi!" he hollered, walking briskly from a brown brick building and toward the curb. He waved his heavily bundled arms furiously, his fingers protected by dark gloves. "Bloody Americans," he muttered angrily when cars continued to whip past. "Steal my wallet, won't get me a cab . . ."

I glanced back at the building he'd come from, catching sight of the letters that were illuminated by a floodlight—Elwood Park Police Department. So that's what his memory had been—getting mugged and then having to take the trouble to report it. Memorable, at least. *Happy Christmas Eve,* I thought ruefully.

A few seconds later a yellow car pulled up before him. He jerked the back door open and lowered himself quickly inside. The door slammed closed, and then the car joined the slow-moving traffic on the icy street.

Though I'd never called for a cab, it looked easy enough. If only my limbs weren't so bundled with the heavy parka, I might be able to freely lift my arm.

Thankfully, Peter wasn't as immovable as I was. He took over by stepping up to the street, attempting to flag down a taxi for us.

I forced myself to follow him, grateful that Hanif pressed up close to my arm. He wasn't the most effective windbreaker, but it helped. The cold was relentless.

We didn't have to wait long. A yellow cab shifted off the road, coming to a stop in front of us, cracking ice in the gutter. Peter grabbed open the back door, waving us briskly inside. I jumped in first, sliding all the way over. Hanif was directly behind me, and as soon as Peter had squished in with us he closed the door firmly.

The sudden heat against my face was almost painful. It

pinched my skin and made me gasp, but it was better than being outside. "Where to?" the cabbie asked. He sounded tired, but he had a pleasantly deep voice.

"Avondale," Peter croaked. "North Bernard Street."

The driver nodded. "Sure thing. You mind if I keep the Christmas tunes on?"

"No," Peter said.

We pulled away from the street, the driver's black head bobbing to the rousing tune of "Jingle Bells." Once my legs stopped shaking with the cold, I looked over the cabbie's shoulder, snatching a look at the dash. The clock read 11:07 PM, and a little calendar showing a pleasant-looking island sported the year 1971.

We didn't speak the whole drive, not that the cabby seemed to mind. He was humming along to "Silent Night" now, and between that and the icy road, he seemed pretty well occupied. I was holding on to the door the whole time, sure the wheels would slip on the icy patches just like I had.

I tried to distract myself from my fear of crashing by peering out the window, taking in the sights of this foreign city. Christmas lights ran along storefronts and houses alike, though many blocks were pretty dark. Golden pools of light fell from tall streetlamps that dotted our path. Snow and ice were everywhere. It looked like a scene from a Christmas movie.

It took about twenty minutes to get to Bernard Street, and once there the cabbie asked for a house number. Peter gave him a false one, but one but one that would get us close to the right house without drawing too much attention to ourselves.

We pulled up to a house with no Christmas lights. It was tall and thin. A small driveway slipped up the side, and it looked like two families lived inside. There was a basement door and an upstairs porch. According to Dr. Radcliffe, we would find the Demon Lord in a similar house, living in the basement portion.

My heart began to pound, knowing we were close. I

fingered the knife in my pocket, but I was pretty sure I'd be too cold and clumsy to pull it out and defend myself in the event of trouble.

Peter paid the cabdriver and we all climbed reluctantly back out into the cold. The driver wished us a merry Christmas before pulling away.

Hanif shivered violently. "Well, I don't know about you, but I say we get this over with as quickly as possible."

"Agreed," Peter grunted.

My lips were too cold to form words. Luckily the wind wasn't blowing as stiffly here, but the cold was sharp. Snow was falling around us, white flurries merging into the frosty piles already on the ground.

Once again, Peter took charge. He led the way down the deserted sidewalk, Hanif and I quick to follow. I felt weird just walking up to the house. What if some Demon saw us and realized we were coming to change the Demon Lord's past? If nothing else, we would fall back on Hanif's plan—pull back to the present at once. I was already tempted to do that, just because of the cold. How could people stand to live in this weather?

We reached the house, hesitating on the front sidewalk to stare collectively at the basement door. There was a wreath on the door, but that paled in comparison to the Christmas spirit the people above them were displaying. Colored lights outlined every window upstairs as well as the roof and the railing on the porch. They made everyone else on the quiet street look like a horrible Scrooge. There was no sign of anyone, anywhere.

Hanif's voice trembled, but that could have been from the temperature. "I-I'm going to go around b-back and get the phone line."

Peter spoke quickly, his voice less influenced by the cold. "Kate, go with him. I'll go around the other side to see if there's anyone suspicious." His shoulders shuddered as a shiver ripped through him. "Make sure you keep your eyes open."

I nodded; we each knew what to do. We'd gone over the simple plan many times.

Peter went left and Hanif and I moved cautiously up the driveway.

I winced when I heard our crunching footsteps. I hesitated, Hanif just behind me. What if someone heard? What if the sound of stupid footsteps got us killed?

Hanif's hand brushed my arm, and he nodded to the ground beside us. "Maybe if we walk in those tire tracks? The snow's pressed down—it might not be as loud."

I nodded and stepped to the side, moving onto the indented track. Our footsteps were muted now, but as we drew closer to the house, I could feel my apprehension growing. If we were right, the Demon Lord was in that house. A young boy, about to face death. If we succeeded, he *would* die.

Hanif concentrated on watching the side of the house, his eyes on the power lines that fed into the house. I found myself peering at the basement windows we began to pass. It was hard to get a good look into any of them, because they were so low to the ground. Also, each one I passed was covered and darkened with hanging sheets, patterned with patches of faded flowers, making it impossible to see inside. As we neared the back corner of the house, I finally found one that was glowing with a halo of light from inside, blocked by a slip of cardboard so I couldn't really *see* anything but the uneven ring of light. I stooped closer, confused by the ill-fitting cardboard. Why not a sheet? My eyes danced over a crack in the glass, near the top of the window. It webbed down the whole pane, and several small pieces of glass were completely missing; the taped-up cardboard would keep the frigid wind out better than a sheet.

I stopped walking altogether, glancing up at the levels above. All of those windows were dark, so I assumed the family up there was asleep. They had no idea such horrible crimes were about to take place downstairs.

According to the police report, the young Demon Lord put the time of the shootings at about 11:40 p.m. I didn't have a watch, but I knew that could be any minute now.

Hanif stepped around me carefully, making a small footprint in the snow when he slid off the tire track. "It looks like it'll be around back."

I nodded but continued to hesitate by the lighted window when I heard a scant cry from inside. Hanif slipped around back while I crouched closer to the damaged window, the sounds louder than I would have expected—probably thanks to the crack.

"No, James, please!" a woman cried desperately, her voice muted by the wall. "He didn't mean it—he won't do it again."

She sounded so broken. So terrified. I swallowed hard but leaned closer to the house.

A man swore, and when he spoke his words were slurred. "No, he won't. I'll make sure of it."

"Please—don't!"

There was a sound I couldn't place at first. And then I heard a small voice shout. "Don't hit my mom!"

"Steven, go back to your room," the woman choked. "I'm all right."

"Listen to your mom, you freak!"

I crouched closer to the window, my heavily gloved hand pressing deeply against the side of the house for balance. I'd never heard anything like this in real life. Knowing that this sort of thing really happened . . . that it was happening right now, and I couldn't do anything to stop it . . .

"Let go of my mom!" the little boy shouted again.

"Shut up!" the man said heatedly. There was an angry footfall followed by a horrible ringing slap.

The boy whined and the mother sobbed, "James, please!"

"I don't want the neighbors hearing anything!" the man snapped angrily. "You got it?"

"I'm not afraid of you!" the boy Steven rasped with white

rage. His emotional voice was nothing like the Demon Lord, but I knew it was him. And in that moment, my heart went out to him.

I swallowed hard, pinched my eyes closed tightly. *Don't aggravate him,* I thought sorrowfully. *Don't do it . . .*

"Leslie!" James growled. "Where's that freak daughter of yours?"

"James, please, she's sleeping . . ."

Someone touched my arm. I jumped and stumbled away from the house, nearly falling back in the snow.

It was only Hanif. "I thought something happened to you!" he nearly hissed.

"Did you cut it?" I asked.

He shook his head. "I thought you were right behind me."

I heard the silenced gunshot inside the house, and the shriek of a small boy in agony.

"Cut it," I choked back on a rush of tears. "Just cut it!"

Hanif wheeled around, almost startled by my tone. Had he even heard the shot, or was I just attuned into to the nightmare unfolding inside? It didn't really matter—he was rushing to follow my orders, as desperate to escape this place as I was.

He disappeared around the corner and I stumbled after him. Before I could round the corner I heard a second shot, followed rapidly by a third. Tears stung my eyes, freezing on my cheeks. The guilt I felt for letting these things unfold when I could have prevented them . . . I'd never yearned for Patrick's warm embrace so badly. I just wanted to get out of here—get back to my own time. Have someone assure me that I'd done the right thing—the *only* thing.

Hanif would cut the line, and we'd wait around until we were sure the young Demon Lord—I couldn't even make myself think of him as Steven—was dead. After that, we could go home. I just had to keep breathing until then. Keep moving, stop thinking . . .

I stepped into the backyard, coming face-to-face with the heavily scarred face of Takao Kiyota, the Demon Lord's most trusted Seer.

"Hello, Kate," he said slowly. His voice was strained and airy from a cut to his windpipe, the reward from a some past knife fight. He was almost my height, though he was older by several years. He had a horribly twisted face, which never smiled. His aura was darkly colored, the slim gold lining around his body the only bright spot. Every inch of visible skin was crisscrossed with scars, and his eyes were cold on mine.

Before I could react he leveled a gun at my forehead. "Don't make a sound."

I saw Hanif forced up against the back of the house, his face turned away from me. But it was his captor that surprised me the most.

My stomach dropped as I saw Peter Keegan's knife pressed against the side of Hanif's straining neck.

Peter glanced my way, his face neutral.

"Peter?" I gasped in shock.

"I'm sorry, Kate," he said softly, voice devoid of emotion. "I had no choice. I had to tell Selena everything. It's the only way to keep Lee and Jeanette safe."

I blinked, shaking my head in blatant denial. "No. No, I trusted you!"

"I'm sorry," he repeated, unmoved.

Takao cocked the gun calmly. "You will return to your own time now. We all will. The Demon Lord will be waiting for us there."

"What?" I whispered, completely dazed.

Takao's arm shifted to the side, his weapon discharging in almost the same second.

Hanif howled as the bullet shot into his shoulder, staining the white camo. Peter flinched back, but his hands continued to support the now gasping Seer.

Takao's words were colder than ice—and I now knew just

how cold that could be. "The next shot claims his life. Now, Kate. Return now."

Shaking so much I couldn't see clearly, I located the internal pull inside my body. Found it and embraced it, letting it jerk me away from this nightmare before anyone else could get hurt.

The next thing I knew I was shivering on the warehouse floor. Lee was grasping my arm, her face completely amazed. For her, I'd gone from sweating in a dry parka to wet and trembling in an instant.

I was slipping into unconsciousness, the rush of distorted time forcing me to black out. I tried to make my mouth work. "Demon . . . Lord," I breathed.

"What?" Lee asked, leaning closer to catch my weak exhale.

But I was already gone. My vision was black, and just before I went under, I heard Toni curse and call out Hanif's name . . .

***

". . . I know. But she's all right. Hanif had the only injury, but Claire was able to stop the bleeding. He's still a little pale, but the damage was pretty superficial." A pause, and then Lee continued, her voice almost meek. "I'm sorry. I should have called you sooner. But relax, okay? She's fine . . . Yeah, about an hour now. Dr. Radcliffe thinks they'll be out for at least another hour or two, if they all came back at the same time, and things went according to plan." Another break. "Well, obviously not perfectly, with Hanif shot. But we won't know exactly until they wake up." Worn sigh. "She wasn't hurt, as far as I can tell. She was shivering, that was all. Peter was the same." Pause. "Of course. I'll have her call you when she wakes up."

I couldn't move my body, but my thoughts were becoming clearer. An hour? How was I this awake after only an hour? Normally I was out for much longer.

And then I remembered why I was fighting so strenuously to get through the fog. Peter was a traitor. He'd betrayed our plans to the Demon Lord. Takao had come back to stop our efforts, and the Demon Lord was waiting for us. What did that mean?

I needed to wake up. I needed to warn them. What else had Peter told Selena? What if the Demon Lord was on his way to the warehouse right now?

"Patrick, will you stop freaking out? Worst-case scenario, they ran into some trouble. But all three of them made it back . . . Yeah. Okay, bye." Lee ended the call.

I struggled to find my voice.

I felt Lee's hands pull up my blankets, tucking me in more securely. Her fingers brushed my forehead, and that simple action lulled me back into sleep.

I lost my only chance to warn them of the incredible danger we were all in.

nineteen

When my eyes finally opened, I knew everything had changed. I didn't need to look around the room to know Lee wasn't with me anymore. In fact, I was pretty sure I was alone in Patrick's room.

Moving came slowly. I laboriously shifted my weight, rolling onto my side before forcing my shaking arms to lift me up into a sitting position on the bed. I was trembling, despite the fact I was now warm and dry. Trembling with an emotion I knew all too well—fear.

I looked to the desk, but my phone was gone; Lee must have moved it. I rubbed my eyes and tried to keep my head steady while my vision spun. The silence rang in my ears, and I fleetingly wondered if I was the only one in the entire warehouse.

Peter Keegan had lied to me. He'd betrayed us. How much had Peter told Selena? Obviously he'd told her about our plans, but did she know where we were? Did she know where the twins were? No. Not possible. I hadn't told him, and I doubted he would have dared ask anyone else. Still, it was a thought that hadn't occurred to me until just now, and I needed to confirm they were safe. I needed to call Patrick.

I needed to find Toni. Claire. Lee. Anyone. I needed to find

Peter and make sure he didn't try to hurt anyone else. If he did, it would be my fault. I'd asked for his help. I should have listened to Patrick. I shouldn't have trusted the Demon Seer.

I glanced at the clock and saw that three hours had passed since I'd gone back to 1971. I'd lost three hours. Hours I could have spent finding the damage Peter had caused. I couldn't afford to stay here any longer. Still faintly dizzy, I forced myself to stand. Blankets slid off my weak body as I gained back the use of my feet, and I shuffled toward the closed door.

I leaned briefly against the door frame, taking a last opportunity to close my eyes and breathe in slowly. My head was pounding, but the pain was noticeably retreating with each throb. I just needed to alert Toni, and then I could crawl back in bed until the ache disappeared completely.

I took in a last shallow breath, then turned the knob, pulling the door open. I stepped out into the makeshift living room and found the Demon Lord's pleased smile trained on me.

"Why, Kate. How quickly you recovered! I hope your headache isn't too severe?"

I stared at him, standing so calmly in the middle of the room. He was holding an apple I imagined he'd just gotten from the small fridge in the corner. The Dmitriev brothers were positioned at the far end of the room, both of their blond heads focused on the man lying on the floor at their feet. My breath caught in my throat—it was Toni. He was curled up on his side, his hands bound behind his back with layers of duct tape. Blood matted his hair and was splattered all over his clothes. A knife was buried high in his back, keeping him from healing and regaining his strength. He breathed heavily into the floor, his whole body quivering with pain.

Lee was on the couch, her eyes red from crying. Her bruised face now sported a few shallow cuts and her arms were wrapped tightly around her stomach as if she were suffering from a sharp pain. She was looking to me, pale and afraid. The white poofy scarf that had once been around her neck now served as a gag. Selena was sitting next to her, studying her manicured nails while holding a small handgun, aimed lazily at my best friend.

Mei Li was near the Demon Lord's arm, her thin body straight as a rod but somehow perfectly relaxed. Her hands were small but deceiving. I knew firsthand what she was capable of.

Far Darrig stood back near the door, wearing a black button-up shirt. He looked so much like his brother, it was uncanny. Sleeves rolled at the elbows, dark jeans, and a firm jaw. His eyes were the same as well; a penetrating blue. He looked to be in his thirties, and he was attractive—except for the black aura surrounding him and his almost haunted expression. He was keeping an eye on Claire, who was tied to a chair with ropes that crisscrossed her chest, and she had a knife in her side. Her face was covered in a sheen of sweat, and like Toni, she had more blood on her than wounds to show for it.

Obviously they'd put up a great struggle. It just hadn't been enough.

Dr. Radcliffe, Hanif, Takao, and Peter were nowhere in sight.

I didn't need anyone to explain what had happened. The Demon Lord had finally come for me, and my friends had lost the fight.

The Demon Lord was dressed immaculately in a perfectly tailored black suit. He had a dark purple tie, and he looked completely harmless. His aura was just as confusing as it had been the last time I'd seen it. There were too many shifting colors to make sense of—they all seemed like a twisting rainbow of confusion.

He was handsome. His face perfectly sculpted with only slight wrinkles around his eyes. He clicked his tongue at me. "Now, Kate, don't look quite so distressed. You really left me no choice. You ran away, and then you defy me by trying to destroy me in the past. For obvious reasons, I can't allow such behavior."

"Let them go," I whispered, my shoulders too heavy to support. "You don't need them. It's me you want."

He winced. "There, see, I knew this would be a problem. I'm afraid you're really not worth the trouble anymore. You can promise to be good and obey, but there will always be a part of you that longs to rebel. I should have seen this from the beginning."

I fought against the trembling in my hands—forced them to stay at my sides. "So what *do* you want?"

He fingered the round apple in his hands, green eyes still on me. They'd turned regretful. My stomach dropped in response. "I hate to waste a Special Seer," he mourned. "But you leave me no choice. You are a liability, Kate Bennett. And I know how to handle liabilities."

I swallowed hard, trying not to let my fear show. I'm sure I failed. "So why didn't you just kill me? Why let me wake up at all?"

"Because I'm a businessman, Kate. I hate to be on the losing side of any deal. The other special Seers the Guardians found, I probably can't use them either. Not after what they tried to do today. So, where does that leave me? To lose three Special Seers in one day? No. It's bad business." He took a bite from the apple and turned to look over the room while he chewed.

His eyes fell on Lee, and he swallowed.

I stiffened.

"This girl," he said calmly. "She's not a Seer, I imagine?" Before I could form words, he was shaking his head. "No, I'm sure she's not . . . But she must be special to you. Why else would she be here?"

He took another bite and twisted back to face me. "Where are your sisters, Kate? And I'm not in the mood for games."

"What do you want with them?" I demanded, trying to

ignore the throbbing in my head. "They have nothing to do with any of this."

"Don't they? I was under the impression your grandfather was a Seer with special abilities. You had them too. Your sisters . . ." He shrugged. "It's just good business. So tell me: where are they?"

I gaped at him, irrationally shocked by his sick intentions. He wanted to turn my sisters into Seers. He wanted to turn my sisters into Seers—just as Selena had made Peter into one. He wanted to almost kill my sisters, to awaken their Sight, and then he was going to make them serve him.

I was shaking my head. "No. You can't do that."

"Can't I?" A single eyebrow rose. "Kate, I think you'll find I'm in a position to do whatever I like. They aren't at your house, and since Patrick isn't around, I'm assuming he ran off with them? Now, I'll ask you again: where are they?"

My mind was scrambling for something to say; anything but the truth. "I don't know. I told him to take them somewhere safe, but I didn't want to know where. They'd be safer that way, if I didn't know."

He smiled, and it was chilling. "I think you've seen one too many movies, Kate. But then, that's a good thing—you won't be surprised by what happens next." He turned on his heel, nodded curtly to Selena.

Toni gasped from the floor where he'd been watching the proceedings through a veil of pain. "Lee!" he panted feebly, choking from the effort it took to lift his head.

Too late I realized what was happening.

"No!" I screamed, letting the shout rip through my throat despite my aching head.

Selena moved casually. Lee's eyes only had time to widen before the bullet pounded into her chest. She was blown back against the couch, blood blossoming through her pink blouse.

Toni snarled and writhed on the floor, unable to push

himself up. Viktor, the Russian brother with long hair, kicked him soundly in the face, stopping the pitiful squirming effort.

I lurched forward but Mei Li reacted just as quickly. She darted in front of me, landing a kick to my stomach before cinching my wrists behind me. She held me in place as I watched Lee slump deeper into the old couch, slipping to lie on her side.

Lee was blinking limply, her eyes slightly unfocused. Selena set the gun on the coffee table and stood, straightening her long black skirt. She leaned over Lee and ripped off the gag so my friend's tortured breaths could fill the room. She tossed the scarf aside and grabbed Lee's wrist, unceremoniously drawing her up from the couch and slinging her body to the floor. Lee slammed hard against the cement, her lungs shuddering at the impact, and an almost surprised cry escaped her.

"Lee!" I sobbed, so shocked by how things were unraveling I could barely breathe.

The Demon Lord stepped in front of me, blocking my view of her. His mouth was a tight line. "My patience is nearly spent, Kate. I will allow one of your Guardians to take her to the emergency room, if you tell me where your sisters are. But speak quickly; she'll be dead in minutes."

The words jumped out of my mouth without thought. "They're staying with one of my grandma's friends. She lives on a small farm—about fifty miles from here."

"Where is it exactly?" he demanded.

I couldn't remember the address. I told him the city and gave him hurried instructions for where to turn. "It's a small yellow house at the end of the road, with a big barn in back," I finished in a pinched rush. "Please, let Toni take her to the hospital!"

The Demon Lord ignored me. He turned to his most loyal servant, Far Darrig, who hadn't budged at all. "You can find it?"

Sean nodded once. "I can find it."

"Take Yuri with you. One of you can distract O'Donnell

while the other takes care of the twins. I will wait for your word, once the job is complete."

Sean nodded again.

I was trying to get a good look at Lee, but Mei Li was holding me too tightly. I heard Toni's voice, cracking and weak. "Hold on, Lee. Please hold on . . ."

Everything we try fails . . .

The door opened and the Demon Lord turned to see the new arrival. My eyes flickered between the door and Lee, whose aura was dimming . . .

Takao Kiyota stepped inside, looking tired. Peter was right behind him, looking troubled. He stopped dead when he saw Lee on the floor.

"What happened?" he demanded, looking first to me and then Selena. "You promised she wouldn't be hurt!"

Selena smiled thinly. "Oops."

Peter pushed around Takao, hurrying to Lee's side. He knelt beside her, touching her shoulder. Lee whimpered when he rolled her over. "She needs help!" he growled, looking to Selena. "You promised she'd be safe!"

She shrugged. "I lied." She stooped over to pick up the gun. "My Lord?" she asked, looking to the Demon Lord.

He nodded once, bringing the apple back up to his lips.

Selena raised the gun, and I was sure she was going to shoot Peter. My stomach clenched, but he wasn't the target.

Lee's body jerked from the second shot, this one catching her in the head. Her aura vanished as she grew still—just like Grandpa.

Peter fell backward, sitting heavily on the floor with a white face.

I couldn't breathe. I couldn't move.

My best friend had just been shot to death in front of my eyes.

Toni was staring at her lifeless body, his rigid shoulders

shaking. He couldn't speak. Couldn't make a sound. A single tear burned a trail down his bloody cheek.

Selena tutted him softly in the sudden silence. "That's one of the biggest reasons *not* to love a mortal, Antonio."

The Demon Lord frowned at Peter, who was reaching to touch Lee's limp arm. He swallowed his bite of apple. "Get up. Go keep an eye on the other Seers. I will see to them later."

Peter's face was blank. He looked up at me. Looked at Selena.

She shook her head at him. "You're pathetic, Peter. Trust me—a stepdaughter wouldn't have been any fun. You'll thank me someday."

His chest rose and fell with a quick, angry burst. He came quickly to his feet, blinking back tears. He stopped short when she raised the gun on him. "I'll kill you next," she said calmly. "And then her mother. Is that what you want? Follow orders, Peter. That's a good dog. Go stand guard with Jose."

It was obvious he didn't want to listen to her, but that didn't stop him from backing away from the gun. He turned abruptly and marched from the room, hands trembling at his sides.

As soon as the door closed Takao shook his head. "He's unstable. Too emotional. You could do better, Selena."

"He just needs to be trained," she disagreed.

The Demon Lord turned to Far Darrig. "Go. When you've finished, call me. These loose ends can be tied after the Bennett girls are secured."

Far Darrig bowed his head stiffly. "Of course, my lord." He stepped away from Claire, gesturing sharply with his chin for Yuri to follow. The huge Russian with spiky blond hair stepped around Toni's broken body, moving for the door. He pulled it open and stepped into the hall. Far Darrig moved behind him, but before he could leave the room I forced my mouth to open.

"Sean, please don't do this. *Please!*"

Surprisingly, he stopped. He didn't turn, but he was listening.

Tears rolled down my face, making my voice crack. "Please. I went to see your father. He doesn't want you to be this person. You don't have to do this!"

I watched for a reaction. I didn't know what I expected. A complete change of heart from a Demon?

His head twisted and he peered at me over his shoulder, taking in my tearstained face. "My father is dead," he finally whispered. "So is Sean."

He strode from the room, shattering the last hope I'd been clinging to.

***

I was sitting in the corner of the room with Toni beside me, my arm sagging around his shoulders in feeble comfort. He now had a dagger in his stomach, making that two knives sticking out of him. His face was covered in sweat and tears. Though I hadn't been bound, I didn't dare move. The Demons were watching me closely, and the fact that I was unbound and yet still completely helpless only made me feel more defeated. Maybe that was why they'd done it.

Toni's head was on my shoulder. He was too weak to support it. He stared unblinking at Lee's body, lying prone in front of us. Her head was turned away from us, but the blood covering her still chest was completely visible. One of her hands had been stopped in the act of reaching for Toni—her curled fingers were inches from his foot, now that he'd been forced up against the wall.

Claire was still in the chair, her bowed head unmoving. None of us had spoken since Far Darrig had left. The Demon Lord was sitting on the couch, Selena beside him. Mei Li was standing alertly near the coffee table, Takao was keeping an eye on Claire, and Viktor Dmitriev was standing next to me.

For a solid hour, my phone—which the Demon Lord held—had gone off almost every five minutes. When I didn't answer, Patrick waited those few predictable minutes, and then tried again. Did he know something was wrong? Was he just anxious? And more important, what did his silence for the past twenty minutes mean? I knew it corresponded with the time Sean would have been arriving. Was Patrick busy fighting his brother? Was he protecting the twins? At least he had Jack. That would take the Demons by surprise . . .

A phone started to ring. I looked up quickly because it wasn't mine. It was a section of Beethoven's Ninth Symphony, but it didn't have long to play. The Demon Lord answered nearly at once.

"Yes?" he said shortly into his phone.

The answer was brief.

The Demon Lord relaxed, and a smile twisted his face. "Good. And he surrendered? Excellent. Bring them all. We'll be ready to go when you get back. Thank you, Far Darrig."

He closed his phone and turned to Selena. "He was successful."

My heart stopped for what felt like the hundredth time today. No one seemed to notice.

"O'Donnell and the twins are secured. Far Darrig's already on his way back. And it seems there was another Guardian, as well as a Seer, and they both surrendered as well."

Claire whimpered thinly from across the room.

"Good news," Selena commented, studying her nails.

"Very." He stood lithely. "Do you feel up to intimidating a few Seers? Perhaps some can still be useful to us."

She grinned, her hand dropping as she stood. "I would love to." She glanced at Lee, the corner of her lip curled. "That human was no fun at all. Completely pathetic."

Toni's limp body tensed. His head rose from my shoulder, his expression black. I'd never seen him so furious. "I will *end* you, Selena," his voice quivered with fervor. "Even if it takes the rest of my existence, I *swear* I'm going to *annihilate you*."

She brushed a hand over her perfectly bushy hair, her thick lips stretching into a grin. "I look forward to such devotion, Antonio. Eternity can be such a bore without some distractions." Her hips swayed as she followed the Demon Lord and Mei Li from the room, leaving Viktor and Takao to guard us. As soon as the door closed behind them, Toni slumped back against me, utterly exhausted. I tipped my head against the top of his, tightening my hold on him, but not daring to bring up my other arm to fully embrace him in case the Demons decided such action merited separation.

"It's over, isn't it?" I whispered unnecessarily.

Toni didn't answer.

The twins had been dragged into this mess. They were going to become slaves to the Demon Lord. Had they already been nearly killed? Patrick and Jack, both captured . . .

Surely this was the end. Winning was impossible now. We'd lost too much.

"Kate," Toni croaked.

I swallowed before answering. Our guards didn't seem to mind if we talked. They had to be able to hear our mumbling, even if they couldn't make out the exact words. "Yeah?" I asked.

"Could you save her?" he whispered. "If you went back?"

I looked to Lee's body, not sure of the answer. Could I? If I went back and talked to Patrick, could I save Lee's life? Maybe if I was more specific this time, if I warned Patrick to make sure Toni took Lee away . . . Maybe I was going to have to use trial and error, constantly repeating these weeks until I managed to save everyone. First I'd delivered the message meant to save the twins. Now I needed to warn Patrick about the twins and Lee.

If I lived this enough times, would it be possible to stop it from ever happening?

I honestly didn't know. But I had nothing to lose at this point. The Demon Lord would probably kill me as soon as he was done with the Seers upstairs. I could go back in time, deliver a final message, a final warning, and then I could die trusting that the endless cycle of time would continue. That, somehow, I would never stop trying to save those I loved, and that someday I'd succeed.

Patrick, I wish you were here. I wish I could have told you one last time . . . I wish I'd said yes. I want to marry you. I want to be yours and I want you to be mine . . .

I pushed away the image of Patrick's face. It was too painful to dwell on.

"I'll try," I whispered to Toni.

I felt him struggle with words. When he did speak, his voice wavered. "Thank you, Kate."

"Hey, what are you talking about?" Viktor asked menacingly.

I lifted my head and Toni straightened painfully beside me. "Take me as far back as you can," I told him suddenly, squeezing his shoulders. "I want to save everyone." If I was going to die, why not save my grandpa too? And Alex and Ashley?

I don't know that he heard me. His eyes were closed and he was concentrating hard.

Viktor stepped toward us, raising his gun and pointing it at me. "Stop moving!" he ordered.

Takao turned away from Claire, catching sight of Toni's aura, which he'd just revealed to me. The Demon Seer paled, making his many scars stand out. "No! She's going to travel!"

Viktor didn't need a direct order. His finger squeezed the trigger of his gun, once, twice, three times . . .

I felt the bullets whip into my body, but I was concentrating on the single emotion Toni was summoning so intently that even the sharp pain couldn't distract me. I was losing myself in the memory when I heard Takao scream in frustration. He was unwilling to follow me, because he didn't know where I was going. He didn't want to travel to a year he'd already lived in. He was afraid to die.

I wasn't.

I was dying anyway.

Viktor had emptied his gun into me, but it couldn't stop me from fading out of time.

I gasped painfully. I was lying in a dark room on the hard floor, and for the first time I was feeling the pain of the bullets. I was dying. Fast. And it hurt. A lot. I could also feel the pull of time, begging me to come back. It was stronger than I'd ever felt, as if it was ordering me to come back quickly, before the fatal damage was done.

I ignored it.

Moonlight filtered through the darkness, silhouetting every shape. I recognized the room almost immediately. I was in Patrick's bedroom. And I wasn't alone. I heard someone breathing—heard the mattress protest against sudden movement.

"Who's there?" a wonderful voice hissed. It was amazing how warm my heart could feel despite the overwhelming trauma my body and mind were going through.

I opened my mouth to answer him. Only a strangled cry could escape. It was a cry of pain, death, and longing. Though I couldn't see him, I heard Patrick ease off his bed. Cautious footsteps brought him around the bed, closer to me. I lifted my eyes, my vision strangely frosted—cloudy. It made it hard to see him clearly. But those blue eyes were unmistakable. They went right to mine, then raked over my bloody body. His mouth was hanging open, a dagger in his hand.

I tried to speak again, this time anticipating the urge that would follow my open mouth; I managed to stifle the scream. "Patrick," I rasped.

The dagger slipped from his fingers, clattering to the floor. He fell to his knees beside me, eyes still dragging across my body, taking in the blood and assessing the damage. I knew he'd realized the extent of my wounds when he suddenly grabbed my hand, squeezing it with a pressure that hurt. His other hand touched my face, pushed my hair back off my forehead. "Kate." He was having difficulty speaking. The words didn't want to pass through his clenched teeth. "What happened? How'd you get in here?"

I cringed against the pain, struggled to swallow back blood or bile or both. "What day is it?" Had Toni understood? Had he taken me back further? Patrick didn't look sick. His face was pale, but he wasn't dying. So when was it?

His face was uncomprehending. "What day . . .?" His body went hard when he figured it out. "Kate, you can't be here."

He looked so worried that I'd risk life by coming back, I gave into the strange urge to laugh. It was a pathetic attempt. "I think I was already pretty done for."

I squeezed his fingers, but it was hard to tell how firmly I managed to do it. I couldn't feel mine anymore. "I'm sorry, Patrick. I know this is hard. But I need you to listen. I need you to change what happens. But to do that, I need to know what day it is."

He kept looking over my body, looking at the blood I could feel soaking every inch of my front. "The funeral," he fairly stuttered. "It was the funeral today."

I pursed my lips and closed my eyes, not that his answer came as a big surprise. "Not far enough," I whispered to Toni, though he wouldn't be able to hear me. "I wanted to save . . ."

The pull was becoming stronger, almost painful—not that it really stuck out from the rest of the torture I was in. I opened my eyes, trying to focus my foggy, pain-laden thoughts. There wasn't any time to waste. He was watching me closely, his expression grave. "Patrick, I don't have much time. Already I'm being pulled back. But you need to promise me something."

"What? Anything!"

My lips twitched at his eagerness, his desperation. He still thought he could save me. I felt like my heart was breaking, but I guess I should just add that to the list of other agonies.

I wasn't exactly sure where to start, but I forced my lips to move anyway, knowing time was short. "I need you to promise that you won't try to stop me. That you'll let me do what I need to do. That you'll save the twins instead. Keep them safe, no matter what. Because you can't save me, Patrick. Not anymore. Not when I've gone back . . ."

His hand flexed around mine. "Kate, you have to tell me what happened—what happens. Who did this to you?"

Of all the things for him to worry about . . . I would have rolled my eyes, if I was conscious enough to do something like that. "It doesn't matter."

He shuddered, which made his breathing ragged. "Doesn't matter? Kate, please—give me anything . . ." He suddenly looked toward the door. "Toni!" he yelled, frustrated and helpless.

I winced at his pain, knowing it was only the beginning.

As if he could sense my spike in pain, he looked back to me, our eyes locking. Though I still had things to tell him, there was something else my heart needed to say, sensing rightly that the last beats were coming.

"I know this is weird for you," I breathed shakily. "But my Patrick isn't here. With me in the future, I mean. So if it's all right . . ." I took a deep breath—as deep as I could manage, anyway. "I love you, Patrick. I love you so much. No matter what, I'll always love you. No matter where I am. Please promise me you'll remember that?"

The door was thrust open, and Toni let out a shocked exclamation. But I wasn't paying attention to him—I only had eyes for the man I loved. The last face I was going to see.

He saw my intensity and was frightened by it. "I promise," he croaked. "I'll always remember."

Somehow I managed a smile. "Save the twins. When

everything goes wrong . . . when everything we do fails . . . just take care of the twins." I swallowed, choked, desperate to warn him about Lee. Toni was in the room now; he needed to hear about Lee. If anyone could save her life, it was him. "And please . . . please, Toni . . . tell Toni . . . he . . ."

Warm blood was climbing up my throat, clogging my words. I couldn't deliver final warnings—I was out of time. I had to hope that the pitiful warning would put Toni on his guard, be enough to save my best friend's life.

Tears were shining in Patrick's eyes. His breath seemed to hitch unconsciously with mine. I couldn't kiss him good-bye—no way I had the strength for that, not when I couldn't even say his name one last time.

I tried to squeeze his hand, failing miserably.

My eyes were too heavy. They closed of their own accord. I felt my heart pound a final time, and then my muscles relaxed. The pain was gone. I couldn't feel anything anymore. Not even the pull I'd been fighting so hard against.

My last conscious thought was that a better death would have been impossible. I'd died next to the man I loved with all my soul. Nothing could compete with that.

twenty

Present Day, Thirty Minutes Earlier
Patrick O'Donnell
New Mexico, United States

I shut my phone, bringing the top to rest near my pursed lips. I stared out the small kitchen window, the yellow curtains accentuating the bright sunlight that shined through. My whole body was tight with an energy and stress I didn't know how to release.

She wasn't answering her phone. No one was. Lee's phone went straight to voicemail, as did Toni's and Claire's. I swallowed hard and tried to get control of myself. There could be a harmless explanation for this extended silence.

But if there was, it was well hidden.

I repeated Lee's last comforting words to me. Kate was all right. Cold, wet, and unconscious, but she was all right. I'd been assured that I would get a call from her the moment she awoke.

So why hadn't she called? She should have been awake by now, if Dr. Radcliffe's estimations were correct. If things had gone smoothly. But I suppose I already knew they hadn't. Hanif had been shot.

I sighed deeply, closing my eyes tightly. I wished more than ever I was with her. I needed to see her—touch her. Know that she was all right. Being away from her when she was putting herself at such risk . . . it was agony. I was forty-seven miles away from her. So close, yet so terribly far.

"Patrick?"

I glanced up to see Jack standing beside the table.

He slid into a seat across from me, his eyes worried. "You all right, mate?"

I pulled the phone away from my mouth, setting it on the table. "No one's answering."

Jack eyed my phone. "There could be a reason for that. There's no sense in jumping to conclusions."

I nodded once. "Maybe."

He leaned back in his chair, huffing. "It stinks something fierce, them being unconscious and unable to tell us what happened. If we knew, we'd be better prepared."

I didn't form any reply.

He shook his head suddenly. "Lilly and Charlotte just left for the store. The twins are out back, playing in the yard."

"They're staying away from the horses?" I asked, surprised. They were loving the small country farm, though their grandmother was pretty adamant that they stay away from the horses unless closely supervised by Jack or one of Lilly's farmhands. Of course, Josie disregarded rules the second they were made, and when it came to horses even Jenna didn't mind a little sneaking. I'd kept an eye on them myself, not that they knew I was here.

He shrugged. "For the moment they are."

"Where's Maddy?" I asked.

"She's still got her headache. I told her to go up to bed."

I nodded slowly, looking back at the phone lying quietly on the table.

Jack's voice was understanding. "I just thought I'd come and see if you wanted to join us out back. Just because you're dead and invisible doesn't mean you need to be a hermit."

I barely smiled, and he sighed. "Look—you can worry all you want, but it isn't going to change anything. So why not step out into the sun. You could use some color," he added jokingly.

"Maybe in a few minutes," I said, reaching for the phone. "I'm going to try Kate again."

He straightened in his chair, shoving a hand into his pocket. "Fine. You do that. I'll try Toni."

Though I was grateful for his show of help, I doubted it was going to do any good. And not just because I'd been on the phone for about an hour without once speaking to another soul. No, it was because of the feeling in my gut. The one that told me something was wrong.

Horribly wrong.

***

Fear Dearg
New Mexico, United States

Slow down," I told Yuri.

He eased up on the gas instantly, slowing the SUV's speed. I could see the farmhouse up ahead, just as Kate had described it; a small, pale yellow house at the end of the road that had turned to dirt about a mile ago. No sign of neighbors. A large barn dominated the flat landscape tucked behind the yellow house. A few trees grew in the yard, and pastures surrounded the land. It was an isolated spot, and though it looked nothing like Ireland I was temporarily reminded of home.

I crushed the thought immediately as I always did whenever memories of my past life cropped up. I was no longer that person. I hadn't been for a long time. If it hadn't been for Kate's reference to my father, back at the warehouse, I wouldn't be thinking about home at all—wouldn't have to push back the sharp feelings such thoughts inspired.

Except I was probably only minutes away from coming face-to-face with O'Donnell—again; maybe that thought alone was what kept triggering my more reflective side. Though that didn't entirely make sense, since lately I'd been thinking of the past far too often. I wasn't one for personal reflection, but since seeing O'Donnell in Vegas, memories had been quick to surface. My mother's face, which I thought I'd forced myself to forget a century ago; my father's voice, which I'd learned to hate even before my death. Even boyhood memories that seemed inconsequential kept surfacing: Patrick and me playing in the cemetery behind Father's church, eating a warm slice of bread in Mother's kitchen . . .

I growled internally. Here I was again, far too distracted by things that didn't matter. Hadn't mattered for years. I needed to focus on *now*. Forget the past. Forget Kate Bennett's fearful face. Forget the odd jerk I'd felt in my gut when that human girl, Lee, had been executed at the Guardian's feet. Forget everything but my hate, my revenge. I'd need my hate if I was going to ruin *him*.

Yuri was easing off the road. I usually hated having partners, but at least Yuri knew how to approach a delicate situation. Surprise would be important, especially when dealing with O'Donnell.

Your brother.

No. My enemy. The one who had forced this fate upon me. The one I should have been able to look up to, depend on.

The one who should have saved me.

"We'll go on foot," I said unnecessarily as he twisted the key out of the ignition.

Yuri nodded, pocketing the keys. "You have a gun?"

I reached into the glove box, knowing I'd find one there. There was also a vial of the virus, the one designed to kill the unkillable Guardians. The Demon Lord believed in keeping his Demons prepared. And if his plans succeeded, every ally he had—every Demon on the planet—would soon have a vial of the miracle substance. The susceptible Guardians would be killed in the first wave, and the others would never be able to keep the Demon population under control. We outnumbered them far too greatly already. We would have complete dominion. Maybe then I would finally find a measure of peace.

Yuri was examining his gun, which he'd pulled from a holster under his arm. The action brought me back into the present.

I left the virus in the glove box, grabbing the sidearm instead. I checked to be sure the gun was loaded and then pushed the door open and stood outside, shoving the gun into the waistband against my back. Yuri exited after me, straightening his jacket after he'd quietly closed his door. I knew he was more heavily armed than I was. It was his style.

I stepped up to the front of the car, surveying the farm yard. It was quiet. The yellow house was relatively small, but the large barn to the side of the house dwarfed everything in sight. I shot a look to Yuri from across the hood. "I'll go around back. You take the front."

Yuri nodded.

I didn't wait for a wish of good luck. Such meaningless things had departed me years ago. And if half the stories I'd heard about Yuri were true, this particular Demon didn't need luck on his side.

I heard Yuri moving behind me, stalking toward the house. I angled for the side of the small home, pushing through a short white gate and treading silently over flat stepping-stones. I followed the meandering path through the side yard and around to the back. I paused at the corner, taking in the scene with a practiced eye.

There was a spacious lawn with weed-speckled grass. There were a few trees, but it was the two giant swings set in the center of the yard that drew my gaze. One small girl with long hair in pigtails was kicking off the ground, trying to pick up speed. She pumped her legs but wasn't swinging to full potential. She was wearing blue shorts, flip-flops, and a white T-shirt with a large blue flower on the front. She couldn't have been more than eleven or twelve years old.

I forced my eyes away, finding the second girl standing near the back porch, lifting her knee to bounce a soccer ball. She repeated the action, evidently bored.

I was almost startled by the sound of her unexpectedly loud voice. "I want to go see the horses."

"Grandma said not until she gets back," the one on the swing countered, still trying to kick her way higher.

The one with the ball snorted. "Jack's around here somewhere. And what about the farmhands? They could watch us. Let's go find someone."

"I want to go higher first."

There was no point in delaying, now that I'd found them. I stepped around the corner of the house, focused on the girl with the ball because she was closer.

The girl on the swing caught sight of me first. But instead of the fear I expected—anticipated—her face flashed with excitement. "Hey!" she called. "Can you give me a push? *Please?*"

I blinked in response, completely taken by surprise. I stared at her blankly, fists loose at my sides. Did she think I was a farmhand? Couldn't she feel the danger? Normally my prey would be screaming by the time they came face-to-face with me.

But she was grinning at me, waiting patiently for me to come give her a push. She wasn't bothering to kick anymore, confident I was going to come over and help her.

The girl with the soccer ball was moving toward me, and I almost flinched back when she stuck out her hand, silently asking for mine. Even if I'd been able to touch her first, I don't think I would have been able to make myself reach for her.

"Come on—I want a push too," she said. She was dressed similarly, but unlike her sister she was not wearing a shirt with a flower. Her T-shirt was black, the name of a band written in shades of gray and white across the chest. Her hair was shorter too, and unbound. Her nose was slightly crooked.

When I didn't take her hanging hand right away she cocked her head at me, fingers curling. "Or were you on your way to feed the horses? Because that would be better than swinging. Can I help you?"

"Wait! I want to swing!" Pigtails protested.

The soccer ball was held in the crook of the girl's arm; her free hand grabbed my wrist.

I barely resisted the urge to jerk back. I hadn't been touched—aside from contact made through fighting or killing—for a long, long time. It wasn't exactly a welcome sensation, but the fact that a child had reached out for me gave me pause. That hadn't happened since . . . before my death, easily.

Her fingers were small, fragile. I could break them in a split second. A simple grab and twist, and each bone in her hand would crack. She would be so absorbed in her pain I could reach her sister without fear of her running away. I could have my hands around the other girl's neck before she could fully scream, and she would be nearly suffocated before her sister recovered enough to stand. If I didn't give Pigtails a near enough brush with death to open up her Sight, Selena could make her a Seer later. She was good at that sort of thing. And after Pigtails passed out in my grip, I could turn around and finish off the other twin. O'Donnell might come to their rescue by then, but Yuri would be able to stop the Guardian from interfering. Mission completed.

I felt her thin fingers flex around my thick wrist, trying to better their hold.

I should grind the bones in her hand. I should get on with it.

No.

Why not?

I couldn't think of a single reason.

So why didn't I act?

"All right," the small girl said, rolling her eyes beside me and breaking into my stilted thoughts, unaware of the illogical debate happening inside of me. "We can feed the horses later. My sister's an impatient freak."

"You're the impatient one!" Pigtails shouted.

Before I fully realized what was happening, I was being pulled toward the swing set, down the increasingly sloped lawn. The gun was pressing up against the small of my back and my free fingers itched to grab it. Anything to defend myself from these strange feelings, this bizarre hesitation.

"I'm Josie," the one clutching my arm said suddenly. "And that's Jenna, my sister."

"We're twins," Jenna confided. "But only in looks. *I'm* more talented."

"Don't listen to her," Josie scoffed, tossing back her head. "I'm *so* much cooler."

She released my wrist as suddenly as she'd grabbed it and my hand hung in midair before I remembered to force it back to my side.

Jenna was almost completely motionless now, waiting for me to move behind her. I did so cautiously, but I couldn't push her—she hadn't touched me, so I couldn't touch her.

"Come on!" Pigtails urged eagerly, glancing over her shoulder at me. "What are you waiting for?"

The gun was still against my back. It would be so easy to pull it out, to wipe the excitement from her face . . .

She moved quickly—twisting on the swing and grabbing my fingers before I could react. I winced at her touch, but she didn't seem to notice. She tugged, and some knuckles popped.

"Give me a good push!" she demanded.

I swallowed hard and jerked my hand from her grip. She didn't seem to find my fast motions ominous, but instead she turned back around, eagerly awaiting my next move.

I ordered myself to reach for the gun, or at least snag her

thin arm and pull her off the swing. I had a job to do, and I was failing. And *Fear Dearg* didn't fail.

I sent the order to my limbs, but instead of grabbing her my fingers settled against her thin back, and I gave her a nudge. She giggled, squirming in the swing. "That tickles," she protested. "Come on. *Push* me!"

I drew back; then I laid a single hand just under her jutting shoulder blades. "Are you holding on tightly?" I spoke for the first time, insanely worried I would make her fall. Didn't I *want* her to fall? What was wrong with me? Why was the thought of pushing her off the swing so distasteful?

She only nodded. Eyes narrowed, I gave her a gentle shove. Her feet left the ground and she giggled. "Harder!"

I pursed my lips, waiting for her to swing back to me. My hand was ready. I gave her a second push, more confident because I knew how much force to use against her small body.

Josie was on the other swing, waiting for me. Her foot tapped the ground impatiently until I moved to stand behind her. I gave her a strong push—stronger than I'd given Jenna.

"Wooo!" she called out, sailing up into the air. When she came back I gave her another push, harder than the first.

I stepped back, watching them swing together, each trying to get just a little higher than the other. A distant part of me recognized I wasn't following protocol. This wasn't the way to run a mission. I wasn't supposed to be playing with them. I was supposed to be *kidnapping* them. Hurting them. Nearly killing them. Making them into Seers for my master. Coming face to face with O'Donnell and making him suffer.

"We haven't seen you around before," Jenna stated suddenly. "What's your name?"

I looked up at her, blinking against the sunlight. Though her question was simple, my answer was not. *Fear Dearg* didn't seem like a satisfactory response.

Sean.

But Sean died. I'd said as much to Kate.

And he had.

The image of myself crouched in a French alleyway, hands dripping with a nameless man's blood, made me want to retch—a painful tug in my gut I hadn't felt for ages. I'd only wanted his money, after all. I was starving. I hadn't meant to knock him down. I just wanted to eat.

I'd cradled his wounded head, stared into his frantic eyes as he'd died, his money still tucked safely inside his jacket. I'd sobbed for hours after he'd stopped breathing—dry heaved until my ribs felt bruised. I'd tried to wipe my soiled hands on the muddy cobblestones. I'd raked my palms over the uneven surface until my blood mingled with the stranger's. I'd begged for my own death. Cried out for my mother's soothing hands, my father's forgiveness, and Patrick's direction.

But they were dead, and I was alone.

My first kill. The only unintentional murder I'd ever committed. Because the will to survive is strong, just as the drive to eat forces a young man to ally himself with ruthless men.

Life became simple. They commanded, and I reacted. I learned not to feel regret for what I did, what I stole—whether it was an object or a life. It was the only way to stay sane. I had my anger, and I focused it on Patrick—the one person I longed for the most. The one person I blamed for everything. Because the only other person I could blame was me, and if I did that, I would starve.

Simple. Sean faded. *Fear Dearg* solidified.

Truth be told, Sean died the night he intentionally took a life. The Demon *Fear Dearg* had truly been born at that moment . . .

"Uh, hello?" Josie asked loudly. My eyes flickered toward her, almost surprised to find myself standing in the yard.

But I'd hesitated too long.

Sean. Your name is Sean.

"Sean," I echoed. But why was I pretending? I wasn't Sean. Not anymore.

"Push me again!" Jenna said happily

"No, Sean, push me!" Josie cried.

I shifted to stand between them, pushing the girls whenever they came to me. But even as my body moved, my mind was racing. I needed to grab the chains, jerk the girls to a stop. Yuri would be here any moment. O'Donnell himself might emerge from the house. I had my orders. Why couldn't I bring myself to complete them?

Why couldn't I get the image of that nameless man out of my head?

Soon the twins were flying through the air. I stopped helping them along, afraid they would go over the bar if I gave them another shove.

"I'm higher!" Jenna yelled to her sister.

"No, I am!"

"You are not!"

"Let's see who can jump farthest, then!" Josie challenged.

No! A long buried voice in my mind shouted. *They'll get hurt!*

I blinked slowly. Let them. They'll be hurt soon enough. I'm going to take them away. I'm going to give them to the most demonic Demons in the world, chief among them, *me*.

Sean, stop them!

No.

"Sean!"

My head jerked up, startled.

It was Josie. "See who goes the farthest! Jenna, on three! One . . ." They pumped faster, desperate to gain more momentum.

"Josie. Don't." The words fell from my mouth, a whisper impossible for her to hear.

"Two!"

My lips quivered. I was rooted in place. "Don't." It was no louder than the first caution.

"Three!"

"Don't!" I yelled, the single word ripping out from deep within me.

Too late. They both vaulted from their swings at the highest point of the arc. They sailed through the air, and it was almost graceful. Until they started downward. I blinked, and I almost missed the moment of impact.

They pounded into the ground. Josie rolled, but Jenna didn't. There was a loud crack as her small body smashed unnaturally against her right arm. She gasped in shock, and then she shrieked in pain.

twenty-one

Fear Dearg

I darted forward, no longer immobile, shoving past the swings that were still flying empty and out of control. I knew instinctively that Josie was all right, so I ran for Jenna, who had shifted into a sitting position; her injured arm rested awkwardly in her lap.

"Ow, ow, ow," she whined rapidly, trying to pull back tears with violent sniffs.

I fell to my knees in front of her, reaching wordlessly for her arm. She gasped and moaned at my touch, large tears slipping down her pale face. "Ow, *owww . . .*"

"It's all right," I tried to soothe her. I knew my voice was too rough. I tried to temper it. "It feels like a clean break." At least there wasn't a bone sticking out.

Josie was shaking at my side, pale. "Jenna, I'm sorry. I'm sorry . . ."

The back door slammed open behind us, and even though I knew who it would be I looked over my shoulder

Patrick looked as young as ever. Maybe a little worn. He was wearing close to the same thing I'd seen him in last, in Vegas. A blue cotton shirt, so light in color compared to my own apparel.

Faded jeans that made his hair appear all the lighter. In a way, it was fitting. He was the angel brother; I was the Demon. All was right in the world—except I was crouched next to a little girl, my fingertips so hesitant against her supple skin. I should have been the one to break her arm. Why was I so desperate to help save her from pain?

Patrick's eyes were filled with panic, his face bathed in white fear. He looked right at us. Right at *me*.

His already tensed body grew harder. Hunched over the small girl, gripping her arm, I must have looked threatening. But, just like me, he seemed incapable of moving. For the moment.

"Patrick?" Josie said, deeply confused. "What are *you* doing here?"

Patrick didn't answer her question, though her voice had broken the spell of stillness. He jumped off the long porch, striding toward us, hands shaking. "Josie, get back!" His voice was a bark, a delayed warning, in my opinion. "Get away from him!" Patrick broke into a sudden run, not that he had far to go now.

I released Jenna's arm and rose to my feet. I nearly stumbled back, knowing I should be reaching for my gun. I could shoot him. Slow him down. Make him suffer. Like I suffered. Grab the girls. Call for Yuri.

"Patrick," Jenna gasped. "My arm, it hurts . . ."

He didn't take his eyes off of me, but I must have backed far enough away because he took the time to stop and reach for Jenna's uninjured arm. He pulled her to her feet. She cried out as her broken arm was jostled. "*Ow*! It hurts!" she yelled up at him.

Patrick had an arm wrapped around her shoulders, and he protectively drew her back up against his chest. Watching me, he tried to examine her injury, staring at her limp wrist.

"It's a clean break," I told him, unable to stop the words from escaping.

He glared up at me. "You've sunk this low? You'll attack a child?"

I bristled, more bothered by his accusation than I should have allowed myself to be. I was *Fear Dearg,* after all.

Josie rose to my defense. "He didn't do anything, Patrick. Jenna and I jumped off the swings."

He wasn't in the mood to listen. "Josie, I need you and Jenna to go inside. Find Jack."

"But Sean didn't *do* anything!" Josie actually stomped her foot against the grass, indignant that I was being wrongly accused. *If only you knew what things I've done,* I thought grimly.

Patrick blinked, glancing quickly away from me so he could see her face. "Sean?" he asked in shock.

Josie rolled her eyes. "That's his name, duh! He was pushing us on the swings. It wasn't his fault."

I watched Patrick's face as he turned back to look at me. Confusion, fear, anger, defensiveness, even pain—it was all there.

I wonder what would have happened if we hadn't been interrupted.

A gunshot sounded inside the house, shattering the momentary stillness. All of us jumped. Josie's wide eyes haunted me as she whipped around to follow the sound. It was obvious she'd never heard a real bullet discharge in her life, but the way she began to shake made it clear she knew exactly what that sound meant.

Patrick's arm around Jenna tightened, as if that feeble gesture could protect her from the imminent danger. From *me.*

His words accosted me. "How many are there? *How many?*"

I didn't answer. I couldn't.

"What's going on?" Josie demanded, fear tingeing her words. "Patrick, what's happening?"

Patrick grabbed Josie's arm, yanking her closer, eyes firmly on me. "Take Jenna," he ordered Josie lowly. "Run to the barn. Hide. Don't come out for anyone but me. Go!"

"But—"

"Go!"

Josie grabbed her sister's left arm, frightened enough by Patrick's fierce tone that she didn't ask questions. They jogged lightly away, obediently headed for the barn.

A strange lump clogged my throat. Without thinking, my legs lurched to follow them, an instinct I couldn't ignore though it defied my whole being. They couldn't go off on their own—Yuri would find them.

Patrick countered my move by mirroring it, and we both froze. We were mere paces away, glaring each other down.

"I didn't come for you," I growled at last. "I came for *them*."

And that means others want them too. Don't send them away. It's not safe, don't you understand? Why couldn't I make myself add the words?

Patrick's hands rolled into trembling fists. "You're not going to touch them."

"You don't understand—"

"What are you *doing* here?" Patrick cut in angrily. "How did you find this place?"

I didn't say anything. I didn't have to.

His teeth clenched tightly. "What have you done? Where's Kate?"

"Probably right where you left her," I said, not trying to soften my words.

His eyes flashed. And then he charged me with his bare hands. I don't know why I didn't pull my gun. I could have. I had enough time. But I didn't. I let him slam into me, knocking us both to the hard ground.

We hit jarringly and he clutched the cloth around my neck, skidding my back over the grass. The gun bruised my skin, but I could feel it healing in the same instant. Patrick slammed my head harshly into the earth and my vision blurred from the impact.

"Where is she?" he hissed, kneeling over me and looking angry enough to kill.

I stared into his eyes, wishing it didn't have to be like this. But that thought alone surprised me. I hated him. I wanted to hate him. I *needed* to hate him.

I loved to hate him.

I went for honesty, since it would be the most painful for him to hear. "With the Demon Lord. Where she's going to die."

His chest expanded harshly, a split second before his doubled fist buckled my nose.

I gasped from the pain and felt the blood cover my face though the bones and sinew were already shifting back into place.

"Where is she?"

Another punch, breaking my nose again.

My eyes were watering, but the pain was doing its job. I was remembering why I was here. I was becoming *Fear Dearg* again.

I kicked him off me, my retaliation so sudden he could hardly prepare himself. He was too emotional, distracted, and frantic. His grip pulled my body over with him, so I was now straddling him. I delivered a powerful blow to his face, affording him a taste of my pain. His cracked nose spurted blood and before it could fully heal I was striking him again. He growled in fury, but his hurt was undeniable. My second punch dislodged his jaw.

I continued to hammer him with my tight fist, my other hand clutching his shoulder, pinning him down.

I heard the back door open, heard Yuri's even yell. "I see them!" His footsteps leaped, making the long jump off the porch, and then he was running after the twins.

Jenna. Josie.

Sean.

Patrick was struggling more desperately beneath me. His blind rage shifted, becoming more focused with the knowledge that the twins were being pursued. Whatever help he thought he'd had in the form of a man named Jack, he was beginning to realize he didn't have it anymore. He tried to lift a knee and take me off guard, tried to claw the flesh from my arm. But I wasn't worried. He would fail, because I was stronger.

I could see to my brother and let Yuri take care of the twins. I could torture Patrick for as long as I wanted, injecting him with a deviant strain of the virus only when I was ready to end his life. I didn't have to agonize over this. I didn't have to think. I could just be *Fear Dearg.*

Jenna.

Josie.

. . . Sean.

It would be easy. Not only that, it would feel so good. To see him suffer. To hear him scream.

Your father loves you.

Only because he didn't know what I'd become.

My eyes were stinging. Had something gotten inside? Sweat, blood, dirt? Certainly I wasn't crying. *Fear Dearg* didn't cry.

But that's not the point. You don't even need to know they love you, really. Not when you *love* them.

I didn't love them. I hated them all.

You love Patrick.

No. I wanted to kill him.

You just want to know that he can still love you, after everything you've done.

No!

I *was* crying. I could feel the tears darting down my face, mingling with the blood. I tightened my grip on my brother, afraid to lose my hate. If I lost that, what did I have? Nothing.

One of the twins screamed.

Something in me snapped.

I shoved away from Patrick, gaining such speed I felt like I was flying. I jumped over a thin flower bed that lined the main backyard, leaving Patrick behind. I swiped an arm over my face, sweeping off a layer of blood. The barn loomed in my view, the wide open doors inviting me to cross the flat land even faster. I could make out the forms of three people, two small and one large, just inside the spacious building. I wasn't sure what I was going to do when I got there, but I needed to get inside. That's all I knew.

Because you can't deny your emotions anymore, Sean. Not when I've finally gotten you to admit they're there.

That's when I realized the voice I'd been hearing inside my head wasn't my own. It wasn't even the long-buried part of me, the part I called Sean. No. It belonged to someone else. Someone, I realized, I'd been hearing since Patrick escaped me in Vegas.

I felt an intense spike of anger, causing me to nearly trip. *Who are you?* I demanded, maintaining a staggering run.

No need to get upset. You're the one who let me in. I couldn't have gotten this much voice if you'd kept blocking me. But we've never been formally introduced. I'm Henry Bennett.

A horrible guilt washed over me as the image of Henry Bennett's face swam before my eyes. It wasn't something I was used to, this guilt; surprisingly, it hurt more than anything I'd ever felt before. More than physical torture, more than betrayal, more than abandonment; I felt more pain than I'd felt that night in the ally, after killing the stranger for a few francs.

You're . . . in my head? The idea was preposterous, no matter who he was. It was insane. Infuriating. Disturbing. Had he been manipulating me for weeks? Had he forced me to feel that guilt?

Not exactly, but frankly it doesn't matter, does it? What matters is, you've opened yourself up to your emotions again. You can't shut out the guilt, the caring. It's a part of you again. You chose to revive your conscience the moment you started running after the girls, and now it can't be silenced.

The gravel shifted beneath me, slowing me down further. Why was I even running? I didn't really want to help those girls. Their dead grandfather was forcing me . . . The man I'd killed . . .

I can't stick around forever, Sean. What's it going to be? Are you going to accept that this was your choice, or are you going to pass along the blame again? It's up to you. You're the only one who can save my girls. You're the only one who can save yourself. So get to work.

His voice vanished. My head felt strangely empty. But my chest felt tight, swollen. The man I'd killed had been forcing me to confront my emotions. And according to him, I'd chosen to be Sean again. But had I? All I felt was confusion. Pain.

The sheer weight of my emotions were going to destroy me.

My legs locked when I reached the massive barn doorway, panting with my arms swinging, unsure of what I was going to do.

They were just inside the barn. The twins hadn't had enough time to hide, and they definitely hadn't stood a chance against someone like Yuri Dmitriev. He had Jenna pinned brutally on the ground, a boot digging into her stomach to keep her there. Her crooked arm was lying near the side of her head at an odd angle. She was sobbing, a combination of pain and fear.

Josie was suspended in a stranglehold, her jerking legs kicking at the man who held her. He was suffocating her—exactly what I'd planned to do to both of them.

That thought caused me to flinch. But I still couldn't move. *Sean or* Fear Dearg*?*

Josie's bare foot swung wildly, ineffective. Annoying, at best. She was grabbing, scratching at his arm with those small fingers, fingers that had touched me only minutes ago, full of trust. She couldn't possibly breathe.

Jenna was hysterical on the ground. "Let her go!" she choked through her tears.

Throat constricted, I stumbled forward.

Josie wasn't in a position to notice my approach, but Jenna caught sight of me. She began to slam her good hand against Yuri's leg. "Sean!" she burst out. "Sean, help!"

Yuri's head jerked around, confused by her cries. He saw me

barreling toward him, and his eyes widened when he realized I didn't intend to stop—something that took me by surprise as well. He threw Josie away from him, unconcerned about how hard she hit the floor. He managed to swivel off Jenna before I tackled him.

We rolled in the loose hay, each of us grappling for a solid grip on the other.

"What are you doing?" he grunted as I pressed him into the ground.

My fist in his face was his only answer.

He replied by chopping the edge of his hand into my throat, cutting off my air for a prolonged second that gave him enough time to shove away from me. We both rolled to our feet, my eyes still flaring with pain.

I heard Jenna shriek Patrick's name. So he'd followed me. I wasn't really surprised. I hoped he had the sense to get them out before I killed Yuri. No young child should have to witness such a thing.

With my peripheral vision I saw Patrick put himself in front of the girls, but he still hadn't armed himself. Did he not have a knife? I could see Josie and Jenna huddled on the ground behind him, neither of them in any condition to run for safety. Patrick knew that, and, even though he had no weapon with which to defend them, he'd still put himself between them and danger.

A few paces away from me Yuri drew out his gun. He aimed it at my defensively crouched brother.

"Stop!" I ordered, though I knew Yuri wouldn't listen. I'd attacked him. He didn't understand my actions, but he intended to follow the master's orders.

I dove for Yuri the same instant he pulled the trigger. The gunshot exploded the air. The girls screamed in unison, and I caught sight of Patrick crumpling. He'd taken the bullet without flinching.

How did I, at the same moment, both hate and admire his bravery? Was it because I was reminded of his death? I'd never seen him get shot in Ireland, only seen his cold body.

But Patrick had always been brave, selfless. That's why he'd tried to leave me behind when our father demanded we joined the United Irishmen. And, if I was going to all this trouble of being honest, it was why he'd become a Guardian in the first place. To protect me.

A memory I hadn't recalled for so long flooded my mind in flashing images. The big yew tree behind Father's church. A dare to jump from the highest limb and onto the roof; Patrick following me, undaunted by his fear of heights. The two of us fighting, though outnumbered, to defend each other.

Patrick had always been there for me. Even when I'd been an idiot.

I growled as I reached Yuri, knocking the warm pistol from his hand with a fluid swipe I'd used hundreds of times to disarm my enemies. Yuri lurched back a step and our eyes met. We both sank into practiced positions, each of us poised to attack, neither of us wanting to make the first move.

It didn't escape my attention that I'd managed to put myself in front of the twins. I was their protector, now that Patrick was down.

"Patrick!" Jenna or Josie cried out in delayed shock. The shout was followed by a wounded groan.

I kicked Yuri's gun back with my heel, hoping it wouldn't hit Patrick but put it within reach in case he could recover enough to use it. I also hoped the twins knew enough about guns to leave it alone.

Yuri's lip curled. "The Demon Lord will not forgive you for this, Far Darrig. He'll personally send you back to Prison for this treachery!"

"I'll save him a spot."

"What's happened?" Yuri snarled. "What are you *doing?*"

"Sean!"

It might have been Jenna. And though I didn't turn, my eyes flickered.

It was the distraction Yuri had been waiting for. He kicked, foot landing on my left kneecap. There was a horrible crack and my whole leg flared in vivid pain. I limped precariously but exaggerated the stagger. Yuri fell for the ruse, taking a step closer. I swung my healed leg up and buried my foot in his stomach, hard, using his forward momentum against him. He nearly buckled but managed to keep on his feet by stumbling back.

"Sean!" Jenna repeated, frightened.

"Get out of here!" I shouted, worried she might try to approach me and get in the way. I lunged at Yuri before he could fully straighten.

Yuri was good—he knew how to fight in close quarters. Hand-to-hand combat was a specialty of his. But that was fine; it was a specialty of mine. And I was better because I had emotion on my side. The image of him shooting my brother, hurting the two girls who'd called for *my* help . . . I was unstoppable.

We were both covered in blood, but I didn't have a way to kill him. I didn't have a knife, since Demons don't generally carry the only weapon that had the ability to kill them. I only had my gun, and I couldn't keep him down long enough to bring it out, not that it would be a permanent solution.

Too late I realized Yuri had a drawn knife. It went against a Demon's basic instinct to have a knife, so I hadn't imagined he'd be carrying one. But then Demons were so treacherous you never knew who was going to try stabbing you—it could be a good idea to have one on hand, in case another Demon attempted to double-cross you.

I guess I should have realized a killer as ruthless and practiced as Yuri would trust no one. Not even me, the Demon Lord's right hand.

His dagger was buried in my shoulder a split second later,

but only because I shifted at the last possible second—it should have landed in my heart.

Still, it was painful. It froze my body, allowing Yuri to kick away from me. He rolled to his knees, a foot away from where I lay on my side, bleeding. Eyes blazing, he reached for a second blade, ready to end me.

His hand patted over empty space. He looked down, shocked that it was gone.

"Looking for this?" Patrick grunted.

I raised my head, looking over at my brother with a wince. His eyes were dark. His grim face was smeared with blood and he was facing Yuri with the handgun extended. In his other hand he clutched a knife, one he'd either snatched from Yuri's belt when we'd rolled nearer to them or one he'd picked up from the floor, lost during the scuffle.

Yuri's mouth twitched angrily. He leaned toward me, maybe thinking he could get the dagger he'd buried in me so he could finish the job.

Patrick was faster. Another gunshot blasted Yuri backward. He tripped over me and fell onto his back. I jerked the knife out of my shoulder and heaved myself up. I saw Yuri's eyes widen, then I shoved the bloody knife into his heart. His head lolled, his expression softened in death.

There was a short silence in the barn. I didn't dare twist around right away. I didn't want to see Patrick level that gun at me. I didn't want him to look at me like I was a monster.

Which was stupid, because that's exactly what I was. It didn't matter that I could *feel* again or that I'd rushed to defend the twins. I was still a Demon.

Why hadn't he shot me yet?

I heard whimpering and realized why he was delaying. The twins were still in the barn. He hadn't taken them out, because he couldn't turn his back on a Demon as dangerous as me.

I closed my eyes and eased up to a standing position. I turned slowly, not sure what else to do but face him.

Patrick was staring at me, the gun still aimed in my direction, supported by a steady arm. Between Patrick's widespread legs I could see the twins huddled together on the floor, both of them watching me as well. My eyes flickered back up to my brother.

A strange mix of emotions contorted Patrick's face: pain, hurt, worry, surprise, hope. I watched him, waiting for him to do it. All he had to do was squeeze the trigger, shoot me to stun me, and then plunge that knife into my heart while I was blinded by pain. It would be so easy. He could ensure the twins' safety. Why wasn't he doing it?

"Well?" I asked him mutely. "Aren't you going to do it?"

Patrick was watching me with a sharp gaze, one that conveyed distrust and . . . regret? So I wasn't the only one to regret the past. Good. Regret was painful.

Even as the thought entered my mind I was plagued by doubt—I wasn't sure I wanted him to feel pain anymore.

Patrick took a step toward me and spoke quietly, trying to keep the words from the young girls. "Why? Why did you do it?"

"Because I hated you," I said, wondering if he'd register the fact that I'd used past tense.

His jaw flexed. "No. Not that. Why did you attack him?"

"Yuri?" I asked, surprised we were even talking about this. Didn't he want to talk about Kate? About the Demon Lord's plans? About my desire to kill my own brother?

Patrick frowned. "Yes. Yuri. Why?"

I closed my eyes, swallowing hard. "He was hurting them."

The confusion was evident in his voice. "But that's why you came here."

My words were spoken in an exhale. "They asked me to push them on the swings. They asked for my help . . ."

Patrick's eyes altered—transformed. His arm gradually fell, lowering the gun until it was pointed at the barn floor. He flexed his fingers around the knife he still held. He wasn't going to kill me.

My eyes met his cautiously. "Why?" I whispered.

The lump in his throat visibly bobbed. "I've never let your stupidity stop me from caring about you before." A single shoulder lifted in a half shrug. "Why should I start now?"

twenty-two

Sean O'Donnell

I was wrapping a towel—a makeshift splint—around Jenna's arm as delicately as possible. It would have to do until her grandmother could return and take her to the hospital. We were gathered in the kitchen of the small farmhouse. Patrick and Jack were covering up a bullet hole with a picture of a lake, and Maddy, a young Seer, was watching me closely, with a healthy amount of distrust. She had a headache, and it had saved her life—if Yuri had found her, he would have shot her like he'd shot Jack. Only she wouldn't have survived.

"Lilly won't notice," Jack was saying confidently, tapping a finger against the picture frame. "She's going blind, and she's got plenty of other wall space."

Patrick just nodded. Yuri's bullet had ripped through his side, but he'd healed fully, though he'd had to explain a few things to Kate's sisters.

I stopped watching my brother and turned back to focus on Jenna's arm. Josie was sitting on the other side of the table, shaking her head, fingering the bruising around her throat subconsciously. "Wow. I mean, *wow.* Why didn't anyone tell us about this stuff? Patrick, you can go invisible? Seriously?

But there's one thing I don't understand. *Why* can you go invisible?"

Jenna huffed loudly. I froze, thinking I'd hurt her, but she was addressing her sister. "Because he's a guardian angel, remember? He told us! He's got superpowers." She twisted her head around so she could look at Patrick. "Even if you got a paper cut, would that heal?"

I had to hand it to Patrick. He'd told the twins just enough of the truth to satisfy them. They didn't know about Seers, which meant they didn't know about Kate. They didn't know about Demons. They just thought Yuri was a burglar who'd decided to target the farm. They had no idea their sister was in a hostage situation. They had no idea they themselves were targets. They hadn't seen me do anything too malicious, so they trusted me. Jack had, of course, sustained injuries, so they knew he was like Patrick too.

"This is so cool!" Josie grinned. "So are you guys really angels? Like, heaven and stuff?"

"Does Kate know you're immortal, Patrick?" Jenna asked seriously.

He nodded once, but his eyes flickered to me. I knew that once the immediate damage was taken care of here, I was going to be questioned. I would have told him everything now, if the twins hadn't been present. But it was obvious Patrick didn't want them knowing too much.

"Yes," Patrick was answering Jenna even as he stepped closer to Josie. "She knows." For perhaps the fifth time in the past ten minutes he touched her chin, prompting her to tip her head back so he could reassess the damage Yuri's crushing grip had inflicted around her throat.

"But you can't be telling everybody," Jack warned them suddenly. "Or we're all going to get in trouble."

"What about Grandma?" Jenna asked.

"She knows—but you can only talk to her about it when other people aren't around."

They nodded again, accepting the terms.

Josie squirmed back from Patrick. "I'm okay," she protested, knocking his hand away with her own. "What are you going to do with that body? Bury it behind the barn?"

"Of course not!" Jenna answered her sister, aghast. "They'll take him to the police. Right?" She looked to me for some reason.

I merely nodded.

Patrick cleared his throat. "Sean, are you almost done? We need to talk."

"Yes. Almost."

Josie was looking between us, as if really seeing us for the first time. Her tone was almost accusing. "Hey, your eyes are the exact same! Are you related? Patrick, is he your older brother?"

Patrick once again glanced at me, but I intended to let him handle that question. He'd done a great job so far.

Patrick focused back on Josie. "Sean is . . . my younger brother."

"Really?" Understanding lightened Josie's expression. "Oh, because he died after you, so he'd be older. Cool." She seemed completely unaffected by the abnormal qualities of this conversation.

I finished with Jenna's arm, complementing the temporary splint with a makeshift sling around her neck. She smiled at me, though she still looked a little pale. Luckily the ibuprofen was beginning to kick in, so her pain would be minimized. "Thanks, Sean. Are you . . . ?" She hesitated, as if embarrassed to ask her question. "Are you *my* guardian angel?"

I blinked, taken aback by the question. I could feel Patrick's gaze, heavy on my face. I knew everyone was listening, waiting. But even though her question was unexpected, my mouth was already moving to form the answer.

"Yes, I am."

Patrick's hand pressed against the table, breaking into the timid conversation. "Jenna, you should wash your face. Josie, could you help her? Your grandmother will be back any minute, and we don't want to unnecessarily alarm her or Lilly. They turned around when they heard about your arm, so they should be here soon."

"But we can't tell them about the burglar?" Josie clarified.

Jenna rolled her eyes. "You *want* to give Lilly a heart attack? Come on, Josie—be brave."

"I *am* brave . . ."

Their voices drifted from the room as they moved to go upstairs. I remained sitting, letting Patrick, Maddy, and Jack sit on the other side of the table. I tried not to squirm under their stares.

"Sean," Patrick said seriously, his voice low. "What's going on? Tell me everything."

For a short moment I feared my mouth was stuck; that I wouldn't be able to get the words out. They were hard to form, now that I could feel my emotions.

I began to speak, pushing the guilt aside as I attempted to tell them everything.

Patrick looked sick by the time I'd finished. "Lee's dead?" he breathed, disbelieving.

I nodded once, unable to ignore the stab of regret I felt.

Jack shook his head. "How many are at the warehouse?"

I thought briefly. "Counting the Demon Lord, there are only six. We didn't need any more. There's also a Seer of Selena's; he was our informant. But he won't be hard to deal with."

"Informant? What's his name?" It was as if my brother already knew the answer; he was just seeking confirmation.

"Peter. Peter Keegan."

Patrick's eyes darkened.

Jack rapped his knuckles on the table, deliberating. "So they're waiting there, for your word. What will they do if you don't call soon?"

"The Demon Lord is impatient. They won't wait long. They'll

kill who they can and then leave. They'll be expecting my call any minute now."

"But Kate is still alive?" Patrick asked again.

I nodded, confident. "She'll be one of the last to go, I'm certain of it. The Demon Lord will find it poetically justifying if she's the last to be killed. He probably wants her to see her sisters in captivity."

"So what do we do now?" Maddy asked grimly.

"We have to move quickly," Jack reasoned. "There isn't time to call for reinforcements. We can call Terence, let him know what's happened, but we're not going to get much help from the Guardians. I could ask Jason to meet us at the warehouse, but it would be suicide. We already have too many mortal people in the situation as it is."

"We need a plan," Patrick mumbled, almost to himself.

"Getting inside the warehouse will be impossible," Jack said. "They'll know we're coming." Patrick shot him a piercing look, and Jack continued quickly. "I'm not saying we abandon them, obviously. But if the Demon Lord brought so few, they must be exceptional fighters." He sighed. "If only we could get to Toni and Claire—free them. Then we'd have a fighting chance at getting the Seers out alive."

"How can we get that close?" Patrick muttered.

I hardly knew my own words because my voice sounded so different from this morning. So level-headed. "I can call him. Tell him I have the twins. That you've surrendered. I can bring you upstairs, tell him Yuri is in the car with the girls. He wouldn't suspect anything. That would get you into the room with them."

Patrick was nodding, acutely aware that time was short and options were limited.

Jack looked uneasy. He spoke to the others, though he wasn't really trying to keep his words from me. "Can we trust him? The Demon Lord's right hand?"

They waited for Patrick. His eyes were on mine. "He saved the twins." He glanced around at the others. "He's my only way to Kate."

It wasn't the most inspiring expression of trust. I was his only way in, so he would *have* to trust me. Logically, I knew I had to earn his trust. And I had a long way to go.

Maddy frowned. "What about me? I'm coming, right?"

"No."

She looked to Patrick, her eyes flashing. He continued firmly. "I know you want to help Claire, but this is too dangerous. Jack's right—this is no place for mortals. Besides, someone needs to stay with the twins. I need you here, Maddy."

Jack faced me for the first time. "Look, no offense, but . . . Honestly, how do we know we can trust you?"

I wasn't offended. After all, he had good reason to be wary. I was almost glad he was wary—one of them should be. What if they *couldn't* trust me? What if—when I got back with my master—I reverted to my old thoughts? What if whatever had driven me to save the twins was fading already?

Henry Bennett had assured me the choice had been mine. And maybe that's what frightened me the most. It was now up to me. Every second of every day, I was going to have to choose. My redemption could only come through my actions.

Jack was still waiting for some kind of answer, some assurance I was no longer an enemy. I wasn't sure what to tell him. How could I convince him when I wasn't even totally sure of myself?

Patrick spoke quietly, his words sure. "He won't betray us, Jack."

Jack and I both looked at him.

Patrick's eyes were on mine. "I *do* trust you, Sean."

I wasn't sure I wanted that responsibility. Yet . . . it felt good. I didn't want to disappoint him. I swallowed and pulled out my phone.

I had a call to make, whether my newfound conscience was ready to face my personal demons or not.

I dialed. My old master's voice filled my ear. "Yes?"

"It's done," I said, staring at the table, avoiding the hard eyes on me. "We have the twins and O'Donnell. We're returning now."

"Good." The Demon Lord sounded pleased. "And he surrendered?"

"Yes. As well as another Guardian and a Seer." I could see Jack's body tensing at my words—my heart pounded in response.

"Excellent. Bring them all. We'll be ready to go when you get back. Thank you, Far Darrig."

I waited until I heard him hang up before disconnecting. I met Patrick's stare. "He'll be waiting. We need to go."

Jack blew out his breath. "Not much of a conversationalist, huh?"

"Not with me," I said.

"Kate?" The words seemed to slip out of my brother of their own accord. His whole expression was edged with desperation. "Did he say anything about Kate?"

I shook my head but spoke before his forehead could wrinkle too severely. "It's a good thing he didn't mention her, Patrick." Hope sparked in his eyes, though he still didn't look convinced. "If he had," I continued, "it would only be because she's dead."

His jaw flexed tightly. He stood. "Time to go. They're all waiting for us."

Jack stood as well, offering to call Charlotte Bennett to let her know that by the time she returned, he and Patrick would be gone. I moved to take Yuri's body to the SUV, and Patrick followed me without a word, as if guessing my thoughts. Or perhaps he just wanted to keep me in sight.

I frowned but pushed the back door open, hooking my fingers around the edge so it wouldn't swing back on Patrick as he exited behind me. I wondered—transiently—if I should tell him about Henry Bennett's voice, if that would help him trust me. Even as I thought it, I knew I wouldn't. Maybe someday I could tell him about the incident, but the time didn't feel right.

Feeling. Something I hadn't done for so, so long. I almost wondered, for the briefest of moments, if regaining my humanity was worth the worry, fear, and pain.

twenty-three

Patrick O'Donnell

My brother's gaze was fixed on the highway. Now that we were off dirt roads we were making better time. Still, nowhere near fast enough.

She was alive. She had to be. Sean said she would be. I had to believe she would be.

In the backseat, Jack was on the phone with Terence, updating him on the situation. I glanced fleetingly toward Sean. He hadn't said a word since we'd climbed into the SUV, and his silence was adding to my growing nervousness. Between the panic and fear I felt for Kate and the hope and confusion I felt for my brother's sudden transformation, I was fast dissolving into a frantic, fidgeting mess. Since I couldn't do anything for Kate at the moment, I tried to focus on the man seated beside me.

When I'd first come face-to-face with my brother after thinking he'd been dead for the past two hundred years, I hadn't been able to find a trace of humanity in him. There wasn't a shred of Sean's personality inside the Demon called *Fear Dearg*. But today, as I'd watched him wrap Jenna's arm, as I'd looked into his eyes when I could have ended his life, I'd seen my brother.

Sean was alive. I was sure of it now. This man was a hardened version of Sean—one who had gone through terrible hardship and lived in so much evil he would never be the carefree brother I used to know. But the light had returned to his eyes. He was no longer the empty body of *Fear Dearg*. He was my brother. He'd had the opportunity to shoot me; I'd seen the gun. He could have stopped me. He could have hurt the twins—he'd played with them instead, defended them. He could have completed his mission, but instead he'd saved us all from another Demon.

If these actions didn't merit trust, I didn't know what should.

Thinking of my father's letter, I marveled at his wisdom. *You cannot hate what you love*. The truth of that eternal statement was now clear to me. I loved Sean. I could hate his actions. I could hate everything he'd done. But I could never hate *him*.

The twins were certainly taken with him. Especially Jenna. When she'd called him her guardian angel, my brother looked more than a little overwhelmed, but his eyes had brightened. That small interaction alone had me confident he could be trusted. Though I wasn't sure how, a little girl had managed to enter his heart and change it. She would never know how grateful I would always be.

But what had started him on this path to change? What had triggered it?

Jack was still on the phone behind us. I cleared my throat; Sean tensed in response. I kept my gaze focused out the windshield.

"So," I began slowly, unsure. "What changed your mind?"

"Hmm?" Sean pretended to be more absorbed in driving than he actually was. I knew, because a muscle in his jaw ticked—a nervous reaction he'd had for as long as I could remember.

Somehow, knowing he was nervous as well made this easier. "In Vegas, you were . . ."

"Consumed with hate," Sean supplied when my words drifted. He shifted behind the wheel, fingers curling tightly, but he didn't elaborate.

"So what happened?" I prompted quietly. "How could you . . . change so much?"

Sean's eyes flickered toward me. He pursed his lips, then took a deep breath. "After Vegas, I . . . I was plagued by thoughts. Memories of you and home, mostly."

"Plagued?"

"Perhaps not the best word." He frowned. "I tried to push them away. But I couldn't. I tried to focus on how much I hated you . . . But it didn't work. Not for long, anyway. And then, today . . ." He swallowed hard. "When Avalos killed that girl, Lee . . . I felt something I haven't for a long time. Guilt. Regret. A lethal combination. And when I was ordered to go, Kate, she . . ."

I realized my hands were shaking. I tried to steady them by rolling them to fists.

Sean must have caught my reaction to hearing her name. "I'm sorry, I shouldn't—"

"No. Please, I . . . I want to know what happened."

"My master . . . the Demon Lord, he ordered me to go, to get the twins. On my way out, Kate begged me not to go. She said she'd been to see Father."

I nodded, trying—and failing—not to imagine Kate's distress and grief at that moment. "Yes. She did. I had her deliver a letter. He sent one in return. When all this is over, I'll show you."

He sighed. "Patrick, I don't know if I can do this. Be forgiven. I've done some . . . unspeakable things."

"We'll figure this out," I insisted firmly. "Together."

My brother bit his lower lip. "He would have mentioned

if he'd killed Kate—over the phone. She's alive." He exhaled sharply. "She has to be."

Not the most encouraging thing he'd ever said to me. Not the most threatening, either. Still, my reflexes had me reacting, grabbing his arm without thinking, my whole body going hard with fear. "Do you know something you're not telling me? Is Kate all right?"

But Sean just shook his head. "I don't know. But we'll be there soon. Another twenty minutes."

I swallowed with difficulty, forcing my fingers to uncurl and release my brother. I settled back against my seat and turned to look out at the rapidly passing landscape.

Please, Kate, hold on. I'm coming. I'm coming.

***

Three blocks from the warehouse, Sean steered into an alley. He cut off the gas and twisted around to look at me and Jack equally. "I'm going to have to tie you up here, just in case someone is waiting downstairs for us." He hesitated, but only momentarily. "I'm going to have to knife you. It's the only way they'll believe you've truly surrendered."

I nodded, accepting his words easily. I would take a thousand knives, if it helped me get to Kate.

Jack sighed behind me. "I'm getting too old for this sort of thing . . ."

Sean opened his door, and I pulled in a deep breath as he rounded the hood. I pushed my door open and climbed out before he'd come to a complete stop. Jack was right behind me, a thick roll of silver duct tape in hand.

He passed it to my brother. "Found it in back, by Yuri."

Sean took it easily and Jack—glancing one last time at me for silent confirmation—turned his back on the Demon, wrists pressed together.

"Hold them a bit apart," Sean instructed. "You'll want some flexibility so you can get free."

Jack complied, holding his wrists about two inches apart, and Sean began to tie him with a proficiency that could only come from repeated practice.

Finished in less than thirty seconds, he asked, "How does that feel?"

Jack tested the binding, moving his hands together to disguise the looseness. "Good," he grunted. "Not too strong, but believable."

Sean turned to me and I twisted around without hesitation. While he bound my hands, I closed my eyes briefly. *Please, please, let me be able to trust you,* I mentally begged. If I'd come this far, only to fail . . . I needed to save Kate. For the moment, nothing else mattered. I had to get her out of there alive. If I was unsuccessful, I would be failing not only as her Guardian but also as the man who loved her. Both failures would be unforgivable.

"How does it feel?" Sean asked me.

I tugged my hands and felt the tape strain against my skin. Perfect. A bit of fidgeting, and I was confident I could free myself. "Good," I said, turning back around to face him.

Sean gestured with his chin to the car. "Your knives are in there?"

I nodded and stepped aside so he could fish the blades out. While he did, I spoke. "Will one knife be believable enough?"

I thought I heard Jack groan.

Sean didn't look at me. "It'll work. They may stick you with another before we have our moment."

"We need to make sure we know where all the Seers are, before we make our move," Jake reiterated.

Sean straightened, holding two knives. I recognized both as mine. His eyes were hard on mine—determined. "I'm sorry," he said.

I tried to roll my shoulders, but they were too constricted by my tied hands. "It doesn't matter," I said.

Sean still grimaced. "Do you have a preference of where?"

I shook my head. Stabbing was stabbing. It hurt, end of story.

My brother lifted the knife, hesitated, then shoved it into my stomach, grasping my arm with his free hand to steady me when I jerked back. I gasped, flinching deeply, but I motioned with my head that I was fine. It had been a clean stroke, and in a place that would make the weapon easy to retrieve when the opportunity came.

I worked on moderating my breathing, trying to ignore the warm trickle of blood while Jack received his knife, and then Sean helped us both into the backseat and retook his place behind the wheel.

Hold on, Kate. Just a few more minutes.

Sean drove slowly up to the warehouse, easing next to the other vehicles sitting motionless near the double doors. Some I recognized, for they belonged to other Guardians and Seers. A couple matched the non-descript SUV I was currently in. They were black and belonged to the Demons. Kate's car was on the end. The sight of it caused my heart rate to spike. I was close.

Sean shifted into park and shut off the car. He looked over his shoulder at us. "Wait to break free until you're near the others," he reminded us. "You'll have to move fast. Leave the Demon Lord to me."

"Right," Jack grunted. "Easy."

"I apologize for any pain I may be forced to inflict."

"Sean, it's really uncomfortable to talk right now," I hissed. I could feel the blade shiver inside of me with every breath, every motion.

"Oh. Yes. Of course." He opened his car door and exited the vehicle. I sucked in a ragged breath. This was it.

Sean swung the door open and grabbed my arm, pulling me out of the SUV. Then he reached in and dragged Jack out as well. He gripped our elbows, standing firmly between us as he herded us toward the warehouse doors.

I hadn't seen anyone yet, but it was obvious my brother thought we would soon. His grip tightened brutally as we stepped inside, and I had to beat back my first true wave of doubt. Could I really trust him?

I didn't exactly have a choice. I tried to focus on the trust Jenna had for Sean.

We stepped onto the cavernous main floor of the warehouse. It was amazing how cold the building felt, though it was still hot outside. Just knowing the evil things that had happened here, the devils that hid inside these rooms . . . It didn't feel like home anymore. It felt like death.

Our shoes scuffed the old factory floor and Jack had bowed his head. I thought he might be praying, but then I realized he was trying to look defeated. I attempted to follow his example, but my eyes kept darting around.

Sean's body grew abruptly stiff. I soon understood why.

"Far Darrig, you've outdone yourself!"

I glanced up, catching sight of Selena Avalos poised on the staircase, waiting for us. She was beautiful, as always. But it was a cold beauty. An empty beauty. She was dressed expensively, as usual, her outfit over the top for daylight hours. This was the first time I'd seen her wear an evening gown of black. Her stiletto heels just peeked out under the folds of her dress, and her hair framed her perfectly sculpted face with an undeniable grace.

I frowned at the sight of her, my eyes burning with anger. Lee's murderer. I wanted to kill her myself, but once Toni was free, I doubted I'd get the chance.

"Is the master upstairs?" Sean asked, his voice smooth and dark.

The sound made me want to shiver, and I know I winced—but that could be dismissed by the knife embedded inside me. He sounded just like *Fear Dearg.*

Selena was smiling at him. "Yes. He's in pretty good sorts, though we've lost a couple Seers since you left."

My stomach clenched, and with the blade stuck inside me the sensation was more agonizing than usual. *It won't be Kate. It can't be Kate. Sean promised . . .*

Sean pulled us up the steps, and once we reached Selena she grabbed Jack's arm, hauling him closer. "Hmm . . . have we met?"

Jack chuckled weakly. "Once, but it was long ago. If it helps, my desire to kill you has only increased."

Her eyes sparkled happily. She fingered the knife handle, grinning when Jack sucked in a painful breath. "Oh, I hope you're not susceptible to the virus. Then the Demon Lord might let me keep you. You remind me of Antonio, but in a more . . . old-fashioned sort of way. I love your accent," she added sweetly. "I just *adore* Australian accents."

Needless to say, no one replied.

We stopped at the second floor. Selena and Jack led the way to our closed living room door, her heels clicking aggressively against the cement at every step. She twisted the knob and pushed the door open, Sean and me right behind her.

My eyes flashed over the scene, trying to gauge the situation with military precision. I saw Viktor Dmitriev first because he was the tallest and most dangerous-looking figure in the room. He was standing near the Demon Lord, who of course was the most impressive person in the room. He was smiling at me, but there was something unhappy about his face. As if things hadn't gone entirely according to plan.

Good. Anything that made him unhappy had to be a good thing.

At his other arm stood Mei Li, her single braid almost as straight as she was. Her beady eyes were watching me closely, sensing my hatred for her beloved master.

I saw Claire next, but only because Selena was pushing Jack in her direction. Claire was tied to a chair with thin rope, a couple knives stuck in her body, keeping her docile. Her head was bowed, but it was lifting. She looked completely defeated when she saw me, but there was more than simple sadness there. She was looking at me with . . . pity?

Sean's fingernails were suddenly digging into my skin. I winced, and then—my head still lowered in what I hoped looked like submission—I peeked at my brother. He was staring somewhere past me, his mouth a firm line, his nostrils silently flaring.

Almost frightened now, I followed his gaze. I saw Lee's body on the floor, her wide pink skirt lying over her twisted legs. I thought I was prepared to see her, after being warned of her death, but I wasn't. The blood, the stillness. No amount of warning could have prepared me for that. She'd been so full of life and energy—one of the most alive people I'd ever met.

What would I say to Kate? How would I console her? She'd lost so much—losing her best friend wasn't fair. My heart burned. Near Lee's hand I saw a worn shoe twitch. I followed the motion, finally finding myself staring at Toni, my long-time partner and greatest friend.

He looked horrible. I'd never seen him so despaired and empty. He'd been beaten badly, though only the blood covering him remained for evidence. His body had healed the minor injuries, leaving only the wounds that were still being penetrated. He had two daggers sticking out of him, and I hoped I would be fast enough to break my bonds, rip out my own knife, and free him before I could be stopped.

And then—as if fate could not keep me from the sight any longer—I saw Kate.

I don't know how I'd missed her until now. She was the one Claire had been thinking of when she saw me. She was the one Sean had been looking at, silently seething. But even putting that together, I didn't understand their emotions: their regret, their pity. Not yet.

She was leaning on Toni. Her hair had fallen across her face in a sheet, blocking her eyes from mine. I looked at her hungrily, trying to take in the reality that I was here, with her. She was real. I could touch her. I could hold her and shield her from these monsters. At last. I was where I belonged—at her side.

I wanted her to lift her head; I yearned for her to look up at me.

She stayed as she was.

That's when I realized she wasn't moving at all. Not even breathing.

And all the blood on her . . . it hadn't come from leaning solely against Toni.

Now that I was forcing myself to take in the details, I realized she looked exactly as I'd seen her that haunting night so long ago. Her body riddled with bullet holes, leaving no chance for life. She'd already done it. She'd gone back. The truth was written clearly in Toni's eyes, now that I knew what to look for.

Kate was dead.

The dagger in my stomach? That pain was nothing now.

The Demon Lord's mocking sigh filled the room. "I know. Disappointing, isn't it, Patrick? I had hoped she would be the last to go, but . . . sacrifices must be made. I suppose I'll survive a bit of disappointment."

I didn't react to his words. I couldn't. Inside, I was screaming. Inside, I was dying.

The Demon Lord looked to Sean. "Where is Yuri?"

"With the girls," Sean said. His voice sounded dry. "I left them in the car. Their screams were annoying."

The Demon Lord chuckled lowly. "You're not exactly a child lover, are you, Far Darrig? And that new Seer you found me is also with Yuri?"

Sean's head jerked in the affirmative.

"Excellent." The Demon Lord stepped up to me, Mei Li at his side. He was smiling. "Well, Patrick, you've looked better. I was hoping to see one final reunion between you and Kate, but . . ." His smile widened when my head lurched up at the sound of his voice flippantly forming her name. "Well, she wasn't exactly cooperating," he finished pleasantly.

I couldn't speak. I wanted to. I wanted to curse him, rail him, rip him apart. But I couldn't. I was too angry, too shocked. Her death didn't seem real. None of this did.

The Demon Lord held out a hand in front of Mei Li, palm up, and she was quick to place a small knife there. He gripped the handle and then grabbed a fistful of my hair, jerking my head up so our eyes met. He was breathing heavily, though my chest was heaving faster. "The Guardians are going to lose this war, you know," he said to me coolly. "You're not all immune to the virus, and the Demons outnumber you. But you, Patrick, aren't going to see the end of the war. Far Darrig is going to administer the virus, and you will die. The Bennett twins are mine now." He tipped his head closer. "I don't think Kate would be impressed with your Guardian skills. Do you?"

My lower lip curled in derision. Blood pounded in my ears. I couldn't see well. Why couldn't I see well? Why was everything blurry?

He plunged the knife into my left shoulder without warning. I howled, but not just from the pain of his knife. It had only caused a fraction of the agony I was feeling.

Sean's grip on me trembled—he was shaking behind me.

"*That,*" the Demon Lord hissed in my face, his breath stinging my skin, "is for all the trouble you've caused me." He plucked the knife back out and I shuddered at its release. "And *this,*" he said, thrusting the blade into my right side just above my hip and driving it in up to the hilt. I heard a harsh cry. I thought it was Sean—then I realized it came from me. "*This,*" he repeated with an additional shove, "is for my own amusement. Guardians may be immortal, but not immune to suffering. And you should suffer. *All* of you. You're not superior." He left the knife in my side and took a step back, releasing his hold on my hair. He slapped my face lightly, trying to get me to look at him.

"All of the Guardians deserve this pain. And that's what I'll give them. That's what I've promised all the Demons who follow me: satisfaction." He tossed a look over my shoulder, past Sean. "Antonio over there was good enough to take a good measure of abuse, but I think it's your turn. And I think Far Darrig should be allowed to go first."

He took a step back and Mei Li offered a knife to Sean. I closed my eyes tightly, knowing he couldn't falter. We didn't know where the other Seers were. We couldn't act yet. The only mortals in here were dead.

Kate . . .

I gasped in anguish as Sean stabbed me in the back.

"How does it feel?" The Demon Lord's voice seemed distant, unfocused.

Sean's deep voice surrounded me. "Good," he replied.

Had he betrayed me? Had he known Kate was dead all along? Had *he* murdered her?

My vision was clearing, and some semblance of reason returned. My loosely bound fingers could feel the knife's handle. He'd jabbed the knife into me, because he'd had to. But he'd placed it strategically. Sean was on my side. He was sticking to the plan. That's what I needed to do—follow the plan. It was the only way to avenge Kate's death. I could worry about how I'd deal with her loss after her murderers were dead.

The Demon Lord turned his back on us, walking toward the couch. "I'm glad. You'll have time for more soon enough. We all will. Now, why don't you offer Patrick a seat? I believe I know where he might like to be just now . . ."

Without Sean lifting all my weight I wouldn't have been able to move. He levered me forward and I stumbled blindly in the direction I was being pushed, almost tripping over my own dead feet.

Sean shoved me to the floor and I fell against Kate's exposed side, my hands pinched painfully by the wall. I cried out when

I hit into her, because her lifeless body started to fall and I was helpless to stop it. Her head slipped off Toni's shoulder, her whole body slumping until she was half lying in Toni's shaking lap, her face turned away from me.

I almost ripped my hands free and ruined the plan—would have, if I wasn't so close to the wall that my movements were restricted. Her leg was stiff next to mine, telling me she'd been dead for a while now. An hour? More?

These Demons from hell hadn't even bothered to lay her body on the floor, let alone cover her up.

I was too shocked to cry. I was too deadened to do anything but stare at her.

Kate was dead.

We'd failed.

Most important, I had failed *her*. I never should have left her. This never should have happened.

The Demon Lord was speaking, though I hardly heard the words. "We're done here. The young Seer—what was his name?"

"Hanif," Selena supplied.

"Yes. Takao—go extend him a last invitation. If he refuses, kill him. Better yet, have Selena's Seer take care of it."

She grinned. "Thank you, my lord. This is just the sort of thing he needs."

Takao bowed to his master and swept from the room to follow his orders.

Jack spoke suddenly, taking advantage of the silence. His voice was strained, and the knife inside him quivered. "What about Dr. Radcliffe? Where is he?"

The Demon Lord winced. Somehow he still looked happy. I wanted to strangle him. "When I learned it was his memory used to get to my past . . . Obviously I couldn't let him live. His body has been keeping the other Seers company. I find that dead bodies help lower the morale in a room—makes the live ones easier to control."

Silence fell after that, except for the quiet mutterings of the Demon Lord conferring with Mei Li and Selena about traveling back to Vegas.

Toni's voice cracked beside me, a thin whisper. "It's my fault. I asked her to go back. Patrick, it was me . . . I asked her to save Lee. I'm so, so sorry."

I couldn't pull my eyes from Kate, not even to look at him. As morbid as it might sound, I wished she was leaning against me. I wished I could wrap my arms around her and kiss her until—like the fabled princesses—she would wake up in my arms, alive and smiling.

My mouth parted shallowly. "It's my fault," I croaked. "I shouldn't have left her."

A sharp gunshot echoed in another room.

Toni's head fell, feeling the pain of Hanif's death acutely. We were supposed to protect humans and Seers. Not let them die.

Failed . . .

The tape cracked behind me, reacting to take the strain I was putting it under. It gave me purpose. I twisted my hands, ignoring the pinching pain as I maneuvered out of the bindings. I squirmed my hands until my wrists tore free, no longer impeded. My shoulders loosened. I could feel a change on my countenance when I lifted my head to make eye contact with Jack. Our eyes met across the room. He nodded once, his face grim as his arms began to twist minutely.

Viktor Dmitriev was standing close to Jack, but he was looking at me. His eyes narrowed at the pure determination hardening my features. He took a step toward me, as if that could help him figure out what I was thinking.

He didn't get far. Jack had ripped free, and with a single motion he'd pulled the knife out of his stomach and risen to his feet. He was too fast, his movements too unexpected—no one could have stopped him. He was able to cut Claire's bonds before Selena saw him and shouted for Viktor.

The Russian turned around quickly, but Jack was ready. He knocked Viktor's gun aside and the two men grappled desperately, wrestling for control of the single knife.

Mei Li jumped forward to stop Claire, but the Guardian was already free of her imprisoning knives. She turned them on her captor, but she was stiff—she'd been tied up too long. Mei Li delivered a few expert kicks and Claire was lying on the floor, defenseless.

I noticed these individual battles through a haze, because I was moving too. I was free, bits of tape still clinging to my wrists. I jerked the knife out of my back first, tossing it aside so I could wrench the other two blades out of my body. I tried to ignore the throb and ache of my body healing itself, sealing up the gaping wounds.

I rolled to my knees and reached for Kate. I knew I didn't have time to linger over her body—I would have eternity to mourn her loss—but I was still gentle as I scooped her up and shifted her body to the floor, away from Toni. I didn't look at her face, though the curtain of hair was slipping away from her cold features even as I twisted away. I couldn't face her. Not yet.

Toni was more than ready for me, already leaning away from the wall so I would have an easy swipe at his bindings. I realized he had another knife in his back—I grabbed it after cutting him free, retaining hold of two knives.

The Demon Lord was shouting for Takao, and Selena was gripping his arm in shock. I stood and faced them, wondering why Sean hadn't already gone for the Demon Lord. I soon realized why. From the corner of my eye I could see him attacking Mei Li, trying to keep her away from Claire so the exhausted Guardian could recover.

I was just fine with his deviation from our sketchy plan. After all, I had Kate to avenge, and though I didn't know who'd pulled the trigger and stolen her life, I knew I didn't have to look any further than the source of all our problems to place responsibility for her death: the Demon Lord.

He was *mine.*

I stepped over Lee's body, content to make him suffer by coming slowly. I could feel my face stretching, and I realized I was grinning.

The Demon Lord backed up quickly, trying to push Selena into my path, but she resisted his shoves. "Far Darrig!" he yelled hotly, eyes still on me and my steady advance. "What are you doing?"

My brother didn't answer. He really didn't have to.

I'd been pushed over the edge. I felt maniacal. I'd never wanted to kill like I did now. If I'd still been eligible for heaven, these intense feelings would have surely disqualified me. Was this the degree of hate one had to feel to become a Demon? These murderous urges were nothing if not demonic.

The Demon Lord was obviously done waiting for one of his bodyguards to rush to his aid. He reached into his suit and withdrew a simple black pistol. He leveled it at me, hooking his finger around the trigger and then squeezing off a round.

I dove to the side and heard the bullet pound into the wall behind me. Near Kate. I roared in barely contained rage, hands shaking as I lengthened my stride to hurry my approach.

His gun swiveled to follow my movements. Somehow I noticed a bead of glistening sweat near his hairline, and it gave me a measure of satisfaction. He was afraid. He fired another shot, and though I shifted my weight this bullet caught me in the upper arm. I thought I heard Sean yell my name, but I was too focused on my prey. The bullet's trail burned, but wasn't incapacitating. It was already healing.

I felt Toni somewhere beside me and knew he was going for Selena. I only had one target to worry about. One point of focus.

As the Demon Lord fired another bullet, barely missing my head, I flung one of my knives, landing it deeply in his right thigh. He cried out and staggered, grabbing at Selena for support. But she'd dived away from him in an effort to avoid the fight, or Toni, or both.

She pulled out a diminutive gun and aimed it at Toni, but I heard my partner chuckle, the sound hard. "Really?" he rasped at her. "*Really?* You think that's going to—"

She let off a shot and his words stopped. I didn't know if he'd been hit, though, because the Demon Lord was limping further away from me, dagger embedded in his leg. I continued my advance, following his backward reel toward the wall by the kitchen area. He couldn't have many bullets left.

I lunged and the Demon Lord's eyes widened, his face washed with pale fear. He emptied the last of his bullets into my stomach, which slowed me down despite my resolve to ignore the bites of lead. At this close range, I could feel the bullets rip right through me. My head ducked instinctively against the pain, but really it just gave me a burst of strength, resolve. This was the pain Kate had felt, and she'd managed to keep going—find me in the past and deliver her final message.

I wouldn't stop until he was dead.

I could still see the Demon Lord jerking the knife out of his leg, gasping in agony. He gritted his teeth, and when our eyes met his fear had fled. He was angry. Beyond angry. He was livid, the pain etching his face into a lethal combination with his fury.

No more lethal than I was. My gaze narrowed.

He adopted a defensive position, barely restraining a wince as he shifted on his bleeding leg.

My own jaw was rigid, my grip on the knife convulsive.

"You're going to lose," the Demon Lord said, voice quaking thinly.

"I'm immortal," I countered.

The corner of his mouth twitched. "Yes, you are. And Kate wasn't. You were too late."

A growl was vibrating through me. My vision clouded. My stomach compressed with grief.

He smiled. "You see, you already lost. You lost her. She's dead, and you weren't here to save her. What good is immortality now?" His eyes sharpened. "I win."

I charged him, crossing the short space in an instant. His knife came up, buried between two of my ribs. I cried out in unrestrained pain as he jostled the knife inside me, goading it up to pierce my heart. If he could embed it there, I'd be immobile. He could escape.

That couldn't happen.

He fished the blade around more frantically when I slammed my arm into his throat, forcing us both to stumble until his back hit the wall, my bedroom to the right of us.

I could still hear the sounds of the others fighting behind me, but I was focused on my own battle. The knife was still inside me. The Demon Lord was unable to breathe, but he tried to kick me—failed because of the close quarters—then harshly twisted the knife inside me.

My body was shaking with pain and adrenaline. I dropped my arm from his jugular and chopped at his wrist, heard something snap, felt the knife stop shifting inside me. He'd lost his grip. Thrust up against the wall, he'd lost all leverage. He was gasping raggedly. He knew he'd lost. I was going to kill him.

His green eyes were almost resigned. Somehow, it made me hate him even more. Shouldn't he be afraid of what awaited him on the other side? After all he'd done? I wanted to see his fear. *Needed* to see it.

"Seers normally go to heaven," I said through gritted teeth. "But I think they'll be making an exception for you."

A ghost of a smile crossed his face, the image only slightly ruined by his audibly racing heart. "Perhaps. But in case they don't, is there anything you'd like me to tell Kate?"

My chest heaved with emotion. The very thought of this

insidious monster getting anywhere near heaven—near my Kate again—drove me over the edge of my tattered sanity. I couldn't stand to let him breathe for another second.

I lifted my knife, plunging it swiftly into his heart as if he were a regular Demon. Because by my reckoning, he was exactly that.

His eyes were dulling. His lips parted. Wavered. He sagged, deadweight.

I stepped back, letting him fall to the floor, the dagger still inside him.

twenty-four

Patrick O'Donnell

With trembling hands I jerked the knife out from between my ribs, shuddering at the sensation. I glanced once more to the body at my feet before turning my back on the Demon Lord's lifeless form. Some of the insanity that had possessed me fled. Not all, but most. I tried to see what I'd missed, doing a quick scan across the room to see if anyone needed my assistance.

Toni had engaged Selena in a fight while I'd taken out the Demon Lord. I say fight, but she didn't stand a chance against Toni, even if he had been tortured for hours today. She was sprawled back on the tattered couch, and I noticed her body was mostly unmarked. Toni hadn't been swiping aimlessly. He was interested only in the kill.

He was standing over her, his whole body stiff.

"Antonio!" she was gasping, propped up on her elbows. "Please! You don't want to do this to me! It's *me*!"

He spun one of the blades he held in his hand, crouching over her. I almost missed the anger-edged words. "I'm pretty sure this is *exactly* what I want to do, Selena."

"Please!"

Toni's stab was clean, effective. She stopped moving, stopped begging.

Selena would never plead for anything again.

"Help!" My head turned toward the frantic croak. It was Claire. She was kneeling next to a still body. It took two heavy heartbeats to realize it was my brother.

As I crossed the room in a rush, I could see the fighting was over. Jack—fingers pressed to Viktor's neck, checking for a pulse—was just reacting to Claire's voice, but I was already kneeling at Sean's side.

I swallowed hard, eyeing the damage. My brother's eyes were open, and he wasn't dead. But a knife was in his heart, the hilt quivering with every shallow breath.

"He stepped in front of me," Claire was mumbling, wringing her hands. I'd never seen her so agitated, so out of control. "Why would he do that? He's Far Darrig! Why would he sacrifice himself for me?"

"He's not dead yet, and he's not *Fear Dearg*," I growled out the Gaelic pronunciation with fury, not intending to sound so fierce. I grabbed hold of his hand, looked him in the eye. "Sean, don't you dare even *think* about leaving me."

Sean was blinking heavily. "Patrick . . . I'm sorry. I'm sorry about Kate."

My breathing hitched. Again, seeing became difficult because of a sudden blur. I finally realized what was causing the sporadic vision problems—my eyes were stinging with unshed tears. "You're not going to die," I said angrily, ignoring his apology. "You can't." I glanced back at the knife. "Are you sure it pierced your heart?"

"I—I think so. I don't know." His whole face scrunched, eyes closing tightly. "It hurts. Bad."

Claire's voice was choked, but more level than before. "There's a chance it didn't get his heart. But if it's that close . . . Even pulling the knife out could kill him."

Jack's voice was right behind me, low. "Only one way to find out."

I tried to pull in steady breaths. But my hands wouldn't stop shaking. Whether it was from fear, anger, adrenaline, or despair, I couldn't tell. I curled them to fists, planted them on my bent legs and looked up at the ceiling. I just needed one minute of strength. Just one more, and then I could collapse.

That's when I heard Toni's strangled cry and I made the mistake of glancing his way.

He'd moved to Lee's side, oblivious to us, and he had her half cradled in his arms. He was pulling her close, sobbing into her shoulder. Kate was lying near him, inert.

His pain mirrored mine. Kate was dead.

My palms pressed against my temples and I scrunched my eyes.

"Patrick," Claire said. "He needs help *now.*"

"I can't," I rasped. "I . . . my hands . . . I can't."

She understood. She looked down at my brother. "Hey," she said, almost too loudly. His eyes flickered up to her. She cleared her throat. "Do you trust me?"

"I don't know you," he returned, short on breath.

"Yes, well . . . if you survive this, I promise you can get to know me." She glanced at me, then looked further. "Jack? Can you help hold down his shoulders?"

I felt the tears slicing down my face. My stupid hands wouldn't stop quaking. I looked at my brother. "I'm sorry," I whispered. "I'm sorry, Sean, I can't . . ."

His eyes rolled to meet mine. "I know," he panted. "I know. It's okay."

It wasn't. He needed me. I couldn't help him if I was shaking. How was I ever going to help anyone again? How could I ever hope to surmount the pain of losing Kate?

Jack was kneeling at Sean's head, placing firm hands on Sean's shoulders.

Claire looked back at Sean. "If this works, you'll start healing right away."

Sean swallowed. "Yeah. And if it doesn't, I die. Get on with it."

Claire's hand hovered above his chest, hesitating. She pulled in a deep breath. Then she wrapped her fingers around the hilt and slid it out cautiously.

My brother groaned deeply, but Jack kept Sean's upper body steady. Claire tossed the bloody knife aside the moment it was free of Sean's body and then quickly peeled the ripped part of his shirt aside, so she could look at the wound.

Her voice was marveling. "It's closing." Her eyes flickered up to his. "You're going to live."

Sean was still pulling in ragged breaths. "Yeah. Thanks." He winced up at her. "What was your name again?"

I saw her lips twitch in a rare smile. "Claire."

He gave a small nod and pushed himself into a sitting position.

Jack stepped back, moving out of my line of vision.

I swiped a hand over my eyes, and when I pulled it back I saw glistening moisture.

Sean's hand was on my arm. "Go to her," he breathed. "It's okay. We'll take care of the rest."

I stared at him, helpless in that moment to form words.

His eyes tightened. "Patrick, I'm all right. Go."

Jack's grunt drew all our eyes. He'd stooped to the floor to retrieve Viktor's gun. He checked it for bullets, then cocked it. He spoke to the room at large. "Where will I find that runt, Tikki, or whatever his name is?"

"Just down the hall," my brother answered. "But I'll go with you—there's another Demon there, one of Selena's."

Claire gripped Sean's arm and he twisted to look at her. "The twins? They're not here? Maddy?"

He shook his head. "They're safe at the farmhouse."

Claire's whole body seemed to loosen with relief.

The two stood and Sean offered me his hand. As soon as I was pulled to my feet, the door swung open.

A woman stepped warily inside, gun in hand. I saw the flash of her pink skirt, but couldn't even think her name. It was too impossible. She was dead.

Her eyes darted toward us, the biggest cluster of people, and she sighed, lowering the gun to her side. "Oh my Oreos, thank *goodness* I don't have to kill anyone. I was freaking out there for a minute."

My eyes sliced to Toni, who seemed frozen, still huddled with Lee's body. Slowly, so slowly, his head lifted—the sound of her voice the only thing that could distract him from his all-consuming grief.

Lee was now wincing at him. Tears burned visibly in her eyes. "Geez, Toni, that's just *weird*. And gross. You're getting my blood all over you."

"Lee?" he gasped.

She pulled in a shaking breath. "Yeah, it's me. I came back to save you all, but I guess you've got that part covered." She was wearing the same outfit she'd died in—a fifties montage.

Toni blinked back down at her body in his arms. His gaze immediately returned to her. "But . . . You're a Guardian?" Toni uttered, shocked.

She almost smiled. "Sure. I mean, if I didn't come back, my mom would have found out about me dying on her. She would have killed me! This way, I have some time to ease her into the idea. As a bonus, I get to tease you for eternity." Her words became more rushed. "Of course, I had to help Peter save Hanif first. So, sorry I'm a bit late for the whole rescue thing. And we've got a couple bodies upstairs. Peter killed them, so I really have no idea how to even hold a gun. The only reason I came charging in here first is we heard gunshots, and you know, I'm immortal now, and I figured I'd make a great shield for the Seers. And, really, while on the subject, I think we should all cut Peter just a little bit of slack, considering everything. And—Toni Alverez, would you *please* put down my corpse? You're freaking me out, and I really, *really* want to kiss you right now!"

He suddenly seemed to realize this was real. She was back. He could have her for the rest of eternity, and no one could take her away. He lowered her mortal body to the ground and stood shakily. He stumbled toward her, like a starving man who'd just been offered a feast.

She was moving too, blindly pushing the gun back behind her. I glimpsed a pair of hands grab the weapon and then Lee was darting to catch Toni as he almost fell into her arms. He embraced her, sobbing, and he tried to kiss every inch of her face at the same time. He was mumbling something in Spanish, but a translation was hardly necessary. Lee buried her fingers in his thick dark hair, trying to pull him impossibly closer. She was crying, whispering his name, trying to soothe his tears. "It's okay," she whispered. "It's going to be okay."

I looked away from them, unable to watch their reunion anymore. I was happy for them. But I couldn't bear happiness right now. I felt as if witnessing another second of this was going to kill me. If only it *could* kill me.

Just then Hanif stuck his head inside, looking more than relieved to see us.

"Hanif . . ." Claire blinked at the sight of him, still trying to process Lee's words. "But—Takao went to kill you. We heard the gunshot!"

Hanif slipped closer. Favoring his injured arm, his good hand gripped the door frame. "Takao *would* have killed me, And if he hadn't, that creep Jose would have. But Peter took care of them first. And Lee showed up just in time to help."

I stiffened at the Demon Seer's name. "Where is he?" I demanded in a low growl.

My roughened voice drew a few looks. Sean's was particularly wary.

Hanif raised a long hand. "Now, now, before you all go off on him, I think you should remember he saved my life. He's in the hall, and I'll let him come in when I think you won't all try to kill him. Where's Kate? I'm sure she'll take . . . my . . ." He'd just spotted her body. He swallowed hard.

Now that my rage toward Peter was distracted I fully remembered my crippling grief. I walked slowly across the room, not caring that everyone was now eyeing me.

The room was near silent as I knelt by Kate's side. I crouched over her, one trembling hand moving to cup the side of her face. The other lifted her hand, my fingers aching to be held by her stiff fingers. I couldn't make myself close her eyes; that would be admitting she was gone, forever lost to me. It was better to see the glossiness, even though her empty eyes cut me to the core.

Knowing she lived on somewhere else did not give me solace. Even though I was armed with the knowledge she would be reunited with her parents, I was not comforted. Because *I* had lost her, and I was too selfish to feel happiness for those who had gained her.

I lifted her cold fingers to my lips, pressed my mouth against her skin with too much force. My other hand brushed her hair from her forehead, and that's when I noticed the remains of the tape on my wrists were grazing against her skin. I jerked back quickly, lowered her hand so I could tear the offensive pieces off, ignoring the flash of pain as they were ripped away and tossed aside. I caught up her hand once more, pressing the back of her hand against my lips. Trembling fingers settled back against her face, wandered over her parted lips. Her beautiful face was frozen, not reacting to my touch.

I choked on a fresh wave of tears. I could feel them streaking down my face, see them splashing onto her still hand. I honestly couldn't stop trembling.

I released Kate's hand once more, only to slip my own beneath her limp body. I lifted her into the cradle of my arms, still kneeling, nearly crushing her against my chest.

I felt someone brush up behind me. A hand pressed to my shoulder. A curtain of pink sank beside me. "Oh gosh." Lee's voice was heavy with emotion. "Kate . . . *Kate*." Her voice pinched off. I lifted my eyes and saw Lee's face, covered in tears; she had one shaking hand clasped over her mouth. Toni was stooped behind her, hands on her shoulders, unwilling to lose contact with her.

"Oh Patrick," Lee's voice hitched. She lowered her hand and looked right at me. "I'm so . . . so sorry."

I pinched my eyes closed. "Please. I . . ."

Lee was crying, unable to speak. Her hand was on Kate's arm.

Toni's fingers flexed their hold on Lee. "Of course," he mumbled toward me.

Sean stepped up to us. He extended his arms, silently offering to help lift her. He understood my intentions: my need to mourn her alone.

Lee backed away with Toni, arms wrapped tightly around each other as Sean helped me up from the floor with Kate. Once I was standing I pulled her tightly against my body. I could carry her. I needed to hold her.

Sean nodded almost imperceptively, honoring my silent wish. He stepped around me, moving for my open bedroom. I followed him.

I knew there were bodies littering this room, but I wasn't going to worry about them. Let one of the other Guardians handle it. I didn't want the responsibility. I was done with this day. Done with this whole life. I was no longer a Guardian. I was a broken man. Nothing more. I'd given everything I could give—I could give no more. Kate . . . *No more*.

This was *my* time. I wasn't going to think about anyone

else's pain at losing her. Not Lee's, not her grandmother's, not Jenna's, not Josie's. For this frozen moment, this last moment, Kate was completely mine.

I stepped into the room, which appeared largely how I'd left it. Only now some of her things littered the floor and the blankets on the mattress I recognized as hers. I barely reacted to the fresh wave of pain the sight of her things brought me.

I laid her on the bed, cringing when her head fell back and I didn't have a free hand to catch it. Sean's hand flashed beside me, reaching out and slipping under her hair, supporting her. He helped me settle her against the mattress before reaching for one of the blankets folded up at the end of the bed.

I grabbed his wrist, stopping him. "No. Not that one." I couldn't soil one of her blankets. It would be criminal to ruin something of hers, something that held her memory.

Somehow, Sean understood my logic. He cast his eyes around the room, spotting a white sheet wadded up in the corner; I'd stripped the bed but hadn't bothered to wash the bedding before leaving.

Sean retrieved the sheet and helped fold it around her, knowing from my silence that he shouldn't cover her head. Shielding her face from me would have been beyond unbearable.

Once she was wrapped, he straightened and put a hand on my shoulder. "I'm sorry, Patrick," he repeated.

I didn't reply to his mumbled words.

He released me and moved back. He paused at the doorway, his voice soft. "I'll keep the others out while you say good-bye."

"Thank you," I forced myself to whisper.

He closed the door, and I was alone. Completely alone.

I knelt on the floor beside her, my hands clasped behind my head, my forearms crushing against my skull in a desperate hold. My elbows were touching—my head was pounding under the pressure. I was gasping—hyperventilating. I couldn't breathe. My lungs felt like they were going to burst. My tense body was going to explode.

But I wouldn't explode with the pain. I wouldn't die. I *couldn't*.

I would never hear her laugh again, never hear her whisper my name. I would never feel her fingers curl around mine. Her warm lips would never touch mine again. She would never cock her head to the side and squint at me, in that way that was uniquely hers. She would never smile at me or confide in me her fears and dreams. She would never do anything. She would just lie here, motionless, lifeless. She was all I had to hold on to—the only thing keeping me from total madness. And her heart would never beat again.

I would be crippled by this pain until the end of time. There would be no release. I could scream. I could curse. But I would not die.

Insanity was something all men feared. It was instinctual to fear the loss of memories and reason. And yet, at this moment—as my sanity was being drained, but nowhere near quickly enough—I only prayed that insanity would take me completely. Perhaps if I was insane, I could forget her. Perhaps if I were mad, I wouldn't feel like this. This torment would vanish, because I would not remember her. I would not remember anything.

I had never so desperately longed for Heaven. For the sweet escape of death. Not once in two centuries—decades of years, full of regrets—had I ever regretted my fate so entirely. I'd never seen the senselessness of eternal life so vividly.

If I was not personally living this agony, I would not believe such hopeless, raw torture was possible. To suffer this much, and still live on; it was impossible. *Should* have been impossible. No one should experience this and survive. It was unnatural.

No word could define my pain. No measurement could describe the depth of my loss. No medication could ease this rending of my heart, mind, body, and soul. I couldn't do anything but hold her and weep.

So that's what I did.

I crawled onto the bed beside her, uncaring about what others might think. She was not just a dead body. She was Kate. There was nothing sick or wrong about my lying beside her. It was natural. Instinctual. It was the only comfort I could see.

It was a feeble balm.

I wrapped my arms around her, pulling her body up against the length of mine. She was too cold. Too stiff. But she was here. She was real. I could hold her . . . She might have only been sleeping—peacefully dreaming. She could wake up. She could come back.

My breathing was slowing. Becoming more even. Maybe I was growing numb. But if that was the case, why was I still burning with pain and guilt?

I buried my face in her hair, pulling in her distinct smell. It lingered strongly, even when she didn't. It seemed wrong. Horribly wrong.

My nose brushed against her cheek as I kissed her nearest temple. When she didn't respond I flinched into her shoulder, letting the torture rip through me in full.

"I'm sorry," I gasped. "I'm sorry, Kate. I'm so, so sorry."

My breathing hitched and broke. I silently cried out for my father, images of the man who'd raised me and that of deity blurring together. I would plead with anyone who would listen. I begged for death to take me.

But my heart continued to break, despite my countless petitions—with no indication that it would ever stop.

twenty-five

Patrick O'Donnell

I was alone, drowning in unspeakable loss. No one was there to help me. The only one with the power to save me—to offer me direction—was gone.

I don't know how long I sobbed beside her, my face buried in the curve of her neck. It could have been minutes or years. Everything was quiet outside, though I was sure the others were taking care of the bodies. As Sean had promised, no one bothered me. I knew this moment of solitude wouldn't last, though. I couldn't stay here with her forever. They would want to take her away from me. But for the life of me, I couldn't make myself let go.

I was no longer crying. My body was too weak to keep up with the torrent of emotions raging within me. All my tears were spent. I'd stopped praying too, since it wasn't doing any good. Or maybe that was why I felt this deadened calm? Some merciful Being had decided to offer me a partial escape from my suffering? If only it could have been total.

I heard the door ease open.

"Patrick?" Toni said, voice cautious.

My back was to the door, and I didn't bother to turn. The

only acknowledgement he received was my body's sudden tensing. My curled grip around Kate's body intensified, my eyes pinched shut against a fresh wave of tears I didn't think I still had in me. They couldn't take her. Not yet. They'd want to bury her in the ground, and I'd never see her again.

"Patrick, we've dumped all the Demons. We're going to take the other bodies to the morgue. I've got a bag, and . . ."

"Get out." My tone was so parched, so dead, there was no inflection or power. Only sheer pain.

There was a short silence. Then the door latched closed, and the silence stretched.

Several minutes later the door opened again. I felt a slight depression as someone sat behind me, near my back. Lying on my side, I didn't even have the strength to raise my head and look over my shoulder to see who it was.

"Please go away," I mumbled stubbornly. *Why couldn't they just leave me alone? Hadn't Sean promised to keep them away?* Couldn't he do that for a little longer?

A small hand was laid delicately on my arm. It was so thin, it could have only belonged to a woman. I closed my eyes and exhaled sharply.

Lee's voice was soothing, understanding. "I know. But you can't keep her here forever, Patrick."

Her words were terribly true.

My mind rebelled against them anyway. "Leave me alone."

Tears colored her words now. "Look, you're not the only one . . . struggling, right now."

"Out, Lee." She had *no* idea how much I was struggling.

Lee sniffed loudly, rubbed my arm briefly, but she eventually left.

My mind may have been blank, but I knew Lee hadn't been gone even two minutes before there was a knuckled tap on the door.

"Go away," I fairly whined, not caring who heard me.

The door opened anyway. Sean's voice was deep, even. "Patrick, it's time. We need to get her body taken care of."

My grip only strengthened. I knew he was right, but my arms wouldn't—couldn't—let them take her from me.

A large hand was pressed against my raised shoulder. "Patrick? Come on. Let go. Let me help you."

"Please," I begged, wincing against her stiff neck. "Please, just leave me alone."

He made the mistake of grabbing my elbow, perhaps thinking he could physically force me to release her. I lashed out unthinkingly. My right arm was still wrapped beneath her, trapped, but my left arm swung wide in what would be a ringing backhanded slap across his face. Would have been, if Sean hadn't effortlessly caught my wrist. "Patrick," he said gruffly. "Look at me."

I did, my eyes leaking steady tears. I knew he could see the raw emotions that distorted my face, see the overall feeling of hopeless grief and loss that had my whole form trembling.

He pursed his lips. "It's time, Patrick. Her family is going to be getting the call soon. You can't keep them away from her. Let Kate get cleaned up before they have to see her. Her grandma shouldn't have to see her like this."

I knew he was right. They'd *all* been right.

My broken words were weak. "I don't . . . I don't think I can . . ."

"Let me help you," he repeated. "You don't have to do this alone."

As if on cue the others trailed into the room. Toni and Jack came around the other side of the bed, Toni fingering a folded black body bag. They stood, waiting for the word.

Lee was standing at Sean's elbow, her face red and puffy. She focused solely on me, as if she couldn't bear to look at Kate. Sean was watching me too, waiting. I closed my stinging eyes, the closest I could get to producing a sign of permission.

They all understood. Sean released my wrist even as Jack bent over the bed, reaching for Kate. Toni was rolling the long bag out across the foot of the bed, peeling back the open sides.

I didn't try to fight them, but I didn't pull away from Kate as Jack and Toni proceeded to compassionately peel her away from my side, her body still wrapped in the sheet. They slid her slowly off my arm, my fingertips brushing her waist one last time. And then my heavy arms were empty.

Sean gripped my shoulder. "Come on. Don't torture yourself. Let's go."

I shook my head and curled into the fetal position, pinching my eyes closed to block out the awful images. I deserved to feel all the guilt, all the pain. And though I couldn't see what was happening, the sounds described everything in horrific detail. Plastic wrinkled as it was pressed down by deadweight, crinkled loudly as it was tugged over her inert form. The long pull of a raspy zipper, sealing her inside. Lee's small hand rubbed my back as the bag was slid off the bed, taken into their arms.

Toni and Jack shuffled out and Sean spoke softly behind me. "What can I do? Do you need to be alone? Can I get you anything?"

I crushed my closed eyes with the heels of my hands. "No," I fairly gasped. My heart was pounding erratically, my gut clenching painfully. I was rapidly slipping into a panic. "I need to be with her."

Sean seemed to debate his answer, not knowing what would really be best for me.

Lee broke into the aggravated pause, eager to agree. "Okay. We can follow them to the morgue. But you need to change your clothes. The twins would have a heart attack at the sight of you. Not to mention what any other humans would do . . ."

Was I ready to face her family? I doubted it. But I couldn't stay here. I needed to be near Kate. So I forced my muscles to obey, willed my body to shift into a sitting position. Lee offered me a fractured smile. "I'll find a car we can use."

"We can take mine," Sean supplied.

"All right." Lee hesitated, as if she had more she wanted to say to me. Another look at my gaunt face had her second-guessing her intentions. "I'll wait for you in the other room," she said dimly, retreating gently.

I tried to ignore the blood on the bed, but as I swung my legs over the side, I couldn't ignore the blood caking my already crisp shirt. It was partially dried, so it cracked sickeningly as I moved. The fact that it was mostly mine didn't keep my stomach from lurching. My eyes flashed to my rickety dresser and Sean was moving a half second later. He pulled open a middle drawer and plucked out a black T-shirt, offering it up quickly for my inspection. I gave a slack nod and he carried it over, not bothering to shut the drawer. I noticed he'd replaced his bloodied shirt with one of Toni's, a basic white T.

My rigid fingers were shaking as I fumbled with the small buttons. Sean laid the shirt beside me and blew out his breath. "I'm sorry, Patrick."

I cringed as I stripped the stained shirt off my body. I tried to answer him—knew he deserved an answer—but my mouth wouldn't work. My jaw was clenched too tightly, my throat too constricted for speech.

Blood had seeped through, so my pale chest was stained with dark pink. Sean immediately offered to find a rag, slipping out of the room and leaving me alone with my thoughts.

Bad idea.

My elbows dug into my quaking knees, the heels of my hands planted firmly against my temples, fingertips clutching my tangled hair.

Her grandmother was going to blame me—hate me. Jenna and Josie—they'd never forgive me. I suppose their reactions shouldn't have had such power to curdle my insides. After all, they weren't going to accuse me of anything I wasn't already blaming myself for. I tried to force myself to think about what tomorrow would bring, but it was hard to imagine. And then the funeral . . .

What was I going to do without her?

My mind was scrambling for answers, for any hint of reason. I would never be able to work as a Guardian again. I was confident of that. No one would be able to depend on me. At least not for the next few hundred years. I wouldn't be in any position to be anything for anyone. Sean hadn't been able to count on me when he needed me to help save his life. I'd just sat there, helpless, useless. My shaking body had betrayed me and rendered me completely unreliable.

I'd need to leave here. Leave everyone behind. Toni and Lee, especially. I couldn't see them every day, an incessant reminder of what I'd had, what I'd lost. I'd ask Terence for money. Just enough to get me a plane ticket, to anywhere. I'd find a place to mourn, somewhere isolated, where I wouldn't be disturbed.

Sean. Could I leave Sean? I honestly didn't know. I had no desire for company, but he and I had so much to reconcile . . .

As my brother returned with a wet cloth and towel I made my decision. I'd need a few weeks alone at least. Then maybe I would be in a better state of mind and could handle his presence in my empty life.

Once I was relatively clean and wearing the fresh shirt, Sean led the way wordlessly into the front room. Lee was perched on the edge of the sofa, head resting in her hands. She glanced up when we entered. She cleared her throat. "I'm going to take Kate's car and drive over to her house. I'd rather tell her family in person. They should be getting there in the next half hour or so."

I simply nodded. Sean was moving toward the bathroom sink, bloody rag in hand. I forced myself to speak. "I'm going to head down. I need to keep moving."

"Of course," Sean said. "I'll be right behind you."

I shuffled out quickly, certain if I lingered that Lee would tell me how sorry she was or tell me that everything would be all right.

Nothing would ever be right again.

As I closed the door, I could hear Lee's muted voice and the indistinct rumble of Sean's answer. Knowing they were probably talking about me made me only more determined to get out of here. As I moved down the wide staircase, I made myself a promise. I was never going to step foot inside this building again. The place where she'd died . . . I'd never be able to stomach it. Someone had pulled the trigger, chosen to take her life up there. And I'd been miles away, completely oblivious. She'd walked up this very staircase, not knowing she'd never walk back down.

I couldn't get out of here fast enough. I lurched into a staggering run, desperate to taste fresh air.

I pushed outside, the heat slicing across my sensitive eyes. I squinted and moved straight for the SUV, parked exactly where Sean had left it.

I jerked open the passenger door and thrust myself inside. Closing the door, I was grateful that the windows were up. Suffocating heat felt good. It tightened my skin, and the overwhelming smothering effect made me feel like I might actually be dying. It was wonderfully therapeutic.

I gasped against my will, choked back a fresh wave of tears, and then decided fighting didn't matter. No one was here to witness my grief. For this moment, I was free to express it completely. I screamed abruptly. Howled into the empty car as loudly as I could. Ears ringing, I pounded the door with my fist, slammed my right foot into the dash in front of me, desperate to express this anguish.

The glove box fell open and my strangled yell died. A vial of clear liquid and a packaged needle were laid out in front of me, begging to be picked up.

I knew it was the virus. What else would it be? It was inside a Demon's car.

A sick surge of hope tingled through my body. Sweat gathered on my forehead, above my lip.

If it was the right strain—a new strain my body didn't recognize—I could be dead in a week, at most two. I didn't have to live forever without her. I could take the virus. Inject myself. Oblivion could be mine.

I was shocked by the intensity of my desire. I'd never considered myself to be suicidal. Besides, Kate wouldn't approve. She'd be disappointed . . . But I'd already failed her in so many ways. Could one more failure really mean anything?

She'd want me to keep going. Keep living. Keep sacrificing . . . What more could I give? I'd been sacrificing for so long—for the past two hundred years I'd been sacrificing. I'd given everything: I'd died for my father, given up heaven for Sean, killed Demons for humans and Seers I could barely recall, and left Kate when all I wanted to do was stay. Would it be so wrong to be selfish, just this once? To finally take the easy path?

No one would have to know. Sean was the only one who knew it existed. If I could keep it from him, I could fool everyone. I could be halfway around the world before any of the telling signs of death appeared. They wouldn't know.

Someone would eventually find my body. Sean or Toni. I knew they'd come looking eventually. But by then I'd be free. By then, I'd be dead.

I glanced out the window, wetting my lips. No sign of Sean. I needed to do it now, before I lost my window of opportunity. I'd be well enough for her funeral. I could pay my last respects, be sure Toni at least would stay to keep an eye on the twins. And maybe Sean could, as well. He could become their guardian angel and find his redemption. And I could find my peace—the only relief open to me—death. Redemption couldn't be mine, not after failing her. Not after killing the

Demon Lord with such relish. Not after giving into such selfishness.

If I couldn't have her, I didn't want to live. Staying alive for anyone else didn't matter. It didn't matter that I couldn't make it to heaven. I didn't need an afterlife. Wouldn't want one, if I couldn't be reunited with her. I only needed an empty abyss.

I snatched up the needle, my hands quivering in anticipation at what I was about to do. Tearing back the plastic I hurriedly freed the needle. In seconds, I was filling the syringe with the only substance that could end my eternal life.

I tapped the side and the small amount of liquid rippled, sloshing inside the cylindrical tube.

I opened my arm, baring the inside of my elbow. The thick vein waited, bulging with tension. As if my body was as desperate for death as my mind.

I took a deep breath, my eyes on the long needle as it descended, touched against the vein.

I heard scuffing footsteps outside, and I knew time was up. Done hesitating, I jammed the needle into my arm and flushed the virus inside.

twenty-six

Kate Bennett
Unknown

My eyes opened slowly, vision blurry—like I'd been asleep for a long time.

I knew I was dead. Not because I was in pain. On the contrary, I felt perfectly fine. Better than fine. No, I knew I was dead because I was in a white room, just like Toni had described to me.

Complete, comforting white. The temperature was perfect. Not chilly, not too warm. The plush bed I was lying on was the sole piece of furniture, though the room was not small. The ceiling wasn't low, but it wasn't high. Everything seemed moderate. Perfectly balanced.

The only difference from Toni's death experience was the person sitting at the end of my bed. It wasn't a little girl. It was Grandpa Bennett.

He looked exactly as I remembered him, though I knew in heaven he would be a handsome young man. Seeing his weathered face and wispy hair caused my heart to burn. His large hands looked just as rough and calloused as they should be. He was even wearing his overalls, though they weren't crusted in dirt from the backyard.

He was smiling at me, eyes edged with melancholy. "Hello, honey."

Though it was probably the least graceful reaction of all time, all I could do was blubber as I pushed up into his arms. He held me tightly, crushing my shoulders in his muscled grip. He rocked me gently and I cried into his shoulder.

"I'm sorry," I finally managed to choke out. "I'm so sorry for everything. For making you die."

"Hey, it wasn't your fault at all. Don't be ridiculous. I'm so proud of you, Kate."

But his reassurances meant nothing to me in my current state. "I ruined everything, Grandpa. Everything. I trusted Peter, and I shouldn't have. I watched them kill Lee—and they went after the twins. I tried to go back but I don't think I made anything right. Wouldn't I know if I had? And Patrick—Grandpa, I made a horrible mistake. I should have told him yes. I don't know what I was thinking. He proposed to me—"

"I know," he cut in. "I was there."

"What? Really?" I pulled back so I could see his face, though the burning tears made his features indistinct.

He set his hand lovingly against my face. "Of course. It's one of the things that makes heaven so great. We're the *real* guardian angels, when it comes right down to it. We watch over our loved ones, so you're never alone. We just live on another plane—one that even Seers can't glimpse. But we're always there."

"Mom and Dad?"

"They saw it too. She was especially thrilled when he used both knees. Called it the most romantic pose. Your father thought he could have at least gotten a ring first, but I think he was mostly joking. As for Patrick's parents, well—"

"They were there too?"

"Of course. It only makes sense, doesn't it?"

If I wasn't dead, I might have been embarrassed to think

we'd had an audience. Still, the idea felt so right. They *should* have been a part of that moment. "I'm glad you were all there." It was almost a whisper.

He smiled, but it was a tired action. "You've been keeping us busy, that's for sure. The last few days have been especially crazy. I left the twins just a while ago . . ."

I paled. "They're not—they're not *here,* are they?"

"You mean dead? No. Patrick and Sean kept them safe."

"Sean?"

He nodded seriously. "He's had more than one angel hovering around him for a while now, working on his conscience, trying to help him recognize his feelings again. His mother, his father—and, most recently, me. He's broken through a lot of barriers today. Emotions he's been hiding from for a long time, he finally decided to face." He seemed to consider something. "Well, I guess Jenna and Josie did the final breaking for him, though, of course, it was his choice in the end. We can go over the whole story later. We've got eternity, after all."

I hesitated, unsure of how to pose my next question. "Can I . . . can I do what you do? Watch everyone? I need to see everyone."

"What do you want to know?" he asked instead.

"Well . . . is Patrick all right?"

He pursed his lips. "He's alive. In his room, at the warehouse, when I left him. He's not taking your death well."

I swallowed hard, trying not to imagine what he must be going through. It was a pain I was confident I'd be feeling soon enough, once my mind adjusted to the fact that I was really dead and I couldn't ever be with him again—talk to him, kiss him, be held by him. It was hard to come to terms with death because I just felt so . . . *alive* right now. It was hard to imagine my body was lying around somewhere, that I'd been dead for over an hour by my reckoning, when I felt perfectly healthy.

I needed to distract myself. "What about the Demon Lord?"

Grandpa patted my hand. "Dead. Along with Selena, the Dmitriev brothers, Takao Kiyota, and Mei Li—all of them gone."

"What will happen to the evil Seers? They haven't gone to heaven, have they?"

He shrugged. "I don't know for sure. They've probably earned themselves a place in Prison forever after all they've done, though. I'm sure they're being treated to the fate they deserve."

"So if the Demon Lord is gone . . . what will happen to the Demon uprising?"

"Since most of his closest confidants were also killed, it's suspected that things will slowly go back to normal. Without anyone to unite them, they'll fall back to their old ways. Different groups of Demons will fight amongst each other, trying to divide the world like regular street gangs. It's nothing the Guardians can't handle."

"But what about the virus? The Demon Lord's been distributing it all over the world."

"Rounding up the vials will probably take awhile, but it's possible to cleanse the world of it. Not all of the Guardians are susceptible, after all."

What he said made sense, so I tried to keep from worrying about it. I still had other questions. "Is Lee here?"

"No."

I waited for him to continue, but he didn't. "I know she's not in the room, but—"

"Lee is not in heaven."

My mind and heart rejected the thought. "But I saw her die. And you can't tell me she didn't qualify—"

"Lee had a long talk with her uncle, and she decided to become a Guardian. She's already returned to that plane, and due to her unique circumstances and death, she has been granted permission to break a few rules."

"Rules?" My head was spinning. I couldn't decide if I was happy for Lee or depressed that I'd lost her again.

He nodded once. "Normally a new Guardian cannot revert out of their invisible state. Not until everyone who previously knew them has also died. The time is usually used for training, but she has been allowed to jump back into her old life. Only Seers would notice the difference, until they realize she's not aging. Her mother will have to be told eventually, but I think Peter's presence will help make that easier."

My eyes narrowed at the mention of the Demon Seer's name. "But he's the one who betrayed us!"

"And he's extremely repentant. He saved Hanif's life."

"Hanif survived? What about Dr. Radcliffe?"

Grandpa's head was already shaking. "But don't mourn him too much. He's absolutely fascinated with Heaven, and the plane of existence we live on. He's only been here a few hours but he's already taking down notes to write a book about it."

"Alex and Ashley?"

"I saw them briefly. They're both fine. Heaven isn't exactly an unhappy place, young lady."

I curled some errant strands of hair around my ear. "So . . . that's it then? I just . . . go on existing?"

"You make it sound so boring. You won't believe all the people you can meet. Aside from that, your parents are eagerly waiting for you, just beyond that door there."

He pointed to a white door I hadn't yet noticed, and I felt my heart tighten. And though I wanted to see them so badly—more badly than words could express—I couldn't make myself stand up. Not yet. I still had too many questions, and they needed immediate answers. "What about the twins? And Grandma? I . . . I can't just leave them hanging."

He sighed deeply. "I know it's hard. Believe me, I know. But it's the way of things—of life. Eventually they'll come along, and we'll all be together again."

I glanced away from him, looking back toward the door. I bowed my head, pinching my eyes closed. "What about Patrick?

I can't just leave him like this. Even if I can watch him, be around him . . . It won't be enough. Not for either of us. I can't leave without saying good-bye. Grandpa, those things I said to him . . . I never got to look him in the eye and apologize."

I looked up quickly when I felt Grandpa squeeze my hand. "Kate, I think it's time to let you in on a little secret. Something Seers aren't allowed to know until they die. Special Seers receive a token of appreciation for all the services they rendered on earth."

When he didn't continue, I frowned. "A . . . 'token of appreciation'? What does that even mean?"

"Well, it's like a special request. A favor, really."

"Seriously?" It came out almost wryly.

He narrowed his eyes at me. "I thought you'd sound excited."

"It just sounds . . . unreal."

"Well, it's quite real, I assure you."

"So you got one?" I clarified.

"I did."

"Can I ask what it was?" I don't know why I was hesitant—he'd always been open with me in life, and that certainly hadn't changed with death.

"Of course. I asked for the chance to interfere with circumstances on another plane, with one person. Specifically, that the selected person could hear my voice."

"How would you even think of something like that?"

He winked. "I'm a wise person, Kate. Ask anyone but your grandmother."

"So who did you choose?"

He almost smiled. "The answer will surprise you, I think. Sean O'Donnell."

He was right—I was more than surprised. "But . . . he's the one who . . ."

"Who killed me? Grudges aren't easy things to hold, Kate, especially here. You gain a lot of perspective after you die."

"What did you do?"

"I helped unbury the emotions he'd been hiding from for so long, forced him to feel *something*. Once he remembered how to feel, it wasn't that hard. He chose to keep feeling, to help save Jenna and Josie from Yuri Dmitriev."

I thought back to Pastor O'Donnell's words, when he told me that somehow I would be the one to save Sean. And maybe I'd helped. Without my final warning for Patrick to save the twins, a lot of things wouldn't have happened; so perhaps I had contributed. Still, it sounded like I was merely one of the keys to his redemption.

I was glad Patrick had his brother back. I was sure they still had a lot to work out, but at least now they had a chance.

Grandpa's voice interrupted my thoughts. "So, if I might ask . . . What will your request be?"

I was almost afraid to voice my deepest wish, but hope won out. "Could I . . . Could Patrick come with me?" Even as I asked, I knew it wasn't right. Not that the idea of being in heaven with him was wrong—but taking him away from his brother, having him lose the title of Guardian, changing a decision he'd made in the distant past—the choice that had brought us together in the first place . . .

Grandpa was shaking his head, confirming my impression. "Patrick made his choice to abandon heaven long ago. That can't be undone now—not by him, and not by you."

He waited for my next question, but I could tell by the look in his eye he knew what was coming. I looked at him, and he looked back at me, waiting for me to say the words.

He didn't have to wait long. "Can I stay with him?" I whispered.

If he was surprised, he didn't show it. "That choice comes with a cost," he warned honestly.

I bit my lower lip, felt tears burn behind my eyes. "I know. Mom and Dad . . . You, and someday Grandma and the twins . . ."

Just saying the words, recognizing the cost, nearly undid me. I swallowed back my emotions. "But I can be with the twins now; be with them as they grow up . . . And I'll have Patrick forever."

"Will that be enough?"

I hesitated to respond only because I was overwhelmed with sudden clarity. It wasn't until now—now that I was truly forcing myself to answer the question—that I realized my answer had been confirmed again and again, every time I was near him.

I nodded. "You'll let Mom and Dad know that I love them?"

He smiled, though there was a flash of something like regret—or pain—in his eyes. "Of course I will. But they already know. And you know? More than that, they understand." He embraced me firmly, planting a quick kiss on my forehead. "I'll be keeping an eye on you, Guardian Seer," he said roughly.

The light in the room was getting brighter. I pulled in a deep breath, knowing time was up. I could feel the tears I'd been determined not to cry spilling down my cheeks. "Grandpa, I love you."

He grinned. "And I love you." He patted my hand. "Bit of advice, Kate. When everything starts to fade, you should look around the room one last time." My brow furrowed, but he only winked, tapping the tip of my nose with one finger. "Tell your grandma I said hello."

The brightness of the room had grown, forcing me to squint. It wasn't painful light, like a brilliant flash that causes blindness—just intense.

Despite not fully understanding my grandpa's advice, I cast my eyes around the room. I slid my gaze over the white walls, curious to understand his vague hint.

His voice was near my ear. "Sometimes I forget to close the door—drove your grandma crazy."

My eyes flitted to the door he'd pointed out earlier—the door that would have led me to heaven, if I'd chosen to go. It was no longer closed, but I didn't bother to look deeply past it.

Glimpsing heaven didn't interest me, because my parents were standing in the doorway, just on the other side of the threshold.

Mom had tears in her eyes, but she was smiling. Dad was wearing his wire-rimmed glasses. They both looked exactly as I remembered, and the sight of them, arms wrapped around each other, caused my heart to warm. They were alive. They were happy. They loved me.

My heart tugged painfully in my chest. *Was* I making the right choice? Could I really leave them behind? Was it worth the pain of losing them again, this time forever?

And then I saw the couple standing behind my parents, and I felt myself smile, though my eyes still dripped with tears. Patrick's parents, who looked exactly like I'd seen them in 1797 were watching me, eyes glowing. His mother—who I'd never really met, only glimpsed—was watching me with an expression of complete affection, and his father was holding her tenderly at his side, his countenance peaceful as he returned my smile.

I had so many things I wanted to say to each of them, but speaking seemed wrong in the face of such a miracle. Instead I lifted my hand and smiled, assuring them that, despite my tears, I was all right. And I knew I would be, even if this decision was laced with pain. Because in the end, it was the only choice that made sense to me.

The light in the room was too bright. I needed to close my eyes. I felt a pressure on my knee—my grandpa's hand, strong and comforting.

My eyes closed, and I could sense the room slowly dissolving around me.

twenty-seven

Patrick O'Donnell
New Mexico, United States

The footsteps outside the SUV grew louder, and I heard Sean's muted yell through the glass. "Patrick!" He tore my door open and wrenched the needle out of my arm.

Strange, it didn't feel like the last time I'd contracted the disease. Last time I'd been exposed my skin had felt irritated. But aside from the pinch of the needle, I felt normal. Better than normal. I was feeling numb. Perhaps this was an advantage of direct injection.

I swallowed hard and let my head tip back against the headrest, eyes on the ceiling.

Sean's presence was oppressive beside me. His breathing spiked as he saw he was too late—the syringe was completely empty.

"You *idiot,*" he bit off angrily, voice low and trembling. "You stupid, selfish *jerk!*"

He threw the needle to the floor by my feet, slammed my door vehemently without another word.

As he rounded the hood, fuming, I finally let myself watch him. He looked more like *Fear Dearg* in his rage, which made me wince. I didn't want him slipping back because of me. The first twinge of doubt troubled me, but it was faint—hardly there, quickly forgotten. Perhaps if I'd had more time to deliberate I would have felt regret. As it was, I'd taken a chance—my *only* chance in the foreseeable future—to end the pain of losing her. I wouldn't let myself feel regret for that.

He violently opened his own door and shoved the keys into the ignition as soon as he was behind the wheel. Hot air flooded the SUV, blowing my hair off my burning forehead.

"What were you *thinking?*" he hissed darkly, not making a move to shift out of park.

At first I thought a drop of sweat was slipping down past my eye. Then I tried to pretend that's all it was. Staring straight ahead, my voice was a croaking whisper. "I can't do this, Sean. I can't. Not without her."

He thumped his palm roughly against the steering wheel. "*No.* You don't have the right to take your life. Not after everything we've gone through. You weren't going to tell anyone, were you? You were going to run, tell us all you needed some space, knowing we'd honor your request—then you were going to die alone."

I ducked my head, staring at the single red drop of blood on my arm. It was the only sign left, since my body had already healed the small entrance of the needle. "That's still my plan. After the funeral . . ." I struggled to steady my breathing. I didn't want to lose it. I needed to convince my brother that I was being calm, perfectly rational. "When things are done here, I'm leaving. There's nothing else I can do."

He was shaking his head. "You're insane if you think I'm going to keep this a secret."

"No one needs to know. They'd try to save me if they found out. Please, Sean. If you care at all—"

"How could you do this to yourself? Would she want this for you?"

I glared at him, let him take the brunt of my anger—anger that had been directed at myself since I first saw her body. "No. But she's dead. She pushed me away. She made me go. She wouldn't say yes, she wouldn't listen—" I was choking. Again, everything was blurry. I knew I wasn't making sense, but I didn't care. "She died, and I'm here, and I'm sick of it. I don't want to be left behind—I *can't* be left behind. Not again. I've done the right thing for the past two hundred years, and I'm sick of it. I'm sick of hurting. I'm sick of losing what I love. I'm . . . I'm just . . . I'm *done*. And you can't make me regret this, because you can't make me feel any more guilt than I already feel for abandoning her. For letting her die in the first place."

While I panted and tried to stop my furious tears, there was silence. The air conditioner was kicking in, the air cool against my sticky face.

He shook his head and muttered to his window, "It wasn't your fault."

My voice was barely in control. "Don't. You. Dare."

He tried a different track. "Patrick, what about the twins? Wouldn't Kate—"

"I've given *everything*," I cut in fiercely. "Everything! I can't *give* any more. Don't you get it? Can't anyone understand? I've got nothing else to give!"

Sean glanced away, unable to meet my glare.

I looked down. My fists were unsteady. My throat felt clogged. I couldn't breathe for a second—I choked. Head bowed, my hands dug into my leaking eyes. Couldn't he see that I was incapable of surviving this? Couldn't he understand?

Sean was looking out the windshield, staring at the warehouse wall. "I'm coming with you," he finally said.

I met my brother's stare but couldn't speak.

He continued, voice grim. "If you don't let me be there with you, I'm telling everyone. They'll have you in a Guardian medical facility within the hour. You'd miss the funeral, and they'd administer a cure before you even started vomiting."

I grimaced at the easiness of his words, though a part of me—a small part of me—looked forward to his company. I would be able to say my good-byes, assure myself he had a place in this world before I left him behind. I wouldn't be utterly alone when the racking pain tore my body apart. I wouldn't have to slip into nothingness alone.

"You won't try to save me?" I asked thinly.

He grunted but wouldn't look at me.

We sat there for a tense minute. The air was beginning to cool, and my breathing was becoming easier.

Finally Sean spoke, and I turned to look at him. "We can leave after the funeral. It will probably be in a couple days. Can you keep it together that long?"

I nodded confidently. Even if the headache set in, I could fake it. I was sure even Toni wouldn't suspect a thing. "Thank you, Sean."

"Don't thank me for doing this. I wouldn't, if I didn't owe you so much. " He blew out his breath, tone changing with the subject. "Lee will be down any minute. She was just gathering a few of Kate's things . . ." He shook his head. "I really can't believe I'm going to let you do this—*help* you do this. I must be completely out of my mind . . ." His words faded as his eyes widened. He was looking beyond me through the window.

I twisted around instinctively, fearing the worst. His look of shock—almost fear—made my stomach clench. And then I was gaping in shock as well.

Two figures were coming out of the warehouse, hand in hand. Lee was easily recognizable in her eccentric outfit. But the girl next to her was . . . *Impossible.*

It was Kate.

Sean swore lowly beside me, still reeling in confusion.

I couldn't breathe.

They were walking slowly but getting closer. I could see Kate's face. Her watery eyes were focused on me, her lips forming a tremulous smile.

My shivering hand grabbed frantically for the door handle, desperate to get rid of the barrier between us. I didn't care if my mind was playing tricks—a hallucination was better than nothing. I shoved out of the car and nearly tripped, barely catching myself on the still swinging door. She paused, only a couple yards away.

I couldn't speak. Not yet. But her lips parted.

"Patrick?"

Her voice was incredibly gentle. Unbearably sweet. Her questioning tone, weighed down from seeing my grief, caressed my ears, my soul.

It must be a lie. I'd stared into her dead face. I'd held her close for so long, begged her to come back, and she hadn't stirred. Perhaps I *had* been driven to insanity.

But no. The others could see her too.

She was standing right in front of me. I was staring into her face—her beautiful, perfect face. Moisture clouded her eyes and a pained sort of smile turned her mouth. Lee was hanging back, her hands clapped over her mouth in joy.

I had to know if she was real. I moved slowly, afraid she'd disappear if I moved too fast. Forcing myself to ease my fingers out to catch her extended fingers, I was thrilled by the warmth I felt. Her hand closed around mine and I swallowed hard, blinking back harsh tears.

"Is this a dream?" I whispered, my throat raw.

She lifted my hand to her lips and pressed her mouth against my pale knuckles. "No," she breathed against my skin. "It's not a dream. If it was, I would be wearing something a *lot* cuter."

I let my eyes wander her face, and then—suddenly realizing she was actually here, that this was reality—I used my free hand to lay unsteady fingers against her face. She reached out to catch my tears with her soft fingertips.

I whispered her name at last, and then I was kissing her. Her arms wrapped around my waist, her lips matching mine easily in deep urgency. I must have been whispering other things, because she was answering me while she ran her fingers through my hair.

"I'm here. It's okay," she said. "I love you too. I'm really here, I promise . . ."

We both needed to breathe. That more than the thought of our attentive audience had me shifting away. I pulled back from her mouth only to snatch up her hands and pull them both to my face. I kissed her palms, her wrists, each precious finger.

"Patrick?" she breathed heavily, her forehead against mine.

"Hmm?"

"I just . . . I wanted to change my answer."

I pressed a last kiss to the back of her hand before holding them both in one of my hands, so I could cup her cheek with the other. "What?" I felt almost delirious.

"When you asked me to . . . marry you? I just wanted to tell you that I meant to say yes."

I lifted my eyes so they could meet hers. She was crying, just as I was crying. I brushed at her tears, and then I pulled her close against my chest. "How is this possible?" I finally asked, my breathing uneven against her neck. "How are you here?"

Her arm smoothed up and down my back and she tipped her forehead against my shoulder. My lips were at her ear now, but I didn't have the strength to question her further.

Her words were soft. "When a gifted Seer dies, they get to make a single request. It's like a reward, for everything they had to go through."

My throat constricted as understanding clutched me. She didn't need to explain the rest. She'd used her wish to see me one last time. Simple.

She wasn't here to stay. She was here to say good-bye.

I pulled in a shaking breath, trying to keep myself from breaking down. There would be time for that later, when she was gone again. It would be an unspeakable crime to waste the precious seconds I had with her. Knowing I still had the virus spreading inside of me assured me that oblivion could be mine, once she was gone.

"How long do you have?" My voice cracked, and I ordered myself to be strong. "Until you have to go?"

I already hated whatever her answer would be. There was no way it would ever be long enough.

She did the last thing I wanted her to do in that moment—she pulled away from me. My stomach ached and my hands reached to frame her face, to hold her there.

She was smiling through her tears. "Patrick, I don't think you understand. I'm not going anywhere."

I blinked but otherwise remained motionless.

She set a single finger against my chin, carefully tracing the shape of my lips, my jaw. "Patrick, my wish was to stay with you. Forever. I'm an immortal now. I'm a Seer living on the Guardian plane. Literally, a Guardian Seer." She shrugged. "I guess even in death I'm abnormal."

My gut tightened. "But . . . Kate, your family. Your parents—?"

She leaned in and placed an easy kiss on my trembling lips. "They understand."

"Understand?" Her words made no sense. They were too perfect, too incredible to grasp.

Her eyes traced every line on my face, the tenderness on her countenance deepening into something that made my heart lurch in my chest. "They know that you're my family now, Patrick. If that's what you want?"

It was the most absurd question I'd ever heard. To prove it, I grabbed her again into my arms and I kissed her hard.

All too soon, reality hit. I pulled back, my face pale. Kate opened her eyes, caught sight of my haunted expression.

"What is it?" she asked, concerned.

She was here, and now my stupidity was going to take me away from her. What if Terence couldn't help me find the cure for this strain of the virus?

I glanced over my shoulder and met Sean's deep stare. As I turned, Kate got a partial view of the car's interior. It was enough. The clutter on the floor easily drew her attention—the discarded needle making her body go still.

"Patrick . . . ?" she questioned, uncertain fear coloring her tone.

Sean addressed me before she could fully ask her question. "You're not in any danger," he said softly.

"But . . . it was the virus," I argued thinly, trying to ignore the pained gasp Kate produced at the confirmation.

Sean nodded. "But it's the same strain I used on you before. That's one of the reasons I didn't take it in with me when I got to the farmhouse with Yuri. I knew it would be ineffective on you."

"But . . . you were upset with me. For using it."

"Of course. You were trying to kill yourself. It didn't matter that your attempt was doomed to fail. You didn't know that. You were obviously in a fragile state of mind."

I could feel Kate's sharp look, but I remained focused on Sean. "But then . . . why pretend I was going to die? You were going to go with me—help me!"

"Yeah—to keep you from trying anything else stupid, once you realized your health wasn't declining."

Kate had found her voice, though it shook dangerously. "You actually tried to . . . ?" She abruptly slapped my hand, and I winced—more from the idea that I'd upset her, than the actual blow. "You boneheaded moron!" she piped, the pain in her eyes somewhat belaying the outrage in her words. "What were you thinking? How could you do something like that to yourself?

And what about my sisters? Toni? Sean?" She looked like she might hit me again. Instead she pulled my head closer and kissed me soundly.

She pulled back too soon, her voice quivering. "You swear to me right now you're never going to even think about doing something like that ever again. *Ever.*"

I swallowed hard and ran my fingers along the side of her face. "Kate, if I have you, I promise I'm not going anywhere."

Her answer was immediate. "You have me, Patrick. Forever."

I wrapped her firmly in my arms again, more content with the idea of forever than I'd ever been before.

epilogue

Thirteen Months Later
Kate Bennett
New Mexico, United States

The colored lights from the Christmas tree sparkled in the brightly lit room. Discarded wrapping paper littered the floor and holiday carols played in the background. Wonderful smells drifted from the kitchen, including buttery rolls and juicy ham. There was also a sweeter scent that could have been strawberry cheesecake, and, knowing my grandma, it probably was.

Though there was plenty of couch space I was sitting on the soft carpet, leaning back against Patrick's chest. His legs were stretched out on either side of me, his arms curled loosely around my stomach. From the sound of it, he'd fallen asleep with his head tipped back against the sofa. I smiled, feeling a little bad for him. The twins were all about waking up at four or five on Christmas morning, and Grandma was such a pushover that she allowed it. Though it was Patrick's second Christmas with my family, he still wasn't quite used to waking up before the sun. He wasn't exactly a morning person, to put it mildly. Still, when the twins wanted something, he was usually pretty quick at giving in.

We were alone in the family room, but the house wasn't even close to being empty. Grandma was in the kitchen, probably with Maddy, who was eager to learn her cooking secrets. Sean was most likely with the twins, since they adored him every bit as much as they loved Patrick. The two O'Donnell brothers were better than celebrities around here. They were the Bennett family's personal guardian angels, though they weren't the only ones.

I could hear Jack's booming voice in the next room, taking up the long time argument with Claire about the pros and cons concerning turkey and ham. It was the same debate that happened every holiday, it seemed, except the Fourth of July—they both loved hamburgers, so there was nothing to argue about.

The twins knew a good portion of the truth about our family now, but not everything. They knew Patrick, Jack, Claire, Toni, and Sean were immortal, but they didn't know that Lee and I were too. Grandma agreed they could wait to learn until they were older. That was fine by me. I didn't want to get too distracted by the supernatural while I had Jenna and Josie in my life, so I'd told Terence I needed a break from Demon hunting. Lee, Patrick and Toni had quickly agreed, all in the interest of enjoying the life we had, now that the Demon Lord was gone

I exhaled deeply, reveling in how great it felt to just sit and not have to think. My first semester of college was finished, and I was more than happy to be done with finals. So far, college was everything I'd hoped it would be. With Lee as my roommate, things never got boring. We lived in a small apartment with Maria Turner and Alyssa Meadows, girlfriends to Jaxon and Aaron—who were roommates with Toni and Patrick. We were all attending the nearby university, and for the record, Toni complained about college a lot more, now that he was enrolled for real.

My eyes swept over the room, taking in the piles of presents that were scattered around. Near the TV was a large plastic tote I'd given Patrick, containing all of my old painting supplies. Now that I was focusing on sketching, I didn't really need them anymore. Of course, art was only my minor. My main focus in school was English—something I was really enjoying so far.

Jack had given my Grandma a new Crock-Pot, extra large in size. His only request was that he needed to be around when she broke it in, and whenever else she used it. Sean had bought sheet music for Jenna and a new soccer ball for Josie. Claire had given Sean a camera, along with an invitation for him to come with her on her newest Guardian assignment in France. Though he'd been struggling for a while to find his niche in the world, I was confident Claire would be able to help him figure it out.

I had many presents in this room, but picking my favorite was simple. It was the one glittering on my left hand. The wedding was set for May, once the school year was over. Though I'd said yes to him a long time ago, we'd decided to at least wait until after I graduated from high school to make the engagement official. I knew some people thought we were young and crazy, but the people who knew us best didn't have a negative word to say about it. Even my grandma cheered when Patrick gently handed me the velvet box, a glowing smile on his face. Even wrapped in red paper with a green bow on top, the gift was no mystery for me. He'd slid the ring on my finger, and the fit had been perfect.

I lifted my hand now, tilting my finger up to view the modest diamond arrangement with the enhancing rainbow effect of the Christmas tree lights. The result was beautiful and hypnotic. The silver band was simple, but better than anything I could have ever imagined.

"Do you need a magnifying glass to see it?"

I looked to the doorway where Sean was standing with his hands in his pockets. His blue eyes were bright and his face was lifted happily. He hardly looked like Far Darrig anymore. It was hard to remember that he'd ever been that person, though it was obvious in the way he grew silent sometimes that he remembered the past well. Maybe a little too well. He was wearing a dark purple shirt, sleeves rolled to the elbows, just like his brother chose to wear his shirts. It was a good look for both of them, showing off their muscular forearms.

When he saw my slight smile he wandered into the room, drawing closer.

"You can joke all you like," I said calmly. "But I think it's wonderful."

He tossed his chin toward his sleeping brother. "He never was much for company."

"He's not really a morning person," I agreed fondly, flattening my hand against Patrick's limp fingers that rested on my leg. I watched Sean sit on the far edge of the couch, and I cocked my head at him. "The twins let you go?"

"They bought up my property and stole all my money."

"Yeah, Josie's pretty competitive when it comes to Monopoly."

"Or anything else on the planet."

I giggled, mostly because having this conversation with him was such a miracle. "They're going to miss you. When you're in France."

He nodded. "Until I promised to bring them souvenirs. Then Jenna offered to go pack my bags."

I pursed my lips, but the smile still escaped. "They do love you, you know."

"I know." He hesitated and then spoke more carefully. "Thank you again—for the letter."

"It wasn't from me."

"I know. But thank you for going to get it from him. It meant a lot, hearing from him."

I smiled. "Your dad was really happy to hear from you. More than happy—he was *this* close to singing praises."

"That, I believe."

"You told him you're going to France?"

He nodded. "And that Claire would be accompanying me."

I grinned. "Ah, that's why he was so happy for you . . ."

The corner of Sean's mouth twitched. "We're taking it slow," he said, and I took that as my cue to stop teasing him for now.

Patrick suddenly snorted and jerked awake. His arms wrapped tightly around me as he raised his head. "Wha . . . ?" he groaned, lifting one hand to rub his face. "I'm sorry. How long was I out?"

Sean was smirking. "Let me put it this way—Happy New Year."

Patrick's body shifted around me as he tried to sit up fully. "Yeah—thanks, Sean."

"No problem."

I twisted around so I could set a kiss against his cheek. "Did you get any rest? That's the real question."

"A little," he said. "Enough to keep me going until tonight, hopefully." He slipped a hand up to my face, holding me in place so he could press his lips to mine. "Mmm," he murmured when he pulled back. "I could get used to that." He glanced down at my left hand and the smile on his tired face was adorably heartwarming. "I could also get used to *that*."

Before I could form any response the doorbell rang, and the twins went running to answer it.

"I got it!"

"No, *I've* got it!"

Not a minute later I heard Lee's excited voice. "Make way! Excuse me! Best friend to the future bride, coming through!"

Patrick and I helped each other to our feet so that when Lee bustled into the family room I was already halfway to her. My eyes popped wide at the sight of her.

She wore a floor length dress of dazzling white and silver. The sleeves were long and draping, reaching as low as the skirt. It was a medieval princess–style dress, with a tight bodice that laced up with thick cords. Her hair was as long as mine now, maybe a little longer, and the only thing that held it back was a shiny metal tiara.

"Uh . . . Lee?"

She didn't seem to hear me or register my shock at all. She snatched up my hand, pulling the fingers close so she could size up my ring. "Oh my *Oreos*—it's so pretty!" she gushed. "Ugh! I just wish I could have been here for the unveiling." She didn't drop my hand, but she lowered it so she could peer over my shoulder. "Patrick, you better have taken pictures of her face. I can't believe my best friend is engaged! It makes you sound ancient."

"Lee . . . Since when did you become a princess?"

Her eyes flitted back to my face. "What? You too? What *is* this?"

"That's what we'd like to know," Sean muttered from the couch.

Lee was shaking her head at me in disappointment. "Geez, Kate, I thought you'd get it."

"You're not a princess?" I guessed.

"Of course not!"

I could feel Patrick standing right behind me. "Lee, are those . . . plastic ears?"

"Yes!" She let my hand fall so she could finger the pointy tips of her plastic ears, just sticking out of her brown hair. "Congratulations, you're the first to spot them without a guided tour. People can be so unobservant."

"Why are you wearing plastic ears?" I asked.

Toni answered that, strolling easily into the room with a sugar cookie in one hand. "She's an elf this week. Abigail, or something."

"Arwen!" she snapped at him. "How in the *world* do you get Abigail out of that?"

He shrugged, taking a big bite of his cookie. "I don't know. How'd you get Arwen?"

Before she could offer a rebuttal he'd caught sight of the ring. "Wow. Not bad," he muttered through his cookie. "Terence spring for that?" he asked Patrick.

"No, as a matter of fact, he didn't."

Toni beamed like a proud parent. "You stole it?"

"I bought it. Is that so surprising?"

"Bought it? With what money?"

Patrick rolled his eyes. "If you didn't spend every cent of your allowance, and if you actually got a job—"

"I'd be considered a big fat stick in the mud," Toni summed up with a nod. He turned to me. "So—you think you can stand him for eternity, huh?"

"I'm here anyway," I joked. "I figured I might as well give it a shot."

Patrick poked my side lightly and I squirmed happily. He was quick to snatch my wrist, to keep me from moving far.

Lee was almost glaring at Toni. "At least *some* men have a grasp of the romantic."

Toni had taken another bite, and he was chewing loudly with his mouth open. "Huh? You say something, hon?"

She snorted low in her throat. "Never mind." She suddenly prodded his arm. "Go eat in the kitchen—you're getting crumbs all over the place."

He obediently returned to the kitchen, passing Jeanette and Peter, who were on their way into the family room. Jeanette's grin was huge as she embraced me and then took a look at the ring. "Oh, it's just *gorgeous,* Kate. Congratulations!" She kissed me on the cheek before folding a faintly surprised Patrick into her arms. "I'm so happy for the both of you. You certainly deserve this."

Jeanette Pearson had taken the news of Seers and Guardians pretty well, considering her unwitting involvement in things. Lee and Peter hadn't been in a rush to bring her up to speed, but before Peter dared to approach her with his proposal of marriage, they'd sat her down for a serious talk. Learning that her daughter was immortal was a bit of a shock, as was discovering Peter's somewhat shady past. Still, she was a good-hearted person and extremely understanding. And since Lee had given Peter the thumbs-up, Jeanette hadn't hesitated. They'd been married for almost five months now, and neither of them had ever been happier. Now that he wasn't being threatened by Selena anymore, Peter had been able to clear everything up with the school board. He was teaching subjects on the high school level, like he used to do before moving here.

Peter took my hand with a smile, his glasses lit with the sheen of colored lights. "Congratulations, Kate. Patrick." They shook hands, and then Jeanette excused herself to go help out in the kitchen.

Peter took a step back to include Sean in his next words. "I spoke with Clyde the other day, and he wanted to let me know that Pierre heard something about—"

"Peter, please," Lee interrupted. "It's Christmas. The Demon hunting can wait for a day."

"Well, yes I know, but—"

She started humming "Jingle Bells" and he got the point.

Claire poked her head into the room, her brow furrowing when she saw Lee. "Kellee, didn't Rapunzel have long hair?"

Lee pouted in my direction. "Really? I thought the ears were obvious! I knew I should have ordered them in men's small."

Toni stepped back into the room, another cookie in hand. "Grandma's calling us all to the table," he said.

We could all hear Grandma grunt from the kitchen. "I'm not your grandmother, Toni!"

Toni grinned at us. "She loves me."

Lee fondly rolled her eyes at him, stepping forward to grab his elbow so she could pull him back into the kitchen. "You're going to get crumbs all over the place, idiot."

"You love me too," he said, just before they disappeared.

"Jenna! Josie!" Grandma called. "Come on, you can finish the game later!"

The twins came pounding into the kitchen, arguing loudly about who would get to sit by Sean for dinner.

Sean smiled at their words, then extended his arm to Claire. "May I escort you?" he asked her softly.

"Of course," Claire said, latching onto his elbow at once. He stooped toward her, planting a light kiss on her forehead before he led her from the room.

Patrick squeezed my hand, drawing me back before I could follow the others. He gave me one of his most disarming smiles. "Did you get everything you wanted?"

I couldn't hold back a wide smile. "I've had you for a while now, so, yes, I'd say I've got everything I could ever want."

He took a step closer, placing my palm against his chest so I could feel the comforting rise and fall of his breath. His hand remained on top of mine, holding me in place.

His voice was low. "Would you mind very much if I kissed you right now?"

I felt my heart warm with happiness at the mere thought, and I let my eyes wander his perfect face, hardly believing he was mine. "You never have to ask."

He grinned, gently tilting my chin up to meet his eager lips.

acknowledgments

The Seers Trilogy has been an incredible adventure for me, unlike anything I've done in my life. Coming to the end of such a journey has left me with a myriad of emotions; closing the door on this life-altering chapter of my life is bittersweet, though new doors continue to open, beckoning me to new adventures. Overall, I feel overwhelming gratitude for my wonderful characters, my loving family, supportive friends, and, of course, for my devoted readers. None of this would have been possible without you, so thank you, everyone!

While there are so many individuals I want to thank personally, I need to begin with my Heavenly Father; He has given me so many blessings and opportunities that I will always be grateful for. I also need to express love and gratitude to my parents, Melvyn and Marlene Frost—your unwavering support has helped me in more ways than you know.

I've been so lucky to have such wonderful brothers and sisters to grow up with (well, grow older with, anyway): Richard, Kevin, Kimberly, Joseph, Emma, Samuel, Lilly, Matthew, and Jacob—just thanks.

A gigantic thank-you must go to my phenomenal beta readers—I'm sure you can each find a place in the book you influenced, and just know that I can too: Crystal Frost, Jill Asay, Laura Hardman, Katelin Gines, Anna Brown, Amber Bowden, Alyssa Quinn, Mindy Holt, Ashley Hansen, Rebecca McKinnon, and Yvonne Manning. I appreciate all the long hours you spent reading, rereading, and discussing things with me.

Special thanks also needs to go to Emily Sinex, for unyielding friendship, and Landen Sinex, for being such a bright spot in my life; Brian Nay, for the amazing work you do for the website; Krista Whitaker, for the endless help you give me with the Facebook fanpage—and everything else you do for me; the Leonard Wells' family, especially Alex; thanks for your courage, faith, and for letting me name a character after you. And thanks must go to the continued support of my first unofficial fan club: James Miller, Rex Davis, Kent Hyer, and Rich Jones! (The final draft is so much better, right?) Also, the awesome librarians at the Garland Library, whose tireless support is greatly appreciated. And thanks to all my wonderful friends who are not only enthusiastic about my writing, but understanding when I become a bit of a hermit. Finally, a big thank-you to Cedar Fort, and all the wonderful people I've had the opportunity to work with. Thanks for making such a dream become reality.

about the author

Heather Frost was born in Sandy, Utah, and raised in a small Northern Utah town. She is the second oldest of ten children, and she has always been an avid reader and writer. She's a graduate of Snow College, and, more recently, Utah State University. She enjoys playing the flute, listening to all types of music, and watching a wide variety of movies. Ever since she wrote her first short story—at the age of four—she has dreamed of one day becoming an author. *Guardians* is her third published novel; her second book, *Demons,* is a Whitney Award Finalist. To learn more about Heather and the Seers trilogy, or to send her a message, visit www.HeatherFrost.com.